Author's Note:

When reading and watching dramatizations of the events that took place in World War Two, the focus is almost always universally centered around Europe, Southeast Asia and the United States. While there are some exceptions to this, the number of stories that involve the European theatre of war far outnumber those that address other areas. In my opinion, one of those neglected areas is Norway.

In planning where to go next in the Shadows of War series, I decided to try to highlight both the importance of this small nation in the war, and also the struggles the Norwegian people faced leading into their occupation. Their story is, I believe, one worth telling. While this book doesn't even begin to scratch the surface of the experiences of the Norwegian people during that dark time, my hope is that it brings awareness to their struggle. Norway was a small nation, often overlooked in history and world politics, but as the war progressed they soon proved that they were a mighty one where it counted the most: in their people.

Night Falls on Norway

CW Browning

CW Browning
Visit my website at www.cwbrowning.com

First Printing: 2020

ISBN- 9798670318020

Night Falls on Norway

"We will not submit voluntarily. The struggle is already underway."
~ *Norwegian Foreign Affairs Minister Halvdan Koht - April 9, 1940*

Prologue

Berlin, Germany

Obersturmbannführer Hans Voss turned from the window as the door opened and a man strode in. He clicked his heels smartly and raised his hand in salute.

"Heil Hitler!"

"Heil Hitler," the man replied, waving him to a seat as he strode towards a large, heavy wooden desk, stripping off his leather gloves. "My apologies for keeping you waiting. It's good to see you, Obersturmbannführer Voss. How was Prague?"

"As we expected, Standartenführer Dreschler," Voss replied, crossing to an armchair placed at an angle before the desk. "The traitors are all detained, with the exception of one. I expect to have him in custody within twenty-four hours."

"That is fantastic news, Obersturmbannführer." Dreschler tossed his gloves into his hat, placed it on the desk, and seated himself. He leaned back and regarded Voss for a moment. "I would say that you didn't have to come straight from the station to give me the news, but that's not why you're here, is it?"

Hans Voss smiled faintly and shook his head. "No, Standartenführer."

Dreschler nodded and leaned forward to unlock a drawer in his desk.

"I assumed as much. Anticipated it, in fact." He pulled out a sheet of paper and laid it on the desk, closing and re-locking the drawer. "You want to know about Operation Nightshade."

"Yes, Standartenführer. It's been over a month since I proposed it. I'd like to know where we stand."

Dreschler sat back in his chair again, studying him.

"Your proposal goes directly against the wishes of the high command. You know that."

"Yes, Standartenführer."

"I won't deny that when I read it I was pleased to see that you're not afraid to voice your opinion," Dreschler admitted. "The Abwehr is incompetent, and their methods are naive. We all know this.

True intelligence can only be gained by getting your hands dirty. They try to work from a distance."

"I'm sure they will have many successes in the war, but the female British agent will not be one of them," Hans said. "She is too smart for them. And too dangerous. She's already shown that she won't hesitate to attack men larger and stronger herself."

"And in so doing, she made an enemy of you."

"And of every honorable SD soldier. She must not be allowed to continue. The Abwehr will not be able to contain her."

"And you will?"

The smile that crossed his face was chilling.

"I welcome the chance."

Dreschler nodded and pressed his lips together thoughtfully.

"I don't doubt you. And, if you are able to hunt this agent down and bring her in, you will have done your duty to Germany, and to Himmler and the SS." He regarded him for a moment in silence. "You will also have interfered with the work of the Abwehr after being expressly forbidden to do so. You will have defied a direct order. You realize, of course, that that carries severe penalties? And that what you propose will cause an uproar from Admiral Canaris if you fail?"

"I won't fail, Standartenführer."

"You had your chance in November, and failed. Why should I believe you now? What's changed?"

"I've had ample time to consider how best to proceed," Voss said slowly. "In November, we were unaware of a few things that have since come to our attention. While that is hardly an excuse for Sturmbannführer Renner's misjudgment, it does give us an edge that we didn't have then."

"Yes, I read your proposal. I saw the new intelligence. But that doesn't explain why you think you can succeed this time."

"It's very simple, Standartenführer. I'll succeed because I will be undertaking it myself."

Dreschler chuckled. "You're always so modest and humble, Obersturmbannführer Voss!"

Hans was betrayed into a quick smile. "The Führer values confidence, does he not?"

"Indeed he does," Dreschler acknowledged, "as do I. And you certainly do not lack it." He tilted his head and grew serious. "But all the confidence in the world won't save you if this operation fails. You understand? I won't be able to shield you from Himmler's wrath."

Hans nodded. "I understand, Standartenführer."

Dreschler studied him intently for a long moment, then

nodded once and sat forward. He picked up a pen and scrawled his signature on the bottom of the single sheet.

"Your operation is approved, Obersturmbannführer Voss," he said, setting the pen down. "Operation Nightshade will commence immediately. There will be no record of it anywhere." He picked up the sheet of paper and got up, walking around the desk to hand it to Hans. "Read it carefully. This is the only copy of the order. I want to be very clear about what is expected."

Hans took the paper and read it through silently. After a moment, he nodded and handed it back.

"I understand completely, Standartenführer."

"Good." Dreschler crossed the room to a large painting of Adolf Hitler and touched an invisible clasp on the edge. The painting clicked and he pulled it away from the wall, revealing a hidden safe. "Should the operation fail, this order will be destroyed and no one will ever know of its existence. If you succeed, the Führer himself will know of your accomplishment, and you will be rewarded accordingly."

Hans watched as the order was locked away in the safe, a deep sense of satisfaction going through him. When he succeeded, his rise into the senior command would be assured.

And the British agent they knew only as Rätsel would be crushed.

Chapter One

RAF Northolt, England
January, 1940

Evelyn Ainsworth watched with a grimace as the latest WAAF recruits piled out of a bus in front of the dormitories. The chattering group of women was loud, and they were dressed in a variety of clothing, all wholly inappropriate for an RAF base boasting fighter squadrons. For that matter, some of the frocks were inappropriate for *any* military base, and most London nightclubs as well.

"Inspecting your new fledgling chicks?"

Evelyn started when a male voice spoke behind her and she turned with a laugh. Before her stood a young man dressed in uniform with a leather pilots jacket slung carelessly over his shoulders, his sparkling blue eyes dancing with unbridled amusement as he peered into the distance.

"They're not mine, thank heavens," she said. "I can't even begin to imagine how I'd deal with that."

"They're a jolly lot, aren't they?" he asked, grinning at the group in the distance. "Good Lord, is that one wearing high heeled sandals?"

Evelyn bit back a gurgle of laughter. The day she met Flying Officer Fred Durton, he'd almost run her over on a bicycle. As an apology, he'd taken her out for a drink at the local pub. That was almost two weeks ago now, and she hadn't been rid of him since. Looking up at him now, she shook her head. In truth, she'd grown quite fond of the Hurricane pilot.

"Yes, and they won't last five minutes."

Fred grinned down at her. "More's the pity. Where are you off too?"

Night Falls on Norway

"I'm on my way to my office to collect my post," she said, turning to continue towards the short, squat building that housed her office. "Then I'm going to the mess for dinner."

Fred fell into step beside her.

"Come out to dinner with me instead," he said. "I've discovered a delightful little pub about twenty minutes from here. We'll go there."

Evelyn glanced at him. "I have a meeting at seven."

He waved the comment away. "Don't worry, Assistant Section Officer. I'll have you back in time. I'll pick you up out front here in ten minutes."

Evelyn started up the shallow steps to the door of the building, then paused and turned to look at him.

"Have you fixed the door on your car yet?" she asked suspiciously.

He grinned and winked. "'Course I have."

Turning, he strode off, whistling cheerfully. Fred drove a beaten up mass of metal, rubber and glass that had been, at one time, a Vauxhall. On the occasion of her last outing in the car, the passenger side door had fallen off when she opened it at the end of the night. After they had finished laughing, Fred had gone off to snatch some heavy twine used on the airplanes from the supply hut. Ten minutes later, the door was tied back on and he had continued on to his bachelor quarters on the other side of the base.

She continued up the steps now, shaking her head with a reluctant chuckle. Fred Durton was a rascal and playboy, but she really did thoroughly enjoy his company.

And if he had fixed his door, she'd eat her hat.

Evelyn sat across from Fred at a small corner table in a crowded and noisy pub. They'd arrived ahead of the evening rush and Fred had snagged the table before she could blink. All the rest of the tables filled up within minutes of them sitting down, making her very grateful for his speed and foresight.

Lifting a gin and tonic to her lips, she smiled as she looked at him. He was attracting quite a bit of attention from the local women in his uniform with the wings sewn above the breast pocket. Then again, he always did. Evelyn had wondered more than once why he kept asking her out when he knew full well that she wasn't interested in any

13

kind of romantic relationship, but he did. And she enjoyed herself too much to decline.

Fred finished lighting his cigarette and tucked his lighter into his breast pocket, smiling at her.

"Do you know what I've been trying to figure out?" he asked, reaching for his pint. "What do you *do*, actually?"

Evelyn shrugged. "I've told you. I train WAAFs."

"Yes, but I never see you actually talking to any of them," he said. "Don't you like them?"

"Of course I do! You're just never around when any of my students are." She swallowed and glanced around the pub. "And besides, the majority of my trainees are at other stations. You know that. However did you find this place? It's absolutely jam-packed."

"I told you it would be. They pour an outstanding pint, and the food is fantastic. You'll see." Fred set down his glass. "And don't think I don't realize what you just did. You really don't like talking about your work, do you?"

She looked at him ruefully. "It's not a matter of liking or not liking. I *can't* talk about my work. I've told you."

"Yes, yes, I know. Top secret and all that." He tilted his head and studied her, his blue eyes dancing. "You don't look very top secret."

"Don't I? And what does top secret look like?"

"Like something I wouldn't look twice at," he said promptly. "Very well. You keep your secrets, Assistant Section Officer. I won't promise not to try to discover them, though."

"Well that's fair, at any rate."

"You said your brother flies? Where is he?"

"He's stationed at Duxford," Evelyn said, relieved at the change of subject. "He flies Spitfires."

Fred brightened noticeably.

"Does he? Now *that's* a jolly nice kite. I'd love to jump in one of those and take it up. I've heard they're terribly fast and handle like a dream."

"He loves it."

"How long has he been at Duxford?"

"Since last summer. His squadron has been doing much the same as you: constantly training."

"And I'll bet they're getting bloody tired of it as well." Fred made a face. "And now the weather's gone and turned beastly. It's bloody cold up there, you know. For that matter, it's jolly cold down here, too. I thought my propellers were going to freeze up today."

"Is that possible?"

He grinned. "Not the faintest idea!"

Evelyn chuckled despite herself. "Miles did write that his windshield had ice on it the other day."

Fred raised his eyebrows and pounced on that.

"Miles? Oho! And who might that be? I thought you said your brother's name was Ron."

"Rob," she corrected him with a laugh. "It is."

"Then who is this mysterious Miles?"

"There's nothing mysterious about him. He flies with my brother."

"Mm-hmm." Fred nodded knowingly. "And now the great riddle is solved."

"What great riddle?"

"Why you, of course!" He leaned forward. "I knew you were hiding something. So, go on. Spill it. How long have you been seeing Miles?"

"Oh for heaven's sake!" Evelyn laughed and reached for her drink. "Don't be absurd. Just because we exchange letters doesn't mean a thing."

"Is that so?" He grinned. "All right. If you want to pretend, we'll pretend. But I know, Evelyn. I've seen that particular look in a woman's eyes before, more's the pity, and I know what it means."

"And what does it mean?"

"That I've got my work cut out for me. I give you fair warning, I intend to fight. All's fair, y'know, and all that."

She shook her head, unable to keep the laugh off her lips.

"Warning acknowledged, but I still think you're being absurd. Just because I don't think you're the be all and end all of my existence, it doesn't necessarily follow that there's someone else."

Fred winced comically. "Ouch! You're awfully brutal tonight."

"You deserved it."

"There's a party at the CO's next weekend for all the officers," he said. "That includes the WAAF officers, of course. Will I see you there?"

"I don't know."

Fred looked at her, amused. "Don't you top secrets fraternize? Don't worry. The other pilots aren't as irresistible as yours truly. You won't be tempted to stray from your Spitfire pilot."

"He's not my pilot, and that's not it at all," she exclaimed, exasperated. "I may not *be* here to attend."

"Ahhh, the meeting you have tonight? Are they sending you

away somewhere? More little chicks to mold?"

"Officers, not chicks, and quite possibly," she retorted, her lips twitching.

"Well, I'll be sure to toast your absence if you can't make it," he said gallantly, stubbing out his cigarette as a barmaid came to the table carrying their dinner.

"So kind of you, I'm sure!" Evelyn laughed as a dish of shepherd's pie was set before her. "That makes me feel all warm inside."

"As it should!"

19th January, 1940

Dear Evelyn,

How are you finding your new station? Are you settling in all right? Quite a good lot of chaps in the Hurries over there. I think you'll like it. Got to be better than where you were, at any rate.

Can you believe the Finns are holding on? The Soviet forces haven't been able to breach the Mannerheim Line defenses. I don't know how long they can hold out, but it's a miracle they've lasted this long. I think Finland has surprised everyone. I know I certainly didn't expect them to put up such a fight. Perhaps they'll pull through after all. Wouldn't that be wonderful?

I wish we were doing as well. If we keep losing our destroyers to the German U-boats, the Navy will be in a bad way. Rob and I were talking to the CO last night and he reckons the U-boats are the worst threat of the war. They're sinking everything, from Danish tankers to our destroyers. We have to find a way to get on top of that. Thank God Churchill is the First Lord of the Admiralty. That man doesn't play around. If there's a way, he'll find it.

This weather is absolutely appalling. Remember I said my windshield had ice on it last week? Well, this morning we took off all right, but when we came in to land, the ground was so muddy that we all barely got in. Rob's kite is still stuck, I think. They were working on it when we came in from the ready. It's a bloody mess out there. Did you hear that the Thames is frozen solid? And now it's starting to snow! They'll be grounding all flights soon if this continues.

    I'm getting very restless. It seems like this war is taking forever to get started. If I have to fly one more formation drill, I think I'll go barmy. We're all getting a bit fed up. Still, if we're in this mess, so are the Jerries. It's just as cold over there.

    I hope you're doing well. When will I see you again? Soon, I hope.

    Yours,
FO Miles Lacey

RAF Northolt

Evelyn looked up from her desk as a short knock fell on the office door and a young WAAF came in.

"Excuse me, Assistant Section Officer, but there's a gentleman to see you. Sir William Buckley."

"Thank you, Sanders. You may show him in."

After the woman left, Evelyn set down her pen and rubbed her eyes. She looked at the clock and stretched. The cover of an Assistant Section Officer wasn't sitting well with her these days. The other officers avoided her, knowing that she was doing some kind of work that was too classified for them to be part of. On the rare occasions that she was on the base for longer than three weeks at a time, such as now, she became very conscious of the speculative looks cast her way. The aircraftwomen assigned to her were friendly enough, but it was clear that they were completely at a loss as to why she was there. They brought her mail and telegrams, provided her tea, and escorted the occasional strange visitors from London to her office. Evelyn might be new to this whole secret intelligence world, but she was fairly confident that this couldn't continue. People would start to get nosy. It was human nature.

The door opened again and her boss strode in with a smile, his hat in his hand and his thick overcoat hanging open.

"Bill!" Evelyn got up and came around the desk, her hands outstretched. "How lovely to see you! Sanders, can you have tea sent up, please?"

"Yes, ma'am."

The door closed softly behind her and Bill grasped Evelyn's hands.

"You look well, Evie," he said. "Not freezing yet?"

She laughed. "Not yet. Let me take your coat. We still have heat in this building."

"Are there some without?" he asked in surprise, shrugging out of his coat.

"A water main broke on the other side of the station," she told him, taking his coat and turning to hang it on a coat rack in the corner. "One of the pilots was in here an hour ago complaining. He has no heat or hot water in the officer's quarters. He said they have to use the enlisted quarters."

"That's uncomfortable," he said, seating himself in a chair across from her desk. "I can't imagine any of them are happy with that arrangement."

"Not very, no." Evelyn went back to her seat. "Officer Durton had some quite scathing things to say about the whole thing. He says if it's not fixed tomorrow, he's going to the inn in the next town."

"Can't say that I'd blame him. It's a right nuisance, this weather. We've got soldiers digging out the train tracks further north so the trains can get through. Whole sections are blocked with snow."

"At least the rest of Europe is in the same boat," she said with a grin. "Hitler can't invade anywhere in this."

He grunted. "There's that, but it's not helping the war at sea. We lost two destroyers within days of each other last week. One to a German mine in the Thames Estuary, and one to a damn U-boat. The German submarines are picking us apart."

"Isn't there any way to track them at all?"

He nodded. "There may be, but we haven't made much headway on that front yet."

She raised an eyebrow questioningly and he shook his head.

"I can't tell you," he told her. "All I can say is that we've got some very smart people working on it."

"Are you talking about code-breaking?"

Bill looked at her in surprise. "What do you know about code-breaking?"

"I know the Poles gave us a machine in September after a few of their code-breakers were evacuated by our government," she said calmly. "I'm assuming that we've set up some kind of section to work on decoding the German traffic. At least, I hope to God we have."

Before he could answer, there was a knock at the door and Sanders rolled in a cart with a teapot, cups and saucers, and a plate of sandwiches.

"I didn't know if you'd eaten, sir, so I had them put some sandwiches on there," she said to Bill with a smile.

"Thank you very much! I haven't, and they are much appreciated."

The young woman flushed with pleasure and looked at Evelyn.

"Will there be anything else, ma'am?"

"No, thank you, Sanders."

Once the door had closed again, Evelyn got up and went over to pour out the tea.

"I should demand to know where you heard about the machine," Bill continued as if they hadn't been interrupted. "No one's supposed to know about it."

She glanced at him, amused.

"You've had me combing Norway, Sweden, France, Belgium and Switzerland for intelligence for two months," she said, pouring milk into two cups. "I was bound to hear things, you know."

"Apparently so."

"Rest easy. That particular bit of information I heard from a Polish refugee in Paris. He has since, I believe, come here and disappeared into the black hole of GC&CS, the Government Code and Cypher School, although why they call it a school, I have no idea."

"What was his name?" he asked after a moment.

"His real one?" Evelyn shrugged and poured tea into the cups. "I have no idea. I was introduced to him as Larry, but I'm sure that wasn't his real name."

"Still, I should mention it to Montclair. We can't have that sort of thing going on. Not with a spy unaccounted for here in London." He accepted the cup of tea from her with a nod of thanks. "If he talked to you in Paris, who knows who else he's told."

"It's true, then? We *are* working on cracking the German codes?" She held out the plate of sandwiches and he took one.

"Yes, it's true," he sighed. "I don't know how much progress they're making. They've got a lot of brilliant people all locked down working on it. Hopefully something will come of it. In the meantime, we need to focus on what we can get the old-fashioned way."

She nodded and carried her tea back to her desk. "I'm sorry I mentioned it now. I can assure you, I haven't repeated that to anyone else."

Bill waved a hand tiredly. "I know. Unfortunately, if you're ever captured by the enemy, they will dig it out of you. They're very good at that sort of thing." He sipped his tea. "Do you remember those two agents I told you about in November? The ones who were kidnapped from Venlo?"

"Yes."

"All of their contacts and most of our European networks have been compromised, and a lot of agents have disappeared. Montclair believes the ones taken in Venlo cracked under Nazi interrogation. There's no other way some of the identities could have been known. It's a bloody disaster."

"All of the networks?" Evelyn asked, her face paling. "Even yours?"

Bill glanced up from his sandwich. "No, thank God. Mine are contained and, as far as I know, safe. None of my agents ever had any contact with the others."

"Well, that's a relief." Evelyn sipped her tea and sat back in her chair. "What will be done now?"

Bill shrugged. "We'll have to start fresh, recruiting and building new networks. It takes time, though. Jasper is concerned about the threat of invasion from Hitler. If he makes it into France before we've had time to rebuild, we'll be working without any eyes or ears in Europe at all."

He finished his sandwich and sipped his tea.

"Which leads me to why I'm here. On the tenth, a Messerschmidt BF 108 crashed in Belgium. One of the officers on board was caught trying to burn documents. Luckily, the border patrol stopped him before they were destroyed. They turned out to contain the invasion plans for Belgium, Luxembourg and France."

"What?!"

"Exactly. There was no date in the papers, or at least none that survived the attempts to destroy them, but the details matched up with intelligence we'd already gathered. So it was assumed that the invasion would begin between the fifteenth and the seventeenth."

Evelyn raised an eyebrow. "I hate to point out the obvious, but those dates have been and gone and there has been no invasion of the low countries."

Bill nodded, a smile crossing his lips. He reached for another sandwich.

"The weather has been just as horrid there as it has here. There's no way Hitler's generals would have advised him to proceed. He's postponed it, I'm sure. Now the question is whether or not they will stick with the same attack plan once the weather improves."

"If they do, they're fools."

"Not if they believe the plans were destroyed. The Belgians

launched a very convincing deception ploy to convince both the pilot and the man carrying the plans that they had been rendered illegible."

Evelyn was quiet. She didn't think the German High Command would be careless enough to risk an entire invasion on the possibility that the plans had been destroyed, but it was certainly a possibility.

"You want me to go to France," she said. "That's why you're here?"

"Yes. You remember Josephine Rousseau?"

She thought of the black-haired Frenchwoman who had helped her escape the SS agents in Strasbourg over a year before.

"Yes, indeed."

"She's in Metz. I'd like you to meet with her. She has a contact in Germany who relays fairly reliable intelligence from time to time on German troop movements. If they're moving troops south, Josephine will know. We've received a few reports that the Germans may try to go through the Ardennes region."

"The Ardennes?" she repeated, surprised. "But that's impossible!"

"That's what the French say as well," Bill said dryly. "But we've now received multiple reports that the Germans are looking at it seriously. In theory, their Panzer divisions could make it through. The difficulty would be crossing the Meuse river, which is why the French have dismissed the possibility out of hand. But Jasper wants to be sure. He wants to know if there is any indication of troops moving south towards the mountains."

She nodded. "When?"

"Not until this blasted weather improves. But as soon as it does, we'll make the arrangements."

"I believe my mother plans on going to Paris in March," she said slowly. "She and Auntie Agatha want to do some shopping, if the situation is still stable, of course. If she does go, she'll stay with Tante Adele. I could join them for a few days."

"Perfect." Bill smiled. "I understand your Aunt Agatha is quite a force to be reckoned with."

Evelyn laughed. "She is, but how do you know?"

"Monty told me. He's the new gardener at Ainsworth Manor." Bill chuckled. "He said he defies anyone to break into the house with your Aunt Agatha staying there."

"That's what Robbie said as well," Evelyn said. "She really isn't all that terrifying. She's just rather blunt. I feel much better knowing that we have someone there to keep an eye on things. Thank you for assigning him to the house."

"No need to thank me. Whatever is in that Chinese puzzle box of yours is a matter of national security. We have every intention of doing what we can to keep it safe." He tilted his head and looked at her. "Have you been back since Christmas?"

"No. I have a long weekend coming up in February and thought I'd take a train up then."

"You do that. The sooner you unlock that box, the sooner we know what your father was onto before he died."

Chapter Two

The man laughed at the parting shot of his colleague and turned to walk down the pavement in the opposite direction. Darkness had fallen over London, and with it, the blackout. A blast of icy wind whistled down The Strand as he strode along the dark sidewalk towards Trafalgar Square and he burrowed deeper into his thick, wool overcoat with a shiver. The weather was appalling. The Thames was frozen and before he left the office this evening the temperature had been posted at -11°C. Another blast of wind gusted into his face and he scowled, pulling his collar up. If this cold streak didn't lift soon, they'd all freeze to death and save Hitler the trouble of sending his Wehrmacht.

And when *was* the Führer going to make his move? They'd all been waiting for it for weeks now, but so far there was nothing. What was he doing? What was he waiting for?

He glanced over his shoulder and peered down the darkened street before hurriedly crossing the road between slow moving vehicles. They had lowered the speed limit to twenty miles per hour because of the increase of accidents and fatalities in the blackout, but it didn't alleviate his discomfort in navigating the streets at night. Just last week a car had driven up onto the pavement when the driver lost his bearings and killed a twenty-three-year-old sailor. The blackout was accounting for more deaths than the actual war was at this point. Bloody ridiculous.

He gained the opposite side of the street and strode around the corner. His umbrella tapped along the pavement in time with his stride and he exhaled as the new direction put the wind at his back. At least for a few minutes his face would be saved from freezing off. As soon as he collected his message, he would hail a cab to take him home. If he'd wanted to live in the arctic, he would have moved to Antarctica.

London was never this cold. His lips twisted briefly. Perhaps it was God's way of punishing them for declaring war.

A telephone booth loomed out of the darkness and the man reached out a gloved hand to open the door, stepping inside and pulling it closed behind him. Out of the wind altogether now, he sighed in relief and picked up the handset. With swift fingers, he unscrewed the mouthpiece and tipped it into his open hand. A rolled up piece of paper fell out and he laid the handset down as he reached into his overcoat to pull out a slim torch. Switching it on, he read the single line of text. A wave of satisfaction went through him and he smiled, nodding in approval.

He switched the torch off, put it back in his pocket, replaced the mouthpiece and hung the receiver back in its cradle. Then, with a swift glance around through the glass panes of the booth, he pulled out his lighter and set the paper on fire. He held it for a moment as the flame licked across it, then dropped the burning scrap onto the floor of the phone booth. Once the paper had been destroyed, he put his foot over the burning embers, putting them out. The smell of charred paper filled the phone booth and he turned to open the door, stepping back out into the cold.

He closed the door to the booth, signaling that nothing had been left in response, and turned to continue down the street, his umbrella resuming the steady tapping. His lips curved again into a cold smile.

Operation Nightshade was a go.

February 20

Miles Lacey tucked his chin into his collar and went into the pub quickly, ducking out of the cold, steady rain drenching Croxley Green. The welcoming warmth of the Fox and Hounds embraced him as the door closed and he exhaled, straightening his shoulders and removing his hat. He looked around as he unbuttoned his coat with one hand. The establishment was crowded and noisy, and the smells of good hearty food mixed with beer filled his nostrils. It was a familiar and comforting sight after the long drive to get here.

Removing his coat and draping it over his arm, Miles elbowed his way to the bar and ordered a pint. There was no sign of Evelyn among the crowd, but he wasn't worried. The rain had made the roads more slick than usual, slowing him down on his drive from Duxford. The same had probably happened to her on her way from Northolt.

"Miles Lacey!" A voice cried from his left and Miles turned in surprise. A young man with curly gold locks nudged and squeezed his way towards him. "My God, it really *is* you! I thought you were off in the army somewhere, fighting in mud."

Miles laughed. Good old Barnaby. They had been up at Oxford together and he hadn't seen him since they'd all come down. Barnaby Langton shoved his hand out, his blue eyes sparkling and Miles clasped it firmly.

"Hardly, dear boy. I'm in the RAF, defending jolly old England's sainted skies."

Barnaby looked surprised. "Never say the old rumors are true for once!" he exclaimed. "You're really flying? I thought that was just lark up at Oxford!"

"It turned into a passion, Barny. I'm flying Spitfires now." Miles picked up his pint and took a sip. "What are you doing all the way out here? I'd have thought you'd be comfortably ensconced in the family pile in Cornwall."

"Not bloody likely," Barnaby muttered, motioning for a pint and joining Miles at the bar. "A man can't say boo in his own home these days, Miles. I've escaped from a swarm of bees, my friend, and it will be some time before I go back."

Miles looked at him sympathetically. "The women are at it again?" he translated. "What's the problem this time?"

Even when they were at Oxford, Barnaby had been plagued by his three sisters and mother every few weeks. A more demanding group of women Miles had never encountered, and poor old Barnaby had to deal with it constantly after his father had, perhaps wisely, departed this earth.

"Aside from the war and this new rationing? Do you know they've rationed butter, bacon, ham and sugar?"

"Yes. Well, they have to do something. We keep losing supply ships. The bloody Jerries are sinking them before they can get to us."

"Yes, well, to hear them tell it, they'll starve to death in a fortnight." Barnaby sighed as a full pint was set before him. "They were already in a tizzy after I broke my news to them last week, now this."

"What news?" Miles asked, his eyes moving to the door as it opened. He lost interest when a couple came in. Still no sign of Evelyn.

"I've gone and joined the RAF in the bombers," Barnaby said with a grin.

Miles snapped his gaze back to Barnaby's face and his

eyebrows soared into his forehead.

"Have you really?!"

"Yes. It's been frightfully dull now that everyone's up and gone into the RAF or the Navy. Even old Ginger went and signed on as ground crew exec in the RAF. Decided I might as well get a piece of the action if they're handing out slices. And Lord knows I'd be no good as a foot soldier. I joined up last month and leave the day after tomorrow."

"Old Ginger went too?" Miles asked, stunned. "Can't imagine why they took him!"

"Well they're looking for anyone these days, aren't they? I say, I'm here with some of the old crowd. We're taking a jaunt into town. Why don't you join us?"

"Sorry, but I'm meeting someone."

"Well bring her along!" Barnaby said. "We're meeting up with Lorry and Tony and some of the others in London. Come along. It's bound to be a good time. We have reservations at the Savoy. I'm sure they'll be able to squeeze two more in. Bound to, anyway, for Miles Lacey."

Miles smiled wryly at the offhand reference to his social stature.

"I'd love to, but I'll have to pass this time."

"Well, we're on the other side if you change your mind." Barnaby picked up his pint. "It's jolly good to see you again."

"If I don't see you, best of luck in the bombers," Miles said, gripping his hand.

"And to you in the fighters!"

Barnaby disappeared into the crowd and Miles shook his head, a faint smile playing on his lips. So Barny had gone and joined up as well. Amazing, that. He'd always been a bit of a bookworm, Barny had. Then again, so was Bertie Rodford, and a better intelligence officer Miles had yet to meet. Perhaps old Barny would do well in the bombers.

The door to the pub burst open then to admit a laughing group of pilots. They exploded into the building in a muddle of flying hats, scarves, gloves and coats. They were singing some song or other, showing that this was not the first stop in their revels. Miles was just turning away with a chuckle when another burst of laughter made him look again. He blinked as Evelyn and three other WAAFs appeared from the center of the group. As he watched, Evelyn tilted her head back and said something in a low voice to the pilot next to her. His face turned a dull red and more laughter rang out.

Night Falls on Norway

Leaning against the bar, Miles was content just to watch her for a moment from a distance. She pulled off her gloves and unwound the scarf from around her neck, trying to look around the pub as she did so. One of the pilots plucked the cap off her head with a laugh and a cascade of blonde hair tumbled around her shoulders in thick waves. Miles grinned as she snatched her hat back and said something sharply to the guilty officer. More laughter greeted her words as the offending pilot grinned down at her, unrepentant.

A sudden rush of contentment went through him and Miles sipped his beer. He'd been waiting for two months to see her again, and he was far from disappointed. Seeing her at ease with the pilots from her new station, he smiled at the simple joy on her face. He realized with a start how lucky he was that she had driven to meet him here halfway between their bases. She had obviously made several new friends among the fighter pilots of Northolt, yet here she was anyway.

And she was here to see him.

Evelyn shook out her hair and turned to look around the crowded pub. The past hour and a half had been almost unbearable. It wasn't that the pilots had been annoying, precisely. They simply refused to believe that she wanted to spend the evening with anyone other than themselves.

When she arrived back late from a training session in Scotland, she found that she'd missed the last bus that would bring her to Croxley Green to meet Miles for dinner. Luck had been on her side though: Fred had been hanging around, waiting for her. He offered her a lift on the 'last bus to town, my dear' and promised to drop her at the Fox and Hounds on the way. The 'bus', of course, had been his condemned car already filled with four other pilots and three WAAFs, sneaking out in the boot. Evelyn had been forced to sit on the lap of the pilot in the passenger's seat, squeezed against the window.

Despite the discomfort, it was a merry group and Flying Officer Greggs was a young man who kept his hands to himself. Once they were well away from the airfield, Fred stopped the car to let the WAAFs out of the trunk. That was the first Evelyn learned of their presence. Enlisted aircraftwomen were not allowed to fraternize with officers, and they were just as shocked to see Evelyn as she was to see them. After a very tense moment, though, she had laughed and shrugged and waved them into the car. They piled onto the laps of the officers in the back and the laughter hadn't stopped since.

After stopping at two pubs on the way, they finally pulled into the parking lot next to the Fox and Hounds. She was supposed to meet Miles here, but all she could see were blue uniforms and wide shoulders.

"Do you see him, love?" Fred's voice asked behind her.

"What do you think?" she demanded, turning to him impatiently. "All I see is blue!"

Evelyn should have recognized the sudden gleam that sprang into his blue eyes. She had seen it enough over the past few months. But she was tired, hungry and longing to see Miles. She'd been looking forward to this night for two months, and all she could think was that he had left, thinking she wasn't coming. Ignoring the glitter in Fred's eyes, she craned her neck, trying to see around the ocean of blue RAF coats.

Strong hands snaked around her waist suddenly and Evelyn's feet left the floor all at once. Gasping, she felt herself hoisted up into the air, where she was planted on Fred and Greggs shoulders. Ducking quickly, she narrowly avoided smacking her head on the heavy oak beam running across the low ceiling.

"Has your vision improved, Assistant Section Officer Ainsworth?" Fred called up to her, a grin on his face and his voice unsteady.

Never one to let an opportunity slip by, Evelyn scanned the interior of the pub from her new advantage of height. Several shocked civilians were staring up at her as she perched on the shoulders of two tall, good-looking RAF officers. She smiled at them blandly, searching for Miles. She finally spotted him, leaning against the bar, laughing helplessly. Relief poured through her and she laughed, waving gaily and calling out a greeting. The shocked silence that had fallen over the establishment broke as every patron, as one, turned to look at Miles before laughter filled the pub. Fred and Greggs set her down, their shoulders shaking with mirth, and Evelyn swung around to face Fred.

"That was a dirty trick to play, Officer Durton!" she exclaimed. "I'm an officer, for God's sake! And there are three ACWs that just saw that!"

Fred just leaned against the wall and roared with laughter.

"Did you see the looks on everyone's faces?" he demanded, gasping for air. "Lord, I wish I'd had a camera!"

"Cor, is that 'im?" one of the ACWs demanded as Miles appeared through the crowd. Evelyn turned to look and nodded.

"Yes, Mary. That's him." She collected her coat and scarf from a still-chuckling Fred and turned towards him. "Miles!"

He closed the last few feet to reach her, still laughing as he reached out to take the coat from her.

"Evelyn, I've never had anyone make up for being late in such a fantastic way!" he exclaimed. "That was absolutely priceless."

Evelyn laughed, drinking in the sight of him. His green eyes were sparkling in the way that sometimes haunted her dreams, and his smile was warm, sending sparks straight through to her toes.

"You have Fred to thank for that," she said, turning to motion to Fred. "Miles, meet Flying Officer Fred Durton and Flying Officer Daniel Greggs. They were kind enough to give me a lift. The others have disappeared already."

"They caught sight of the bar, I'm afraid," Fred said with a grin, grasping his hand. "Nice to meet you. Evelyn nearly had my head for stopping at that last pub. She was sure you'd leave without her."

"As if I ever would," Miles said with a laugh, shaking his hand.

"That's what we told her," Daniel said, holding out his hand. "Said you'd have to be an out and out looby to leave without her."

"And I said you were and that's why we had to hurry!" Evelyn said with a grin, turning to Miles and tucking her hand into his arm.

"Durton!" A voice exclaimed loudly behind them. "I don't believe it! Never would have either, if Frosby here hadn't caught sight of me!"

Evelyn turned to watch as a young man with curly blond hair came towards them. He carried a pint in one hand and a cigarette in the other, the picture of idle privilege. One of the officers from the backseat of Fred's car followed behind him.

"Barny!" Fred exclaimed, his face lighting up. "Whatever are you doing here?"

"Same as you, I imagine." Barnaby grasped Fred's hand. "I didn't know you knew Miles!"

"I don't. We've just met."

"Barnaby, this is Evelyn Ainsworth," Miles introduced the smiling newcomer. "Evelyn, meet Barnaby Langton. Don't believe a word he says. He's a shocking flirt."

"Oh, I say!" Barnaby shook her hand warmly, holding it a little longer than necessary. "Don't listen to Miles. He's still cheesed off over a little serving maid from school."

"Barny!" Fred exclaimed in mock horror. "There's a lady present!"

Evelyn laughed at them. "Oh, don't mind me!"

Miles looked at her, his eyes dancing.

"That's the problem, my dear," he murmured. "They do mind you. Come on. Let's go eat and leave them to their own devices."

After they had said their goodbyes to the laughing pilots, he steered her towards the back of the crowded pub where another door led into the dining area.

"I was beginning to think you'd changed your mind about coming," he said with a smile, glancing down at her. "I'm glad I was wrong."

"I got back late from a training stint in Scotland," she told him. "I'd missed the last bus, so Fred very kindly offered to drop me on his way to town."

"That's where Barny's headed as well," he said, guiding her to a quiet table in the far corner of the restaurant. "We were invited to go along, but I'd rather spend our few stolen hours alone. I hope you don't mind?"

"Not at all," Evelyn said with a smile as he pulled out her chair. "I love Freddie, but I've had just about as much of him as I can take for one day."

Miles grinned and turned to hang their coats on a coat rack nearby, then returned to sit across from her.

"He seems a very jolly fellow. How did you meet?"

"He nearly ran me over."

Miles stared at her. "Pardon?"

Evelyn laughed at the look on his face.

"I was crossing the road to get to the officer's building and he came flying around the corner on a bicycle. He swerved just in time to miss me, but he crashed into a particularly thorny bush. I had to help disentangle him. The entire time he was wailing about losing his race."

Miles chuckled, familiar with the pranks bored pilots got up to when they weren't flying.

"Shame he lost," he murmured. "Did you make it up to him?"

Evelyn twinkled across the table. "They had it again the next day and he won. He swears to this day that it was because he wore my tie tied round his forehead."

He choked and burst out laughing. "He must have looked an idiot!"

"Yes, of course he did. They all do it around there." Evelyn looked up as a bar maid approached their table. "Odd bunch, the fighter pilots of Northolt. Still, I expect they're like it everywhere," she added pointedly.

Miles grinned. Apparently Officer Fred Durton had won her approval.

30

"Of course we are," he said. "Stands to reason we've got to be. We voluntarily chose to fly with our hair on fire to meet an enemy who's faster and more experienced than us. We all must have a few screws loose."

The barmaid joined them and handed them menus while they ordered their drinks. Once she'd gone, Evelyn looked across the table and smiled at him.

"It's so good to see you," she said suddenly. "How are you fairing up in the great blue yonder?"

"Piece of cake." He tilted his head and his lips curved. "What about you? I know the pilots aren't the only ones having a grand old time in our down time. What are you doing to keep yourself amused during this horrid winter?"

Evelyn chuckled. "Me? Why nothing! I'm a pillar of respectability."

"Mm-hmm. If that were so, Durton would never have dared hoist you up on his shoulders. Come on. Fess up. What pranks have you got up to? I know there must be at least one."

Evelyn met his gaze and couldn't stop her lips from pulling up at the corners.

"Oho! That's a mischievous look if I've ever seen one!" he exclaimed. "Spill it."

"Well, I may or may not have dressed up as a man a few weeks ago," she said slowly, her eyes dancing.

Miles grinned and leaned forward, resting his arms on the heavy oak table.

"Do tell!"

"Fred and I were talking and he was on his way to the officer's mess. I mentioned that I didn't think it was fair that WAAF officers aren't allowed in their mess. We're stuck in a moldy old shack at the back with cold tea and stale biscuits."

"Stale biscuits?"

Evelyn smiled sheepishly.

"Well, perhaps it's not that bad, but it's pretty horrible." She cleared her throat. "I was complaining to Fred about it and the next day, he shows up in my office with an RAF uniform and dares me to put it on and come to the mess with him."

Miles stared at her, his mouth dropping open. "You dressed up as an RAF officer?!"

"Well, I wasn't about to let him think I wasn't up for it. Besides, I wanted to see how much better your side of things is."

"And?"

"And I'm appalled at what they expect the WAAFs to settle for," she said promptly.

Miles choked back a laugh. "You actually went through with it?"

"Yes of course I did, and had a fantastic time. After a few glasses of brandy, I stopped worrying about being caught. Well, until the CO showed up, at any rate."

"No!"

She nodded soberly. "Fred helped me out a back window while one of the other pilots stalled him in the front."

After a stunned silence, Miles burst out laughing. He was still laughing a few minutes later when the barmaid returned with their drinks.

"Oh God, Evie, please don't ever change!" he gasped as the glasses were set down before them.

Evelyn reached for her wine.

"Oh, don't worry. I don't plan to." She sipped it and smiled across at him. "I do believe I warned you that you might regret getting to know me."

"You also told me that you and Rob were the boring ones in your family," he retorted. "If you're boring, I absolutely must meet the fun side of your family!"

Chapter Three

Evelyn tucked her arm into his and ran with Miles through the rain to his low slung Jaguar SS100 on the far side of the parking lot. Her RAF issued coat and hat kept most of her warm and dry, but did nothing to combat the rain blowing into her face. All she could do was put her head down and hope she didn't trip on the gravel.

They reached the sports car and Miles opened the door for her. She ducked inside and he slammed it closed before running around the hood to the driver side.

"It had to turn to rain today, didn't it?" he gasped, getting in beside her.

"At least the snow has stopped," she replied. "And I don't mind the rain."

"Don't you?" he glanced at her as he started the engine. "Tell me, Evelyn, is there anything you *do* mind?"

She thought for a moment.

"Do you know, I can't think of a single thing," she finally decided. "It must be all those glasses of wine."

Miles laughed and pulled out of the parking lot. "In that case, remind me to invest in barrels of the stuff."

Evelyn smiled and leaned her head back on the leather seat.

"I'm so glad we did this," she said. "I'm sorry that you have to drive me all the way back to Northolt, though. Next time I go home, I'll take the car back to Northolt. Robbie won't miss it. Then you won't have to do this."

"I don't mind." He glanced at her with a smile. "It's not that far."

They were silent for a moment, then she chuckled.

"Were you very shocked when Freddie put me on his shoulders?" she asked, turning her head to look at him.

He grinned, his eyes on the road. "Not in the least."

"He really is a bit much sometimes, but he makes me laugh."

"He flies Hurricanes?"

"Yes." She glanced at him with a smile. "Although he says he'd love to hop in a Spitfire and take one up. He's heard such wonderful things about them."

"It's a fantastic kite," he said with a shrug. "It's faster than the Hurricane, but Hurries have better range. There's also a lot more of them. I did a few hours in one last year. They're easier to fly."

"Are they?"

He nodded. "Yes. There's a learning curve to the Spit, but I love it. It turns like a dream, and is more maneuverable."

Evelyn smiled. "I suppose it's all what you're used to."

He looked at her. "I'd love to take you up in one," he said with a grin. "You'd love it."

"Oh, I wish!" She sighed. "Maybe one day. After the war. Except then I expect it wouldn't be a fighter plane."

Miles turned his attention back to the road. "No, but I'll continue flying after the war. I'll take you up with me one day."

Evelyn looked out the window over the dark, dripping countryside. They spoke so easily about after the war, assuming that they would both survive it. She sobered, unable to ignore the fact that they probably wouldn't.

"Did you hear about the German ship we seized?" Miles asked suddenly.

"*The Altmark*?" Evelyn pulled her gaze away from the window. "Yes. We seized it in Norwegian waters."

"And freed three hundred prisoners of war."

"Yes, but we did it in neutral waters. Norway is furious."

Miles glanced at her. "So is Germany. Did you see they've accused Britain of piracy?"

Evelyn couldn't stop herself from laughing.

"Yes. And murder. As if they haven't murdered thousands in Poland alone." She sobered. "Although, it's not really funny. Norway has always been our ally and now they're furious because we breached their national waters. I can see their point. They're trying to remain neutral. Now Germany is demanding reparations for one of their ships being attacked in Norwegian territory."

"Do you think Germany will go after Norway?" he asked after a moment.

"I think it's a fair bet," she said slowly. "If they have control of Norway, and the Soviets gain control in Finland, they have total control of the North and Baltic Seas, as well as the North Atlantic."

Miles looked at her, a strange expression on his face. She caught it and raised an eyebrow.

Night Falls on Norway

"What?"

"Nothing." He shook his head. "It's just strange to hear you talk about strategic positioning. It's not what one usually hears coming out of the mouth of a beautiful heiress."

She grinned. "Are you intimidated?"

He met her gaze and smiled slowly. "Not a bit."

"Good."

"I'm surprised we haven't made any move to try to protect Norway, actually," he said after a long moment. "We could be mining the water around them, at the very least."

"I don't think Chamberlain wants to get any further involved in this war than he's forced to," she said, unable to keep the derisive tone out of her voice. "He's too afraid to do anything."

"We have to do something, and soon. Finland is falling. It's only a matter of time now. And once they do, they will have no choice but to align themselves with Germany. All we've done is send some planes and munitions. France has done the same, but it's a half-hearted effort at best. What else are the Finns to do? They can't hold off the Russians alone."

"We've done a bit more than that," she protested weakly. "You make it sound as if we're just sitting and watching them fall."

"Aren't we?" He glanced at her. "I'm not saying we should have sent all of our forces up there, but we bloody well could have done more than we did."

Evelyn was quiet for a moment. He was right, of course. Finland would have no choice but to ally with Hitler, and if Hitler took Norway, most of Scandinavia would fall under the cloak of the Nazi regime. She thought of Anna Salvesen, the woman in Norway who had helped her in November, and frowned. She would be trapped.

"You don't agree?" Miles asked, mistaking her silence for disapproval.

"Oh no, I do," she assured him. "I was just thinking about what would happen if Scandinavia falls under both Hitler and Stalin. If that happens, I'm afraid both France and Britain will have been responsible."

"And yet Chamberlain does nothing." He shook his head in frustration. "We'll never make it through this war if he doesn't grow a backbone."

Evelyn nodded in agreement and they were silent for a few miles. Then, with a heavy sigh, he glanced at her.

"I'm sorry. This always seems to happen. We have a fantastic time together and then end up discussing miserable world affairs."

"I'd rather that than have a lovely time together and then end up quarreling," she said with a smile.

He laughed. "That's true. And I have the strangest feeling that you would be deadly in a quarrel. I feel like you would fight dirty."

She shot him a sharp look under her lashes, inwardly wincing. He had no idea about her training in what many called 'dirty warfare,' or about her study of the Chinese art of Wing Chun. In fact, he had no clue how accurate his offhand comment really was.

"Oh Miles, you have no idea," she murmured, drawing a smile from him.

"You don't scare me, ASO Ainsworth," he said with a flash of white teeth. "I think I'll hold my own just fine."

Paris, France
March 4

Evelyn ran lightly across the side street, gaining the pavement on the other side a moment later. She carried a clutch purse in one hand and a bag from her favorite fashion house in the other. The weather was mild and the sun shone brightly over the city, coaxing Parisians and visitors alike outside to throng the streets. As she moved through the chattering crowds spilling along the Champs-Élysées, she breathed deeply and couldn't prevent the wave of contentment that went through her. England was her home, and London her playground, but Paris would always hold a special place in her heart.

It was where she felt alive.

"Evie!" A woman called from a table outside a café, waving. "We're here!"

Evelyn smiled and made her way towards the outdoor seating where her mother, Aunt Adele and cousin Gisele were seated with cups of coffee, enjoying a short respite from an entire morning spent shopping.

"I'm sorry it took so long," she said as she reached the table and dropped into an empty chair. "Madame Beaupellier insisted on showing me the latest summer patterns."

"Did you see anything you liked?" Mrs. Ainsworth asked.

"Of course I did, and placed an order. It will be delivered on Thursday, just in time for me to return to England," she replied with a laugh, setting her bag by her feet and laying her purse in her lap. "But where are your packages? I know the three of you didn't spend the past hour shopping and not buy anything!"

"Oh George has already collected them and taken them back to the house," Gisele said gaily. "He'll come back for us. They filled the entire back of the car!"

"It's been too long since I was here," Mrs. Ainsworth said with a sheepish laugh. "I'm afraid I may have got carried away."

"And you deserve to," Evelyn said promptly, reaching out and squeezing her hand. "Who knows when you'll be able to get back."

"That's what I told her," Adele agreed, motioning to a waiter. "Will you have coffee, my dear?"

"Yes, please!"

"Do you really think you won't be able to come again?" Gisele asked once the waiter had gone. "They're saying the Germans won't make it past the Maginot Line."

"They also said they wouldn't take Poland," Evelyn couldn't resist pointing out.

"Who can tell, Gisele? But I have to assume that if this war goes on for much longer, then it will be more and more difficult to get over," Mrs. Ainsworth said, casting Evelyn an exasperated look.

Evelyn dropped her eyes, her lips tightening. Despite the fact that everyone was preparing for the storm that they all knew was coming, her mother insisted on not discussing the very real possibility of her beloved France being invaded by the Nazis. France was her mother's home country. She was born and raised here, and it wasn't until she married Robert Ainsworth that she had moved to England. While Evelyn could understand her reluctance to acknowledge the dangers France faced, she couldn't help but think that her mother was burying her head in the sand to some degree.

"Never mind, Madeleine," Adele said cheerfully. "If things do get bad, we'll come to you. I suppose I can tolerate London if I must."

Evelyn laughed at her aunt's mild teasing. Adele's love for the London theatre was well known, and when she did come to England, she enjoyed herself immensely.

"We have ample room for all of you," Mrs. Ainsworth said with a smile. "There's nothing I would enjoy more, and I know Robbie and Evelyn feel the same."

"Of course we do! It would be lovely to have you all stay at Ainsworth Manor," Evelyn agreed.

"Maman, you won't really leave France, will you?" Gisele demanded.

Adele looked at her and something akin to sadness crossed her face.

"I wouldn't want to, you understand, but if it's the only way to remain safe…"

"Don't worry yourself, Gisele," Mrs. Ainsworth said, reaching out to pat her hand. "It won't come to that. Not that you wouldn't be very welcome in any case."

"Where is Auntie Agatha?" Evelyn asked suddenly. "Didn't she come out with you?"

"She went back to the house with George. Her feet were hurting her. It was the new shoes. I told her not to wear them, but you know Agatha. She's as stubborn as a mule."

Evelyn grinned and nodded in thanks as the waiter set a cup of coffee before her. She sipped it thankfully.

"Mmm…this is delicious," she murmured. "How is she enjoying Paris?"

"I think she's having a fabulous time. If she eats any more pastry, though, she's going to gain ten stone."

"I'm so glad the two of you were able to come over," she said, setting down her cup and smiling at her mother. "You needed to get out of that house."

"Just them?" Gisele stared across the table at her. "What about you? I haven't seen you since last August!"

"I'm afraid I'm not a lady of leisure anymore, Zell. The WAAF is a very serious business," Evelyn said with a wink. "I'm lucky I got the time that I did."

"Madeleine says you're a training officer?" Adele asked, sipping her coffee. "What does that entail?"

"Oh, it's terribly boring. I train enlisted ACWs, that's short for Aircraftwomen. I'm stationed on one airfield, but I travel to others to lead the training. In fact, I think I spend less time at my posting than I do traveling around England!"

"That sounds exhausting," Gisele said decidedly. "What do you train them to do?"

"I can't say."

"How mysterious!"

"Not really, I assure you."

"Well, we're very happy to see you again," Adele told her. "It really has been an age since you were here. And, do you know, I think you even look more mature?"

Evelyn laughed, tossing her head. "I can't imagine why that would be!"

Mrs. Ainsworth tilted her head and studied her daughter thoughtfully.

"I think she's right," she said slowly. "I hadn't really noticed it before, but now that she points it out, you do look more…I don't know. Worldly."

"I think military life must agree with her," Adele agreed. "Although the thought of women working alongside the men on active military stations still seems very odd to me."

Evelyn swallowed and reached for her coffee. If she looked more mature and worldly, she supposed she could thank the war for that. Sneaking around in the shadows and fleeing from SD agents in strange cities was bound to leave its mark somehow.

"Do you think you'll continue when the war is over, Evie?" Gisele asked.

"Goodness, I hope not!"

"Perhaps that nice Miles Lacey will have an alternative," Mrs. Ainsworth said slyly, her eyes twinkling.

"Miles Lacey?" Gisele latched on to the name. "Who's that?"

"He's a pilot who flies with Robbie," Evelyn said, shooting her mother an amused look. "And before you start making wedding plans, he is just a friend."

"He's one of the Yorkshire Laceys, you know," Mrs. Ainsworth told Adele, ignoring her daughter. "Very handsome. He's been to the house twice now, and I was impressed each time. Robert would have liked him."

"One of the Yorkshire Laceys?" Adele nodded, impressed. "And he's a pilot?"

"Yes. Well, they're all having to do their bit now, aren't they?" Mrs. Ainsworth shrugged. "Look at Robbie."

Gisele looked across the table at Evelyn, her lips curved wickedly.

"One of the Yorkshire Laceys?" she repeated, eyes dancing. "Oh he doesn't stand a chance, does he?"

Evelyn couldn't stop the laugh that bubbled out.

"Not with these two sitting here with that look in their eyes!" she agreed, finishing her coffee. "Come on, Zell. Let's go and leave them to it. I want to look for a hat to go with the suit I just ordered."

Gisele nodded and finished her coffee, then stood up and pulled on her gloves.

"You realize they will have your entire wedding planned before we get home?" she asked with a grin.

Evelyn picked up her bags and stood, glancing at her mother and aunt.

"Can we please get through the war first?" she asked with a laugh. "I refuse to make any plans when I don't know where I'll be next week."

"We're not making plans, dear," her mother said complacently. "We're simply noting that Miles is an excellent prospect."

"Of course you are." Evelyn leaned down to kiss her mother on the cheek. "I'll see you later."

"Have fun." Mrs. Ainsworth waved her away with a smile. "Don't forget the Buckleys are coming for dinner with Marguerite."

"I won't."

She turned away from the table and smiled as Gisele tucked her arm through hers. It was lovely to be back in Paris with her family, even if the purpose of her visit wasn't pleasure. The smile faded somewhat. Bill was coming to dinner tonight and, while he was there, would give her the address in Metz where she could find Josephine Rousseau. The war continued, even in Paris in the spring.

And she had work to do while she was here.

Chapter Four

Evelyn looked up when the door to the music room opened and Gisele's twin brother Nicolas strolled in carrying a sketchbook in one hand. His step checked when he saw her.

"Oh! I didn't know you were in here," he said. "Would you rather be alone?"

"Not at all." She closed the book in her hands. "I was just reading. Auntie Agatha and Mum started arguing and I had to get away."

He grinned and closed the door, crossing the room to drop his sketchbook on the table near the window. During the day, sunlight poured through the glass panes, making the light ideal for drawing. Now darkness had descended and the curtains were pulled across the bay window, blocking out the night.

"She's your father's sister, isn't she? I thought they seemed to get along well."

"They do, for the most part. Auntie Agatha is very outspoken and stubborn, but Mum tends to balance her somewhat. It's only occasionally that something sets them off."

Nicolas crossed to the piano in the corner and perched on the bench.

"And tonight was one of those times," he finished. "Well, it's bound to happen, I suppose. She's staying with Tante Madeleine now, isn't she?"

"Yes, for the time being. She closed her house in London. Said she couldn't abide the blackout and the war preparations." Evelyn set her book on the cushion beside her. "I think the company is good for Mum. It's been an adjustment for her since Dad died. Robbie gets home as often as he can, of course, but it's still difficult."

"I can only imagine." Nicolas lifted the cover to the keys and pressed one absently, and then another, picking out a random tune. "It was a shock when he died. We were all completely stunned."

"So were we," she said dryly.

"Couldn't have happened at a worse time, could it?" he asked. "I mean, not that any time is a good time to lose your father, but with the war just starting and everything getting thrown up into chaos, it seemed a bit much at the time. At least Tante Madeleine has Agatha with her now to help her through it all."

"I'm happy she's not alone," Evelyn agreed. "And I know Robbie is too. He was worried about her."

"How is he? Still flying Spitfires?"

"Oh yes."

Nicolas was silent for a moment, playing the piano half-heartedly with one hand, then he got up restlessly.

"What do you think of this whole business?" he asked, glancing at her. "With the war, I mean. Do you think it will get started now that winter's over?"

She watched as he crossed the room to a side table and opened a sturdy wooden box. He pulled out a cigarette and held it up questioningly. She nodded and he pulled out a second one, walking over to hand it to her.

"I think it's bound to, don't you?" she asked as he held out his lighter for her.

"I suppose so." He lifted the lighter to his own cigarette as she sat back on the love seat, blowing smoke up into the air. "Everyone's saying the Nazis won't make it past the Maginot."

Evelyn looked up at the tone in his voice. She raised an eyebrow and studied her cousin's face.

"You don't agree?"

He shook his head and tucked his lighter back into his pocket.

"No." He turned to retrieve a crystal ashtray from the table and carried it over to set it on the small, round table near her elbow. "Zell does. She thinks this will all be over by summer. She listens to Marc Fournier and his crowd. They're idiots."

Evelyn laughed. "They're amusing idiots, though."

He flashed a grin. "Yes. And Marc still asks about you. You'll have to see him before you go back to England. I'll never hear the end of it if you don't."

"I think Gisele already arranged something for later in the week. Don't worry." Evelyn tilted her head looked at him thoughtfully. "What do you think will happen? Do you think the Germans will try to invade France?"

She knew that Hitler had every intention of invading France. The documents recovered in Belgium in January proved it, along with scores of other intelligence pouring in from around the continent. But she couldn't tell Nicolas any of that. All she could do was pretend to speculate with everyone else, and keep her thoughts to herself.

"Of course they will, and they won't go through the Maginot." Nicolas shook his head. "If they have any sense, they'll come through Belgium. The fortifications were never completed there."

"I'm sure both our governments have made defensive plans for that."

Nicolas made a rude noise and began pacing. "I don't have very much faith in Daladier. He's a fool," he muttered. "There's an uproar right now because he didn't do anything to help Finland and now it looks like they're going to fall to the Soviets. He says there is no immediate threat of invasion. Ha! Hitler will come for France. He has no choice."

Nicolas stopped pacing and faced her, pointing his cigarette at her to emphasize his point.

"And when he does, it will be nothing like the last war."

He was right, of course. Hitler had been in the front lines when Germany and France collided in the Great War. He wouldn't repeat the same mistakes his predecessors had made.

"You've given this a lot of thought, haven't you?" she asked. "I didn't know you were interested in any of it."

"We all have to be interested now, don't we?" He resumed pacing. "We can't just sit and wait for the war to come to Paris."

Her lips tightened and she thought of the address in Metz that Bill had given her the night before. She would drive out and meet with Josephine tomorrow because, as Nicolas so aptly said, they couldn't just sit and wait.

"I don't think you have to worry about the war coming to Paris," she said calmly, inwardly wincing at her own words. "The combined forces of the British Expeditionary Force and your army will stop the Wehrmacht from getting this far in."

"Will it?" Nicolas stopped again and glanced at her. "I don't know."

Evelyn studied him from under her lashes, surprised. Her cousin had changed since she'd seen him last August. He'd grown more serious and, as was evidenced by this very conversation, more concerned with the very real threat Herr Hitler posed to France. This set him apart from the majority of his acquaintances now, as she well knew. While it was only natural for the people of Paris to be nervous, most of them were quite happy to trust their government and army to protect them. If the government said there was no immediate threat, then there must not be.

"I'll tell you this much," he said. "If the Germans make it past our initial defenses, France will be lost."

"And if that happens?" she asked, stubbing out her cigarette in the ashtray beside her.

"I don't know." He blew out his cheeks and exhaled. "I honestly don't know. Maman and Papa have mentioned going to England."

"Yes, it came up yesterday as well." Evelyn watched as he put out his own cigarette. "We'd be more than happy to have you, of course. Mum would be overjoyed."

Before he could respond, the door opened and Gisele swept in in a swirl of silk and perfume.

"Here you are!" she exclaimed. "I've been looking everywhere for you. What are you doing in here?"

"I came in to escape the argument in the parlor," Evelyn said with a laugh, "and then Nicolas came and found me."

Gisele crossed the room to drop carelessly onto the love seat beside her.

"Are you coming out tonight?" she asked, looking at Evelyn. "I think we're going dancing."

"I'll have to take a pass, I'm afraid. I promised a friend that I would take a package to her Aunt in Metz."

"Metz!" Nicolas exclaimed. "When?"

"I thought I'd go tomorrow, if I can borrow your car, Zell."

"I don't mind." Gisele yawned and picked up the discarded book on the cushion beside Evelyn, glancing at it cursorily. "Long drive, though."

"That's why I'm staying in tonight. I want to get an early start in the morning."

"You may need to get petrol. I don't remember the last time I filled it up."

Evelyn smiled. Gisele's car was a Bugatti 57s Atlantic sports car that she and Nicolas shared. However, neither of them drove it much while they were in Paris. They were always quite happy to have her borrow it when she wanted, and she unabashedly admitted that she took advantage of their generosity whenever an opportunity arose. It was fast and sleek, and she loved it.

"I'll take care of it."

"Do you want some company?" Nicolas asked suddenly. "I'll come along if you like."

She blinked in surprise, but before she could say anything, Gisele clucked her tongue.

"You can't go to Metz tomorrow," she said. "We're expected at the Gautier's for their spring luncheon."

Nicolas made a face. "Completely forgot about that. Do we have to?"

"Yes. You know we go every year." Gisele grinned. "Perhaps they won't have it next year." She looked Evelyn. "It really is the dullest thing, and it's so packed that you can't even move. We hate going."

"Then why do you?"

"Traditions, I suppose." Gisele shrugged her slender shoulders. "Especially now, we have to try to keep up whatever semblance of normality that we can."

Evelyn raised her eyebrows. It was unlike her pretty cousin to bring up the war. She tended to avoid discussing it as much as possible.

"Paris seems just the same as ever to me," she said.

"It's not," Gisele said, surprising her. "This war is like the big elephant in the room that no one wants to acknowledge is there, myself included. But we all know it's looming over us. The clubs are a little too noisy now, the restaurants a little too packed. Everyone is trying to go on as before, but underneath…" She shrugged. "We're all waiting."

"For what?"

"Why, for the invasion, of course." She got up and wandered over to the piano, pressing one of the ivory keys. "You know, Evie, I'm a little jealous of you and your new job with the…what is it called again?"

"WAAF. It's the Women's Auxiliary Air Force."

"At least you can do something. I'd love to join the army, but the only thing I can do is be a nurse or drive for the Red Cross." She turned and leaned against the piano, staring pensively across the room. "I suppose if things continue, I'll end up driving. I don't think I'd make a very good nurse."

"You?" Her brother grinned. "No. But you can drive. If you want to do something, why don't you?"

"I don't know. Why don't you?"

"Papa is trying to get me into the diplomatic service," he said unexpectedly. "If that doesn't pan out, I'll have to join something. I'm surprised they haven't called me up already, to be honest."

Gisele looked startled. "But you've already done your two years service!"

"We're at war, Zell. They're calling people up now." Nicolas sat on the love seat next to Evelyn. "If I have a choice, I suppose I'd rather go into the air force. If things don't work out the way Papa wants, then perhaps I will."

"Oh, this whole thing is horrible," she cried. "Maybe we should just go to England with Maman and Papa and wait it out there."

Nicolas frowned. "And leave France?"

"It would be better than you having to do something you hate and maybe be killed!"

Evelyn looked from one to the other.

"Are Tante and Uncle seriously considering going to England?" she asked. "I know it's been mentioned, but are they really serious about it?"

Gisele nodded. "Yes. Papa is worried."

"What about the chateau?" Evelyn asked.

"That's where we will go if we have to leave Paris," Nicolas replied. "It's far enough south that it will be safe enough, at least temporarily. I think Papa is worried that it will be like Poland."

Evelyn was silent. If and when Hitler finally moved, if the joint efforts of Britain and France didn't stop him, it very well could turn into Poland. Uncle Claude was right to be worried.

"Nicki, I know we agreed that if they go to England, we would stay. But if there's a real possibility that you will have to fight, perhaps we should reconsider," Gisele said slowly.

"There was always that possibility," he pointed out. "What's changed?"

"*I* wasn't aware of that possibility!" she exclaimed, her blue eyes flashing. "We've always done everything together, but I can't fight with you. And I'll be damned if I'm going sit at home alone while you go to war."

Evelyn couldn't stop the grin that crossed her face.

"I think perhaps you're both getting a bit ahead of yourselves," she said soothingly. "Zell, if he gets a spot with the diplomatic office, he won't have to fight. And if he doesn't, well, they still haven't called him up yet."

"I don't know how you can be so calm all the time," Gisele complained. "Aren't you worried about Rob flying his fighter planes?"

"Every day, but worrying isn't going to change anything. All it will do is make me look haggard, and then who will dance with me?"

Gisele choked on a laugh. "Marc Fournier will always be willing to dance with you, Evie."

"As would any man in his right mind," Nicolas agreed with a grin. "How did we get so melancholy all of a sudden? This is will never do." He stood up and looked down at Evelyn. "Are you sure you won't come out with us? I think we need a few drinks and some dancing to forget about all this for a few hours."

"I'm sure." She smiled up at him. "I'll come out next time. I promise."

Nicolas nodded and glanced at his sister. "Come on, Zell. Let's forget about all this for a few hours."

She nodded and Evelyn watched as they left the room, closing the door behind them. She picked up her discarded book, but it sat on her lap unopened as she stared across the room, a frown on her face. If France was invaded, and Gisele and Nicolas remained in France, they would be in a perfect position to help her feed information back to MI6. With their connections, they would be able to move freely and see and hear all kinds of things. While she, on the other hand, would be in France under a completely different guise.

Her lips pressed together thoughtfully. She knew they could never know about her own activities, but perhaps Bill could find a way to pull them into a new network. They were trying to rebuild the networks that had been destroyed by the Venlo incident, and here were two perfect candidates that could be invaluable. They both wanted to do something for the war, but had no idea what. They were exactly the type of people Bill was looking for. Why had neither of them considered it before?

After a long while, Evelyn finally set the book aside and stood up, moving towards the door. Gisele and Nicolas couldn't know about her or Bill, but that didn't preclude them arranging for an introduction to someone else. Someone who would report back directly to Bill.

Someone like Josephine Rousseau.

Chapter Five

Evelyn steered the Bugatti to the side of the road and turned off the engine. It was a little after noon when she entered the medieval city of Metz, driving through picturesque streets that took her breath away. She'd never been to the city, and now she gazed about in appreciation. The narrow, curving streets were lined with old, beautiful buildings that had stood for centuries along the Moselle River. As she progressed through the city, following Rue de la Tête d'Or, Evelyn continued to be impressed by the sheer beauty of the old streets. It reminded her forcibly of Strasbourg and she wondered why she had never ventured east to explore these regions before now.

Reaching over to the passenger seat, she picked up her purse and got out of the low-slung sports car, closing the door and looking around. She was to meet Josephine at the Porte des Allemands, or the German's Gate, which spanned the River Seille. It was part of an old fortress constructed in medieval times, and she could see the bridge leading to the turreted, fortress-like gate at the top of the street. With a swift glance around, she started up the street towards the bridge.

It was another beautiful day and the sun shone over the ancient streets while a soft breeze blew off the river, stirring her blonde hair under her hat. Breathing deeply, she inhaled the scent of aged stone mixed with the river and sighed.

Oh, how she loved France!

As her fashionable heels clicked along the pavement, Evelyn sobered. Metz was close to the German border, and one of the most heavily fortified regions in the Maginot Line. When the Germans came, and they would, this city would be one of the first to be attacked. She looked up at the buildings next to her and wondered, suddenly, if they would be spared the wrath of the Luftwaffe, Germany's Air Force.

It had been well over a year since she last saw Josephine Rousseau. The young woman had been in Strasbourg on that fateful day in August, 1938, when Evelyn had gone to pick up a package for Bill. If it weren't for Josephine, she wasn't entirely sure that she would have made it back to Paris. When she arrived to meet the man from

Munich, it was only to find out that he'd been followed out of Germany by an SD agent. Hans Voss.

Evelyn shivered despite the mild spring day. It had been her first experience with the Nazi Sicherheitsdienst, the intelligence division of Himmler's SS, and Josephine had helped her escape. She had hoped that would be an end to her dealings with the SD, but she had run into them again in Oslo this past November. It was a different agent, but he had been even more persistent and determined than Voss.

As she made her way up the street towards the bridge, Evelyn wondered if Josephine had been surprised to hear that she was still working with Bill. When she last saw her in the streets of Strasbourg, there had been no guarantee that Evelyn would continue down this road. At the time, she was simply doing an old friend of the family a favor. Her lips curved faintly. She had often wondered in the months that had passed if Bill had already known what her decision would be the day he asked her to go to Strasbourg.

She paused on the corner and waited for a break in the traffic before running lightly across to the bridge on the other side. The sun glinted off the waves of the Seille, an off-shoot river from the Moselle, and the breeze pulled at the little rose-colored hat on her head. It was all in the past now, in any case. She *had* decided to continue with SIS, now called MI6 since the war began, and now she was meeting the French intelligence agent who had saved her neck all those months ago.

She started across the ancient stone bridge, the round tower of the medieval gate looming over the bridge like a sentry. An ornate iron railing ran along the bridge on either side, allowing an unimpeded view of the river in either direction. A group of tourists stood in the middle, clustered together at the railing while they gazed over the water and chattered together in what sounded suspiciously like Dutch. As she approached the center of the bridge, a woman emerged from behind the large group and walked towards Evelyn. Her black hair was tied back with a ribbon and covered with a brown hat. She was dressed in a simple brown suit and looked just like any of the other Frenchwomen moving around the city. Evelyn smiled, meeting her dark gray eyes over the distance.

Josephine smiled and, as she approached, held both her hands out to her.

"Mon vieil amie!" she exclaimed, grasping her hands and leaning forward to kiss the air beside her cheek. "It's been so long! How are you?"

"It's been too long!" Evelyn replied, returning the greeting. "It's so nice to see you again! You look fantastic."

49

Josephine laughed and tucked her arm through hers, turning to continue across the bridge towards the gate.

"I couldn't believe it when William told me you were going to be in Metz," she said. "I never thought I'd see you again. When we parted company in Strasbourg, I was convinced that you would return to Paris and never be seen again. What changed your mind?"

"You did," Evelyn said, surprising the other woman.

"Moi?"

"Well, and Karl," she qualified. "How was I to walk away and go back to my parties and my shopping knowing that people like you were out there doing unbelievably brave things in support of Liberté, Equalité, Fraternité?"

Josephine smiled and glanced at her, her dark eyes squinting in the sunlight.

"I'm glad you continued," she said. "We're in desperate need of people like you."

They reached the end of the bridge and Evelyn looked up at the medieval fortress gate before her.

"Incredible," she murmured. "Just amazing."

"Have you never been to Metz?"

"No, I'm ashamed to admit. I can't think how I never came to explore the city."

"It's quite beautiful. It doesn't have the same feeling as Strasbourg, but it still has plenty of the old world charm." They walked towards the arched entry to the gate. "I've been here for a few months now."

"Why did you leave Strasbourg?"

Josephine glanced at her. "I didn't have a choice," she said after a moment. "If I had stayed, the SS would have discovered my identity."

"How?"

"Not everyone in Strasbourg is as patriotic as we are," she said with a twisted smile. "I knew it was getting dangerous for me, but I foolishly didn't think it was unsafe yet. When one of my contacts from Stuttgart was arrested at the border, I knew it was time to leave. As it turns out, I heard that the police came to my apartment the day after I left. They had two Gestapo agents with them."

Evelyn's lips tightened. "It's beginning already," she murmured. "They haven't even invaded yet and they're already using the French police."

Josephine shrugged. "There is nothing new in that, as you saw yourself. The Gestapo have been coming and going freely, and it has only intensified since the war began. They've increased their presence in the city, and their influence. They are building many supporters. It is their way, no? They convert a few, and then use them as an excuse to march in."

They passed out from under the arched stone fortress and into a cobbled walkway between the gate and the two tall stone turrets of the castle. Stone arches stretched to their right, and on their left was what remained of the low medieval wall with its curved alcoves. There were a few other people in the walkway joining the two gates, but Josephine ignored them as they strolled towards the other gate. Beyond it, Evelyn could see the street.

"I suppose Bill wants to know if there's been any activity with the German troops," Josephine said in a low voice. "Is that why you're here?"

"Something like that, yes." Evelyn glanced at her. "We have the reports from the fortifications and the French army, but I don't think he quite trusts them."

Josephine let out a sound suspiciously like a snort.

"And he would be right not to," she muttered. "The forces at the line are being shuffled around and there is talk of the bulk of the Metz forces withdrawing and moving east along the Maginot towards Belgium. If they do that, there was no point in establishing these fortifications at all."

"Why would they do that?" Evelyn asked, startled. "With the weather turning mild, it can't be very long before Hitler moves."

The other woman shrugged.

"Your guess is as good as mine. Perhaps because the Germans haven't built up their forces on their side? They haven't, you know. There's no real change in the troops positioned along their border."

They walked under the second gate and emerged onto the street beyond. Evelyn paused and turned to look up at the two towers behind them now.

"I'd have thought they would have been attached to something," she murmured.

Josephine laughed and glanced up at them. "You would, wouldn't you? They were at one time, I'm sure."

"Why is it called Porte des Allemands?"

"They say there was a house of German knights near here in the 1200s. So the gate became known as the German's Gate." Josephine smiled wryly. "If they have their way, it will be theirs once again. This region has always gone back and forth between the French and the Germans, throughout history."

"And now it will begin again." Evelyn turned and fell into step beside her as they moved away from the gates and down the street. "There hasn't been any change at all on the German side of the border? Are you sure?"

"As sure as we can be without going over ourselves and looking. We receive news from people all along the border and there haven't been any indications of increased troop movements yet."

"What are they waiting for?" Evelyn wondered, her brows creased in a frown.

Josephine glanced at her. "They may not be waiting for anything," she said slowly. "I said there have been no troop movements along the borders with France."

Something in her tone made Evelyn look at her sharply. "Meaning?"

"There has been significant movement in other parts of Germany." Josephine paused to look in the window of a hat shop. "They're moving large amounts of troops and supplies north."

"North!"

She nodded. "Yes. Several divisions in the past few days alone."

"But the only thing north of Germany is…" Evelyn's voice trailed off and Josephine nodded.

"Precisely."

Evelyn exhaled. So Hitler was going for Sweden or Norway next.

"He will eventually turn his attention to France, but right now Hitler seems more preoccupied with Scandinavia," Josephine continued. "It won't last long, but it seems that our borders are safe. For now."

Evelyn nodded. "For now. But as you say, it can't last long."

"The North?" Bill stared across the desk at Evelyn, his brows pulled together in consternation. "Is she sure?"

"That's what I said," she replied with a short laugh. "She's sure. The Germans have been shifting whole divisions and supplies to the north of Germany."

She paused and opened her purse to pull out a slender tube much like a lipstick. She twisted the top off and tipped it upside down. An oblong roll of paper slid out and she stood up to pass it to Bill.

"She sent these. They're detailed lists of trains and mobile convoys carrying supplies north."

Bill raised his eyebrows and unrolled the papers, glancing through them.

"Where did she get these?"

"She didn't say. Only that they came from a verified source in Germany." Evelyn sat down again and crossed her legs. "She said they were to go to her own government, but she thought they would be of more use if they came to you instead. I'm afraid she doesn't seem to have a very high opinion of her own people at the moment."

Bill grunted and set the sheets down on his desk.

"I'm not sure that I blame her," he said. "Deuxième Bureau has been consistently ignoring certain information, while accepting less than reliable intelligence as fact. However, at least they are trying. The Netherlands are a disaster in that department. Unfortunately, much of the information the Deuxième passes on to the generals is discarded."

"That's what Josephine said as well." Evelyn frowned. "I don't understand. Why would they ignore information from their own intelligence service?"

Bill sighed and sat back.

"It's very difficult right now. They have leaders who are set in their ways and determined to fight this war the way wars have always been fought. They don't acknowledge that perhaps the enemy has changed and evolved. There is significant in-fighting going on at all levels in Paris. Many are calling for Daladier to step aside. They're disgusted with his handling of Finland, and have lost confidence in his leadership." He rubbed his forehead tiredly. "It's frustrating, but hardly surprising. This, however, will interest Montclair greatly." He indicated to the papers on the desk. "He's convinced the Germans will go after Norway. He's been pressuring for us to move first, but while Chamberlain and the House agree that Norway should be a priority, they have yet to actually do anything. Churchill has been ranting about mining the Norwegian waters for weeks, but again, nothing has been done."

"If Hitler attacks Norway, what about Sweden?"

"Sweden will remain neutral for as long as possible. They want no part of this war."

"Neither did Finland, but look at them now. They'll surrender any day now. They have to." Evelyn frowned. "Can the Norwegian army withstand a German offensive?"

"Not without us to help them," he said bluntly. "They would be out-manned and far out-gunned. They haven't made any attempt to rearm or build up their forces. Their army is strictly a defensive force, and not a very large one. Hitler knows that."

They were silent for a moment and then Evelyn looked up.

"Could it be a diversion?" she asked. "Could they be moving forces north to make us think they won't invade the lowlands?"

Bill smiled faintly. "Yes."

"But you don't think they are?"

"Who's to say?" He shrugged and sat forward again. "That's for London to decide. We did our job. What they do with the information is up to them. How did you find Josephine? Is she well?"

"Yes, she appears to be. We had lunch in a café before I left."

Bill's eyes met hers. "And did she arrange to stay in contact?"

Evelyn smiled. "Yes. Just as you predicted. How did you know?"

"The French aren't stupid. They know that if Germany invades and the battle is lost, they will lose their intelligence network. Agents like Josephine will want to ensure that they have another way of getting information out."

"I gave her the drop address in Paris, just as you said. If she needs to contact me, she'll arrange for a message to go to that address."

"Good." Bill looked at his watch. "It's getting late. Your mother will be wondering where you are."

Evelyn laughed and stood up, accepting her dismissal with good grace.

"I doubt that. She and my aunts have gone to the theatre. I'm meeting Nicolas and Gisele for dinner, though, so I have to be on my way." She turned towards the door, then paused and looked back over her shoulder. "Am I still returning to England on Friday?"

"Yes. Enjoy the rest of your time in Paris. I know you love it here."

Evelyn smiled. "I do, and I will."

She left the office and made her way through the embassy to the entrance. Her smile faded as she stepped out onto the Rue du Faubourg Saint-Honoré and turned to walk along the busy thoroughfare. The tension was palpable in the embassy and with Bill. They knew Hitler would move, and move soon. When he did, his Blitzkrieg, or Lightning War, would sweep across Europe. Paris would become dangerous, and Nicolas and Gisele would have to decide what they were going to do, as would her Aunt and Uncle.

Evelyn pressed her lips together as a chill went through her. She had a terrible feeling that, very soon, everything was going to change drastically, and she suddenly wanted nothing more than to enjoy her last few days in Paris with her family. She may not have the opportunity again for a very long time.

And when it was all over, the Paris she loved may be irreversibly changed, or gone forever.

Chapter Six

Liège, Belgium

Obersturmbannführer Hans Voss squinted against the sun and peered up at the cathedral before him. Of all the places in the city that he could meet with his informant, they had to pick a church. He hated the places and avoided them whenever possible. They filled him with a kind of dread, a throwback to his youth when his father would drag him by his ear every Sunday to listen to an old man expound upon the hopelessness and evils of humanity. That same old man was later caught raping a four-year-old girl in the woods. As far as Hans was concerned, the clergy could keep their hypocrisy. He would take his chances with the afterlife after living this life as he saw fit. And that did not include attending services on Sunday.

He started up the steps to the entrance of the sprawling example of Gothic architecture. He had come to the city on other business, intending only to stay for two days. Upon hearing of his arrival, however, Mira had contacted him to arrange this meeting. He agreed when he saw the last word in her message: Rätsel.

The mysterious Englishwoman had got under his skin. He freely admitted that. Twenty minutes in her company had been enough to convince him that she was intriguing. The subsequent weeks and months that followed had proven that she was also dangerous. The Maggie Richardson he met in Strasbourg had passed all the background checks that the SS had issued, except one. The woman he spoke with outside a café in Strasbourg claimed to have family in Berlin. The Margaret Richardson employed by the *Daily Mail* had no relations in Germany at all.

It was a small thing, overlooked by the British Security Service, but it was enough to convince them that she was a British agent. When Karl Gerst, the German traitor she'd been meeting with that day, disappeared less than twenty-four hours after crossing back into Germany, it only strengthened their suspicions. While they had been busy confirming the Englishwoman's story, Karl managed to slip away and, to date, still hadn't been found. They had been played by a pretty, young blonde.

Night Falls on Norway

Hans Voss did not take kindly to that at all.

He strode into the church, the sun disappearing as the heavy door swung closed. The dim gloom of the sanctuary engulfed him as he scanned the rows of empty pews stretching all the way to the nave at the back. The only sources of light came from the candles burning near the altar and the stained-glass windows high in the walls. The rest of the cavernous space was thrown into shadows, and it was within those shadows that he finally located Mira.

She was seated at the end of a pew next to a large stone pillar about halfway down the main aisle. A small functional hat covered dark hair, and she had her head bent as if she were in prayer.

Hans stripped his gloves off as he strode forward and down the center aisle. When he reached her pew, he continued to the next one before moving into the row seating himself in front of her. As he did so, he heard her shift and then her head appeared near his shoulder as she settled on the kneeler behind him.

"Guten Morgen, Frau Lutz," he murmured.

"Guten Morgen, Herr Schmidt," she replied. "How are you finding Liège?"

"Very busy," he said pointedly. "You have something for me?"

"Yes. As you requested, I've been remaining in close contact with our associates in Paris," she said, abandoning small talk. "I took the liberty of advising them to monitor the airports and train depots in the region."

"And?"

"Rätsel arrived at Orly on a British Overseas Airways flight two days ago."

Hans turned his head, glancing at her face sharply. "You're sure?"

"Yes. Our man there was certain. He described her perfectly." Mira kept her face towards the altar, not looking at him. "She arrived alone and went straight to a waiting car."

"Did she have anything with her?"

"A single suitcase and her purse."

"And where did she go?"

There was the faintest of hesitations and his eyes narrowed.

"Marcus lost her after they entered Paris."

Hans' lips tightened and he turned his head back to stare forward.

"He's watching the airport and alerted the men at the train stations. If she leaves Paris, they'll know."

"I'm not concerned with where she goes when she leaves Paris," he snapped. "I want to know who she sees while she's there."

Mira was silent and, after a moment, Hans sighed imperceptibly.

"Tell him to watch the embassy and passport control offices," he finally said. "If she's in Paris for any length of time, she will go to one of them. The SIS keeps their agents there. We can pick her up again when she checks in."

"And if she doesn't?"

"Then we have to wait for another opportunity." He began to pull on his gloves. "Tell Marcus not to lose her next time."

"If she does resurface, what then?"

"I want to know who she sees, where she's staying, and what she does. I want to know all of it. But under absolutely no circumstances is she to be approached! Contact me directly if we regain contact."

"Yes, Herr Schmidt."

He nodded and stood, moving out of the pew. He walked back down the aisle without a backwards glance. Mira would relay his message and if Rätsel reappeared, he had no doubt that he would know of it within a few hours.

As he emerged back into the sunshine and went down the steps of the church, Hans felt a familiar feeling of elation. The hunt was on again.

And this time he would not fail.

RAF Northolt
March 25, 1940

Evelyn watched as Bill shouldered his way through the people thronging the narrow, dockside street. She was seated in the back of a black Vauxhall, waiting to board a ship bound for Oslo. If there were nerves, she was trying to very hard to ignore them. Instead, she was concentrating on the fact that the trip had been moved up unexpectedly, resulting in her leaving directly from Scotland rather than London as originally planned.

When her liaison officer on the RAF base in Scotland had come into her office yesterday morning, Evelyn had been expecting instructions to go to London. Instead, she'd been handed a train ticket to Aberdeen. When she arrived at the station an hour ago, Bill was waiting for her. Aside from saying that the timetable had been moved up, he'd been unusually quiet on the ride to the docks. Now, watching him make his way back to the car with a paper-wrapped package under his arm, she chewed her bottom lip thoughtfully. What had happened to make it imperative that she go to Norway a full two-weeks ahead of schedule?

Bill reached the car and climbed into the backseat next to her, handing her the paper-wrapped package.

"This is all your identification and press credentials," he told her, closing the door. "You'll be staying in a boarding house run by one of our agents, but you may need those to verify your identity while you're going about the city."

"Are we still going with Maggie Richardson?" she asked, opening the package and pulling out a bill-fold. Opening it, she found identification papers, press credentials for the *Daily Mail* in London, and over five hundred pounds in Krone notes.

"Yes. That identity is established, and will work well in Oslo." Bill glanced at his watch. "We have a few minutes before it's time to board. I suppose you're feeling rather confused."

"A bit, yes." Evelyn tucked the billfold into her bag. "Why the sudden rush?"

"Shustov contacted us through the embassy in Helsinki. His scheduled trip to Oslo was changed. He's there now." Bill looked at her. "When you arrive, you'll check in with this contact at the embassy. Daniel Carew." He passed her a business card. "He will let Shustov know that you're in Oslo with a pre-arranged signal. Beyond that, Shustov refuses any and all other contact, so the assumption is that he will find you."

"He'll find me?" Evelyn stared at him. "I don't even know what he looks like! How am I supposed to know it's him?"

"That's an excellent question, and he's already provided the answer. When he does make contact with you, he'll ask you how the weather was in London when you left." He reached into the inside pocket of his coat and pulled out a small notebook. Flipping it open, he thumbed through until he reached a particular page. "Your reply should be the following, word for word: 'I carried an umbrella because it looked like rain, but left it on the train.' Got it?"

"Yes."

"Good." Bill tucked the notebook away again and looked at her. "Once you have the package, let Carew at the embassy know and he'll arrange for your return trip."

"That's it?"

"That's it. You should be back home in no time at all."

Evelyn exhaled and nodded. It certainly seemed straightforward enough. Check into her rooms, contact the embassy, wait for Vladimir to find her, and then go home. Her mind inadvertently went back to Strasbourg last summer. That also had been an easy and straightforward plan, and look at what a fiasco that had turned out to be.

"And everything's arranged with my posting in Scotland?" she asked. "In case anything comes up? They know what to do?"

Something like a smile passed over Bill's face.

"This isn't our first time out, m'dear," he assured her. "Believe me when I say that your liaison officer there is more than capable of taking care of any surprise visitors or family emergencies. You left your pre-written letters to be sent if you're delayed for some reason? Good. Then there's nothing to worry about. Should Rob or anyone else drop in, they'll be told you're away on a two-day training exercise."

They were silent for a moment and then Bill looked at her.

"Are you ready? It's time."

Evelyn took a deep breath and nodded, raising her blue eyes to his. "It doesn't matter if I'm ready or not, does it?" she asked humorously. "I have to get my feet wet sooner or later."

"The nerves will pass," he told her. "You'll be just fine. I've told you before that you're a natural. Some people were made for this kind of work, and you're one of them. Keep it simple and remember your training. You'll be on your way home in no time."

RAF Duxford
November, 1939

Evelyn hunched her shoulders against a brisk, stiff wind and put her head down to make her way across the road to her office building. She'd returned to London three days ago, but had ended up staying and going through a rather rigorous training refresher on code recognition. As a result, she'd just arrived back at Northolt this afternoon. She was tired, cranky, and wanted nothing more than her bed.

"Ooof!" Evelyn gasped as she collided with something tall and solid.

Night Falls on Norway

"Well well, if it isn't Assistant Section Officer Ainsworth!" She tilted her head back and peered up at Fred. "How goes the training?"

"You mean, how went the training?" she asked, extracting herself from his arms and grimacing when a blast of wind smacked her in the face. "Where did you come from? I didn't even see you!"

"I'd noticed. Funny how we keep running into each other this way. Only I recall that the last time you did that, you apologized."

"I'm terribly sorry." Evelyn tucked her arm into his and hurried him along towards the office building. "This wind is going to blow me away. Aren't you bothered by it?"

"Lord no. These flight jackets are terribly warm, y'know." Despite his words, Fred hunched his shoulders against another blast of wind. "'Course, the wind *is* jolly brutal today."

They ran together up the steps of the building and sighed in unison as they burst into the warm interior.

"Come into my office and have some tea. You can tell me what exciting news I've missed," she said, unbuttoning her coat.

"Where *have* you been?" he asked, following her down the hallway towards her office at the end. "I feel like I haven't seen you in weeks."

"It's only been two weeks, and you know I took some leave to visit my family," she replied, opening the door and going into her office. Fred followed, closing it behind him as she took off her coat and hung it on the stand behind the door. "I was in Paris for a week, if you must know, having a wonderful time."

She crossed to the desk, glancing at the stack of mail in the center before reaching for the telephone.

"Are you hungry?" she asked, glancing at him.

"Not a bit. Just tea, thanks."

Evelyn nodded and dialed the canteen, requesting tea to be sent round. When she hung up, she looked up to find that he'd shrugged out of his flight jacket and was straightening his uniform.

"Paris? That sounds marvelous. Who do you know in Paris?" he asked, perching on the edge of her desk.

"My mother is from France. Her sister still lives there with her family."

"Did you spend the whole week going to parties?"

"Something like that." She paused and looked at him suspiciously. "Why do you ask?"

"I thought so. You look tired."

"Well, thank you very much!" she exclaimed, affronted.

"No, I didn't mean it like that," he said hastily. "You just look a little pale, that's all."

"That's every bit as bad as tired!" Evelyn glared at him. "Are you saying I look like an old hag?"

She swung around and marched to the small mirror that hung on the wall a few feet away.

"Evelyn, I don't think you will ever look like an old hag," Fred announced. "You're beautiful, and you know it."

She frowned and examined herself in the small, cheap mirror. He was right. She did look tired and pale. Who would have thought that a week in France and three days of code recognition would take so much out of her? Lifting her hands, she pinched her cheeks to try to get more color into them, noting the dark shadows under her eyes. As she did so, Fred's face appeared in the mirror next to hers.

"Darling, I really didn't mean it. You're beautiful."

Evelyn met his worried gaze in the glass and smiled.

"But I'm not looking up to my usual standards. No, you're right. I do look tired." She sighed and turned away from the mirror, going back to the desk and dropping into her chair. She leaned her head back and stared up at him. "If I'm like this now, whatever will I look like if this war finally gets going?"

"You'll bloom!" Fred said promptly. "You've been working very hard. You're always off somewhere training someone. I'm glad you got some time off to enjoy yourself in Paris. I shouldn't have said anything. I don't suppose that Lacey chap would have, would he?"

"No. I don't suppose he would have," she said with a small smile.

"You missed a jolly good party at the officers' last night," he said, returning to his perch on the edge of her desk.

"Did I? Was anything broken?"

Before he could answer, a knock fell on the door. She called to enter and a young WAAF came in bearing a tray with a teapot and cups and saucers.

"Tea, ma'am," she said smartly.

Evelyn got up and met her to take the tray. "Thank you."

The WAAF nodded and saluted, then turned to leave the office, closing the door quietly behind her.

"Nothing was broken. Only a few hearts," Fred said with a wink.

"Then was it really even a party?" she demanded with a laugh, carrying the tray over to the desk and setting it down. "Didn't someone knock over a table at the last one? I could swear you told me something like that."

Night Falls on Norway

"It wasn't a table. It was the punch bowl." Fred grinned. "Nothing so exciting last night, but there was a fantastic band. Oh! Have you heard the news?"

"What news?" Evelyn poured out a cup of tea and handed it to him.

"Thanks. We've finally gone and done it!"

She looked at him blankly. "Sorry? Who's gone and done what?"

"England. The RAF. Us. We've finally done it!" His eyes were shining and Evelyn recognized the look in them. It was a look she'd seen in Robbie's eyes countless times when talking about his flying. It was a look of unsuppressed excitement.

"What have we finally done? Really, Fred, sometimes you're worse than a child!"

Her dancing eyes and fond smile took the sting out of her words as he grinned, unrepentant.

"We've gone and bombed Hörnum. It's a German airfield on some island or other."

"Sylt."

"Pardon?"

"The island of Sylt," she said, sitting down with her tea. "It's where Hörnum is."

"Then you know of it?" he asked, his eyebrows raising. "I had to look it up."

Evelyn shrugged. She knew all about the raid on Hörnum. She'd heard about it while she was still in Paris, but she couldn't very well take the wind out of his sails.

"What happened?"

"Fifty of our bombers flew over there and bombed them." Fred sipped his tea. "With bombs! Not bloody pamphlets! We've finally started showing some teeth. After all the convoys and patrols Jerry's been bombing, we're finally dishing some of it back."

"I'm not sure we should be so happy about that," Evelyn murmured.

Fred stared at her. "Why on earth not?" he demanded. "Do you have any idea how dangerous it is to fly over Germany and Poland? They don't exactly roll out the welcome mat. We've been sending over pilots with nothing but paper. They could be killed all for a cargo full of pamphlets saying we're right and Hitler's wrong!"

She sighed and nodded. "Yes. I know. I realize that, of course."

"Evie, don't you realize what this means? It means that we're finally going to get to do something other than fly useless training exercises. I'll be able to see action at last!"

Evelyn looked at him and saw the unbridled excitement in his eyes. She understood what it meant, all too well. But did he?

"Is that what you want?" she asked.

"Doesn't every pilot?" he replied. "I want to get up there and give Jerry what for! And I'll wager so does your Miles Lacey, and so does every other pilot worth his salt. They can't be allowed to just take whatever they want."

She nodded. Of course he did, and he was right. It was what he, Miles, Robbie and hundreds of others had been trained to do. And they wanted to do it. They wanted to fight for their country. Everyone in England did. So why was she suddenly so unenthusiastic?

"You're right," she said. "I just worry about what the war will bring now that the weather is improving."

"You worry too much," he told her with a wink. "It's because you work too hard. I think you need some time off. Come out to dinner with me tonight."

"I just had a week off!" she protested. "I can hardly claim to be overworked after traipsing off to Paris, can I?"

"All right. You're a slug who wastes her days," he retorted, finishing his tea and sliding off her desk. "In which case, you need someone to keep you in line."

"And that's you?" she asked with a laugh.

He grinned and reached for his jacket. "None other. I'll pick you up here at six."

"Have you got that door fixed yet?"

"Why'd I do that? It lends a certain charm, don't you think?"

"I think it's a disaster waiting to happen," she said, watching as he shrugged into his flight jacket. "Mark my words, Fred Durton. It won't be in a plane that you meet your Maker; it'll be in that car!"

Chapter Seven

Broadway Street, London

Evelyn got out of the taxi and went up the steps to the nondescript, drab building. She didn't even glance up at it anymore. The first time she'd come here, she'd thought she was in the wrong place. Now she was a regular.

She went in and nodded to the young man behind the front desk. He nodded back and lowered his eyes to his work, dismissing her. Evelyn strode past the desk and opened a door that led down a corridor to a flight of steps, and the labyrinth that was MI6's headquarters in London.

After glancing at her watch, she jogged lightly up the steps and smiled at the armed soldier at the top.

"Good morning, Harry," she said cheerfully, holding out her identification card for inspection. "How are you today?"

"I'm well, Miss Ainsworth, thank you." He nodded and looked at her card. "It's always nice to see you. It's been a few weeks, hasn't it?"

"Two, but you already knew that," she said in amusement. "I doubt very much gets past you at all, Harry."

"I do my best." He looked up and finally smiled, stepping back so that she could proceed. "Have a nice day."

She nodded and moved down the long corridor. When she'd first visited, she'd been shown the way to Jasper Montclair's office by a moody woman whom she'd never seen again, but Harry had been on duty then, and every day since. She honestly couldn't image ever coming to the top of the stairs and not seeing his curly black hair. Once she'd asked Bill if the personnel ever changed in the house on Broadway. He had looked faintly shocked and replied that if the personnel ever changed, they would be in dire straights indeed.

Coming to the last door before another set of stairs, Evelyn knocked once and reached for the handle.

"Come in!"

She turned the handle and entered the large corner office, a ready smile on her face.

"Good morning, Mr. Monclair. It's a lovely day outside." She closed the door and turned to look at William Buckley, who had risen at her entrance. "Good morning, Bill."

"Good morning." He nodded to her. "Did you have a pleasant drive in?"

"I did indeed! Fantastic driving weather!"

Jasper Montclair had stood up behind his desk and, as she spoke, he moved out from behind it to come forward, holding out his hand.

"I've been here since five. It wasn't as pleasant then," he said with a laugh. "I'm glad you came. Have a seat."

"Thank you." She shook his hand and moved to take the chair across from Bill. "You should really get out at least for a walk."

"A walk?" He raised his thick eyebrows and looked at her askance. "Really, my dear. This is London. We drive."

Evelyn laughed and set her purse beside her on the chair.

"You're wasting a gorgeous spring day," she told him, removing her gloves. "But to each his own."

"You'll never convince him," Bill told her. "He takes the car to the post office, which is right around the corner. It takes longer for his driver to pull around than it takes me to walk."

"I'll leave the exercise to the youth," Jasper retorted, seating himself again. "How was France?" he asked, turning his gaze to Evelyn.

"It was very nice. Paris was lovely, but then it always is. Metz was stunning. I can't think why I've never gone before." Evelyn finished removing her gloves and laid them on her lap, smiling across the desk at the man who ruled over them all. "But I don't suppose you care about the scenery, do you? Everything is in my report."

"Yes, I read it. Tell me, how did you find our French associate?"

Evelyn raised her eyebrows. "She seemed the same as she was the last time I saw her, but I'll admit that I've changed since then. She may have as well. Why do you ask?"

Jasper sat back in his chair and gazed at her pensively for a long moment. His bushy eyebrows were pulled over his eyes, giving him the look of an unsettled bulldog.

"Bill has shared with you the state of our networks in Europe, yes?"

Evelyn swallowed and glanced at her immediate boss. He shrugged.

"Yes."

"We're trying to rebuild them as quickly as we can but, as I'm sure you understand, we have to be necessarily cautious in our recruitment of agents. The Nazis know we're trying to rebuild, and they will be trying to insert people into any new system that we form. It's even more imperative now that we protect and maintain the networks we have left."

"Are you concerned that she might be turned by the Germans?" Evelyn asked. "I think that a very remote possibility. She's doing everything she can to pass on information about them to the outlets where she thinks it will cause the most damage."

"Yes, thank God. Deuxième Bureau is in something of a muddle at the moment, or so I'm told. They're still gathering intelligence from their agents, but how that information is being disseminated is rather disjointed."

"I've received the impression that Paul Reynaud is sympathetic to the efforts of the intelligence community," she said slowly, a frown knitting her brow. "Is that not the case? I thought him taking over as Prime Minister would be beneficial to the war effort."

"Yes, yes, he is. In fact, he's already put forth some rather bold ideas for collaboration between Britain and France that show he is serious about fighting this war, and winning at all costs. But he's kept many members of the old cabinet in positions that make it difficult to get the right people to listen to the right intelligence." Jasper sat forward and his frown grew. "I have no doubt that the dust will settle soon, but for now we have to maintain and build what contacts we can, and make sure those contacts are viable and, above all else, reliable."

"I believe that to be the case, at least as far as Josephine is concerned." Evelyn looked at Bill. "You would know better than me. I've only met her twice. You've seen the intelligence she's been gathering for the past two years."

"Yes, and I agree that she falls into the category of both reliable and stable," he agreed with a nod. "Her information has always been verified as correct by independent sources. This last lot was confirmed by an agent in Poland that she couldn't possibly have any knowledge of or association with."

"Good!" Jasper's countenance lightened somewhat. "That's what I want to hear. Do we have many more like her in France?"

Bill nodded.

"I have about four others, but they all report to the DB," he said. "It was the only way I could set up the extensive network that I did before the war began."

Evelyn was silent as they talked, her mind going to Nicolas and Gisele. This was the perfect opportunity to mention them, but she hesitated to do so. While she had no doubt that her cousins would be perfect agents, she was reluctant to drag them into this world of hers unless it became clear that France was going to fall. The danger was too real, and the cost too high to subject them to it unless it became absolutely necessary.

"It's a start, at least." Jasper turned his attention back to Evelyn. "I understand you've been learning Norwegian and Swedish."

"It seemed appropriate after November," she said with a sheepish smile. "While my translator was lovely, it wasn't ideal being unable to understand the language."

"I agree. How is it coming?"

"I'm fluent in both now."

He blinked and stared at her in astonishment. "Pardon?"

Bill was betrayed into a low chuckle.

"Welcome to the linguistic mystery of Miss Evelyn Ainsworth," he said, his eyes dancing. "I think we all gave up trying to comprehend how she does it a long time ago."

"You're completely fluent?" Jasper repeated.

She nodded. "Yes. My accent could use some work, but if I'm not trying to pass myself off as a Norwegian, it is acceptable."

"And if you were passing yourself off as French? Or German?"

"More than sufficient."

Jasper sat back in his chair and shook his head, a reluctant smile crossing his face.

"Is there anything else I should know? Have you gone and mastered Swahili as well?"

She laughed. "Not yet."

"I do enjoy how she says yet," Jasper said to Bill with a grin. "How's the Japanese coming?"

"I'm still working on that. I haven't had very much time to devote to it. Norwegian and Swedish seemed to be the more pressing need."

"Agreed, especially now." Jasper nodded. "You're going back to Norway, I'm afraid."

Evelyn raised her eyebrows in surprise. "Sir?"

"It's why I called you here today." He got up and went over to a tall filing cabinet against the wall, pulling out a key from his waistcoat pocket. He unlocked a drawer and pulled a file out. "I know Bill usually takes care of these briefings, but this one is a bit sensitive. And there are some aspects with which he is not at all familiar with at the moment. He's being briefed as well as you. Some of this was just finalized this morning, as a matter of fact."

He turned from the cabinet and returned to his seat, setting the folder down on his desk.

"I've decided to send you back to Oslo because, to be frank, you're the only agent that Daniel Carew has anything good to say about," he said, glancing up. "You made quite an impression in November, and I'm told you made solid contacts in the city."

"I only made one that I'm aware of," Evelyn said. "He said I made more than one?"

Jasper smiled faintly. "Perhaps you were unaware that the Kolstads are considered agents?"

"The landlords? I knew they were aware of my activities to some extent, but Carew specifically warned me that they lend rooms to agents of other countries as well."

"Yes they do, under our advisement." He flipped open the folder. "They keep a close eye on the activity that occurs in Oslo, both ours and others. That activity has increased substantially over the past few months."

"Isn't that to be expected?" she asked. "They're a neutral country. As such, they're bound to attract everyone. It's safer to conduct business there than in, say, Finland at the moment."

Jasper glanced up sharply. "Speaking of Finland, I have some news about your source there. Niva."

"Oh yes? How is he?"

"We believe he's dead." He sat back. "He never returned to Turku after your meeting with him in Sweden."

Evelyn stared at him, feeling the blood drain from her face. "What?"

He nodded soberly. "He seems to have disappeared. However, and this came from a not very reliable source, someone matching his description was seen being helped onto a ship in Stockholm. He was accompanied by two men, believed to be Soviet NKVD."

"But...no one knew he was meeting me," she stammered. "How could he have been caught? The only person who knew was..."

Her voice trailed off suddenly and Jasper nodded.

"Precisely. Shustov was the one who offered to arrange the meeting, correct?"

"But he wouldn't give up one of his own, would he?" Evelyn asked, looking from Bill to Jasper in consternation. "What would he have to gain by it?"

"We don't know, and there's no proof that he did," Bill said. "Neither of the men seen getting on the ship match the description you gave me of Shustov. I don't think he was there."

"That's if it even *was* Niva spotted getting on the ship," Jasper added. "As I said, the source isn't completely reliable. The ship was bound for Russia, and we've confirmed that it did sail on that date from Stockholm to Leningrad."

"But he definitely didn't return to Finland?"

"No."

"Well, that's all very disconcerting," she muttered, sitting back in her chair and exhaling. "If he was taken by the Soviets, and Shustov wasn't involved, he's at risk as well. Have we heard anything from him?"

Bill shook his head. "No. That's not unusual, though. Your father would go for months before he was contacted again."

"So I just wait?"

"Yes. And in the meantime, you go to Oslo," Jasper said. "I'm getting concerned about the increased activity there, especially from the Germans. The situation is very delicate, though. Norway is officially neutral, and they aren't happy with us at the moment."

"Because of the *Altmark*," Evelyn said, nodded. "You can't blame them, really. Not only did we breach their neutrality by engaging the Germans in their waters, but then Germany demanded reparations from them for allowing it to happen."

"Agreed, but it has put a strain on our relations with them. Furthermore, we will be straining that relationship even more in the coming weeks. With Reynaud taking over in France, there are significant plans being made with regards to Norway."

"Are we going back to the plan to lay mines in their waters?" Bill asked, startled. "I thought that was abandoned."

"It was. Reynaud has revived it, and added to it substantially." Jasper sat back and looked at them both soberly. "The fact is that Hitler gets his iron from the mines in northern Sweden. If we can take away the possibility of the Germans moving that iron through the Norwegian ports, we can cripple their supply lines. I'm sure you understand how vital iron ore is to them. Not only that, but if they gain control of the ports along the western coast of Norway, the German navy will have unrestricted access to the North Atlantic. Given the havoc their submarines are wreaking on our shipping already, that is to be avoided at all costs."

Evelyn stared at him. "You're talking about Hitler invading Norway."

"It's believed that he will try. Well, it stands to reason, doesn't it? He'd be a fool not to."

"So we're going to mine the waters to try to disrupt the German naval movements? That will infuriate the Norwegians, and it will force Hitler to retaliate," Bill pointed out.

"Exactly. That's why I said that things are about to get even more strained."

"If Hitler retaliates, we'll go into Norway," Evelyn said suddenly. "That's what they're thinking, isn't it? That we'll go in first."

Jasper looked at her in surprise. "Very good, Miss Ainsworth."

"It's what Hitler and Stalin have both done. They've created an incident and then used that to justify taking control of countries. We're going to do the same thing."

"Perhaps. Nothing is settled, and a lot can happen before it gets to that point."

Evelyn pressed her lips together. The thought of using their own tactics against them didn't disturb her as much as the thought of Norway paying the price for it. Norway was a country filled with thousands of innocent people. Jasper was discussing forcing war onto those people without any emotion, as if they wouldn't be the ones to pay the price for it.

"Now that you're aware of the situation," he continued, oblivious to her simmering discomfort, "let's discuss what you'll be doing in Oslo. With all of this up in the air, we have to think about what happens if the Germans get to Norway first. As it stands right now, if Hitler invades Norway, we have no one there to get information out."

"You want to build a network in Norway?" Bill asked incredulously.

"I want to gauge what the response would be if we tried. Things are shaky between our governments, but I want to know how that translates into the people themselves. If we can build even a small group to pass information, it will be critical in the event that Hitler does invade."

"And you want *me* to do this?" Evelyn asked, staring at him in astonishment. "I don't know the first thing about gauging people's interest or building networks!"

"You know much more than you think," he said dryly. "According to Carew, you have a willing disciple in the translator you worked with in November. You also managed to cultivate a new and unknown asset in the NKVD. He's since disappeared, but the fact remains that you gained his trust. Bill says that your French associate spoke very highly of you after meeting you in '38, and it doesn't appear that that opinion has changed since. That isn't something that can be learned, my dear. We can teach you how to recognize possible recruits and how to approach them, but that's where it ends. Gaining their trust and respect is something that can't be taught. And you appear to have that rather invaluable skill."

"But…I wouldn't even know where to begin!"

"Which is why you will begin a crash course training tomorrow morning. Bill will give you directions and the appropriate credentials to access the facility. It's not far, only about an hour's drive."

"And when do I leave?" she asked, resigned. There was no arguing with them. That much was clear.

"You'll have three days of intensive training, then you'll be on your way. We've arranged for you to leave from London. You should be on your way by Sunday at the latest. Time is of the utmost importance."

"I understand."

He nodded and his face relaxed into a small smile.

"Good. Then Bill will take care of the rest."

Chapter Eight

Zurich, Switzerland

"Here you are, Herr Pemberton," the concierge said with a smile, handing over a room key. "Please enjoy your stay. If there's anything you need, don't hesitate to inquire."

"Thank you." The man took the key and picked up his suitcase, turning away from the desk. He went a few steps, then paused and turned back. "Actually, there is something. I need to send a telegram. Do you have that ability here?"

"Yes, of course." The concierge reached under the counter, producing a pad. "If you fill out the form, we can send it directly from the hotel."

Mr. Pemberton went back to the desk. "Thank you. I'll take it to my room and drop it off when I go out for dinner."

"Very good, sir."

He took the slip of paper from the concierge and turned away again, moving towards the lift, waving away the services of a porter. A short time later, he unlocked the door to his room and went inside. The hotel was one of the best in the city, and the room was large and comfortable. After a cursory look around, he set down his suitcase and crossed over to the window.

The sun was setting, casting the mountains in the distance in varying shades of pink and orange. He stared at the breathtaking sight for a moment, then turned to drop the slip of paper on a desk positioned near the window. He had to compose a message to Berlin, but it could wait a few minutes.

Crossing back to his suitcase, he lifted it onto the bed and undid the leather clasps. The journey from London had been long and he was tired, but he had to meet the Swiss attaché for dinner in an hour. That meant changing into dinner clothes. He glanced at his watch and opened the case.

This was his first official trip to Zurich. He'd been twice before, but both times were for skiing and relaxation. This was his first time being sent by London on official business. His lips twisted faintly. If nothing else, war was good for advancement, at least in Whitehall.

Zurich had always been Robert Ainsworth's domain, but his death had left a void that few expected would ever be filled. He was hoping to change that way of thinking.

Fifteen minutes later saw the man dressed impeccably in a black formal suit. He adjusted his cuffs and looked at himself critically in the full length mirror. It would do. Percy Pemberton, as he was known to the hotel, was a traveling salesman from London and, as such, would have to wine and dine his clients. If the suit made him look more like the upper-class English politician that he was he doubted that anyone in the hotel would notice. Perhaps in the restaurant someone would recognize the cut of the suit as that of an English tailor, but in the restaurant he would be known by his real name; no one would question him.

He turned and went back to the desk, seating himself and picking up a pencil. This Zurich trip had turned out to be rather perfect timing, really. Not only would he have the opportunity to meet with his German handler in person, but he could also assure them of his eventual success in making good on his promise to retrieve what Robert Ainsworth had stolen. Unfortunately, he had been unable to do so as of yet. They were getting impatient in Berlin, and who could blame them? He'd said he could deliver, and then he hadn't. The only thing saving him right now was the obvious fact that while he had been unable to locate the missing package, so had everyone else. The secrets were still safe, for the time being.

But that wouldn't last for long.

The man thought for a moment, staring sightlessly across the room. How to word the telegram? He wanted to make sure that the information reached Berlin immediately, before he met with his handler the following day. He wanted no surprises here in Switzerland. More than one agent had died here recently, and he had no wish to join them.

Lowering his eyes to the paper, he wrote quickly, filling out the spaces.

ARRIVED IN ZURICH. EVERYTHING ON SCHEDULE. PRODUCT STILL IN PRODUCTION. RÄTSEL MODEL ADVANCING QUICKLY. KNOWN AS JIAN BY THE WORKERS. NEXT PLANNED STOP IS OSLO.

When he had finished, he sat back and set the pencil down. There. That would buy him time with Berlin. His current standing would be assured as long he continued to provide information that would aid with Operation Nightshade. And, lucky for him, he had access to information that would prove useful.

Night Falls on Norway

It wasn't as easy as it had been five months ago. They had shut down access to that entire section of the security service in November, followed closely by several others. It was difficult now, but not impossible. The spy the Germans called Rätsel was still active and, as such, information could be found.

One just had to know where to look.

Dorchester Hotel, London
March 31, 1940

Evelyn looked across the table at Miles and smiled. He was dressed in his uniform, which was impressive in its own right, but his careless elegance seemed more apparent than ever this evening. From the time they'd arrived at the exclusive restaurant and he'd given his name to the maître d', he'd done nothing but play the gentleman to her and everyone around them. It was a strange shift from the laughing, carefree man she was getting to know, but it was a shift that seemed to be just as much a part of him as the reckless pilot. This was Miles Lacey of the Yorkshire Laceys.

"That dress is far from RAF issue," he said with a grin. "Not that I'm complaining, mind you!"

"I came to London on Friday for a meeting with the solicitors," she said easily, reaching for her glass of wine. "I could hardly wear my uniform all weekend. They're dreadfully uncomfortable, you know."

"Do you think so? They seem fine to me."

"Of course they do. You're used to wearing a tie!" she retorted. "Although, more often than not, you're not wearing it when I see you. Why *do* you wear a silk neckerchief?"

"It's a sight more comfortable, for one thing," he said. "I've also learned, as did most of the other pilots who went before me, that turning your head constantly in the cockpit tends to rub your neck raw. One of the chaps who trained us flew in Spain. He gave us the tip about the silk scarves or neckerchiefs."

"I would never have thought of that on my own," Evelyn admitted, pursing her lips thoughtfully. "It makes perfect sense, though."

"They also make us look dashing and set us apart from everyone else," he added with a wink.

She laughed. "So they do."

"How is Fred Durton? Are they flying patrols now as well?"

"Yes. He's just like a schoolboy, all giddy with excitement." She tilted her head and looked at him. "I can't imagine you like that, but I suppose you must be happy to be doing something other than fly training sorties."

"I am," he admitted. "I think we're all glad that the waiting seems to be almost over. But I'm also a bit more pragmatic than some of the others. I don't think it will be quite what we're all expecting. How can it be? The Luftwaffe pilots are much more experienced than we are. They've already seen battle in Spain and Poland. All we've done is hours of formation flying."

"Not all the Luftwaffe pilots have seen battle," she said. "I'm sure there are just as many who haven't yet."

Miles shrugged and let out a noise suspiciously like a grunt. "Perhaps."

"Do you believe in luck?" she asked suddenly. "I mean, like lucky charms and that sort of thing?"

He raised his eyebrows in surprise. "You mean like a lucky rabbits foot?"

"Yes. Fred does. He wears a chain round his neck when he flies with a medal on it. St. Christopher, I think. Says it was his fathers. He won't go up without it, apparently."

"I never have before," he said slowly, "but I don't suppose I ever gave it much thought. Slippy, one of the other pilots in my flight, has a lucky sharks tooth that he takes up with him."

"And you don't have anything?"

Miles winked. "I don't need luck, m'dear. I'm a fantastic flier."

Evelyn laughed. "Of course you are."

"What do you think about the situation in France?" he asked after a moment.

"You mean with the prime minister?" When he nodded, she shrugged. "I think people were fed up with Daladier. My uncle says that more should have been done to help Finland, but that Daladier didn't have the courage to do it."

"And Reynaud does?"

Evelyn couldn't help but think of Reynaud's immediate push to maneuver into Norway before Hitler did and her lips tightened imperceptibly.

"I think so," she said slowly. "I think he's more in line with what people like my uncle want in a leader. He's keeping Daladier on in his cabinet, so he's being sure to appease everyone."

76

Night Falls on Norway

"I can't help but wonder if the same thing will happen here," Miles said unexpectedly. "There is a very large portion of the House that doesn't think Chamberlain's the man to lead us in this war. After all, he did everything in his power to prevent it, and now he hasn't done anything really to show that we're serious."

"I know you don't like him," she said with a quick smile. "I don't much, either, but Lord Halifax would replace him and I don't know that that's any better. At least we know what we have with Chamberlain."

"Yes. We have our bombers flying over Poland dropping pamphlets instead of bombs." He reached for his whiskey and soda. "It's ridiculous. We're at war and we're bombing them with paper! I can guarantee that any fighters that come across our bombers won't be shooting spitballs. The crews are risking their lives, and for what?"

"To not incite Hitler's wrath."

"Exactly. And at what cost? I heard that there was a bombing raid over Poland and the pilots had to fly back over Germany. Can you imagine? Not one bomb on the plane and they were flying over the Fatherland as bold as you please." He sipped his drink. "Do you know what happened? One of them thought they had crossed back into France and landed. Turns out he wasn't in France at all. He was still in Germany!"

"No!" she gasped. "What happened?"

"The poor sod had to take off again, didn't he?" Miles shook his head and a reluctant smile came to his lips. "Can't imagine what the farmers thought. Supposedly there were a lot of astonished peasants watching."

"Thank God he was able to take off again before anyone got there!"

"Yes, bloody lucky. I wonder if he had a good luck charm on him? He ended up landing safely in France, at any rate."

"I see your point, though," she said after a moment of thought. "All that could have ended much differently and all his mission had accomplished was to drop tons of propaganda over Poland."

"Precisely."

"But we did have at least one bombing run with bombs. Freddie told me about it. He said we bombed Hörnum."

"Yes, and do you know what we did?"

"I believe his phrase was that we 'showed them what for,' " she murmured humorously.

"Oh, we showed them all right. We showed them that some of our navigators are idiots. One of the planes bombed the wrong island! In fact, they went to the wrong bloody country!"

Evelyn's mouth dropped open. "What?"

"Somehow the navigator managed to guide his pilot to Bornholm."

"Isn't that a Danish island?" she asked, her brows knitted together.

He raised an eyebrow, impressed. "Very good. Yes. Most people don't know that. You remember your geography."

She grinned. "I'm good at some things," she replied. "But…Bornholm isn't even in the North Sea! It's in the Baltic!"

"I know! That's what makes it even worse! They went to the wrong island, in the wrong country, and in the wrong sea!"

"Denmark must have been furious!"

"I don't think any damage was done, not really. They probably hit an empty field somewhere. It's bloody embarrassing, though."

Evelyn was silent for a moment, then her lips trembled. He saw it and gave her a mock stern look.

"Are you laughing, ASO Ainsworth?" he demanded.

"You must admit, it *is* rather funny," she said, the trembling turning into a chuckle. "They're finally allowed to drop something other than paper and someone goes and mucks it all up."

"I suppose we should be grateful it wasn't the Soviet Union they hit," he said thoughtfully, his own lips curving. "I don't imagine that would have ended well at all."

"Oh Lord, no!"

"I suppose these things are bound to happen, but it really does make me feel like we're trying to win the game from behind." He sighed. "At least we're starting to do something, though. We've spent the entire winter doing nothing."

"So have they," she pointed out. "It was a particularly bad winter. I'm glad it's over, personally. Now we can get down to business."

He smiled across the table. "And are you getting down to business?"

"More than ever," she said, inwardly wincing at the irony in her tone. Before he could notice, she continued, "I'm off to Wales tomorrow to give an extended training class."

"Wales!" he exclaimed. "How long will you be there?"

"I'm really not sure, to be honest. It's a week long course, but there's always something that comes up to delay things."

"Now what could possibly delay a training course?" he wondered, his eyes dancing. "No! Don't say it. I know. Taboo subject. My apologies."

Evelyn laughed. "I think I'm finally getting you trained, Miles Lacey," she decided.

He looked horrified.

"Good Lord, is that what's happening? We can't have that." He pushed his chair back and stood up, holding his hand out to her. "Let's dance and forget all about the war for a bit."

She placed her hand in his and allowed him to pull her out of her seat. Meeting his green eyes, Evelyn felt a rush of contentment as his fingers closed warmly around hers. Yes. They would forget about the war for a few hours and enjoy each other, as they would if none of this was happening. Tomorrow would come soon enough, and it would see her on her way to Oslo and him back to Duxford.

But tonight they had music and each other.

Oslo, Norway
April 2, 1940

The door to the tall boarding house opened as Evelyn climbed out of the taxi that had carried her to a quiet street, just a block from the busy Bygdøy Allé in Olso's West End. The boarding house was just as she remembered it from the previous November, and she smiled at the sight of Josef Kolstad filling the doorway.

"God ettermiddag!" she called cheerfully.

The man's eyebrows rose in surprise and something resembling a smile curved his lips.

"God ettermiddag," he said, coming across the pavement to take her cases from the driver. "You learned Norwegian?"

"I did," she said, turning to pay the driver. "But you will have to correct me if I get something wrong. I've not had anyone to practice with."

"Did you have a good trip?" he asked, turning to carry her bags into the house.

"Yes, thank you. I flew in so it was very quick and very uneventful." She followed him into the house. "How are you and Else?"

79

"We're well. She's at the market doing the shopping. She asked me to show you to your room." He started up the narrow stairs. "She's put you in the same room you were in the last time. I hope that's acceptable?"

"That's perfect," Evelyn assured him as they reached the top of the stairs and turned left. "Are there many guests here?"

"Not many. It is a slow time right now."

She nodded and watched as he opened the door to her room and went inside with the bags. Hopefully she wouldn't have to worry about any SD agents like Herr Renner this time around. Her lips tightened at the thought of the German agent. That was an experience she had no desire to repeat any time soon.

"I started the fire for you earlier," Josef said, setting her cases down near the door, "so it should be warm in here now."

"Thank you very much," she said, looking around the familiar room with a smile. "It was a bit of a shock to come back to winter. Spring has already begun in England."

"We're still some way off from spring. There will be snow again yet." He turned to leave. "I'll leave you to get yourself settled. Welcome back."

"Thank you."

He paused at the door and turned to look at her.

"Daniel Carew reserved the room under the name Marlene Elfman. Is that what you wish to be called at present?"

"Yes please." Evelyn turned to smile at him ruefully. "I was told you would understand."

A wry smile cracked his face and he nodded brusquely. "I understand perfectly, Miss Elfman."

He left, closing the door behind him, and she turned to gaze around the room. It was just as she remembered. A large hearth dominated one wall and a four-poster bed was set opposite it. A desk stood next to the bay window overlooking the street, and a single chair was placed near the fire. An upright armoire was in the corner near the door. Everything was neat and clean. Although sparsely furnished, the room was warm and cozy, and Evelyn felt comfortable here.

She picked up her suitcase and carried it over to set it on the bed. Unfastening the leather straps, she unlatched the case, flipping it open to reveal her clothes neatly folded inside. She would unpack and hang the clothes in the wardrobe, then she would make arrangements to see Daniel Carew.

He would be her contact while she was in Oslo. She had dealt with him the last time she was here and had found him to be very helpful and efficient. Evelyn was grateful that he was still the attaché in Oslo. It would be easier to approach this mission surrounded by people she was already familiar with, especially in a strange country.

Her lips curved faintly as she began to unpack. Not that this was a strange country anymore. Driving through the streets on her way here, Evelyn now felt as if the city was becoming familiar to her. Knowing the language this time around certainly helped make her feel comfortable as well, she admitted to herself. Everything wasn't quite so strange as it was in November. She hadn't expected to return to Oslo, yet here she was, on a mission to recruit potential spies for England.

Shaking her head, she took a deep breath. The training course she'd gone through last week had been intensive and surprisingly thorough. While she still didn't feel entirely comfortable, at least she now had more confidence in her ability to recognize potential allies and recruit them accordingly. It was something she hadn't expected to be doing, but Evelyn was quickly coming to the realization that this war would be filled with tasks that she never thought she would have to do.

When she first began this journey with Bill and MI6, she'd had only a vague idea of what she would actually be doing. She had imagined a life of picking up packages and delivering them, nothing more. Her lips twisted now as she emptied her suitcase. Oh, how naive she had been! She was much more than a simple courier now, and she was expected to do whatever was necessary in support of King and Country.

And she had every intention of doing just that.

Chapter Nine

Hotel Bristol, Oslo

The restaurant was slow but Evelyn assumed that that was to be expected for a Tuesday evening. She had been shown to a table in the corner, partially concealed by an immense potted fern, and that suited her perfectly. She would be lying to herself if she pretended that she hadn't been looking over her shoulder ever since getting off the plane that afternoon.

They still hadn't found the spy in London who had been responsible for leaking her whereabouts in November. Bill had taken every precaution in the intervening months to protect her. That had included restricting access to the section of MI6 where she worked, and adding another layer of security to her already classified personnel file. Even so, she was well aware that nothing was foolproof until they located and apprehended the mole. Until then, she had to have eyes in the back of her head and take every possible precaution.

Coming to the Hotel Bristol for dinner on her first night back in Oslo didn't seem to her to be very cautious, but she'd had little choice. This was where Daniel Carew had suggested they meet. The embassy was out; too many eyes and ears. From now on, she was to avoid embassies unless there was an emergency. It was better for everyone involved that way.

Evelyn looked up as a shadow fell across the table. She smiled and stood, holding out her hand.

"Mr. Carew! How lovely to see you again!"

A man with dark hair graying at the temples smiled and grasped her hand.

"How are you? I'm glad you made it to Oslo safely," he said, seating himself across from her. "We're very happy to see you back."

"I'm very happy to be back. Although I must confess, I did not miss this cold."

He laughed. "I'm used to it now. But I understand you had quite a bit of cold yourself this winter in England."

"Yes indeed. The Thames froze, if you can believe it. I've never known that to happen in my life."

Night Falls on Norway

A waiter approached and Daniel ordered a whiskey and soda. Once he had gone, he turned his attention back to her.

"And how was it when you left?"

"Much warmer."

"I hope you don't mind, but I've invited Anna Salvesen to join us," he said.

Evelyn raised her eyebrows in surprise. "Anna? No, I don't mind at all, but why?"

He smiled. "A lot has happened since you were last here. Anna no longer works for the law firm. She works for me now."

Evelyn couldn't stop the smile that came to her lips.

"That does not surprise me one bit," she said. "When did that happen?"

"Just after Christmas when she returned to Oslo. When she left you in Stockholm, I arranged for her to leave the train as soon as it crossed into Norway. From there, a car took her north, where she stayed until your German friends had left the city." Daniel shifted in his seat and crossed his legs. "Even after they left, I insisted she stay away until I could confirm that no one had come to replace them. She spent Christmas with her family. When she returned, I convinced her to come work with me. I needed a good translator in my office, and she was getting bored working for the solicitors."

"I'm glad. Without her help, I would have been hard pressed to get out of Stockholm as quickly as I did. I'm eternally grateful to her for all her help."

Daniel smiled. "She told me that she had the time of her life. She found it all very exciting."

Evelyn made a sound suspiciously like a snort. "It was that, if nothing else."

The waiter returned with Daniel's whiskey and soda, and they fell silent as he set it on the table.

"Are you ready to order?" he asked, looking from one to another.

"We're just waiting on one other person," Daniel told him easily. He glanced at Evelyn's glass of wine. "Would you like another glass of wine?"

"I'm all right for now, thank you."

The waiter nodded and smiled and moved away again.

"I understand you escaped Stockholm by taking a merchant ship to Copenhagen," Daniel continued once he was gone. "How did you find Denmark?"

"I didn't have much of an opportunity to form an opinion, to be honest. I traveled across the country by train and car to reach Esbjerg. I had a very friendly guide who went out of his way to point out various landmarks and tell me about the country as we went, but one can only see so much through a window." She smiled wistfully. "For all the traveling, I don't seem to have the time to enjoy the new countries I'm visiting."

Daniel sipped his drink. "Certainly not that trip," he agreed. "Do you remember when you first arrived and I told you that you had nothing to worry about in Oslo?"

Evelyn nodded, her eyes dancing. "Yes. You told me that I would never run into a Gestapo or SS agent the way I had in Strasbourg."

"Yes. It seems I owe you an apology," he said with a sheepish grin. "We never had any problems before then, and we haven't had any since."

"Of course you haven't," she said with a laugh. "I'm beginning to think it's just me."

"Oh, I wouldn't go that far quite yet. Now, if something goes awry this time, perhaps I'll reconsider." He winked. "Now, before Anna arrives, I should tell you that she knows that you're a British agent."

"I'm fairly certain she figured that out before we ever went to Sweden together," Evelyn said. "What have you told her?"

"Me? Absolutely nothing. She figured most of it out herself. When I told her you were coming back to Oslo, she asked if she could see you again. I didn't think you would have any objections."

"No, of course not! In fact, she could be very helpful, if you're willing to share her for a few days."

Daniel raised an eyebrow and looked amused.

"My dear girl, why do you think I invited her along this evening?" he asked. "I don't know why you're here, but I do understand how helpful a local can be. She's all yours for as long as you need her. Just don't go getting her embroiled with the SD again, will you?"

"I'll do my best not to."

"I've told her that you're going by the name Marlene Elfman, so you don't have to worry about any slips there. I haven't told her what your cover is because, to be honest, I don't know." He tilted his head and looked at her. "What *is* the official reason for your visit?"

"I'm a Belgian national here to visit my old friend."

"Ah. Very generic," he said approvingly.

"Marlene!" A voice cried and Evelyn turned to watch as a tall brunette crossed the restaurant towards their table. "How wonderful to see you again!"

Evelyn stood up as the woman approached. "Anna!" she exclaimed, a smile stretching across her face. "I'm so happy you could join us!"

"Oh I'll never turn down dinner!" Anna Salvesen said with a laugh, greeting Evelyn with a warm hug. "You couldn't have kept me away. Hello Daniel!"

"Anna," Daniel said with a nod and a smile. He sat as the two women took their seats. "I've been telling Marlene how you work with me at the embassy now."

Anna nodded and her brown eyes danced as she glanced at Evelyn.

"You're not surprised, I'm sure," she said, setting her purse on the chair beside her. "When I came back to the city after Christmas, the law firm seemed very dull."

"No, I wasn't surprised." Evelyn said, sipping her wine. "How have you been?"

"I'm well! I was very relieved to hear that you got away safely in November," she added, lowering her voice. "I was worried. Although, when they all showed up at the train station, I knew it had worked just as you said it would."

"I couldn't have done it without you. I owe you for that."

Anna waved her hand dismissively. "Nonsense. I had a fantastic time! I'm just glad I could help. Is this trip going to be as fun?"

Evelyn laughed. "Goodness, I hope not! I want a nice, easy visit this time. Nothing unexpected and no enemies lurking in the shadows!"

"I'll drink to that," Daniel said, lifting his glass. "Here's to an uneventful week!"

Anna stared across the small table at Evelyn, a cigarette in her hand and a look of stunned disbelief on her face.

"You're here to do what?"

Evelyn shrugged and sipped her drink. Daniel had departed after dinner, and she and Anna had moved into the cocktail lounge to have a few drinks before calling it a night. Evelyn had taken the opportunity to confide the true purpose of her visit to Oslo.

"Daniel doesn't know," she said now. "It's better if he doesn't. It's less complicated that way."

Anna shook her head and rubbed her neck, a reluctant smile crossing her face.

"Well, that's certainly not what I was expecting to hear," she said, reaching for her drink. "And I hate to be the one to break it to you, but you'll have a bit of an uphill battle. No one wants to get involved in the war, especially to do anything that might incite the Germans to retaliate."

"I understand." Evelyn hesitated for a moment, then leaned forward. "The thing is, Anna, they might not have a choice. All of our intelligence suggests that Hitler will try to move north into Sweden or Norway, or both. If he does, not only will we need eyes and ears here, but you will need help from England and France as well."

Anna blew out smoke and frowned. "I know," she agreed. "I've seen the reports. I know the threat is real. The problem here is that most of us don't think there is any need for us to be involved. They don't believe that Germany will bother with Norway. The general feeling is that if we don't poke the bear, the bear won't notice us."

"And if it does?"

She shrugged. "Then they will face that problem when it arises." She paused for a moment thoughtfully. "Although, there are some that might be willing to consider the possibility. I've just remembered someone who went to school with my brother. He might be worth approaching."

"Oh? Why?"

"He's a wireless radio enthusiast," she said unexpectedly. "Been mad about the things for years. My brother still sees him occasionally when he's in the south and speaks very highly of him. If Erik respects him, I can assure you that there is more there than just a man who likes to play with radios."

"He uses them for a living?"

"God no." Anna laughed. "He's a fisherman by trade. The radios are just a hobby, but according to Erik he's a genius with the things."

Evelyn tilted her head thoughtfully. "Does he know you?"

"Oh yes. I haven't seen him for a few years, but he knows me. Would you like me to contact him? He might be a good place for you to start. Erik said that he has some very strong political views and it was my impression that he is very concerned about this war."

"If you could, that would be wonderful. I'd like to begin getting a feel for how people are feeling and what they will do if, God-forbid, Germany does come after Norway."

"Of course." Anna stubbed out her cigarette. "And I'll see if I can think of anyone else. I assume you're looking for people with useful skills?"

"Not necessarily. Anyone can be helpful, even workers in factories. Intelligence can be gleaned anywhere. You just have to know where to look and how to recognize it."

"And Daniel knows nothing about this?"

"No."

Anna tilted her head and looked at her questioningly. "Why?"

"There's no reason for him to know, and it would only cause complications with his job at the embassy. There can be no suspicion that he may be aiding in violating Norway's neutrality, especially now."

"And if he has no knowledge of your actions, there can be no accusation of him trying to undermine the government's stated policy," Anna said slowly. "England isn't supposed to have any active agents in Norway, yet here you are. Of course, neither is Germany and look what happened in November."

"Exactly."

"It's all rather ridiculous, really, isn't it? It's like a game where everyone knows what everyone else is doing, but everyone pretends that nothing is going on. What's the point?"

"To avoid an all-out conflict," Evelyn said promptly. "We all know that Hitler will use any excuse possible to justify walking into a country and taking control. There's no point in handing him one."

"Do you think he will attack us anyway?" Anna asked suddenly, her dark eyes probing Evelyn's.

Evelyn swallowed. She'd forgotten Anna's uncanny ability to put her on the spot suddenly and unexpectedly.

"I don't know," she said finally. "All I know is that, despite your country's determination to remain neutral, there are too many reasons why it would behoove Hitler to come here."

"You're talking about Sweden's iron mines," Anna said. "They supply Germany with all of their iron, and if they come into Norway then they can protect them. But then why not invade Sweden?"

"Norway has the Atlantic Ocean."

Anna sat back in her chair heavily. "And ports."

"Yes."

She stared at Evelyn thoughtfully for a long moment.

"England would have the same benefits if they established themselves here," she finally said. "They would be able to block the iron from getting to Germany, as well as limit access to the north Atlantic."

Evelyn resisted the urge to squirm uncomfortably and instead laughed shortly.

"Chamberlain won't even bomb Germany. Do you really think he'll deploy troops against a neutral country?"

"I think a lot of leaders are doing things that, at one time, we all thought were impossible and ill-advised," Anna replied dryly. "The fact that you're here shows that England is thinking of Norway in strategic terms. I don't blame your government, understand, but there are many who would. They don't understand what's at stake."

"I don't think that's something you have to worry about," Evelyn said, reaching for her drink. *Yet*, she added silently.

"I think it's something we all need to worry about," Anna said, leaning forward. "As I understand it, we have a choice between Hitler or allowing our waters to be mined and our ports blockaded. Neither scenario will sit well with my countrymen, and that is what you will be facing in this quest of yours."

Evelyn pulled a cigarette case out of her purse and extracted a cigarette.

"Are you having second thoughts about helping me this time?" she asked with a quick grin.

Anna laughed. "Not at all. I've already told you that I understand what is at stake. I've seen the Gestapo up close and heard the stories firsthand. I know what lies in store if the Nazis are allowed to continue gobbling up territory. I'm just trying to illustrate what you may run into here. We Norwegians may seem nice and easy-going, but we have a particularly stubborn streak in us when it comes to our business."

"As do the English." Evelyn lit her cigarette. "Let me ask you this. If Hitler sent his army and invaded Norway, do you think there would be a fight? I don't mean by the army. Of course your army would defend Norway. I mean by people. If all else failed and you were occupied like Poland was, would your countrymen organize and fight back?"

Anna pressed her lips together thoughtfully and was silent for a long time. Then, finally, she nodded slowly.

"I think we would," she said. "Perhaps not everyone. There would be those who would go along to keep what they have and protect their families. But there would be others, like my brother Erik, who would do everything they could to resist. And there might be more like him than we think."

Evelyn blew smoke upwards, her eyes never leaving Anna's face. The other woman was being truthful, she decided. There would be a resistance if Germany invaded. That is, if the Gestapo and SS didn't round up all the people like Anna's brother first.

"And you?" she asked, her lips curving. "Would you be with them?"

"Do you really need to ask?" Anna demanded with a short laugh. "I'm going to help you find spies for your government while we're still neutral. Of course I will. I'd fight until they killed me. And then I'd probably come back and haunt the bastards."

Evelyn laughed. "Let's hope it doesn't come to that."

"What about you?" Anna asked after a minute. "What if Hitler invades England? Would you fight?"

"If Hitler invades England, I won't have a choice. There is no happy ending for me if England falls."

"No, I don't suppose there is." Anna sighed. "When did the world become such a mess?"

"When people got desperate. They began to starve and when their governments wouldn't help them, they turned to men who could."

"And now you're at war and I'm caught somewhere in between my country and my convictions."

Evelyn nodded slowly. "Something like that."

Anna picked up her glass. "Well, at least we know exactly where we stand," she decided. "Here's to us. May we always have our convictions and the will to continue!"

"Cheers to that," Evelyn said with heartfelt sincerity, lifting her glass.

Chapter Ten

Evelyn looked out the window as the train rocked and swayed over the countryside. Anna sat across from her in the first class compartment reading a magazine as they traveled south. The day after they'd had dinner together, Anna had telephoned her brother's friend. After speaking to her, he agreed to meet them for supper the following day.

Now, looking out of the window as the winter scenery sped by, Evelyn was having second thoughts about her ability to do what Jasper had asked of her. How on earth was she going to convince someone to send information to them at the risk of their own freedom and, quite possibly, their own lives? If the Germans did invade Norway, and if they were caught, they would be killed. How exactly was she supposed to sell that?

"Cheer up," Anna said, breaking into her thoughts.

Evelyn looked at her, startled, to find the other woman peering at her over the top of her magazine.

"What?"

"You look as if you're on your way to the gallows." She closed the magazine and tossed it onto the seat next to her. "What's the matter?"

"Nothing." Evelyn hesitated, then shrugged. "Well, nothing that can be fixed, at any rate."

"Would you care to share? Maybe I can offer some insight."

"I'm just wondering how on earth I'm going to convince your fellow countrymen to do something so potentially dangerous," she said reluctantly. "You've seen how quickly things can go off the rails, especially if the SD gets involved. Why on earth would anyone voluntarily jump into this war?"

Anna looked at her for a moment, a faint smile on her lips. "You did."

"Yes, but I…well, I had my reasons."

"And so will they. It's not your job to convince them to be patriotic. It's your job to give them an option to help their country if the worst happens. That's all."

Evelyn nodded slowly, shifting her gaze to the window again. She was right, of course. It wasn't her job to convince them to take the risk. All she could do was offer them a way to move the information that they would come across in the course of their daily lives. It was up to them to decide whether or not the risks were worth it.

"What's his name?" she asked, glancing back at Anna. "This friend of your brothers?"

"Kristian," she replied. "Kristian Nilsen."

"And he doesn't think it's strange that you're coming down to see him suddenly out of the blue like this?"

"Not that he said, no. It's not as if he doesn't know me, after all. I told him that I'd seen Erik recently and that he'd mentioned him. One thing led to another and I brought up his radio." Anna grinned. "I'll warn you right now: he gets very passionate about his hobby. I didn't understand most of what he went on about. When I said I had a friend who was interested in speaking to him about what he was picking up on the thing, he didn't seem surprised at all."

"Does he know you're working for the British Embassy now?"

"Yes. I think he's probably put two and two together. Kristian was always very clever." She looked at her watch. "We should be there soon. He said that he was looking forward to meeting us both."

"I hope he's not disappointed," Evelyn said with a short laugh.

Anna looked at her, obviously amused. "I doubt that he will be. I've seen how you turn heads," she said dryly.

Evelyn waved that away, turning her attention back out the window.

"Don't wave me away," Anna said with a laugh. "It's true. The problem with you is that you don't see it as a weapon."

"A weapon?" That got Evelyn's attention again. "What *are* you talking about?"

"You! You're sitting over there worrying about how you're going to recruit people, especially men, to your cause and you've never once considered the biggest advantage you have!" Anna shook her head at the blank look on Evelyn's face. "You, you silly goose!"

"But I'm not up for grabs!" Evelyn protested, laughing despite herself. "I may be a very independent and modern woman, but I'm not *that* modern!"

"You don't have to be. They don't have to know you're not available. Trust me. They don't even have to necessarily want anything from you. Sometimes it's enough just to know that they're doing something that will make a beautiful woman very happy." Anna leaned forward. "I'm being very serious. If this war continues, and you and I both know that it will, you're going to have to use every weapon you have available. We all will. And yours is the face and body that you see in the mirror. Use it to bend people to your will."

Evelyn frowned. "You make it sound so calculating."

Anna threw her head back and laughed. "But it is, Marlene, my dear! And so are you! You have to be. You may not think of yourself as a calculating woman, but you are. You're trying to build a network of people who will die to get information to help your country win a war that they have nothing to do with. If that's not calculating, I don't know what is."

"Oh God, you make it sound so cold and heartless!"

"But it is," she said practically, sitting back on her seat. "War is cold and heartless. Its warriors must be as well. And please don't make the mistake of thinking you are not one of England's soldiers because you are every bit as necessary and formidable as one of your British Expeditionary Forces, or one of your fighter pilots. You're just fighting in a different way, and in a different theater of operations."

Evelyn stared at her for a moment.

"When did you become so wise?" she asked finally, her lips twisting wryly. "I thought I was the one with all the experience here."

Anna shrugged.

"I've learned so much over the past few months," she admitted. "And it began in Stockholm. On the train back, I realized that I was wasting my time translating boring court documents for solicitors and doing an odd job on the side for Carew. I decided I wanted to do more. You were blazing all across Scandinavia in service of your country, and I was doing nothing for mine." She paused for a moment, then grinned. "I suppose I'm still not. I'm doing it for yours."

"Which will benefit yours in the long run," Evelyn said.

The other woman nodded.

"That's the hope, yes. And so I've been learning as much as I can under Daniel Carew and doing what I can. And in all of this I have come to realize that what you do *is* warfare. The threat to your life is every bit as high as it is for an infantry soldier holding a rifle. Perhaps even worse because there is no respect or quarter given to spies, whereas prisoners of war are simply interned until the war is over."

Evelyn swallowed, uncomfortable with hearing herself referred to as a spy. She had grown used to thinking of herself in terms of the word agent, or even more generically as a courier. But she had gone far beyond the scope of a courier now.

"Well, I do try not to think of that," she admitted. "I'd rather just focus on what needs to be done."

"Do you know, I think my brother would really like you," Anna said suddenly. "He's a no-nonsense army lieutenant. He thinks in much the same way."

"Well, since the odds of our ever meeting are non-existent, I don't suppose we'll ever know."

Anna grinned. "Pity. That's an introduction I would have loved to have made."

When Evelyn and Anna walked into the waterfront restaurant, the Friday evening crowd was just starting to roll in. As Anna searched for Kristian, Evelyn looked around, taking in the low ceilings and warm atmosphere of the establishment. It was warm and cozy after the bitter wind coming off the water and she felt herself relaxing as the heat began to seep through her coat.

"Anna!" A voice called. "Here I am!"

A man of medium height pushed his way through the crowd, his curly blond hair shining in the muted lighting. Evelyn watched as he approached Anna, a wide smile on his boyish face, and she liked him immediately. He had an open countenance and his curly hair reminded her of a puppy somehow.

"Kristian!" Anna greeted him, holding out her hands. "How are you?"

"I'm well, I'm well!" He grasped her hands and leaned in to kiss her cheek. "You look fantastic. City life agrees with you."

She laughed. "Thank you! Kristian, this is my friend Marlene. Marlene, this is Kristian Nilsen."

Evelyn smiled and held out her hand. "Hallo!"

"Hallo!" Kristian grasped her hand, his eyes meeting hers as he smiled at her. "It's very nice to meet you."

He withdrew his hand and turned to Anna. "Come. I've got a table in the back corner where it is a little quieter and we can talk without shouting."

She nodded and they followed him through the throng to the back of the restaurant. As they made their way through what turned out to be a very large establishment, the crowds thinned out and the volume lowered considerably as they drew further away from the front. Looking around, Evelyn realized that there were actually two restaurants. The one where they entered was closer to what she recognized as a pub setting, while the back restaurant where they were obviously sitting was less casual; and much quieter.

"I'm so glad you came down to visit," Kristian said once they were seated. "I haven't seen Erik in almost a year. How is he?"

"Same as ever," Anna said with a smile. "He's stationed up near Trondheim. I saw him over Christmas."

"Is he worried about the war? If we get dragged into it, he'll be in the thick of it. Still, I suppose that's what he signed up for."

"You know Erik. He's very practical about the whole thing. If war comes, he's ready. If it doesn't, he's ready for that as well."

Kristian looked at Evelyn. "Anna tells me you're visiting from Belgium," he said with a smile. "How does it look there at the moment? As far as the war?"

"About the same as it always has," she said with a shrug. "There are bomb shelters in the cities now, and the threat of a German invasion has some people nervous, but for the most part, life goes on."

"That's good. I hope you never have to make use of the bomb shelters."

"So do I!"

A waiter approached their table to take their drink orders and Kristian glanced at her.

"Are you a beer drinker, Marlene?" he asked.

Evelyn swallowed. While she had had an odd pint or two in the past, it wasn't something young women of her class drank when they were out and about. In fact, if her mother had ever caught her with a pint in the pub, she was fairly sure she would have a heart attack.

"Not particularly, but I'm not opposed to it," she replied.

"You must try a glass of Aass while you're here," he said. "It's a local beer. The brewery is right here in Drammen."

"Oh?"

Anna grinned and added her voice to Kristian's, a devilish twinkling in her eyes.

"You really should try it. It's very good, and something you won't find outside of Norway."

"At least, not yet," Kristian said, ordering three glasses of the beer.

Evelyn smiled graciously and accepted that she would be drinking beer with her meal. She supposed she would have to adjust to the company she found herself in as the war progressed, and now was as good a time as any to begin. After all, when in Rome, and all that.

"What brings you to Norway, Marlene?" Kristian asked once the waiter had left. "Your Norwegian is very good, by the way."

"Thank you. I'm here to visit an old friend of mine from school. She's married and lives in Oslo now."

"How did you and Anna meet?"

"That's a funny story, actually," Anna said. "She was here last year to work on an article she was writing for a newspaper. She's a journalist. Did I tell you that? Anyway, she was in Oslo last year and needed a translator because she didn't speak a word of Norwegian. Not a word!"

Kristian raised his eyebrows and looked from one to the other. "Not a word?" he repeated. "But…you speak it very well now!"

"That's what's so funny!" Anna agreed with a laugh. "I acted as her translator last year and we became friends. When she came back, I met her for dinner, fully expecting to be translating the menu again. But there was no need!"

"That's quite amazing." Kristian grinned. "You must have a very good ear for languages."

"I do." Evelyn smiled. "But I must confess I still have some difficulties. I gave the landlord of the boarding house I'm staying in a good laugh this morning. I mixed up my words and told him the lice in the hallway was out."

Both Anna and Kristian burst out laughing and Evelyn grinned and shrugged.

"There will always be mistakes," Anna assured her, still chuckling. "I was in a jewelers once when an American came in. He was looking for a gold chain for his wife. He asked for a gold vagina! I didn't think the salesman was ever going to stop laughing. I finally took pity on the American and went over to help."

"Oh my goodness!" Evelyn gasped. "I hope I don't ever say that!"

"As I said, mistakes will be made. It's to be expected."

Evelyn sobered, looking up as the waiter returned with their drinks. Mistakes were to be expected, but if she made them in front of the wrong person, it could be a deadly. She had to do better.

"Here's to mistakes!" Kristian said, lifting his glass of beer. "May they always cause laughter and not offense!"

She smiled and sipped her beer, turning her attention to the menu. After studying it for a moment, she decided on salmon with roasted potatoes and set it down. While the other two were still deciding, she took the opportunity to look around the restaurant. The tables around them were filled now, but the closest ones were not within hearing distance. They might as well be all on their own, which suited her perfectly. If she was going to try to get Kristian to talk about what he was listening to on his radio, she didn't want any curious ears listening.

"I think I'll gain a ton with you visiting," Anna announced after a few minutes, setting the menu aside. "I hardly ever go out to eat, and this is the second time this week!"

"Don't you?" Kristian looked up. "That surprises me. Why not?"

"I'm a working girl now," she said with a grin. "I don't have the time or the funds for a wild life anymore."

"Did you live a wild life before?" Evelyn asked in amusement. "Do tell!"

Anna laughed. "Hardly. But I did used to go out quite a bit."

Kristian set the menu down. "I think we all did," he agreed. "This is a rarity for me as well. When you're on a fishing boat at four in the morning, you don't want to stay out late the night before."

"You both make me feel very decadent and irresponsible," Evelyn said decidedly.

"Why? You're on holiday. You're allowed to be decadent and irresponsible," Anna retorted. "Besides, I'm not complaining! I'm enjoying it."

"Do you have to be out early tomorrow?" Evelyn asked Kristian.

He shook his head. "No. My brother is taking the boat out for me. We rotate weekends so that we can have some kind of a social life."

"It's a family business," Anna explained to Evelyn. "Kristian is partners with his two brothers. His father used to work as well, but he's getting on in years now."

"He keeps the nets repaired and helps with the boat maintenance, but he doesn't go out anymore." Kristian reached for his beer. "He keeps his hand in, but we're all glad he's finally agreed to stay ashore. After his heart trouble last year, it's best."

"How *is* business?" Anna asked, and he shrugged.

"It's the same as its always been, which is a good thing. We make it work."

"Do you still live in the village?"

"No. I moved into a small house just outside. I have a wonderful view of the river and the village is below me." Kristian nodded. "The height is perfect for my radio, and I enjoy the quiet. My brothers are still in the village with my parents."

"Anna said you're a wireless radio enthusiast," Evelyn said with a smile. "I've played with one myself, but I don't know that I would consider myself a student just yet."

"Have you?" Kristian leaned forward, his eyes widening in interest. "Anna didn't tell me."

"Anna didn't know," that lady said dryly. "I did tell you she was interested in talking about it, though. I remember distinctly!"

"Yes, of course."

"Did you build your radio?" Evelyn asked.

"Yes. I've always been good at things like that. It's much more practical to build it yourself."

"The one that I played with belonged to my friend. He built his as well. He did a tremendous job. He could listen to broadcasts all the way from America!"

"Oh yes. I listen to the German broadcasts, as well as the Danes and the French. I've even managed to pick up some of the Soviet ones, but of course I have no idea what they're saying. I don't speak Russian." He sipped his beer. "The signals are fantastic now. I haven't managed to get a BBC one yet, but I think that's more due to my set than anything else. I want to make some adjustments, and once I have, I hope to tap into those as well."

"I've always found it amazing that we can listen to broadcasts from across countries," Anna said. "It seems rather fantastic, somehow."

"It's quite simple, actually," he told her. "The signals travel from the towers, you see. As long as there is a tower within a certain distance, you can pick up the frequency and listen in."

"Your radio is just a receiver, then?" Evelyn asked, reaching for her beer. "You can only listen?"

His blue eyes sharpened and something like a grin pulled at his lips.

"Oh no. I can send as well."

Evelyn felt her pulse leap and she forced her hand to remain steady as she sipped her drink. He had a wireless set that could send messages as well as listen to broadcasts. That was precisely what she had been hoping for.

"Can you?" Anna sounded suitably impressed. "And you made it? Who can you send messages to?"

"Anyone I want to. I have a friend in Sweden and we exchange messages several times a week. I can send a message to anyone if I know what frequency they're on."

Evelyn set her glass down. "And can you also intercept messages sent by others?"

Kristian nodded. "Yes."

"Well no wonder you're so fascinated with it!" Anna exclaimed. "It's like having your own private way of communicating, isn't it?"

"Not so private, but yes." He looked from one woman to the other. "You're both very interested in all this, but I don't think it's because of the technology, is it?"

Evelyn met his gaze and swallowed, then slowly shook her head.

"No."

He nodded, unsurprised. "I didn't think so."

"I'm very interested to know what you've been listening to," she said slowly.

"You want to know what I've been listening to?" he repeated, his brow furrowed. "Why?"

She took a deep breath.

"Because I think you're probably hearing a lot more than you realize," she said, "especially what's coming out of Germany."

"You want to know what I've been hearing from Germany?" When she nodded, he looked at her sharply. "Do you work for the Germans?"

"No."

"The Russians?"

"No."

"Then who?"

"England." Evelyn raised her eyes to his and took another deep breath, plunging in. "And we're very interested in what you might be able to pass on to us."

Chapter Eleven

Kristian stared at Evelyn, his face a comedy of disbelief mixed with astonishment.

"You can't be serious?"

"Yes." She smiled faintly and reached for her beer again. "I'm very serious."

"You work for the British government?" he asked skeptically.

"Yes."

He blinked at her bluntness and reached for his beer. "This is unbelievable."

"Not really," Anna said. "Of course the Brits are going to have an interest in what's happening. They're at war, after all."

"Yes, but they don't normally send young women to fishing villages in Norway to recruit amateur radio specialists, do they?" he retorted. Then he paused comically and looked at Evelyn. "Do they?"

She couldn't stop the chuckle that bubbled out. "Not usually, no."

"There. You see?" He looked at Anna. "As I said. Unbelievable. Did you know about this?"

"It may have been mentioned," she murmured.

"And you naturally thought of me."

"Well, you *are* a wizard when it comes to wireless communication." Anna grinned. "Besides, who else would I suggest? I know you're a good man. I'm hardly going to offer up someone I don't know, am I?"

Kristian ran a hand through his hair and finished his beer, signaling the waiter for another round.

"If that's supposed to make me feel better, Anna, it doesn't." He sighed and looked at Evelyn. "You *are* serious? This isn't some kind of joke?"

"No, it isn't a joke." She leaned forward. "We know that Hitler is planning something, and we believe that he will move against either Norway or Sweden, or both. If he does, the only chance we'll have at

99

gaining information is through people like you. People who are already in place and who have the skills and ability to get the information out."

"You're talking about more than one," he said, lowering his voice. "You want to recruit multiple people in Norway?"

"I'm looking for a small number of key people who can be counted on to resist if, God-forbid, the Germans invade Norway and cut it off from the Allies."

He studied her thoughtfully for a long while, then sat back as the waiter approached. He ordered a fresh round of drinks for all of them and watched as the man retreated again. Once he was out of earshot, Kristian returned his eyes to Evelyn's.

"You're going to have one hell of a time convincing people to help," he told her. "Your government isn't making life easy for us. They're not honoring our neutrality, and now there's talk of mines in the waters. If they do that, they'll force Hitler to move whether he intends to or not."

"Let me ask you this," Evelyn said. "If Britain didn't show an interest in Norway, but instead honored your neutrality, do you believe that Hitler will really continue to do the same?"

His eyes wavered and he shook his head. "Probably not," he admitted.

"Then which is the lesser of the evils, us or the Germans? Because I can assure you that if the Germans come, the SS will not offer you a chance to keep your freedom and your radio. They will take your radio and shoot you for being a spy, even if you're not."

"And if I help you, and I pass on information that I gather, I will be shot anyway for being a spy." Kristian sighed. "I suppose if I'm going to be shot, it might as well be for something I'm guilty of."

Anna met Evelyn's gaze across the table and a very faint smile curved her lips. They had him.

"This is all assuming that Hitler invades Norway," Evelyn said. "He may not, in which case there is very little risk to yourself."

"You don't believe that or you wouldn't be here having this conversation with me."

"It really doesn't matter what I believe," she said with a shrug. "The only one who knows the Führer's intentions are the German High Command, and I've heard that sometimes even *they* aren't told what he has planned until the last possible moment."

The waiter returned then with their fresh round of drinks, setting them down and asking if they were ready to order. After they placed their orders, he smiled and departed again.

Night Falls on Norway

"Do you ever wonder if waiters listen to the conversations at the tables they serve?" Anna asked suddenly. "I mean, no one ever pays them any attention."

"I'm sure they do," Evelyn said. "That's why you should always be mindful of where they are."

"I've been watching for him ever since we began this conversation," Kristian assured her. "He hasn't heard anything."

"I know." She smiled. "I've been watching as well."

"If I agree to this," he said after a moment, "where would I send the information?"

"Because you come equipped with your own radio, you would send it directly to London," Evelyn said. "You'll be provided with codes and a schedule, and you would transmit anything to us directly."

"No middle man?"

"Not unless you want one."

He shook his head. "No. I'd rather it was just me. In fact, I'd rather no one in Norway outside of this table know anything about my involvement."

"I'm sure that can be arranged."

He sighed heavily.

"You're right about the Germans. They're planning something," he said in a low voice. "I've been listening to their traffic out of Poland and Germany now for over a month. I was listening before that, but it took some time to figure out their code."

Evelyn raised her eyebrows in surprise. "You deciphered the German codes?"

He hastily shook his head. "No, no. Well, not in the sense that you think. I figured out the rudimentary code that they use for unclassified messages."

"That's still impressive," she murmured.

"Perhaps, but not very useful in the end. They were mostly sending messages about the weather and updates regarding the amount of foodstuffs they were maintaining. For instance, they were running out of coffee a few months ago. So, as you see, nothing very exciting. But then, a few days ago, the code changed. Everything changed. The number of messages more than tripled, and now they're all heavily encrypted. I can't make head or tail out of them."

"These are the ones coming out of Germany?" she asked sharply.

"Not just Germany, but also Poland. It's like they've suddenly locked everything down."

Evelyn's lips tightened. "That's not good."

"No."

"Have you told anyone about this?" she asked, shooting him a sharp glance under her lashes.

"No, of course not. No one knows I've been listening to the Germans. Even my friend in Sweden doesn't know."

"Good. I advise you to keep it that way." Evelyn reached for her drink. "In the meantime, even though you can't understand them, continue to monitor the signals. I'll contact London and see what we can find out."

"There's more," he said after a moment, and she raised her eyebrows. "I think there's a build-up of ships happening in German ports."

Evelyn stared at him. "What makes you think that?"

"After all the messages I've listened to, I've managed to pick up certain call signs and figure out where the transmitters are." He drank some beer and lowered his voice even more. "Each branch has their own unique call signs. I've figured out the German navy and the Wehrmacht ones, but not the Luftwaffe."

"You know who you're listening to?" Evelyn demanded, her heart thumping. "You can actually tell where the messages are coming from and going to?"

He shrugged and nodded. "To a certain extent. I've learned just about all the navy call signs. I know when they are navy signals, but I can't understand a thing they're sending. I've learned most of the Wehrmacht signs, but again, I can't understand what they're sending."

"What about the diplomatic messages?" Anna asked.

"Those are the easy ones. The embassies all have their own signs, and their messages were the ones I was able to decode. But, as I said, they've changed them now and I can't understand them."

"But you know when it's a diplomatic message as opposed to, say, a navy one?" Evelyn asked.

"Yes." Kristian smiled ruefully. "I suppose I should have told someone before now, but to be honest, I didn't think anyone would believe me."

"I'm very glad you didn't!" she said fervently.

"I thought about telling Erik the last time I saw him," he said, glancing at Anna. "But then something stopped me. I think I thought perhaps he would feel obligated to report it to his superiors, and then they would take my radio away."

Anna bit her lip thoughtfully. "I don't honestly know what he would say," she said slowly. "He does tend to operate very strictly in accordance with the rules, but then sometimes he surprises me. I think you did the right thing in not telling him."

Kristian looked at Evelyn. "And what will your government do with this information?" he asked. "Will they take my radio as well?"

"Goodness no," she assured him. "I don't know how they will want to proceed, but I can guarantee that they won't take away your radio. What would be the purpose? If you don't have it, you can't pass on the information."

"I can't pass on the information now," he muttered. "I don't have any clue what they're chattering about."

"You've managed to gather much more than you think," Evelyn told him. "I'm not even sure where to start with all of this. I'll contact London first thing in the morning and find out how they want to proceed. I'll forward on everything you've told me."

"And then what?"

"Do you have a telephone?"

"Yes. That's how Anna reached me."

"I'll phone you tomorrow and we'll arrange something."

Kristian made a slight motion with his head, his eyes over her shoulder, and Evelyn fell silent. A moment later, the waiter approached with two others and they began laying out their dinner. She watched as her dinner was set before her, her mind spinning. How on earth was she supposed to eat when her stomach was tied up in excited knots? She had never dreamed that she would hit a jackpot like this. When Anna said she knew someone who was an amateur radio operator, she certainly hadn't been expecting this! She'd thought he might be listening to news out of Germany, but had assumed it would be the news broadcast by Goebbels' propaganda ministry. While that still would have been helpful for gleaning information about life in Germany and possibly the true state of their economy and social structure, it would have been nothing compared to this relative cash cow of intelligence. If Kristian was able to distinguish between the diplomatic signals and the naval signals, they could begin to put together a clearer picture of what Hitler's plans were and, more importantly, where he was building up troops.

The waiter finished and made sure they were settled and didn't need anything before departing once again. Evelyn picked up her knife and fork and glanced at Kristian.

"You think they're amassing ships in their ports?" she asked. "Tell me what makes you think that."

"There has been a massive increase of signals going between the naval call signs," he said, cutting into his pork medallions.

"Rostock, Stettin and Swinemünde, in particular, have seen huge amounts of traffic. The only reason I can think of for that amount of sudden traffic is an increase of ships in, or leaving, the ports. There are others, as well. Kiel has increased the traffic substantially."

"If that's true, then Hitler's definitely up to something," Anna said with a frown. "What if he *is* going to attack us?"

Kristian looked at her and they were all silent for a moment. Then he sighed.

"I suppose we face that if it happens," he said. "There's nothing else we can do. Our army will defend us, but they are no match for the German forces."

"I think perhaps it's a very good thing that we came down here today," Anna said. "If they are going to attack Norway, I'd rather know what's coming, to be honest. At least now we know that something is definitely in the wind."

Evelyn chewed her fish, not tasting it. If Kristian was correct and there was a build-up of ships in German ports, that could only mean that they were going to attack Norway or Sweden, unless Hitler was going to move to France next and wanted his Kriegsmarine to lend support. Of the two options, she was leaning heavily on the former. There were too many indications to support an invasion of Scandinavia to ignore them.

"There is someone in Oslo that you might want to talk to," Kristian said after a few minutes of silence.

Evelyn looked up from her dinner questioningly. "Oh?"

"His name is Peder Strand. His family has a shop on Uranienborgveien, I believe. He also has a wireless set." He glanced at her. "I have no idea if he would be willing to assist you, but I can vouch for his skill with a radio. I trained him."

Anna looked up, surprised. "This isn't the Peder that Erik got into a fight with last year, is it?"

Kristian laughed. "I'd forgotten about that! Yes, it's the same Peder. What was that about again? I don't remember."

"Too much whiskey," she replied with a laugh. "They were both perfectly happy the following morning. I don't remember what sparked the argument, either. I don't know if I ever really knew. One minute they were drinking and the next they were swinging fists outside."

"Well, as I said, I don't know how he feels about the current state of affairs in Europe, but if Hitler is going to make any moves towards us, it won't hurt to have another radio at your disposal."

"No, indeed," Evelyn said with a nod. "Thank you!"

Kristian shrugged. "No need to thank me. It is purely selfish on my part. If the German army comes, I would rather have people I trust working alongside me. At least then I know I'll die in good company."

British Embassy, Oslo

Daniel Carew strode into his office, stripping off his gloves as he went.

"Where is it?" he demanded of the assistant who followed him.

"On your desk, sir," the young man replied. He wasn't upset by the sharp words from his boss. He was getting used to that particular tone of voice. Mr. Carew was notoriously bad tempered when he was called back to the embassy late at night. "It came an hour ago. I notified you as soon as we received it."

"This is getting bloody ridiculous," Daniel complained, tossing his gloves onto the desk and rounding the corner to pick up the sealed message sitting in the center of his blotter. "Every other day we're getting some warning from somewhere. They all contradict each other, and no one can even agree on a location."

He tore open the message and scanned it quickly.

"Is it the same as the others?" the assistant asked after a moment.

"Just about." Daniel dropped into his chair and reread the message before tossing it onto the desk. "A respected member of a legation in Berlin advises that an attack on Norway and Denmark is imminent."

"How imminent?"

"Well, this one says the ninth," Daniel said, glancing back at the message. "The other day it was the eighth, and last week it was Holland, and it was the tenth. As I said, this is getting ridiculous."

"At least we know the Germans are planning something," the assistant pointed out.

"Oh, they're planning something right enough," Daniel muttered. "The question is what and where. And when! All these reports all have different dates and different locations. The only consistent theme in any of them is that Hitler is moving. But moving where?"

"What do the Norwegians say?"

Daniel made a disgusted sound and looked across the room at his assistant. "They don't believe any of it. They're ignoring the warnings. They think the sources are unreliable, the information faulty, and they refuse to consider the possibility that their precious neutrality might be breached."

The assistant stared at him blankly. "But…that many reports can't all be false," he protested. "Where there's smoke and all that. How can they simply ignore it?"

"Which one would you have them act on?" Daniel rubbed his eyes tiredly. "I think it's a mistake to dismiss all of them, but I can see their point. With this many warnings, it's damn near impossible to pin down which ones might be true."

"And London? Have we heard from them?"

"Yes. They believe an invasion is imminent. They've begun mining the waters off the coast to try to prevent German ships from getting too close to the shores." Daniel looked up. "You'd better go make some tea. I'll contact London with this latest message from Berlin and we'll see if anything new is known."

"Yes, sir." The young man turned to leave the office, but paused inside the door. "Should I call in Anna?"

"No. She's not in Oslo. She's gone down to the coast." Daniel shook his head. "This is a hell of a time to have someone from London in. Send a car round to the Kolstad's house first thing in the morning. I'll write out a message for Jian. She should at least be aware of this latest report."

"I'll tell the driver to be ready in the morning," the assistant said. "If you write out the message, I'll take it personally."

A smile cracked Daniel's face. "Thank you, Peterson. I don't deserve you. Now go get that tea and let's get to work, shall we?"

Peterson nodded with a grin and left the office. As soon as the door closed behind him, Daniel leaned forward and picked up the message again. It had come from Berlin, from an assistant to the Danish delegation there. It was a source he had cultivated on his last visit to Copenhagen, and so far the information he'd sent to Daniel had been accurate. Daniel stared at the date typed in the message: April 9th.

Four days from now.

He dropped the paper on the desk again and stared across the room, his lips pressed together. This was the third time the 9th had been mentioned. *Was* Hitler sending his forces against Norway in four days? Or was this just another red herring?

Night Falls on Norway

And if it wasn't, how the hell was he going to get Jian out of Norway in the midst of it all?

Chapter Twelve

Oslo, Norway
April 6

Evelyn looked up when Josef entered the dining room where she was sipping her morning coffee. She had finished eating her light breakfast of toast with cheese and fresh fruit, and was enjoying her coffee while she turned the pages of a newspaper.

"This came for you just now," he told her, holding out an envelope. "The car was from the embassy. I didn't recognize the man who brought this. He looked young."

Evelyn couldn't hide her smile at the disgruntled note in Josef's voice. He sounded almost affronted.

"He can't be very young if he's working for the embassy," she said with a grin, taking the envelope. "They don't hire children."

"Don't they?" Josef snorted and turned to leave the room. "You could have fooled me."

Evelyn laughed and tore open the envelope, pulling out the single sheet of paper. None of the other guests had come down yet and she had the dining room to herself this morning. Scanning the message from Daniel, her smile faded and her brows came together sharply. After reading it twice, she swallowed the rest of her coffee and pushed her chair back quickly. Carrying it with her, she crossed the room and went out into the hall, glancing at the front door. It was closed. The messenger hadn't waited for a reply.

Evelyn turned and went down the short hallway to the kitchen door and poked her head inside. An older woman with dark hair beginning to streak with gray was standing at the large island chopping vegetables. When Evelyn stuck her head in, she looked up in surprise.

"Marlene! God morgen," she greeted her, her face breaking into a smile. "Is everything all right?"

"Yes, thank you, Else. Everything was delicious," Evelyn said, stepping into the kitchen. "I wonder if I can use your telephone?"

"Yes, of course. It's in the front parlor. I'll show you." Else put down her knife and wiped her hands on her apron before moving around the island towards the door. "How was your trip to Drammen yesterday? Did you enjoy yourself?"

Evelyn smiled. "It was very nice. The scenery on the way down was wonderful. Norway is a beautiful country."

"Parts of it are, indeed," Else said, leading her out of the kitchen and back down the hallway towards the front room. "If you really want to see something, go north. That's where our real beauty lies."

"I don't know if that will be possible this time, but I'll remember it for next time. I'm on a rather tight time schedule this trip." *Especially now,* she added to herself silently, glancing down at the folded paper in her hand.

"Josef's people are from Trondheim. Beautiful country there, but of course that's in the central part of the country. I call it the north because I was born here in Oslo. He gets annoyed, but to me anything in that direction is north."

"Trondheim? Isn't that where Anna's brother is stationed?"

"Yes, that's right. There's an army base not far from there." She went into the front room and motioned to the desk on the other side. "There it is. I'll close the door so you can have some privacy."

"Thank you."

Evelyn waited until Else had closed the door behind her, then crossed over to sit in the chair before the desk. Picking up the heavy handset, she listened for a dial tone and then dialed the number to Anna's flat. A moment later, she was listening to the telephone ring on the other end. After several rings, she picked up.

"Hallo?"

"Anna, is that you?" Evelyn asked, frowning at the muffled voice coming through the handset. "Good heavens, I can barely make you out!"

"I'm sorry," Anna said, suddenly much louder and clearer. "I had a towel wrapped around my head. I just finished washing my hair. Is that better?"

"Much! Would you like to meet for coffee? Say, in an hour?"

There was a short pause on the line. "All right. I'll see you in an hour."

Evelyn hung up and opened the paper in her hand, rereading the message swiftly. This wasn't the first time she'd seen reports of Germany moving towards to Norway, but after their talk with Kristian last night, this one gave her pause. If what Daniel had said was true, then she had three days to recruit as many people as possible, knowing that they would be thrown into action immediately. If it was another false alarm, then there was nothing to worry about, but she had no way of knowing for sure which it was, or how she was expected to proceed. She had to contact Bill in London, and she didn't want to go through the embassy now. If Germany was about to invade, she couldn't risk anyone learning what she was doing in Oslo.

Getting up, Evelyn crossed the room swiftly and went out, heading for the stairs. There was one way to contact Bill, and it involved getting changed and meeting Anna for coffee in an hour.

6th April, 1940
Dear Evelyn,

How's the training going? I know you're away at a different station and won't get this until you get back, so I hope it went well. We're flying patrols more frequently now. The other day we flew a reconnaissance flight. It's all very dull, to be honest. We're all rather keen to sight some Jerries, but so far we haven't had even a wingtip to shoot at.

The Yank had a spot of excitement today. He was flying back from a patrol when one of his propellers snapped clean off! He had to land at an airfield in the south with only one prop. Turns out dry rot set in, so now they're replacing all the propellers in the squadron to make sure it doesn't happen to anyone else. The CO says we were due for the new propeller kit anyway. Chris swears that termites attacked his Spit! He really does seem to have the worst luck. Thank God he's a good flier!

I read in the newspaper this morning that the Dutch troops have been put on full alert along the border. It won't be long now. Do you think Hitler will move soon? Rob thinks he will try something up in Sweden or Norway first, then turn his attention to France. I think he'll just go straight for France. We have a small pool riding on it. Care to join? It's a ten quid buy in, and I'll put in for you if you tell me your choice! The pot is already over a hundred pounds.

I hope you're well. I had a dream last night that we were in London and the air raid sirens went off. When I turned to grab you, you were gone and I couldn't find you to get you to the shelter. You'd simply disappeared. Strange things, dreams. I can never make head or tail of them. They're supposed to mean something, but I've no idea what the meaning could possibly be behind that one.

I'm off to sleep now. We're back to patrols in the morning. Take care of yourself.

Yours,
FO Miles Lacey

Hotel Bristol, Oslo

The lobby of the hotel was nearly deserted in the early afternoon. Aside from the tall man checking in at the desk, the only other occupants were two porters and a couple crossing the tiled floor from the direction of the attached restaurant. It was unusually slow for a Saturday, but the lack of traffic suited the newcomer signing the registration card just fine. Less people meant less exposure, and that was something he preferred whenever possible. He finished filling in the card and handed it to the manager.

"And how long will you be staying with us, Herr Gruber?" the manager asked.

"I am not sure. Perhaps a week. Perhaps longer. It depends upon my business." The man smiled apologetically and the concierge nodded.

"Yes, of course." He turned to get a key from a slot on the wall behind him. "I understand. Have you stayed with us before?"

"Yes, indeed. I was here last summer."

"We thank you for returning." He handed him the key to his room. "Shall I summon a porter for your bags?"

"No, I'll take them. Thank you."

"Very well. Enjoy your stay, Herr Gruber. If there's anything you need, please don't hesitate to ask."

"I won't."

He inclined his head politely and turned from the desk to walk across the lobby to the lift. As he walked, his dark eyes scanned the faces of the few occupants in the lobby out of habit. He carried a suitcase in each hand and his brown overcoat was unremarkable. He looked like any other businessman checking into another hotel in a line of cities. And that was exactly how he wanted to appear. He had made a successful career out of disappearing into crowds. Despite his height, no one ever looked twice at the weary businessman. They never noticed his eyes with their exceptionally keen gaze, or the way he moved with purpose that bespoke a confidence rarely seen in mid-level sales and businessmen.

And they certainly never realized that he heard and saw much more than most.

The man going by the alias Herr Gruber stepped into the lift, nodding to the attendant.

"The third floor," he told him.

The attendant nodded and closed the gate, pulling the handle. As the lift jerked into motion and moved upwards, Herr Gruber set down his suitcases and looked at his watch. The ride from the airport had taken less than half an hour and he was well ahead of schedule. He wasn't due to check in with Hamburg for another hour. Perhaps he would have time to grab something to eat before his scheduled transmission.

"Is the restaurant still open for lunch?" he asked the attendant.

The man looked at his watch and nodded. "For another hour, sir."

Herr Gruber nodded and bent to pick up his suitcases again as the lift came to a stop and the attendant opened the gate.

"Danke."

The attendant nodded and watched as he stepped out of the lift before closing the gate again. The motor whirred and the lift began its journey back down to the lobby. Herr Gruber turned and went down the wide hallway, looking for the room number on his key, finding it at the end of the hall.

The room was small, but well-appointed and comfortable. After a cursory look around, he set his cases down and went over to the window. He glanced at the busy street below before pulling the heavy curtains closed, blocking out the mid-day sun, and turning to lift one of the cases up onto the small writing desk. He would set up the wireless radio and send a message with his arrival. Then, after lunch, he would return for his scheduled transmission.

Gruber pulled a set of keys out of his pocket and unlocked the case, unsnapping the two clasps and lifting it open. Inside was a portable, wireless transmitter and receiver. He lifted out a long cable and unwound it, attaching an adapter to the end and then going over to plug it into the outlet on the wall behind the desk. After ensuring the power source was working, he pulled out an antenna and carried it over to the window, setting it on the sill behind the curtain. He crossed back over to the desk and sat down, lifting out the headset and putting it on.

Night Falls on Norway

After adjusting the earpieces over his ears, Herr Gruber settled down to begin his transmission.

He sent the message, alerting Hamburg of his arrival in Oslo and his intent to begin surveying the infrastructure. While he had arrived in the city ahead of schedule, there was still much to be done. The Abwehr had sent him to gather and relay very detailed information relating to the train routes and major arteries through southern Norway in advance of Operation Weserübung, the German invasion of Norway and Denmark. With the information that he would send, the Germans would be able to accurately sever all escape routes and communications throughout southern Norway, easing the way for their troops and containing any resistance from the Norwegian military. But before that could happen, he had to gather the intelligence, and he had to start tonight.

Operation Weserübung would commence in two and a half days.

Herr Gruber finished his transmission and was just removing his headset when the earpieces crackled and a signal began coming through. He frowned sharply and reached out to adjust the knobs on the machine, sharpening the receiver so that he could hear it clearly. There wasn't supposed to be a transmission for another hour. That was the schedule. Why, then, was he receiving one now?

He picked up a pencil and pulled the pad out of the case, quickly jotting down the code that was coming through the headset. It was definitely Hamburg, and they were definitely transmitting early.

The frown grew as the transmission continued. It was too long to be a simple acknowledgment of his arrival. When it finished, he waited a few moments to make sure nothing else was coming through, then removed his headset. He pulled out the codebook from the case and set about decoding the message. When he'd finished, he sat back, staring at the message in surprise.

INFORMATION RECEIVED SINCE YOUR DEPARTURE. JIAN IN OSLO. PROCEED WITH MISSION. FOLLOW ENEMY AGENT PROTOCOL. JIAN IS PRIORITY. ACKNOWLEDGE RECEIPT OF INSTRUCTION.

The English spy was in Oslo? Gruber's brow furrowed and he lifted his eyes to stare across the room. Why would she be here? The last he knew she was in France, meeting with a member of the French Intelligence in Metz. Why come to Norway now?

His lips tightened. The British must know about Operation Weserübung. That was the only explanation for Jian's presence on the eve of the operation. How had they found out? It was impossible! Even the crews on the ships setting sail didn't know where they were going yet. How had the English discovered it?

His gaze shifted back to the message. Enemy agent protocol. They wanted him to watch and report on every contact the English spy known as Jian made. He wasn't to apprehend unless absolutely necessary. They wanted to know who she was meeting, where, and when. Once they knew her network, they could roll it up and, eventually, take her down with it.

Herr Gruber got up restlessly and took a turn around the small room. He had been given Jian's case six months ago, and he had been looking for leads ever since. Aside from a few random references, all of which turned out to be false, it was as if the spy had disappeared. After slipping through the SD's fingers in Stockholm in November, she had dropped out of action. Until last month. A radio transmission from Paris had alerted them to the possibility of her surfacing there, and upon further investigation, it had turned out to be the first genuine sighting in four months. Unfortunately, he had arrived in Metz a day too late. She had already disappeared again, along with the member of French Intelligence whom she had been meeting. He had returned to Germany under the impression that she was now working in France. It made perfect sense, of course. The French and British knew they would go after France. It was only a matter of time. And he and his controllers were perfectly content to wait until they were there to focus on Jian.

But now here she was in Oslo, and that changed everything.

Gruber went back to the radio and sat down, replacing the headset and beginning his acknowledgment transmission. A familiar rush of excitement went through him. Finally, he would be able to lay eyes on the spy that had the SD and Abwehr both chomping at the bit. At last, perhaps he would find out what was so important about this one spy.

INSTRUCTION ACKNOWLEDGED. WILL COMMENCE SURVEILLANCE IMMEDIATELY. - EISENJAGER

Chapter Thirteen

Anna stared at Evelyn in disbelief across the small table in the back corner of a café.

"Are you serious?" she demanded, her steaming cup of coffee forgotten on the table before her. "You really think they're coming?"

"Why do you seem so surprised?" Evelyn asked, raising her eyebrows. "You heard what Kristian said last night."

"Yes, but it's one thing to debate the possibility and quite another to have it confirmed by the embassy," she replied, sitting back in her chair and exhaling heavily. "We've heard these reports before, but they were never accurate."

"I think this time they might be," Evelyn said slowly. "There are too many of them now. There has to be some truth there."

Anna pressed her lips together.

"If the Germans are coming, and I'm not saying I believe that they are, then we're completely outnumbered," she said slowly. "They'll roll right in, and it will be a complete disaster. Our government hasn't prepared for this, and our army is certainly not ready to take on the Wehrmacht."

Evelyn was silent. They both knew that if Germany invaded, Norway had no chance of surviving without the immediate aid of England and France. Evelyn knew that England already had ships on the way, and now it was simply a race to see who reached Norway first: England or Germany.

"You can't possibly consider continuing," Anna continued after a moment, her dark eyes probing Evelyn's. "If you really think there's something to all these reports, you need to get out of Norway."

"I can't, not until I've done what I came to do."

"Don't be stupid, Marlene!" Anna exclaimed, lowering her voice hastily when it came out louder than she intended. "You can't continue to try to recruit people for a network in the middle of an invasion. It's suicide!"

"I agree, but an invasion hasn't begun yet, and it may not," she pointed out. "Just because I think it's likely doesn't make it so. We need

115

to prepare for it, but I also need to continue working until I can't work anymore."

Anna shook her head and reached for her coffee.

"You're absolutely insane," she muttered. "But if I can't convince you, I'll have to help you. What do you have in mind?"

"I need to contact London," Evelyn told her, leaning forward, her voice low. "I don't want to go through the embassy. It's too risky."

"Then how are you going to…" Anna's voice trailed off as understanding lit her eyes and she smiled slowly. "Of course. Our new friend with the radio."

"Actually, I was thinking more of the one here in Oslo. I don't have time to go back to Drammen, as much as I would prefer to use Kristian."

"What if he won't do it? It's entirely possible that he won't want to have anything to do with any of this."

"Then I'll have to go back to Drammen," she said with a shrug.

Anna sighed and drummed her fingers on the table thoughtfully.

"I'll go round to their shop on Uranienborgveien when we leave and speak to Peder," she finally said. "He'll remember me, and with Kristian's recommendation I may be able to work something out. I'll tell him I have a friend who needs to send an urgent message to England and see if he can help."

"I'll come with you."

Anna shook her head.

"No. It's best if I go alone," she said, holding up her hand when Evelyn looked as if she would protest. "Be sensible. If the Germans are indeed on their way here, the last thing we need is you making yourself known all over Oslo. If Peder is willing to help and seems predisposed to be sympathetic to the idea of using his radio in defense of France and England, then I'll bring you to him. But if he isn't, then the only one compromised here is me."

Evelyn frowned in displeasure but didn't argue. She couldn't. Anna was right. If an invasion was imminent, the less people who had actually seen her and could identify her, the better.

"Very well," she agreed.

"Good," Anna said with a nod. "If he's willing, then I'll come get you and we'll go together. If he's not, I'll contact Kristian and arrange for you to meet with him. Perhaps he can meet you halfway."

Evelyn looked across the table at her friend. After a moment, she set her cup down.

"Anna, we need to discuss what you will do if there is an invasion," she said slowly. "You can't stay in the city. If the Germans come, so will the SS, and they already have you on their radar."

"I know." Anna met her look and smiled faintly. "If that happens, I will leave Oslo."

"Where will you go?"

"North. If we're invaded, there's no way we can hold out for long. Norway will fall. If I go North, there are places I can hide until I can change my appearance. I'll change my name and continue on."

"Continue on doing what?" Evelyn pressed. "The embassy will close and Carew will leave Norway. You'll be out of a job."

"I'll be out of that job, yes," Anna agreed. "But if we are invaded, believe me when I say there will be other opportunities. You're not the only one willing to fight for your country."

"You're talking about a resistance."

"Yes."

Evelyn was silent, studying the other woman. If the worst happened, and Norway was occupied, having Anna in a resistance movement would be something that MI6 could make good use of. With her skills in translation, she would be a huge asset to have already in place.

"Why are you looking at me like that?"

"I was just thinking that any resistance movement would be very lucky to have you," Evelyn said with a quick smile, finishing her coffee. She wasn't about to tell her what she was really thinking. There would be time enough for that if an invasion really did occur. "While you talk with Peder, I'll send a message to the embassy and tell Carew that I'm staying in Oslo for the time being."

"Are you sure I can't talk you out of it?"

"Yes. I'll worry about leaving when it becomes apparent that there is no other choice."

Anna frowned and shook her head as the two women stood.

"I just hope that won't be too late."

Evelyn followed Anna into the shop on Uranienborgveien and looked around, the bell over the door jingling as it swung shut. The small store seemed to both sell and repair everything from radios to bicycles. As she came in, a man about Kristian's age looked up from where he was bent over a household radio behind the counter, a screwdriver in his hand. He nodded to Anna and his eyes went to Evelyn.

"Is this the one?" he asked, straightening up. "She's not what I was expecting."

"And what were you expecting?" Evelyn asked in Norwegian, raising an eyebrow.

The man looked startled, then grinned.

"She said you were English," he said, setting down the screwdriver and wiping his hands on a clean rag. "My apologies. I didn't know you spoke our language."

Evelyn nodded, a reluctant smile coming to her lips. "Apology accepted. But what were you expecting?"

"I'm not sure," he admitted. "Someone older, I think, and much uglier."

Anna laughed. "Now I know I never said anything that would give you that impression," she said. "Don't listen to him, Marlene. He's just trying to stir up trouble."

"I never stir up trouble," Peder retorted, coming out from behind the counter and moving forward with his hand outstretched. "A pleasure to meet you, Miss Elfman. I'm Peder Strand."

Evelyn took his offered hand. "Please call me Marlene."

"I understand you're trying to get a message to your uncle in London. Why not send a telegram?"

"It's rather complicated," she said with a smile. "I'd rather send it directly to his office."

His brown eyes met hers and he considered her thoughtfully for a long minute before releasing her hand. Turning his head, he looked towards the back of the shop.

"Rolf!" he bellowed.

Evelyn started and he turned back to her.

"I'll have my brother mind the store while we go to the back," he told her. "I can't promise anything, but I'll try."

She nodded and looked to the back of the store as a young man with dark hair emerged from an open door.

"Rolf, watch the store for a few minutes," Peder said, leading them towards the back. "I won't be very long."

His brother nodded, glancing at Anna and Evelyn curiously as he went behind the counter.

"What's the story with this radio?" he asked over his shoulder.

"Mr. Brevig said that it's not receiving," Peder said. "I was going to open it and take a look. You can do it, if you like. See if you can discover what's wrong with it. Just don't change anything until I return. I'll check to see how you did."

Peder held open the door at the back for the two women, motioning them to go through.

"He's still apprenticing," he explained, following them through the door. "He's good, but still has a lot to learn."

"Is everyone in your family good with radios?" Anna asked, looking around the small storeroom they were in.

"Not everyone, no. Rolf and I are the radio experts." Peder moved through the small storeroom to another door and opened it, motioning them forward. "Come. The office is back here."

Evelyn glanced at Anna and followed, her shoulders unconsciously stiffening as she went through the second door. No threat waited on the other side, however, and she relaxed as she stepped into a spacious office with two desks and a large window overlooking a tiny patch of grass.

"Kristian said you've been doing this for a long time," Anna said, looking around. "Did you start in school as well?"

"Yes. We both became interested in radios around the same time." Peder went over to a tall cabinet and opened it. "Your brother thought we were crazy."

"My brother thinks a lot of people are crazy," she replied with a flash of teeth.

He pulled out a large case and carried it over to the desk closest to the window, setting it down carefully.

"In our case, he wasn't too far off," he said with a short laugh. "We were very silly in those days. I suppose we did seem rather insane."

"Is that it?" Evelyn asked, walking forward as he opened the case. "It's not very big."

Peder glanced at her. "It doesn't need to be. I've designed the transmitter to be more powerful while taking up less space."

"How heavy is it?"

"About fifteen pounds." He pulled an antenna from the back of the case and unwound the cord, carrying it over to attach it to the window. "I wanted to make something portable that I could transport easily to the conferences and meetings that I attend. I got tired of lugging thirty pounds of equipment with me."

"Thirty pounds!" Anna exclaimed. "I should think so! Is that how much your old one weighed?"

"That's how much most of them weigh," Evelyn said, bending down to examine the radio on the desk. "At least, from what I've heard," she added hastily.

"The ones that are powerful enough to transmit over long distances, yes," Peder agreed. "There are smaller ones that are short-range and they are much lighter. With this one I retained the range while lightening it up. I think it worked out very well."

He plugged the machine into an outlet and looked at Evelyn.

"I can send a message for you, but I need to know what frequency and where to send it."

Evelyn nodded and opened her purse, pulling out a slip of paper and passing it to him. "This is where it needs to go."

He took the paper and read it, nodding. "Pull up a chair," he said, seating himself before the radio. "Let me see if I can make contact. If I can, then you can tell me what you want to say."

Anna pulled a chair over and motioned Evelyn to sit.

"What about you?"

"There's another one over there."

Evelyn nodded and sank onto the chair, watching as Peder put on a headset and began to fiddle with knobs on the machine. She had gone through basic training on a wireless radio in Scotland, with another crash course in December. She could operate a radio in a pinch, but she was very grateful to have someone who obviously knew what he was doing willing to help her.

Silence fell over the office as he worked, and Evelyn glanced at Anna. She was watching Peder with avid curiosity. Catching Evelyn's look, she grinned sheepishly.

"I'll admit I find it very interesting," she whispered. "I wouldn't mind learning myself."

"I'm happy to teach you," Peder said over his shoulder, making her start. "If you really want to learn, that is."

"I do, actually," Anna said. "I'm beginning to realize how handy it could be."

Peder shot her an unreadable look and Evelyn's eyes narrowed. He wasn't a stupid man. If he had built this machine from scratch, and it appeared that he had, he was far more brilliant than most. He had to know what Anna was referring to, and after that briefly searching look he'd given her in the shop, Evelyn was confident that he knew something was out of the ordinary with her as well. He would have to be an idiot to think that none of this had anything to do with the war.

"I think I've got through," he said after a few more moments, looking at Evelyn. "That was much faster than I was expecting. What do you want to say?"

"Are you ready to start transmitting now?"

He nodded. "I'm ready when you are."

Evelyn cleared her throat and glanced at Anna. She wished Anna wasn't in the room, but there was no help for it.

"Uncle George, I heard about Aunt Martha. I'm sorry I can't be there. How sick is she? Do I need to come back?" Evelyn watched as Peder began transmitting the message, tapping it out in Morse code on a single metal paddle. "A storm is on the way and in three days, the good weather here will turn bad. I'm enjoying myself and meeting a lot of new people. If I must return, I'll be sorry to leave, but happy to do so if it will help you." Evelyn paused, watching, then, "Sign it as Jian."

"Jian?" Peder repeated, glancing at her. "How do you spell that?"

"J-i-a-n." She hesitated, then smiled. "It's a nickname from when I was a girl."

He nodded and finished a minute later. "Am I waiting for a reply?"

"If you don't mind."

"How long does that usually take?" Anna asked.

Evelyn shrugged. "It depends. Sometimes right away, and sometimes longer."

Peder removed his headset and turned to face Evelyn.

"While we're waiting, why don't you tell me why you're really here?" he asked pleasantly, crossing his arms over his chest and settling his dark gaze on her face.

Evelyn raised her eyebrows. "Pardon?"

"I just sent what I'm pretty sure was a coded message to London," he said. "You could have done that from any other radio in the city, or from the embassy. Why me?"

She swallowed and saw Anna look at her out of the corner of her eye.

"Kristian said you were the best radio operator in Oslo," she said slowly, keeping her eyes on his face. "I wanted to see for myself."

Peder raised his eyebrows. "And?"

"And your machine is superior to anything I was expecting to find."

"Who are you? And don't tell me you're Anna's friend. Who do you work for?"

"I think you've already figured that out, haven't you?" she asked softly.

There was a long moment of charged silence and then a reluctant smile pulled at his lips.

"I think so, yes," he agreed, uncrossing his arms and reaching into his pocket for a packet of cigarettes. "Do you mind?" he asked, holding them up questioningly and she shook her head.

"No."

"What are you doing in Norway?" he asked, offering them each a cigarette. Evelyn took one but Anna declined. "Are you here because you think the Germans will come? Or are you here because you think the British will come?"

He leaned forward to light her cigarette and Evelyn couldn't stop the faint smile that came to her lips. She'd known he wasn't stupid. He was just the type of person they could use.

"What do you think?" she asked.

He lit his own cigarette before shaking out the match and sitting back.

"I think Hitler will try anything. He's arrogant, and his forces need the Swedish iron to keep going. Everyone knows Germany has none of their own. I don't know if it will be Norway or Sweden, but I think he will try something." He paused, then shrugged. "All the radio traffic out of Germany says as much."

"You've been listening to them as well?" Anna asked. "Are all the amateur radio operators listening to the Germans?"

Peder grinned. "Well, they make it so easy," he said with a laugh. Then he sobered. "I don't know that all of the others are listening, but a few of us are. And I don't like the amount of traffic that's been going between the Kriegsmarine and the Wehrmacht lately."

"What do you think it means?" Evelyn asked.

"I think it means that Hitler is planning something big for Scandinavia, but I don't know what." Peder frowned. "He's guaranteed that he will not breach Norway's neutrality. Perhaps it is Sweden he is looking to."

Evelyn studied him for a minute. "What if it isn't?"

His lips tightened.

"Then that's a problem, and one that I think we'll all have to face sooner rather than later." He met her stare. "Is that why you're here today? To know what I will do if the Germans try to invade Norway?"

The blunt question took Anna aback and she let out a soft, involuntary gasp, but Evelyn smiled slowly, unsurprised.

Night Falls on Norway

"I think I know what you will do," she said. "Am I wrong?"

There was a long, heavy silence, then he grinned. "Somehow I don't think you're wrong very often."

Evelyn let out a short laugh. "Oh, I'm wrong more often than I like to admit," she told him. "But I don't think this is one of those times."

Anna looked from one to the other, a frown on her face.

"Will you stop speaking in riddles, please?" she asked. "What will he do?"

"It's more a matter of what he *won't* do," Evelyn said. "He won't accept a German government, and he certainly won't allow them to take away his radio."

"Ah yes. The radio. It all comes down to that, doesn't it?" he asked. "That's why you're here, after all. Tell me if I've worked it out correctly. You want me to transmit information to the British that will help them in their war. And, if the Germans invade Norway, you want me to continue to supply your government with information on German movements and installations. Am I correct?"

"Yes."

"And why does your government suddenly care so much for Norway?" he asked. "They violate our neutral waters regularly, and they've made no secret of the fact that they're not opposed to preventing ships from bringing supplies into our harbors. Why would they suddenly care about what happens to Norway?"

"Because if Norway falls to the Germans, the Kriegsmarine will have unlimited access to the Atlantic Ocean, and Hitler will have complete control over the North and Baltic Seas."

"And if we fall to the British?"

Evelyn swallowed. "There is no talk of England invading Norway."

He gave her a skeptical look. "There was no talk of Hitler invading Poland either, until he did it," he pointed out. Then he sighed. "I'm well aware of the danger of the war coming to our shores and, if it does, rest assured that I will do everything I can to help you and your country. If that means transmitting information, then I will do so happily."

He held up a finger when she opened her mouth to speak.

"But I will *not* do so until that war comes to our shores," he continued. "I will not break my government's neutrality and risk my countrymen for the sake of playing secret agent for Britain."

Evelyn stared at him and slowly nodded. "I can understand that."

Before he could say anything, a sound came from the headset and he grabbed it, putting it on as he swung around to the radio. The room fell silent as he listened intently and began writing down the signals coming through. Evelyn watched him, her heart pounding. The answer had come quickly, which told her that they were already aware of the situation and had been waiting for a message from her. Would she be ordered back to England?

After what seemed like forever, but was in reality only about three minutes, Peder removed the headset and turned to hand her the piece of paper.

JIAN: AUNT MARTHA'S CONDITION HAS BEEN EXAGGERATED. YOUR RETURN NEXT WEEK AS PLANNED IS FINE. ENJOY YOURSELF AND BRING BACK A SOUVENIR. - UNCLE GEORGE

Evelyn exhaled and stubbed out her cigarette in the ashtray on the desk.

"Well?" Anna asked.

"Everything is fine," she said, smiling at her. "Nothing to worry about."

"Well that's a relief!"

Evelyn turned her eyes to Peder.

"I appreciate your candor," she said. "I'm sorry that I won't be seeing you again, but I really do understand your position."

He nodded. "Should anything change, so will my answer," he said, standing. "However, until then, I will remain a passive observer."

Evelyn nodded and turned towards the door, tucking the paper he'd handed her into her purse.

"God willing, nothing will change," she said, "but if it does, Anna will know how to reach me."

Peder hesitated and Anna looked at him questioningly.

"What is it?" she asked.

Evelyn turned to look, raising an eyebrow.

"Before you go," he said slowly, his forehead creased in a thoughtful frown, "there's someone you might want to talk to."

"Oh?"

"He's right here in Oslo." He hesitated again, then sighed. "He's an artist. He's very...outspoken politically. I think he would be someone you would find useful. His name is Olav Larsen and he lives in Kampen."

Peder turned and went back to the desk, bending to scrawl something on a piece of paper. Returning, he held it out to Evelyn.

Night Falls on Norway

"This is his address. You'll find him there during the day. At night, he works. When you go, tell him I sent you about his artwork."

Evelyn took the address and smiled, her eyes meeting his warmly. "Thank you."

He nodded.

"I wish you luck, Marlene, and God speed."

Chapter Fourteen

London, England
April 7

Bill nodded to the guard at the top of the stairs and held up his identification. The man looked at it and nodded, stepping aside to allow him through.

"Good afternoon, sir," he said. "Enjoying your Sunday?"

Bill snorted as he tucked his wallet back into his coat pocket. "I'd be enjoying it a lot more if I wasn't here," he replied. "Is Montclair in his office?"

"I believe so, sir. I haven't seen him leave."

Bill nodded and strode down the corridor towards the office at the end. The last place he wanted to spend his Sunday afternoon was in Broadway. When the message calling him to Jasper's office was delivered shortly after they returned from church, Marguerite hadn't said a word, but her silence didn't fool her husband. She was annoyed, and he couldn't blame her. They were supposed to be on their way into the country for a few hours away from London and the war. Instead, he was here. Again.

He reached the door and knocked once. Jasper called for him to enter and he went in, stripping off his gloves as he went.

"Hallo, Buckley. Thanks for coming in." He looked up from his desk. "I know it's a nuisance on a Sunday."

"It's not convenient, no, but it's to be expected," Bill replied, walking forward. "What's going on?"

"A reconnaissance flight spotted a large formation of German ships moving north," Jasper said, sitting back in his chair and waving Bill into a seat. "They were in the North Sea."

Bill scowled. "When was this?"

"Earlier today. The RAF scrambled some bombers, but between the two of us, I will be very surprised if they succeed. Have you heard from your agent in Oslo?"

"Yes. She made contact yesterday from an unknown source." Bill ran a hand over his face. "She said German forces were moving towards Norway, but I disregarded it."

Night Falls on Norway

"What?"

He dropped his hand and shook his head. "We've been seeing these reports for weeks. You know that. They're never accurate. I thought it was just another unsubstantiated report. The consulates have been flooded with them lately."

Jasper frowned, then sighed. "I don't suppose I blame you," he admitted. "What did you tell her?"

"To stay put and finish her mission." Bill got up restlessly. "Are we sure they were moving north?"

Jasper nodded, watching him pace. "Yes. And the amount of ships is significant. Hitler's got an invasion force on the move. The only question is whether it's going to Norway or Sweden."

"If they're in the North Sea, I think it's safe to wager it's Norway," Bill muttered. "Damn! What about our own fleet?"

"On their way to lay mines." Jasper hesitated, then sighed. "They went in two groups, one for the northern waters and one for the southern. The first group is already in range of where they're dropping the mines, but the southern group was recalled when we got news of the German convoy. The Prime Minister doesn't want to risk an open sea battle."

Bill stared at him. "And the others?"

"Too far north to run into them. They're laying their mines, then they'll head back."

Bill was silent, pacing. Jasper watched him for a moment, then cleared his throat.

"Any word on how Jian is doing with the locals?"

"She said she's making progress, but no details on how much." He stopped and glanced at Jasper. "Even if she does manage to put together a few people, it won't be enough if the Germans invade Norway altogether."

Jasper nodded. "I know. But it will be a seed, Bill. And seeds grow."

"Only if they're in the ground long enough to root," he retorted. "The Germans will dig them out before they can set."

"Perhaps. Perhaps not." Jasper pursed his lips thoughtfully. "Carew sent a message this morning. He said Vidkun Quisling has been making noises again. He was in Germany last month. If Hitler does invade, I won't be surprised if he sets him up as the head of a puppet government."

"Will the people follow him?" Bill asked, going back to his chair and resuming his seat. "I always got the impression he didn't garner very many followers."

"He doesn't, and I know King Haakon can't stand the man. The Norwegian military is loyal to the King. Quisling won't be able to take control of them so easily, not while the King is still alive."

Bill looked up sharply. "You think the Germans will try to assassinate him?"

"They'd be fools if they didn't," Jasper replied. "He commands the loyalty of the military and the people. He is a beloved leader. If Hitler wants to control Norway, he needs to remove the king."

"Is King Haakon still in Oslo?"

"Yes."

"Oslo will be one of the landing points if they do try to invade. If the king is still there…" Bill's voice trailed off and he shook his head. "I wish I had known all of this yesterday."

"Would you have pulled Jian out?" Jasper asked, watching his face.

Bill was silent for a long time, then he sighed heavily.

"I don't know," he admitted. "She's clearly making progress, and in the absence of irrefutable proof of an invasion, it might be premature to pull her out. The ships could be going to Sweden for all we know."

"And if they do go to Norway?"

"Then I'll contact Carew and have him get a message to her," Bill said after another long silence. "He'll know how to find her; one of his translators is working with her."

Jasper nodded slowly. "As long as you get her out in time," he said. "I don't want to lose her in Norway. We're going to need her, and more like her. You know that."

"Yes."

"If she does manage to put some kind of network together, and the Germans do invade, we'll already have something in place," Jasper said thoughtfully. "Chamberlain will send troops to support the Norwegians. He won't have a choice. When he does, we can send in equipment for the people she's organized. That will go a long way to establishing our seeds."

"As long as the Germans don't get to them first," Bill said. "Let's not get ahead of ourselves just yet. I have every confidence that Evelyn can succeed, but I have less confidence that a sudden invasion won't make her new recruits scatter. And who would blame them?"

"Even if they do, you and I both know that when the dust settles, they'll emerge again. People like that always do. They wouldn't agree to do it otherwise."

Bill nodded slowly.

Night Falls on Norway

"And they would be fighting to get their country back. I can't think of a better motivation than that," he agreed. "I'll keep Jian in place as long as I think it wise, but then I'm pulling her out, whether she's finished or not. As you said, we're going to need her. I don't want to risk losing her in Norway."

"Agreed."

Moscow, USSR

Vladimir Lyakhov opened the door of the large, three-story building that occupied half of the section of Ulitsa Bol'shaya Lubyanka and stepped outside onto the pavement. A sharp wind howled down the city street and he fastened his coat before turning to walk towards the corner. It was April, but the wind still carried the bite of winter, and the heavy clouds in the sky threatened an onslaught of rain or snow. Even so, the fresh air was welcome to the NKVD agent, who had spent the last four hours in an interrogation room with a man who reeked of rotting onions.

Taking a deep breath, Vladimir reached the corner of the building and glanced down the intersecting street to his right. A short man in a dull brown overcoat and hat nodded to him, and Vladimir nodded once in acknowledgment before stepping off the curb and crossing the street. His departure had been noted.

Reaching the pavement on the other side, he strode along the busy street towards the square. It was nice to stretch his legs and get clean air into his lungs. He would pass the square and then continue to the small restaurant where he preferred to take his solitary meals. Vladimir glanced at his watch. He just had time to eat before going home to pack. He was booked on a train leaving for Poland in three hours, and would not be back in Moscow for at least a week, perhaps longer. He had his new friend who smelled like onions to thank for that.

He shook his head as he walked. It was amazing what damage a mere ship mechanic could do when given the right amount of incentive. And the Nazis had given him plenty of incentive. Vladimir's lips tightened. If he hadn't tracked him down when he did, the damage would have been much worse. At least now, he could contain it. To do so, he would be forced to spend a few unpleasant days hunting down the man's fellow collaborators in Poland, but then it would be done and he could turn his attention to the more pressing matter that had also come to light during the interrogation.

It had been a single name, and he was positive that the man had no idea what it meant. But Vladimir did, and he had been shocked to hear it tumble past bloody, cracked lips.

Eisenjager.

The German agent had become a legend in the SS and the NKVD alike, and something of a thorn in Vladimir's side. Each time he came across the name, it inevitably resulted in complications with one of his own investigations, or an investigation in which he had an interest. That the agent really did exist was beyond doubt. This wasn't just another made-up story that had been blown up beyond the realms of reality. The agent was real, and so were his results. Not only a formidable spy, but trained by the elite Waffen-SS; the agent blended intelligence gathering with more forceful methods. Not very different from what Vladimir did himself, but where he was part of an entire system, the German agent was a lone wolf under the Abwehr umbrella. No one seemed to know how he ended up with the German intelligence agency rather than the notorious SD, but that he had thrived there was an understatement. He was as efficient as he was ruthless. If Eisenjager was looking for you, you would be found. And that would be the last anyone ever heard of you.

Reaching the square, Vladimir strode past without sparing a glance for the impressive facade of the Kremlin in the distance. It was a sight that had long ceased to stir any kind of emotion in him other than that of knowing he was home. But home had taken on many meanings over the past few years, and so that word had also ceased to stir an emotion. Perhaps it was just as well. In his life, he had no time for sentiment. In fact, in his experience, sentiment had led directly to the downfall of more than a few good men and women. He had no intention of becoming one of them.

He was crossing the road to get to the restaurant a few moments later when he caught sight of a tall man out of the corner of his eye. He was getting out of the back of a black car, dressed in the same uniform that Vladimir wore.

"Comrade!" he called as Vladimir reached the pavement a few yards away.

Vladimir stopped and turned, watching as the man walked towards him. His coat hung open over his uniform and he carried his gloves in one hand. The sharp wind didn't appear to bother him, and as he reached Vladimir, he held out his hand with a friendly smile.

"It's been a long time, Vlad," he said. "How are you?"

Night Falls on Norway

"Comrade Grigori." Vladimir shook his hand and nodded in greeting. "I'm on my way to dinner. Would you care to join me?"

"Thank you." Grigori fell into step beside him and they continued to the entrance of the restaurant a few feet away. "Congratulations on your promotion. I'm sorry I missed it. I was in Leningrad at the time."

Vladimir nodded. "So I heard. Thank you. You didn't miss very much."

"Just barrels of vodka, or so I'm told. Was Beria really there? He didn't come to mine in December."

"He didn't stay long," Vladimir assured him as they walked into the restaurant.

"So now we are equals again," Grigori said with a grin. "I'll have to work harder on the next promotion."

"As if you ever stopped," Vladimir said with a chuckle. "You were always the ambitious one. I've never sought these."

"And yet they just keep handing them to you."

"I don't know why."

Grigori slapped him on his shoulder. "You are too modest, my old friend. You've deserved each and every one. You're a true Tovarisch."

Vladimir grunted and turned to walk towards his usual table at the back of the restaurant. It was unoccupied. It was always unoccupied when he arrived, a reflection of his status in the government hierarchy. He came here when he wanted a good meal. When he wanted anonymity, he went to one of the many crowded canteens in the city.

"What brings you out today, Grigori?" he asked, unbuttoning his coat and removing it. He hung it on a rack near the table and stripped off his gloves. "It's not like you to hunt me out."

"Can't an old friend say hello?" Grigori asked, hanging up his own coat and turning to seat himself. "If I waited for you to come find me, I'd wait forever."

"I've been very busy," Vladimir said, sitting down. "I'm leaving again tonight and won't be back for several days. You caught me at a good time."

"I know." Grigori ran his eye over the menu. "You're going to Poland. Or, rather, what was Poland."

"Yes." Vladimir didn't question how the other man knew his travel plans. There were eyes and ears all over the city, and nothing was secret anymore. "I don't know when I will return. Perhaps in a week. Perhaps more."

"Lucky you. I'll be here until the end of the week, and then I'm back to Leningrad." Grigori set the menu aside and focused his dark gaze on Vladimir. "You're correct, though. There was a reason I sought you out today, Comrade. Something I thought you would find interesting."

"Oh?"

"I received some information from the Germans the other day. Do you remember the British agent in Oslo last November? Blonde woman?"

Vladimir raised his eyebrows in surprise. "Yes. The Germans interfered to such an extent that she got away from you."

Grigori scowled at the reminder. "Yes."

Vladimir made a slight gesture with his hand and they fell silent as a waiter came over to take their order. Once he'd left again, Grigori looked at Vladimir.

"We never did pick up her trail again. She disappeared."

"I doubt that she disappeared, Grigori," Vladimir murmured, amused. "She's not a ghost."

"Perhaps not, but we were unable to find any trace of her. Until now. The Germans think they know where she is."

Vladimir looked across the table, his face not betraying anything but mild interest. "Really?"

Grigori nodded. "Yes. They say she is in Norway again."

"Why would she go back to Norway? There is nothing there to interest the British."

"Why was she there in November?" Grigori retorted. "It doesn't matter why. What matters is that the Germans have sent Eisenjager."

"That's the second time I've heard that name today," Vladimir said, his brows drawing together.

"Is it?" Grigori didn't sound surprised. "I find it interesting that the Abwehr has become involved."

"It was the SD that lost her in Stockholm. I would think that didn't sit very well in Berlin."

"Very true." Grigori nodded and sat back as the waiter returned to set down glasses of clear liquid. "They are obviously serious about apprehending her if they've sent Eisenjager," he continued after the man had gone again. "His reputation doesn't allow for the kind of sloppy carelessness that happened in Stockholm."

"No. It does not."

Night Falls on Norway

"If the Nazis get her, we will look like fools," Grigori said after a moment. "I mentioned it this morning in a meeting. I'm pushing for one of us to be given the task of finding her."

Vladimir raised an eyebrow. "I thought they determined that she wasn't a threat?"

"Do you really believe Canaris would send Eisenjager if she wasn't?" Grigori demanded, reaching for his vodka. "I don't pretend to know why they want her so badly, but if they do, there must be a good reason."

He took a drink, then pushed his chair back. "I have to piss. When I come back, we toast to your new rank."

Vladimir nodded and watched as his old friend made his way to the door leading to the restrooms. He reached for his glass and took a sip of the vodka, his eyes narrowing. So the Germans were getting close to tracking down Evelyn. How the hell had they found her? What was MI6 doing? Were they really that careless? Didn't they know what they had in Robert Ainsworth's daughter?

His mind went back to the library in Oslo last November. His conversation with the pretty young woman had been brief, but it had been long enough for him to realize that she was following in the steps of her father. And, unless he was mistaken, she would far exceed what her father had been capable of. Jian was a raw talent, but she was one that would learn quickly and become invaluable to whatever government controlled her.

And clearly the Nazis wanted to be that government.

Eisenjager was only sent for one of two reasons: to assassinate or to turn. If the Nazis wanted her dead, they would have stuck with the SD. That was what they were trained for, to hunt and kill. No. The very fact that Eisenjager was on Jian's trail told him that they wanted her alive. If they got their hands on her, there was a very real possibility of them being able to turn her into one of their greatest weapons. It was something his own government excelled at, and Himmler had shown a definite flair for the process. If he had his way, the Nazis would soon be almost as good as the Soviets were at psychological manipulation.

Vladimir took another drink. It was time for him to begin setting his own plans into motion. He had to take precautions against Jian being captured by either the Nazis or his own agency. She had the potential to be far too valuable to him. He couldn't risk anyone else gaining control of her.

It was time to contact her again.

Chapter Fifteen

Oslo, Norway

Evelyn looked up at the tall building skeptically. While it wasn't shabby, precisely, it was not the type of building that she was used to frequenting. In fact, the whole neighborhood was bordering somewhere between the fading grandeur of times past and the encroaching poverty of a depressed economy. She looked at Anna.

"This is it?"

Anna nodded. "Yes. He's on the fourth floor, according to the letterboxes."

She opened the door and Evelyn swallowed a sigh, following her into the apartment building. Inside, the light was dim but the entryway was clean and the paint, while not fresh, wasn't peeling from the walls. She forced herself to relax. She had no doubt in her ability to defend herself if needed, but she would rather not have Anna see that side of her just yet. She already knew far too much about Evelyn as it was.

The two women climbed the stairs to the fourth floor. They didn't pass anyone and the only sound came on the second floor where someone was playing a radio behind one of the doors. When they reached Olav's floor, Anna looked around before leading the way down the narrow hallway to a door at the end.

"This is it," she said, lifting a gloved hand to knock briskly on the door. "Here's hoping that he's at home."

There was a moment of silence and then they heard a muffled noise on the other side of the door. Footsteps followed and the lock clicked before the door opened partway and a young man with a mustache peered out at them.

"Ja?"

"Mr. Larsen?" Anna asked with a smile. "Peder Strand gave us your name and address. He suggested we come see you about some artwork."

Olav Larsen raised a thick dark eyebrow and opened the door a little wider.

"He did, did he?" he asked, looking at both of them more closely. "Then you'd better come in."

He swung the door open and stood aside so they could enter the small apartment. Evelyn swallowed as she stepped inside, but was pleasantly surprised by the neat and tidy living area she found herself in. The furniture was simple, with only a small sofa and two chairs and a long, low table in the center. Late afternoon sun streamed through the window, brightening the room considerably after the dim light in the hallway.

"Thank you. My name is Anna Salvesen, and this is my friend Marlene. Peder sends his regards and says that you should come by the shop one day."

"How is Peder?" Olav asked, moving around them. "I haven't seen him in a few weeks."

"He's well." Anna looked around curiously. "I'm sorry to have come without sending a message first. I hope we aren't disturbing you."

Olav motioned them to the chairs.

"No. I was just finishing up some work," he said, waving vaguely in the direction of a door to their left. He sat down on the couch and looked at them expectantly. "Why did Peder send you to me? What can I do for you?"

"Actually, he wasn't very clear about what kind of artist you were," Evelyn said, working her gloves off her fingers. "He seemed to think that I would be interested in your work."

Olav studied her for a moment. "And so here you are?"

"Yes."

"You speak Norwegian very well, but I don't think you're from Oslo, are you?" he asked.

"No."

"Are you German?"

"No."

"Thank God for that," he said. "I had a German once who didn't pay me. I haven't worked with any since."

Evelyn smiled faintly. "I can't say that I blame you."

"What kind of artist are you, Mr. Larsen?" Anna asked.

A faint smile crossed his face. "Portraits, mainly," he said. "I used to do landscapes, but there was no money in those."

"And is there a lot of money in portraits?" Evelyn asked.

"A surprising amount, if you have the right clients." Olav tilted his head and considered her thoughtfully. "Where are you from, Miss…"

"Elfman. I'm from Belgium."

"And what brings you to Oslo?"

"I'm visiting an old friend."

"Ah. Of course." Something in his smile told Evelyn that he didn't believe a word of it, but he didn't seem inclined to pursue it. "Are you enjoying yourself?"

"Immensely," she smiled. "It's a wonderful city. Anna took me down to Drammen the other day. I had a wonderful time."

"Drammen? Did you try the beer?"

"Yes. We had dinner on the water and then came back," Anna said. "I told her she had to try the Aass, as it was a local brewery."

"Drammen seems a strange place to go on a visit to Norway," Olav said. "Do you know someone there?"

"A friend of my brother lives there," Anna said smoothly.

Olav nodded. "Ah. That makes more sense, then." His eyes went back to Evelyn. "Did you like the beer?"

"It was different from what I'm used to," she said truthfully, "but I enjoyed it."

He laughed. "I must say that you don't strike me as much of a beer drinker. In fact, I'm having a hard time figuring you out, Miss Elfman."

"Whatever do you mean?"

"Let's just say that you're not the normal clientele that gets referred to me," he said humorously. "I'm usually quite good at reading people, but you're different. I'm curious why Peder thought I might be able to help you."

Anna looked at her and Evelyn cleared her throat.

"I think perhaps he thought you would be sympathetic to something I'm trying to do," she told him. "But I'm not sure why he thought an artist would be helpful, to be honest."

"Perhaps if I knew what you were trying to do?"

She looked at him for a long moment. There was nothing but polite interest in his face and she wondered, not for the first time since coming into this small flat, why Peder thought Olav would be helpful to an intelligence network. But he obviously knew something that Olav hadn't shared with them yet, and she didn't think he would send them here on a whim. He seemed far too sensible for that.

"I'm trying to locate people with, shall we say, skills that would lend themselves to a particular task," she said slowly. "Unfortunately, without knowing precisely what your particular skill is, I have no idea whether or not we can be of any benefit to each other."

Olav was quiet for a long moment, then he raised his eyebrows. "And what kind of task is it that would need doing?"

Night Falls on Norway

"Well, that would depend entirely on your skills," she said with a smile and a shrug. "So, you see, it would appear that we're at an impasse."

He chuckled and suddenly stood.

"Come with me," he said, turning towards the door on the left. "If Peder trusts you, then I suppose I can."

Evelyn glanced at Anna and stood, following him. Anna was right behind her, her eyes wide with curiosity. He opened the door and went in, motioning for them to follow. Evelyn stepped into a smaller room, looking around. A large table dominated one wall, stretching the length of the room, with bright lights on either end. Spread across the center was a variety of paper and what looked like card stock, along with boxes filled with pens, ink, stamps and assorted seals. On the far side, the wall was completely bare and a tall lamp with an adjustable neck stood to the side, angled to shine on the wall.

Evelyn's brows came together and she turned her head to find a camera set up on a tri-pod opposite the blank wall. After staring for a second, her eyes flew to Olav's face and a grin began to pull at her lips.

"Oh!" she exclaimed softly. "Of course! Portraits."

He nodded.

"But...Peder said you were an artist," Anna said, looking around in confusion.

"He is," Evelyn said, moving over to the long table and glancing at the papers. "It takes a significant amount of artistic skill to create identification papers."

Anna gasped. "You're a forger?" she demanded.

"I never much cared for that term," he said with a shrug. "I provide people with a means to a new life."

"What kind of means?" Evelyn turned to look at him. "What kinds of identification do you provide?"

"Whatever they are willing to pay for," he said. "Passports, identification cards, papers. The more difficult they are to get, the more I charge. I can do almost anything, as long as I have an original to work from." He went over to a box on the table and rummaged around inside before pulling out a slim case. He opened it and held it out for Evelyn to look. "I've even made a few of these."

She stared down at a Soviet identification card, issued in February, before raising her eyes to his in surprise.

"How did you get this?" she asked. "These are impossible to get outside of the Soviet Union!"

He chuckled and closed the case.

"Nothing is impossible, Miss Elfman, only difficult." He replaced the case and leaned against the table, crossing his arms over his chest. "Is this something that would be beneficial to your particular task?"

"Yes, it would," Evelyn said decisively. "How much do you charge for Norwegian identification papers? And perhaps a Norwegian passport?"

"For you?"

She nodded.

"Eight hundred kroner."

Anna let out an involuntary gasp but Evelyn didn't blink. "How soon can you have them finished?" she asked.

"When do you need them?"

"As soon as possible."

He studied her for a long moment, hesitating, then nodded.

"I'll take your photograph now and I can have them for you by tomorrow afternoon. They will need to cure overnight."

"You can't be serious!" Anna exclaimed, looking at Evelyn. "Eight hundred kroner?! That's ridiculous."

Olav didn't take his eyes from Evelyn's face.

"You can get them cheaper elsewhere, but they won't be as good," he said with a shrug. "Peder didn't send you to me for average work."

She smiled slowly. "No, he didn't."

"Then let's get started."

Oslo, Norway
April 8

Eisenjager watched as the blonde woman walked past the alley where he stood concealed behind an iron gate. She was heading towards the tram stop on the next block. He waited a full minute before slipping out behind her. She had already reached the corner and was crossing the side street. He turned up the collar on his coat against the brisk wind blowing down the narrow street and started up the pavement, following her.

He had located the boarding house where Jian was staying easily enough. She had returned to the same lodging she had used in November, where Sturmbannführer Renner had failed to apprehend

138

her. That was a beginner's mistake, and one that he had thought she would make. She hadn't disappointed. According to the very little information he had on the English agent, she was new to this game. As such, at least for the time being, he could count on her making the fundamental mistakes that all new agents made. They tended to cling to the familiar, using the same lodgings and same contacts as they had previously. Those that survived the first few months of active duty learned very quickly to never use the same lodging twice, especially when it had already been exposed. Jian hadn't reached that stage yet, but she would. And quickly. Until then, however, her ignorance was to his advantage. It had made finding her a very simple matter.

Jian moved through the mid-morning traffic on the sidewalk with a confident stride. She never once glanced behind her, but she held her chin up and he could tell from the rigid line of her back and shoulders beneath her coat that she was fully aware of her surroundings. She was alert, and that would work in her favor if she made it past the next few days. It also explained why she had been so difficult for Renner to pin down. The agent may be new to the shadows, but she had the instincts of a professional, and that counted for far more than people realized. He knew this better than most, for he had started in the same manner. It was only because of his instincts that he was still alive, and had had the success that he had.

Eisenjager's lips tightened imperceptibly as he followed the woman towards the tram stop. He had been studying what they knew of her for six months, but seeing her for the first time this morning had been something of a shock. He supposed it was her youth that had surprised him, but he couldn't in all honesty attribute the lingering feeling of shock solely to that. There was something about the woman that made him think there was far more to her than they realized. This wasn't simply a mere pawn recruited by MI6 to gather information. This was a weapon. He had no idea why he thought that, nor could he pinpoint what it was that made him so sure that Jian was a formidable foe, but as he spent the morning watching her, Eisenjager became more and more convinced that this young, green agent was a threat to the Third Reich.

And all threats to the Third Reich were to be eliminated.

She joined a small cluster of passengers waiting for the tram at the stop ahead, and he picked up his pace when he glanced behind him and saw the tram approaching the stop. He had no doubt that the order would come soon enough to terminate the British agent, but for now he was instructed only to watch and report. So far, the only person she had seen today was the young woman that she met for coffee.

Eisenjager had recognized the woman from the descriptions in Herr Renner's reports. It was the translator Jian had used in November. Once again, she had clung to the familiar. It would be a small mistake like that that would get her killed, he decided, joining the small throng at the stop as the tram pulled to a halt. This was going to be easier than he thought.

They all climbed onto the tram, and Eisenjager moved to the back corner where he could observe her easily without being noticed. Once he saw where she was going and who she was meeting, he would report back to Hamburg with his findings on both Jian and the airports and train stations in and around Oslo. The information on the infrastructure would be forwarded to the SS and the invasion troops, enabling them to secure the capital quickly tomorrow, when Operation Weserübung commenced. By nightfall, Oslo would be in German hands. Then he could concentrate on Jian.

But first things first. He would see who she was meeting and where she was going today. That would give him a good idea of her purpose in Oslo, and of the network that she was in contact with here. Once the Gestapo had rolled up the network, they would know exactly what the agent's plans were.

And then he would go to work.

Evelyn lifted her hand to knock on the door. Olav's building hadn't improved with the knowledge of what to expect, and she was fairly certain that the strong smell of garlic in the hallway hadn't been there yesterday. As her gloved knuckles fell on the wood, she resisted the urge to wrinkle her nose and instead glanced over her shoulder towards the stairwell. All of her instincts seemed to be in overdrive this morning. She had felt unusually on edge ever since leaving the boarding house, and yet there was no reason for her to feel so uneasy. Everything was going surprisingly well on this visit to Oslo, despite her initial reservations about attempting to build a network for MI6 on foreign soil. Perhaps Bill was right. Perhaps she *was* made for this.

Olav opened the door and nodded to her, standing aside so that she could enter the apartment. As he did so, he grimaced.

"I'm sorry for the smell," he said, closing the door behind her. "Mr. Lotte at the end likes to cook and, as you can tell, gets carried away with the garlic at times. He spent a month in Sicily last year, and that was all it took."

Night Falls on Norway

Evelyn laughed. "At least it confines itself to the hallway," she said.

"That is true. Come. Everything is ready for you."

He led the way through the living room to the small room on the other side and went in. Evelyn followed, blinking in the dim light. The curtains were pulled tight over the window and only a single lamp shone in the corner.

"Oh. Let me open the curtains," he said. "I pull them closed when I'm working, but it makes it very dark in here."

Olav crossed to the small window and threw open the curtains, letting in the murky daylight from the overcast sky. The room brightened considerably, and Evelyn looked at the long table along the wall. Most of the clutter had been pushed to the end, but in the center was a passport and two identification papers.

"May I?" she asked, motioning to the table.

Olav nodded. "Please."

Evelyn walked over to the table and picked up the passport, examining it closely.

"Here." He walked over to the bright lamp he'd used the day before when taking her photograph and switched it on. "Bring it over here and look under the light."

Evelyn did so and stared at the passport in surprise. It was a perfect duplicate of a real passport.

"This is fantastic," she murmured, turning it over. "It looks just like the real thing."

Olav smiled faintly. "That's what you're paying me for."

She glanced up and nodded, a smile coming to her lips. "So I am."

She turned and went to pick up the identification papers, finding that they were of the same superior quality.

"You have quite a talent," she said, turning to face him. "Really, it's quite exceptional."

He inclined his head. "Thank you."

Evelyn set them down and opened her purse, pulling out a stack of bills. She held them out to him.

"I appreciate this," she said, "and thank you for doing them so quickly."

Olav took the money, counting it quickly.

"You're welcome." He lifted his eyes to hers. "But I have a strong feeling that you didn't come only for identification papers."

Evelyn smiled and shook her head.

"No, I didn't. I would like to ask if Anna can use your services in the future," she said. "You will, of course, charge your usual rates, and you would be paid extra for your discretion."

He studied her thoughtfully for a long moment.

"How much extra?"

"Ten percent?"

He raised his eyebrows in surprise. "Simply for my discretion?" he asked. "Discretion is already part of my business."

"Consider it as added insurance against any…possible unpleasantness."

To her surprise, he chuckled.

"That also is already part of my business," he told her, tucking the money into his pocket. He crossed his arms over his chest and leaned against the wall, his eyes on her face. "Let's dispense with the games, shall we? Who do you work for and why are you really here? I know it wasn't just to get a passport and papers. Tell me what you're really asking me to do, and I can give you an honest answer."

Evelyn nodded.

"Very well. I work with the British embassy, and I've been authorized to arrange for certain safeguards in the case of a German invasion of Norway." She paused, then shrugged. "There are many who believe such an invasion is imminent. If it is, then Norway will need people who are willing to help others oppose the Nazis."

His face was unreadable as he stared at her across the room.

"And those people will need identification to move freely," he said slowly.

"Something like that."

"And why is England so interested in helping the people of Norway?" he asked.

Evelyn's lips twisted dryly. "England is interested in anything that will help her win the war."

Olav was silent for a long moment, then he sighed.

"If the Nazis come to Oslo, I will have more problems besides this," he finally said, waving towards the equipment in the room. "I have been very outspoken in the past about my political leanings, and the Nazis don't tolerate communists."

Evelyn raised her eyebrows. "You're a communist?"

He nodded. "Yes. So, you see, this places me in a rather awkward position."

She pursed her lips thoughtfully. "I'm not sure that it does," she said slowly. "What do your political leanings have to do with aiding your fellow countrymen?"

Night Falls on Norway

"Is that what I would be doing?" he asked her softly. "Would I be aiding them, or the British government?"

"Both, but the immediate benefit would be to Norway. If the Germans invade, and it really does seem likely that they will try at some point, the only hope will rest with your people. They will have to be the ones to resist."

Olav was silent for a long time, his lips pressed together into a thin line. Evelyn watched him, unable to read his expression. He was clearly in two minds over the proposition, but she had no idea which option he would choose.

"And Peder?" he finally broke his silence. "Is he also lending his support to this scheme?"

Evelyn shook her head. "Not yet," she said. "He doesn't want to oppose his government until there is no other choice. If there is an invasion, then he will use his radio to help us. Until then, he remains neutral."

Olav's lips twisted. "That sounds like Peder. Always practical and loyal to what he perceives as the right thing." He was quiet again for a long moment, then he sighed. "Peder will be invaluable if there is an invasion. His skill with radios is exceptional."

"Just as yours is with this," she said softly.

Olav smiled. "I am one of the best in the city," he agreed, "but there are others. I am not the only one. However, they might not even consider this. What you're asking isn't just for me to provide identification for enemies of the Third Reich, but for me to risk my own freedom and life to do so."

"Yes."

They were silent, staring at each other. Evelyn couldn't say anything else. He was right. That was exactly what she was asking of him. It was up to him whether or not he felt the cause outweighed the risks. After what seemed like a very long time, Olav exhaled and straightened up, dropping his arms to his side.

"I will do it," he decided. "Tell Anna that she can come to me, and we can arrange it. Unlike Peder, I see no reason to wait. I believe it is only a matter of time before Hitler turns his eyes north to us. When he does, there will be many who will need my services."

Evelyn hadn't been aware that she was holding her breath until he spoke, then she exhaled silently in relief. She nodded and smiled, holding out her hand to him.

"I will let Anna know. Thank you."

He grasped her hand, shaking it. "Don't thank me. I do it for my country, not for you. Just as you are here for *your* country, and not for me."

She met his gaze.

"One is not necessarily exclusive of the other," she said softly. "I am here for my country, yes, but that doesn't mean that I don't care about yours. The Nazi threat is something that affects us all. It is something we all must resist."

Olav smiled faintly and released her hand.

"And we shall."

Chapter Sixteen

Drammen, Norway

The large fishing boat bobbed in the water as the men finished securing the day's catch before preparing to go back to shore. Kristian looked over the water, taking a deep breath of salty air before turning away from the others.

"I'm going below deck," he said over his shoulder. "Set a course for home. We've had a good day out."

"Going back to your machine?" his brother called with a laugh. "You're obsessed."

Kristian shrugged and went through the opening and down the wooden steps to the lower level of the boat. He was used to his brothers teasing him about his radio. They didn't fully understand why he preferred to spend his spare moments with the radio, but they did understand that it was his passion. And more recently, they had begun to realize how useful his wireless radio could be.

He went into the tiny room he used as a combination office and chart room and sat down before the radio. This morning, the traffic between the naval yards in Germany and Poland had been heavy, making him think that something was changing. Something was going on, and Kristian was very much afraid that it wasn't anything good.

He lifted the headset and settled it over his head, switching on the radio and turning the knobs. After playing with the frequency for a moment, he found the one from this morning and settled down to listen. The flurry of activity was still going strong and he frowned, picking up a pencil and pulling his notepad towards him. The messages were still in the new code that he couldn't make head or tail of, but every once in while he got lucky and was able to piece together words that meant something. With any luck, perhaps now would be one of those times.

Fifteen minutes later, Kristian took off his headset and stared down at the pad of paper. There were several phrases scrawled down and he studied them intently for moment. One word was used in all of them: Weserübung.

He frowned, staring at it. Why was there so much traffic going between the ports about a river exercise? It had to be a code for something else. He underlined the word and turned his attention to the others on the paper. There was something here. He just had to find it.

Oslo, Norway

Peder held the door open for the customer carrying his newly-repaired radio.

"Thank you, Mr. Brevig. I think you'll find it works much better now," he said with a nod.

The old man smiled. "You're a genius, Peder, and a life-saver. My wife listens to this every evening. She's been miserable since it's been gone. I'll admit, I've missed our nightly program as well."

Peder laughed. "Go home and enjoy it, then. And tell Mrs. Brevig hello for me."

"I will."

Mr. Brevig departed and Peder closed the door, locking it and turning the sign in the window to say that they were closed. It was fifteen minutes past closing time, but Mr. Brevig had been a loyal customer for many years. When he'd come to pick up his radio just as he was preparing to close, Peder knew it would take a few minutes. Mr. Brevig liked to chat, and Peder always enjoyed their talks. He didn't mind staying a little later for him.

Turning, he went back to the counter to collect the till and take it into the back. He would settle the drawer, lock it in the safe, and then go join his family for dinner.

Peder was just opening the safe ten minutes later when the radio on his desk in the back room came alive with the unmistakable sound of a message coming through the receiver. He glanced at his watch and frowned, setting the cash drawer in the safe before closing and locking the heavy door. Who was trying to reach him? He usually didn't go on until later and most of his fellow radio enthusiasts knew that.

He crossed over to the desk and sat down, picking up the headset. Settling it on his head, he flipped a switch on the radio and listened for a moment. His eyebrows soared into his forehead in surprise. It was Kristian. He'd just heard from him on Saturday and he hadn't mentioned contacting him again so soon.

146

Night Falls on Norway

He lifted out the signal paddle and answered the signal, then settled down to wait. Perhaps he had learned something new about what was happening across the sea in Germany. Personally, Peder thought he was insane for trying to decode German messages, but he admitted that if anyone had a shot at that, it was probably Kristian. He was one of the smartest men Peder knew, even if he did spend most of his day on a boat with fish.

His lips twitched at the thought. When Kristian elected to return to Drammen after they finished school and join the family business, they had all been dismayed. With his brains, he could do anything. Why fishing? Surely that was a waste of his talent and education. But Kristian had proved them all wrong. Returning to Drammen, he had taken over the family business, growing it from two small fishing boats to five large ones over the course of two years. The business was growing and doing well, and so was Kristian. Not only had he taken the helm of the business, but he had continued his radio hobby, and often traveled to Oslo to speak at meetings for the many societies he was still a part of.

Peder picked up his pencil as a new message began to come through. It was in the code that he and Kristian had developed while they were still in school. They were the only two who used it, making it perfect for transmitting messages that they didn't want anyone to know. It had started as a fun game for the young students, but now Peder frowned. If Kristian was using the old code, it wasn't a game anymore.

A few minutes later, he stared down at the message on the paper, stunned. He felt the blood draining from his face and he dropped his pencil as his hand began to shake. It was impossible. Kristian had to have got it wrong. Even as the thought entered his head, though, Peder knew it was wishful thinking. This wasn't something Kristian would have got wrong. He was too good for that.

DECODED PORTIONS OF SEVERAL TRANSMISSIONS TODAY. THERE CAN BE NO DOUBT. GERMANS SENDING INVASION FORCE. THEY EXPECT TO BE IN OSLO TOMORROW.

Peder took a deep, ragged breath and got up, running shaking hands through his hair as he paced restlessly around the office, his mind spinning. How had Kristian cracked the German code? He knew that he had been working on it, and knew that he had broken the diplomatic code months ago. But he never really thought that Kristian would learn anything very important. Yet, if what he just said was true, he had figured out something that Peder doubted their own government even knew. The news today had been dominated by

Norway's strong protests against Britain mining waters off the coast. Not a word had been mentioned about any possible German fleet movements.

Peder dropped back into his seat and rubbed a hand over his eyes. Yet it made perfect sense. The English were busy laying mines in the waters to prevent German ships from moving freely through Norwegian waters. Why would they do that if not because they believed that Germany would try to invade Norway?

This was exactly what Anna and Marlene had been warning him of just two days ago. Marlene had been convinced that an invasion was inevitable, but he hadn't wanted to believe that it could be possible. At least, not without some kind of warning.

He put his headset on again and began to reply to Kristian. He needed to know everything Kristian knew. And then he had to let Anna know.

If the Nazis were coming, Marlene was in danger. They had to get her out of Oslo, and they would need his radio to help.

"So that makes two definite and one possibility," Anna said. "That's not bad for your first attempt!"

"*Our* first attempt," Evelyn corrected her. "I couldn't have done it without you."

She and Anna were seated at a table in the restaurant of the Hotel Bistro. Monday night was not a busy evening and the tables around them were empty. They weren't the only diners, but it was a far cry from the busy dining room Evelyn was used to. Opposite them, on the other side of the large room, a businessman sat alone with a newspaper while he waited for his dinner. Not far from him, an older couple who looked as if they were tourists were dining with gusto, while two men who had the stamp of foreign diplomats upon them were seated towards the doors. In all, only about ten of the tables were occupied, making it seem as if they were safely isolated from each other.

"I think you could have, but I'll admit that I enjoy helping," Anna said, lifting her glass. "To an early success!"

Evelyn smiled, raising her glass in an answering toast and sipping the crisp, white wine in appreciation. While she was used to dining in fashionable, busy restaurants, she was enjoying the relative quiet this evening. This was exactly what she needed after the tense afternoon in Olav's back room, trying to convince him to become part of something larger than himself.

"I've had some ideas on other people to approach," Anna continued, setting her glass down. "Olav's unique…skills got me thinking. I hadn't really considered it before, but people who are perhaps not on the right side of the law may actually be the perfect people to approach."

Evelyn's brows furrowed. "We need to be careful when it comes to people like that," she said slowly. "They would undoubtedly know ways around things and that could prove invaluable, but they also, by and large, can't be trusted."

"Would you rather not explore the possibilities?" Anna asked after a moment. "We don't have to. It was just a thought."

After a long pause, Evelyn looked at her. "Who did you have in mind?"

"There's a woman I met when I first came to Oslo. She lived in the flat above me. She used to work at night and I thought she was a nurse. It turns out that she was, but not quite the kind that I thought."

"What does that mean?"

"She was a nurse, and a very good one by all accounts. But then she discovered that there was much more money to be made by working in private practice." Anna lowered her voice and leaned forward. "She works with a doctor. They provide special care. Their patients are prostitutes."

Evelyn blinked. "Special care?" she repeated, mystified. "What does that mean?"

Anna cleared her throat and looked a little uncomfortable. "They take care of the medical problems that arise from…well, being a prostitute."

"You mean disease?"

"Among other things."

Evelyn was silent, her mind spinning. She had never given the profession of prostitution much thought, but she supposed that they would need doctors, perhaps more than most. She was well aware of the various diseases that could be contracted in the oldest female profession. Her mother, of course, would be horrified if she realized that she knew, but Evelyn had always been a very forward-thinking individual. Even so, what Anna was discussing was still rather shocking to her.

"How would this woman be useful to us?" she finally asked. "I don't understand."

Anna leaned forward again. "If the Germans do invade Norway, there will be a lot of soldiers a long way from home and in a strange country," she said in a low voice. "Where do you think they will go for...companionship?"

Evelyn gasped softly. "Of course!" she breathed. "And if the nurse is in the confidence of her patients..."

Anna smiled. "Exactly."

"That's...that's brilliant."

"I'm glad you think so. Shall I try to hunt her down? I'm sure she's still working with the same doctor. She had no intention of stopping when I last saw her."

"Do you think she would be sympathetic?"

"If the Nazis come? Yes. I think she'll be furious. She was very outspoken about her opinion of Herr Hitler." Anna shrugged. "I don't think she'll take much convincing, especially for you. You've clearly got a knack for talking people into this."

"I don't know how. I'm still at a loss, to be honest."

"Well, it doesn't show."

Evelyn met her gaze and smiled, remembering how skeptical she had been when Jasper and Bill had given her this assignment. And yet here she was, sitting on two definite recruits and one probable. She was already ahead of where she'd thought she would be.

"Enough about work," she said, reaching for her glass. "This is supposed to be a celebration, not a meeting. Let's talk about something else. Tell me about your brother."

"Erik?" Anna looked surprised. "What do you want to know?"

"You said he was in the army?"

"Yes. His unit is just outside of Trondheim." Anna sipped her drink. "Although, I believe he's going up to Narvik next month."

"What does he do?"

"He's a Lieutenant. I have no idea what kind of officer he is, but I know he's very good with his rifle. It's strange because I can't think of him as a leader and an officer. He's the older brother who used to hide snakes in my galoshes when I was little."

Evelyn smiled. "Do you miss him?"

"Yes, I suppose I do," Anna said after a moment of thought. "We were always very close, though we tend to disagree on many things nowadays."

"Do you? Like what?"

"Well, for one thing, he's very firmly of the opinion that I should be home with my parents and not in Oslo working for the

British Embassy," she said with a quick grin. "He has very strong opinions on the British at the moment."

"I imagine many Norwegians do," Evelyn murmured, her lips twisting dryly. "We're not very popular right now."

"No, but I understand why your country is doing what it is. Unfortunately, Erik isn't interested in trying to see the other side of it. That's where we part company on many subjects. His is very single-minded and stubborn."

She tilted her head and studied Evelyn across the table.

"And what of your brother?" she asked. "You said you had one in the RAF."

Evelyn swallowed and nodded, uncomfortably aware that Anna fully expected her to be as candid about her own brother as she had been about hers. Yet she was reluctant to do so. The less Anna, or anyone else, knew about her the better.

"Yes."

"And do you get along well with yours?"

"Yes. Like you, we've always been close." Evelyn reached for her wine. "But we agree on most things. We're a lot alike."

"What's his name?" Anna asked after a moment of silence.

"Robert."

"Do you miss him?"

"Dreadfully," she admitted with a sad smile. "He's always good for a laugh."

"Do you worry about him?" Anna asked after another moment of silence.

Evelyn lifted her gaze and met the other woman's eyes. In an instant, she felt as if she was joined with Anna in solidarity.

"Every day."

"I do as well," Anna said with a sigh. "Especially knowing that we will likely be facing off with the Germans sooner rather than later. Our military is not prepared for war. Despite everything that has been happening in Europe over the past few years, our government has not mobilized the army or navy, or even provided updated equipment. They are trusting in our continued neutrality."

"They haven't done anything at all?" Evelyn asked, startled.

Anna shook her head. "No. Erik has been complaining about it for almost a year. He, and others, can see what's coming, but they won't have the means to fight properly against it."

Evelyn was silent. She had known the Norwegian forces were no match for the Germans in numbers, but she hadn't realized that they weren't prepared to go to war at all. She had just assumed it was as it was in the rest of Europe, that the government was scrambling to be ready if the need arose. Apparently, that wasn't the case.

"But they will fight?" she finally asked.

"Oh yes. They are loyal to King Haakon. As long as the King remains king, they will fight as one for him. Of that, you can have no doubt."

"What about this Vidkun Quisling fellow?" Evelyn tilted her head and looked at her questioningly. "Would they follow him?"

Anna scoffed. "Quisling? Not likely. The man's a puppet for the Nazis, and no one ever did really like him very much. It's a mystery to me how he's even still in the government. His party is so small, and it never gains any traction in the elections."

Evelyn looked up as the waiter approached their table with their dinner. She smiled and waited while the plates were laid out on the white cloth before them, then nodded and murmured her thanks as he refilled her wine glass. Once he had ensured that they had everything they needed, he left, and she looked across the table at Anna.

"Here's to a speedy end to this war," she said, raising her full glass, "and to our brothers, who will do their part to help bring it to a close."

Anna raised her glass with a smile.

"To the brothers!" She drank, then set her glass down. "Tomorrow, I will hunt down Sylvia, the nurse I was talking about. Shall we meet for lunch?"

"Yes, okay," Evelyn agreed, picking up her knife and fork and preparing to cut into her fish. "I plan on spending the morning getting more acquainted with Oslo. By lunch I will be more than ready to get back to work."

Anna grinned. "Enjoy your morning off," she said. "You've earned it."

"I don't know about that, but I am looking forward to taking a few hours and spending it sightseeing," Evelyn said with a smile. "The last time I was here, I didn't have the chance at all."

"Well, now you will! And just think, you won't have any Germans right behind you!"

Evelyn laughed despite herself.

"Thank heavens for that!"

Chapter Seventeen

April 9
12:15am

Evelyn's eyes flew open and her heart leapt into her throat as she came awake with a start. The room was dark, with only a faint glow coming from the hearth where the embers still smoldered orange in the dying fire, and she sat up quickly, her heart pounding. She had no idea what time it was, or even what had awakened her so abruptly from a deep sleep. Shaking her head to try to clear the lingering fogginess caused by a deep slumber, she frowned, listening. Something had pulled her from sleep. What?

As soon as the thought entered her head, she jumped as a knock fell on the door to her room. With a soft gasp, she threw the covers off and got out of bed, her heart pounding once again. Who on earth was knocking at her door in the middle of the night?

Grabbing her dressing gown from where it lay across the foot of the bed, she pulled it on quickly, tying it tightly around her waist as she went across the room to the door.

"Yes?" she called.

"Miss Elfman, it's Mrs. Kolstadt," a voice called softly through the door.

Evelyn exhaled and threw back the bolt, opening the door quickly. Else stood in the darkened corridor clad in a dressing gown, her hair covered by an old-fashioned sleeping cap. Beside her stood Anna, bundled in the same winter coat she had been wearing earlier with a hat over her dark hair. Evelyn gaped in surprise at the two women standing there.

"Is everything all right?" she asked, looking from one to the other. "Anna, what are you doing here?"

"No, everything isn't all right," Anna replied. "Can we come in?"

Evelyn nodded and stepped back quickly.

"Of course! I'm sorry. I'm still half asleep. Come in!"

They stepped inside and Evelyn closed the door behind them before turning to go across the room to switch on the lamp. As soon as light filled the room, she turned to look at them.

"Marlene, you have to pack quickly," Else told her urgently, her voice strained. "You must leave!"

Evelyn stared at her. "Leave? What are you talking about?"

"Peder is downstairs," Anna said, unbuttoning her coat and looking around the room. "There are German warships approaching Oslo. They are outside the Fjord now, but they're undoubtedly heading into Oslo. Where is your suitcase?"

"How…how do you know?"

"Peder got a message today from Kristian. He came to my apartment shortly after I arrived home tonight," Anna explained. "Kristian was able to piece together enough from numerous radio messages to determine that a German invasion force is on its way. When Peder found out, he began monitoring radio traffic as well. He heard from a friend in Horten that large ships passed there not three hours ago."

"Marlene, dear, you must hurry," Else told her, walking over to her and grabbing her hand. "If the Germans are coming, you must leave! You can still make it to the border with Sweden, but only if you leave now."

Evelyn stared at the older woman, trying desperately to think clearly. Her mind was clamoring to make sense of what she was hearing. Even though she had suspected it was coming, hearing the confirmation now was almost surreal.

"Yes," she said, forcing herself to focus. "Yes, of course."

"Suitcase?" Anna prompted.

"It's under the bed." Evelyn took a deep, ragged breath and turned towards the bed.

"I will help you pack," Anna said, turning towards the wardrobe.

"I'll go downstairs and tell the young man you will be down shortly," Else said, turning to the door. "Hurry!"

She went out the door, closing it softly behind her, and Evelyn blinked. With the closing of the door, the fog in her brain seemed to evaporate and she gasped softly as the severity of the situation suddenly became clear to her.

"How do we know that this isn't a false alarm?" she asked, pulling the suitcase out and lifting it onto the bed.

Night Falls on Norway

"We don't," Anna admitted, coming away from the wardrobe with an armful of skirts and blouses. "Although, I don't see what else German ships would be doing coming up Oslofjord, do you?"

Evelyn took one of the warmer skirts from Anna and tossed it onto the foot of the bed before turning to go to the wardrobe to pull out a blouse and sweater to wear with it.

"I suppose not," she admitted. "I don't know why I'm so taken aback. We knew it was coming."

Anna glanced at her. "I don't think either of us expected it to happen tonight," she replied, quickly folding the clothes she'd taken from the wardrobe and setting them in the suitcase. "I know I didn't."

Evelyn dressed quickly, her mind spinning, while Anna pulled the rest of the clothes from the wardrobe. Not only could she not be here when the Germans came into the city, but she had to get out of Norway before they closed the borders. The Gestapo and SS were already aware of her and what she looked like. She had to get out before they knew she was here. But could she reach the border in time?

"Can I make it to the Swedish border?" she asked, bending to slip on her shoes.

"Peder has his car, so it's possible," Anna said. "Let's make sure the threat is real, although I'm sure it is, and then we'll decide which is the best way to go."

"How will we do that?"

"I know a place on the edge of the city that overlooks Oslofjorden. If there are ships, we'll be able to see them from there."

Evelyn nodded and stood up, crossing to the desk next to the window. She opened her square toiletries case and began packing her toiletries away quickly. Strangely, her hands were steady and she realized with a start that her heart was beating normally. The shock had worn off already, and in its place was a quiet sense of purpose. It was time to move. She had known this could happen, and now that it had, she seemed almost prepared.

"And Peder?"

"He said he will help get you out of Norway." Anna looked up from the suitcase with a faint smile. "And that he is now willing to trade information to the British."

Evelyn nodded curtly and finished packing her belongings into the toiletries case. She closed and locked it, then turned to look at Anna. The other woman was just closing the suitcase.

"Thank you."

Anna nodded. "Don't mention it. Now, is that everything? There's nothing left?"

Evelyn looked around and shook her head, reaching for her coat.

"No, that's everything. I travel light."

"Thank God for that. The less we have to get out of the country, the easier it will be." Anna lifted the case off the bed and turned towards the door. "I brought one case with me and crammed it with everything I could fit. I don't know if I'll be able to come back for the rest."

Evelyn looked at her sympathetically. "What will you do?"

Anna shrugged. "Go to my parents. They are near Trollheimen. Beyond that, I don't know. I'll worry about that later. Right now, let's get you out of Oslo."

Evelyn nodded and they turned towards the door.

"We need to move quietly," she said. "If none of the other guests have woken already, I don't want to wake them now."

"If the Germans are in Oslofjorden, they'll be woken soon enough," Anna said, reaching for the door. "But I agree. Let's get you out of here and leave the others to their own fate."

2 am

Evelyn stared through the binoculars and felt her blood run cold. She pressed her lips together, her heart thudding in her chest. She counted three...no, *four* large, silent ships in the water beyond the opening to inner Oslofjord. The dark shapes were unmistakable in the moonlight, and their very silence was more ominous than if they had their guns blazing.

"Not a false alarm, then," she murmured, studying the ships. "What are they waiting for?"

"Dawn," Anna said. "At least, that's my guess. The German ambassador will have to issue a statement to our government. They won't do anything until then."

Evelyn lowered the binoculars and glanced at Peder, leaning over his radio a few feet away.

"Did your friend say anything about more ships passing?" she asked him.

He looked up and shook his head. "He only mentioned those. That was a few hours ago, though. More may have gone by him since then."

Night Falls on Norway

Evelyn handed the binoculars back to Anna and stared pensively out over the dark fjord.

"There could be many more behind them," Anna said.

"I'm sure there are," Evelyn said, turning away from the rise and looking at her. "They'll land forces all up the western coast, not just in Oslo." She looked at Peder again. "Will you be able to reach London?"

"I don't know. I'm trying. Before I left, I made a crystal for the radio with your frequency. It will help, and make any connection more stable. Do you know that someone will be there to receive it?"

"Yes. Someone will receive it. We just won't get an answer right now." She shook her head and glanced back over the dark water far below them. "By the time they find out what's happening, I have to be well away from here. I think Sweden is the only real option. After we get through to London, how quickly can we reach the border?"

"A couple of hours," Peder replied.

"Good. I just might make it."

"I think we should consider something else," Anna said slowly. "I'm not sure going straight to the border is the best thing."

Evelyn stared at her. "Why on earth not?" she demanded. "If we can make it in a couple of hours, I can cross the border well in advance of the Germans even getting a foothold on land." She lowered her voice. "You know I can't be caught here by the Gestapo or the SS."

Anna nodded, her brows pulled together in a frown.

"I know, and that is my worry. If, for some reason, we don't make it to the border in a couple of hours, you will be trapped. If we go east, we are severely limiting where we can go if we don't make it in time. And, even if we do, there is no guarantee that we will be allowed to cross the border."

"What do you mean?" Peder asked, looking up. "Why wouldn't we be allowed to cross?"

She looked from one to the other, then sighed.

"I've heard some rumors at the embassy," she said reluctantly. "Sweden was very willing to help Finland against the Soviets, but the general feeling is that they won't be as sympathetic to us. If that thinking is correct, they could very well close the border as soon as they realize Germany is invading. And even if they don't, there's nothing to say that we will be at liberty once we're in Sweden."

"Meaning?"

She shrugged. "They could put us in a holding camp, and then hand us over to the Germans. Who knows. That's what Romania did to the Polish."

Peder scowled. "I don't think that is something that will happen. The Swedes aren't like the Romanians," he muttered. "And she's not even Norwegian," he added, nodding to Evelyn. "They wouldn't dare detain a British national."

Evelyn pressed her lips together, her mind spinning. If even part of what Anna suggested was possible, she couldn't take the risk. Her identity couldn't be discovered, not here and not in Sweden. And especially not by the Germans.

"What, then?" she finally asked, looking at Anna. "What do you suggest?"

"I think we should go north, at least until we can determine if the border is a possibility," Anna said. "If they keep it open, we can cross to it further north. In the meantime, we'll be ahead of the German forces."

"That will depend on where they land," Evelyn pointed out. "If they land up the coast, they will be coming inland as we are going north."

"Actually, she has a point," Peder said thoughtfully. "It takes time to land troops, and they will have to get past our army before they can come inland. We'll have a start on them. It could buy us enough time to learn what the situation is on the border."

Evelyn looked from one to the other and then shivered as a gust of biting wind blew in off the water. As far as she could tell, it was six of one and half a dozen of the other. She could risk being trapped near the eastern border or in the middle of Norway. Neither option appealed to her.

"And if we can't make it to the border at all?"

"Then at least you will be moving north and closer to the coast. It will be up to your people to get you out."

"I'm through!" Peder suddenly announced, looking up again from his radio. "I've connected to London. What do you want to send?"

Evelyn went over to him quickly and crouched down beside him.

"German invasion force outside Oslo Fjord. Swedish border in doubt. Heading north. Will attempt to make contact again once safe. Sign it Jian, as before." She paused and squinted down at her watch in the moonlight. "It should be more heavily encoded, but I wasn't given instruction for this eventuality."

Peder glanced at her. "This simple encoding will be sufficient for the invasion forces," he assured her. "They won't be worried about single messages going out like this."

Night Falls on Norway

She was silent and stood up again, turning away. Under normal circumstances, Peder would have been right. The incoming troops would have more important matters on their minds over the next few hours. This wasn't a normal circumstance, however, and if the SD were monitoring radio signals out of Norway in advance of the invasion, she had just sent up a flare.

Shaking her head, another shiver went through her that had nothing to do with the cold. It couldn't be helped. While she had been given very cursory training in sending encoded radio transmissions, she hadn't been given a current codebook or even a list of coded phrases to alert Bill to an invasion. She was completely unprepared to be caught in the middle of a German offensive, and there was absolutely nothing she could do except what she was doing.

"When he's finished, we need to get moving," Anna said as she joined her again at the car. "You do understand why I'm so reluctant to go directly to the border?"

Evelyn nodded. "I understand. It is a risk I can't afford to take, not until we have some kind of idea of how the Swedish government will react."

"I wish I had a better plan to offer you. At least we're moving north and towards higher ground. The mountains will offer more protection in the short term, until we can form a better plan of action."

"What of Carew?" Evelyn glanced at her. "Have you contacted him?"

Anna shook her head. "When he finds out what's going on, if he hasn't already, he'll know I'm helping get you to safety. There is nothing else I can do. I'll be of no use to him now."

"He'll be evacuated to England. The entire embassy will be. They will be safe. They're protected by international law."

Anna let out a short laugh. "Yes, if Herr Hitler still respects that."

Evelyn shrugged. "He did with Poland."

"Probably because he doesn't want to fall afoul of the United States." Anna exhaled loudly and looked up at the sky. "God, what a mess. This is really not how I thought this night would go. When we left the hotel, I had no idea what we were in for."

"Nor did I." Evelyn was quiet for a moment, then she looked at Anna. "At least we had one last good meal."

Anna was surprised into a laugh. "Very true. And Else was kind enough to put together that big basket of food for us. God bless her for that! Who knows if we'll be able to get food as we go."

Evelyn nodded, watching as Peder packed up his radio and came back towards the car.

"It's done," he told them. "Now we go?"

"Yes." Anna nodded and turned to open the passenger door. "Let's get out of here."

Evelyn took one last look at the silent, dark water of the fjord. Beyond the shores, lurking in the darkness, were the forces that had been spawning warnings from all around Europe for weeks. Warnings that ambassadors and leaders alike had dismissed as unfounded and not credible. Warnings that had been ignored. A wave of anger went through her, making her inhale sharply as her hands clenched at her sides. Now German ships waited menacingly offshore to violate Norway's precious neutrality. Here was the invasion that everyone said was unlikely.

And she was stuck right in the middle of it.

Chapter Eighteen

5 am

The door to the office swung open with force and Daniel Carew strode in, stripping off his gloves as he went, his face creased into lines of anxiety. He flipped on the light and tossed his gloves and hat onto a chair.

"What do we know?" he demanded, unbuttoning his coat. "Aside from the obvious fact that Jerry is banging on the front door, that is."

"At 4:20, the old Oscarsborg Fortress on Drøbak Sound fired on a German cruiser," his assistant said, following him into the office. "They hit the lead ship, the first of four so far. The shots caused heavy damage, but the ship continued on until it passed the torpedo installation of the fortress. The Norwegians fired two torpedoes, hitting the cruiser again. As of the last report, it is critically damaged and sinking."

"And the other ships?"

"They've retreated and are landing troops outside the range of the Oscarsborg batteries."

Daniel tossed his coat over the back of the chair and ran a hand over his face.

"And so it begins," he said. "Do we have any word from the palace yet? How about the installations on the west coast? What else do we know?"

"Not much yet," the young man replied. "The phones and machines are going berserk with sightings and landings, but it's all rather a mess. This is all we have so far."

He handed him a stack of messages. Daniel took them and strode around his desk to his chair, flipping through them as he went.

"The King has issued orders to resist," he said unnecessarily, dropping into his seat. "Good. That will give London and Paris time to respond."

"Yes, sir." His assistant cleared his throat. "Because the battery at Drøbak slowed down the initial landing in Oslo, it gives the King and his government time to evacuate before the Germans arrive."

Daniel glanced up and nodded.

"Thank God. If the Jerries get hold of King Haakon, it's all over. It's amazing those old weapons at Drøbak are still functioning. Stroke of luck, that was, especially considering the entire fortress is manned by trainees and fresh recruits." He finished scanning the messages in his hand and then tossed them onto his desk, exhaling heavily. "You're right. These are a mess. I can't make head or tail of where the Germans are right now. According to these, they're everywhere."

"Yes, sir."

Daniel stared at the top of his desk pensively for a long moment, then looked up at his assistant.

"The Norwegians won't be able to hold out for long," he finally said, "if at all. The city is protected by unseasoned soldiers. All of those with any experience and training are in the north. We have to assume that Oslo will be occupied by the end of the day. We'll proceed with the appropriate protocols. Gather anything sensitive from your office and bring it here. We'll go through it all and destroy what we can. I'll do the same in here."

"What about the civilians who work with us?" The assistant asked. "Like Miss Salveson?"

Daniel glanced up and a fleeting smile crossed his lips.

"Worried about her, are you?" he asked. "Yes. I can see why. Send someone round to her apartment to get her. She will be better served to flee the city, but if she chooses to stay, she can hunker down here with us. Perhaps we can get her out when we go."

The young man nodded and turned towards the door. Before he had gone a few steps, Daniel stopped him.

"Rodney, before you do that, ring the Kolstadts, will you? Have them send Jian here. She'll have to come here until we can arrange something to get her out of the country."

His assistant glanced at him sharply, then nodded and left the office. Daniel sat back in his chair with a frown. He would be very surprised if she came. She was probably making her own arrangements to get out of Norway. There could be no doubt that she knew of the invasion. Those guns at the battery had alerted half the city already. She had proven in November that she was able to escape tight situations, but she had had help from their embassies then. There was nothing he could do to help her now. As soon as the Germans entered the city, all of his power would be useless.

He got up and strode across the office to the door. Before he began sorting through his files and destroying anything that absolutely could not fall into German hands, he had to send a message to Buckley. While he had no doubt that London was being flooded with messages, Bill needed to know exactly what was going on. He would alert him to the status of the invasion, then return to get his office in order.

Shaking his head, he moved down the long corridor towards the telegraph and radio room. That last warning claiming that an invasion on Norway and Denmark was scheduled for the 9th had turned out to be the one that was correct. They had all disregarded it, along with all the others.

And now they were out of time.

London
6am

Bill scanned the decoded and typed message, his lips tightening imperceptibly. So it had begun. The Germans were invading Norway and Evelyn was caught right in the middle of it. Her communication was very much to the point. The Germans were outside Oslo and she was going north. His brows creased into a frown. Why she thought the Swedish border was in doubt was another question for another day. All that mattered was that she wasn't in Oslo now.

"When did this come in?" he asked the young man who had handed him the message when he strode into the radio room.

"Just after one in the morning, sir."

"So two in the morning there," Bill murmured. "Very well. Listen for another communication. This is critical. If they contact again, I want to know immediately. And add that radio to the list of contact sources. I want to make sure their messages get through. Understood?"

"Yes, sir."

He nodded and left the small room, striding down the long corridor towards the stairs. He had been awoken by the telephone ringing at the ungodly hour of four in the morning. Within an hour of the call, he was on his way to the building on Broadway as a gray dawn broke over the city. Marguerite had watched him get dressed, her face creased in concern. She hadn't asked what was happening. She didn't need to. She knew she would find out soon enough on the wireless.

Bill started up the stairs. He had known Hitler would move soon. They all had. That it was Norway shouldn't have been a surprise, but he was conscious of a stunned feeling nonetheless. Somehow, they had all managed to convince themselves that Norway would remain safe, whether through neutrality or through England's protection. Instead, Hitler had beat them to the punch.

His lips thinned as he approached the top of the stairs, pulling out his identification for the guard on duty. If Chamberlain hadn't pussy-footed around with whether or not to mine the Norwegian waters, they may have been able to avoid this. But he and his war cabinet were a bunch of imbeciles, and now Norway was paying the price. It was absolutely inexcusable.

Bill held out his identification and the guard examined it, then nodded and stepped out of the way so that he could proceed to his office halfway down the hall. If he were to be honest with himself, he supposed it wasn't entirely Chamberlain's fault. They had certainly had enough warnings regarding a German offensive on Norway, but they had all ignored them. For one reason or another, every warning had been deemed not credible. But none of that would have mattered if Chamberlain's cabinet had moved decisively from the very beginning, instead of hoping for peace. For that was all they had done. They had remained indecisive and inactive, all the while hoping that Hitler would just sit down and go away like a good little corporal.

Bill snorted as he unlocked his office door and went inside. As if Herr Hitler had ever had any intention of doing anything other than exactly what he *was* doing: spreading out and claiming more and more living space for his bloody Third Reich. He closed the door and took off his coat, hanging it on the coat rack. Hooking his hat on the knob above his coat, he turned to go to his desk.

Evelyn was moving north and, if she could stay ahead of the landing troops, they had a shot at extracting her. He had to contact Jasper. He was sure he would be able to arrange something, but until he heard from her again and had a better idea of her location, they wouldn't be able to make any definite plans. All he could do was wait.

And pray.

Just as he was reaching for the phone to call Jasper, his office door flew open and Wesley Fitch, his intrepid assistant, burst in out of breath, his jacket askew and his hair falling into his eyes.

"Denmark has surrendered without a fight!" he exclaimed. "They've accepted Hitler's terms, and his protection."

"And so it begins," Bill said, sitting back. "What of Norway?"

"They refused in no uncertain terms, apparently," Wesley told him. "Minister Koht told the German ambassador that they would not submit. What army they have will fight."

Night Falls on Norway

"Thank God for that!" Bill got up and took a restless turn about his office. "And King Haakon?"

"He and his entire government have escaped Oslo."

Bill looked at him sharply. "Oh?"

Wesley nodded. "The first German ships were engaged at the mouth of Inner Oslofjord at 4:20 this morning, their time. The batteries near Drøbak sunk the lead cruiser, forcing the rest of the ships to retreat and land their troops outside of the range of the old fortress. It cost the Germans a few hours, which the King used to get out of Oslo."

"That's fantastic news!" Bill exclaimed. "The Norwegian forces are loyal only to King Haakon. As long as he is alive and on the throne, they will continue to fight."

"Yes, and I'm sure the Germans were expecting to neutralize him along with his government."

"And they all got away? Every one? The ministers as well?"

"Yes." Wesley cleared his throat. "That's the good news."

"And the bad news?"

"Reports are beginning to come in. The Germans have landed at Trondheim, Bergen and Stavanger. They also landed a large force at Narvik."

Bill scowled. "What of the local commanders?"

"Norway is woefully unprepared to rebuff the Wehrmacht. They put up resistance, but were quickly defeated. The German forces are through and advancing already." He paused, then cleared his throat. "In Narvik, the local commander ordered his troops to allow the Germans to land and not to resist."

"What?!"

"That being said, I believe that the commander is a Vidkun Quisling supporter," Wesley said. "If he is, that would explain his eagerness to let the Germans in."

"And to lose Norway their largest port in the north!" Bill exclaimed. "Not that they could have held out for long, but every hour would help."

"Forgive me, but help what?"

"Chamberlain will be forced to send troops now. The cabinet will approve lending aid and troops to fight with the Norwegians. Every hour the Norwegians hold on brings our boys closer to them."

"But Narvik has already fallen and the Jerries are already advancing through the country."

"Don't underestimate the value of Norway," Bill told him. "It may be small, but it is mighty in this war. Without it, Hitler can't get his precious iron from Sweden, or have access to the North Atlantic. Even Chamberlain won't allow it to go without a fight."

Wesley grunted and watched as Bill went back to his seat behind his desk.

"Any word from Jian?"

"She got a message out at 2am that the Germans were outside Oslo and she was going north." Bill shook his head. "She somehow found out before they attacked, thank God. I'm waiting to hear more."

"At least she got out of Oslo in time. Why did she go north and not east? The Swedish border isn't far from Oslo."

"She said there was some doubt as to the border." Bill frowned. "I don't know why, but I'm sure she had her reasons. Jian may have nerves of steel, but she does tend to err on the side of caution rather than the other way around."

The phone on Bill's desk jangled shrilly and Wesley turned towards the door.

"I'll let you know developments as they come in," he said over his shoulder. "Shall I put the radio boys on alert?"

"Already done," Bill replied, reaching for the phone. "A few earnest prayers wouldn't be amiss, though."

Wesley nodded grimly.

"Already done."

Knutshø, Norway
7am

Evelyn climbed out of the back of Peder's Volvo and shivered in the cold morning air. It was decidedly colder here than it had been in Oslo, and she quickly buttoned up her coat. Peder had pulled into a petrol station in a small town with a single main street, boasting a bakery and butcher's shop alongside the filling station. The other stores weren't open for business yet, and she looked towards the small building behind the gas pump.

"Do you think they know yet?" she asked Anna, nodding towards the building. Through the window, they could see a couple inside, the man behind a counter and the woman sweeping the floor near the door.

"It depends on if they have a radio," Anna replied, climbing out of the car. "If not then no."

Night Falls on Norway

"Should we tell them?"

She looked at her in amusement. "To what purpose?"

"Well, so they can leave if they want to," Evelyn said with a shrug.

Anna's smile grew.

"And go where? Most people have nowhere to run to," she said. "However, if it makes you feel better, we can tell them before we leave."

"It would, yes."

"While we're stopped, do you want me to try to reach London?" Peder asked over the roof of the car. "If we're going to try, now is a good time."

"Yes, please." Evelyn turned to look at him. "But stretch your legs first. You've been driving for over four hours."

Peder shrugged and went to open the back of the car where their suitcases and his radio were stored.

"I'm all right," he said, pulling out his case. "I'll see if I can get through to them. If I do, I'll knock on the glass."

He climbed into the backseat of the car and closed the door. Evelyn watched as he sat sideways on the seat and began to set up his radio.

"I'll take care of the petrol," Anna said, walking over to the pump. "Why don't you walk for a minute and stretch your legs?"

"It's too cold to walk far," she retorted, burying her hands in her coat pockets. "What I wouldn't give for some coffee!"

"We should be able to find an open café in another hour or so. We'll stop then." Anna glanced at her. "The further north we go, the colder it will get."

"Don't you know it's supposed to be spring?"

"Not in Norway," she retorted with a short laugh.

Evelyn shook her head and turned to walk a few feet away, loosening up muscles cramped from sitting. It could be worse, she supposed. At least Peder had this car. She could be without transportation altogether. Or without friends willing to help get her away from Oslo and the oncoming Germans. She glanced back at Anna refilling the tank of the car, and was suddenly extremely grateful for her once again. She could never have escaped Stockholm in November without the woman's help, and now here she was, making herself invaluable once again. How could she ever repay her?

And where on earth was she going? Evelyn continued walking, her hands in her pockets and her head down against the brisk wind. They couldn't just continue to flee north ahead of the Germans with no

167

clear destination in mind. Eventually they would run into the advancing forces. They had to have a destination well before that happened.

She pursed her lips thoughtfully. Perhaps she should try for the Swedish border after all. Peder had been right when he said that it was unlikely for the Swedish to detain a British national. However, if Anna was correct and they refused any refugees at all, then she would be trapped at the border in the face of the advancing German army and, more importantly, the Gestapo and SS. Was it worth the risk? On the other hand, what were her options?

Evelyn exhaled and glanced back at the car. If Peder could get through to London, Bill would be able to advise her. She had no idea what the best course of action was anymore, except to keep moving and avoid the Germans.

Strangely, she wasn't in a panic over the thought of the advancing enemy troops. So far, aside from the sight of the silent warships in the water outside Oslo, she hadn't seen any of the troops, nor heard any bombs or gunfire. Of course, they were nowhere near the coast where the invasion forces were undoubtedly landing, and that distance encouraged her to think that perhaps she would be able to get out of Norway without coming face to face with the Germans after all.

"Marlene!" Anna called.

Evelyn turned to find her waving her back. She hurried back to the car, her brows raised in question.

"What is it?"

Anna waved towards the car where Peder had unrolled the back window.

"The Germans have landed at Bergen and Narvik," he said, looking up from his radio. "After we left Oslo, the batteries at Oscarsborg Fortress sunk one of the ships. The rest retreated and landed troops further south. They'll reach the city soon."

"Where else have they landed?" Evelyn asked, leaning against the car.

"I don't know yet. That was all I managed to get so far. I'm still trying to get through to London, but no luck yet."

"What if he can't get through?" Anna asked Evelyn.

"I'll have to keep trying as we go," she answered with a shrug.

"My brother's unit is near Trondheim," Anna said slowly. "I think perhaps we should try to reach them. If nothing else, the army may have a better chance of reaching London."

"They would have to know why and who they're contacting, and that's impossible," Evelyn said, shaking her head. "No. I still think

Sweden is my best course, but I want to wait and hear from London first. They may have something else in mind."

"Yes, but in the meantime, we need to keep moving. If we head towards Trondheim, we will be moving into territory held by the Norwegian forces."

"If they haven't fallen," Peder said from the car. "There's no guarantee that Trondheim is safe. It's a harbor, and for all we know, the Germans may have landed there."

"Then we continue on, but we must try to move towards friendly forces," Anna argued. "If the Germans do sweep inland, we'll never make it on our own."

"That's true, too," he admitted.

Evelyn exhaled.

"All right. We'll go north until I can reach London," she said reluctantly. "But if we run into any fighting, I'll argue that we move east towards Sweden if I haven't got through to my handlers."

"Agreed," Anna said with a nod. "Peder, how much longer do you need? I've finished filling the tank."

"I'll try for a bit longer," he said. "If I haven't got through in ten minutes, we'll continue. Do either of you know how to drive?"

"I do," Evelyn said. "Do you want me to drive?"

"If you do, I can sleep."

"I don't mind," she said with a smile. "In fact, I enjoy driving. You stay back there and sleep. As long as Anna is willing to tell me where I'm going, we'll be fine."

"Good. I'll sleep and then continue trying to get through on the radio for you," Peder said, stifling a yawn.

"I'll go pay for the petrol." Anna turned towards the building on the other side of the small pump. "And I suppose I will warn them of what's going on."

"Do you want me to come with you?" Evelyn offered, but Anna waved her away with a smile.

"No. Go familiarize yourself with the car. I'd rather not end up in that ditch over there."

Evelyn was betrayed into a laugh and turned to go around to the driver side door. The likelihood of her landing them in a ditch was virtually non-existent, but Anna had no way of knowing how skilled a driver she was. Her only regret was that she didn't have the speed of Gisele's Bugatti or her own Lagonda. Or Miles' Jaguar.

Evelyn slid behind the wheel of the Volvo, her smile fading with the thought of Miles. He would be horrified if he had any inkling of where she was or what she was doing. He thought she was in Wales on a training course. Instead, while he was flying his Spitfire on patrols over the English Channel and having drinks at the pub, she was fleeing across Norway ahead of the German army with two compatriots who were risking their own lives to help her. Miles could never learn the truth, and as the war went on, the secrets and the lies would only continue to build until she didn't know if he would ever forgive her.

And that was almost as terrifying as the prospect of being caught by the advancing Germans.

Chapter Nineteen

Oslo, Norway
8am

Eisenjager glanced up at the apartment building before him and moved out of the way as the door swung open and a man rushed out, carrying a suitcase in either hand. His hat was askew on his head and he looked startled to see someone standing on the pavement outside the building. After a quick glance, he turned and hurried up the street. Eisenjager watched him go, wondering if the man had a plan or if he was simply fleeing with no clear idea of where he was going to go. His lips twisted faintly. He would be better off staying put in his apartment. The Germans would be here soon and then life would continue as normally as possible. Unless, of course, the man was a Jew. If that were the case, the faster he fled the better for him.

Turning back to the building, Eisenjager walked up to the door and went inside. He had gone to the boarding house where Jian was staying, only to discover that she had fled in the night ahead of the invasion. Hardly surprising when the guns at the battery on the fjord had begun firing at four in the morning. The advance warning had come earlier than any of them had expected, and as a result his pigeon had flown the coop. It couldn't be helped, of course. All he could do now was try to determine in which direction she had gone, and then follow. And to do that, he had to begin with the woman she had been having dinner with last night at the Hotel Bistro.

Going over to the mailboxes on the lobby wall, he searched for the woman's name. Salvesen. There it was. She was on the third floor. He turned and started towards the stairs. She worked at the British embassy, but he thought it very unlikely that she would have gone to work this morning. After all, the city was under siege, or very soon would be. Going to work would be the last thing on her mind.

He climbed the stairs, looking up as a couple came clamoring down from the second floor. They carried suitcases, and he moved to the side as they ran by. The man nodded to him, and Eisenjager nodded back pleasantly, turning to watch as they continued down the stairs to the ground floor. Another couple running from the advancing

Germans. The streets were clogged with them, people trying to get out of the city and away from the invading troops they knew were coming. What they didn't realize was that there was nowhere to go. Norway was being overrun and the borders secured. There was no way out.

Reaching the third floor, he turned and moved along the corridor until he reached the door with a little nameplate next to it that read Salvesen. Lifting his hand, he knocked loudly and waited, listening. There was no sound from the other side of the heavy wooden door and he frowned, lifting his hand to bang again.

"She's not there."

A voice spoke behind him and he turned to find an older woman standing in the doorway across the hall. He hesitated, then smiled.

"I'm sorry if I disturbed you," he said in Norwegian. "Do you know Miss Salvesen?"

"Yes. She's been my neighbor for over a year now." The woman looked him up and down. "Are you from the embassy?"

"No. I'm a salesman. I had an appointment with her this morning." He moved across the hall until he was standing before her and removed his hat politely. "Do you have any idea when she'll return?"

"No. She had a visitor very late last night." The woman frowned. "A young man. I don't approve of men coming to visit single woman like that. It's not decent. I've never known Anna to have one up that late before. She's a nice, good girl. Of course, now I know he was probably coming to warn her."

"Warn her?"

She looked surprised. "About the Germans, of course."

"Oh yes, of course." He smiled apologetically. "Did she leave with him?"

"Yes. I saw them get into his car in the street." She tilted her head and looked up at him. "She had a case with her. I don't think she's coming back very soon. She locked everything up tight. I can't say that I blame her. Most of the building has left already. Doors have been slamming and people running out of here for the past two hours or more."

"You aren't leaving?" he asked.

She shrugged. "Where am I going to go? This is my home. I've got nowhere else."

He nodded and his face softened slightly. "You will be just fine. I've traveled extensively in Germany over the past year. They are a good people. They will not bother you."

"I hope you're right."

"I think you'll find that I am," he said with a smile, replacing his hat and bowing slightly. "Thank you." He started to turn away, then paused and turned back. "You don't happen to remember what kind of car they were in, do you?" he asked.

She thought for a moment. "Yes, as a matter of fact I do. It was a black Volvo. A '37 PV51, I think."

He raised his eyebrows in surprised. "You know the make and model?"

"My son has one and I remember thinking to myself, oh that's just like Stefan's car. Of course, Stefan's is much nicer. He runs a factory in Asker and can afford to maintain his automobile. The young man last night clearly could not. Or perhaps he purchased it from someone who didn't take very good care of it."

"It wasn't in very good condition, then?"

"It's not so much that it was in bad condition, but it looked…worn, if you know what I mean. Like it needed a good clean and a shine." She shrugged. "I suppose they are expensive to take care of, though. Everything is these days."

"One last thing, if I could," Eisenjager said, smiling apologetically. "I don't suppose you saw the plate number, did you? You see, I'm rather anxious to ensure that Miss Salvesen is all right."

The woman frowned and thought for a long moment, her brows pulled together.

"A, of course, and I think it was followed by a 5, but it could have been a 6," she said slowly. "I was looking out the window and it was at an angle, you see. I'm sorry."

He smiled engagingly and tipped his hat to her. "That's quite all right, ma'am. You've been very helpful. I wish you the best of luck."

London
10am

Bill strode into his office and took off his coat. He'd just returned from a meeting in Whitehall and his mood was even more grim than it had been when he departed two hours before. After hanging up his coat and removing his hat, he turned to go to his desk. Picking up the telephone, he dialed the radio room.

173

"This is Buckley," he said when it was picked up. "Anything yet?"

"Not yet, sir."

"Thank you."

He hung up and the scowl on his face grew. It had been over eight hours since Evelyn's last transmission. She should have contacted again by now. Where the devil was she? Daniel Carew had sent three messages over the course of the past four hours, keeping him updated with the progress of the Germans. Things were not looking good at all, and he would feel much better once he'd heard from Evelyn.

The door opened and Wesley came in carrying a tray with a teapot, cups and saucers.

"I saw you come back and thought you could probably use some tea," he said, carrying the tray over to the desk. "How did it go?"

"It's not good." Bill dropped into his chair. "The Germans have taken control of all the airfields in Norway. Paratroopers secured them at the same time that the Luftwaffe was busy dropping bombs on all the major ports. Their Blitzkrieg is carving the Norwegians up, and it all looks like child's play." He pinched the bridge of his nose and leaned his head back tiredly. "Narvik has fallen, as well as Bergen, Trondheim and Stavanger. Oslo is overrun. They marched in behind a bloody brass band, for God's sake!"

Wesley glanced up from where he was pouring tea into the cups. "What of Kristiansand?"

"The same. The Germans are already past the landing points and moving inland." Bill dropped his hand and exhaled heavily. "No word yet on the King. As far as we know, he's still safe."

"If the Germans manage to get him, rest assured, they'll crow it loud enough for the world to hear," Wesley said, handing him a cup of tea. "No news is good news, I'm sure."

"I wish I could say the same with confidence about Jian," Bill muttered, taking the cup and saucer.

"Still no word?"

"No. We should have heard something by now."

"Do we know what she's using for a radio?"

"It's a private wireless. I have no idea whose it is, or who's transmitting, but they know our call signs, frequency, and her code, so they must be with her." He sipped the hot tea and sighed again. "One thing working in her favor is that no one knows she's there, so no one will be looking for her. If she can avoid the advancing troops, she'll be safe enough until we can get her out."

"How will you do that, sir?" Wesley sat down with his tea. "If she can't get to Sweden, how do you propose to extract her from Norway in the middle of all this?"

"Montclair is arranging it. The navy has ships on the way. One of them will land Royal Marines at Namsos. If she can get there at the same time, the captain has agreed to take her aboard and get her to Scapa Flow."

"When are they expected to land?"

"On the 14th."

Wesley shook his head. "That's five days from now," he said. "Will she last five days?"

"She'll have to." Bill set down his tea and rubbed his face. "Carew thinks that translator who helped her in Stockholm is with her. If she is, then I like Jian's chances of making it out of there."

"Could the translator be the one with the radio?"

"It's possible."

"It could be that they just haven't been able to get through," Wesley said after a moment. "It must be insane there right now. Perhaps they're trying and just can't get a signal out."

"That's what I'm pinning all my hope on," Bill told him grimly. "The alternative is…well, you know what the alternative is."

His assistant nodded soberly and sipped his tea. After a moment, he glanced up.

"What of the Norwegian forces?" he asked. "What will they do?"

"The King is still alive and urging resistance. They'll regroup. Hitler caught them unprepared and surprised them, but they will rally quickly behind their king."

"And if the King is captured?"

"Then God help them all."

RAF Duxford

Miles watched as the ground rushed up to meet him and felt his wheels bounce once before the Spitfire settled onto the grass and began to coast along the landing strip. He reached up and slid the canopy back, taking a deep breath as fresh air rushed into the cockpit. Chris was coming around to land behind him and he steered the plane to the end of the strip, turning it to park it alongside Rob's kite.

Shutting the engine down, he stood up and turned to climb out of the cockpit onto the wing.

"Have a good flight, sir?" called Jones, one of the ground crew sergeants, running over to push chocks in front of the wheels.

"It was extremely uneventful, Jones," he replied, jumping off the wing onto the ground.

"Don't worry, sir. It'll pick up now."

Miles looked at him curiously, but before he could question the man, Rob called to him from across the grass.

"Ho, Miles!" he yelled. "Hurry!"

Miles raised his eyebrows and started towards the dispersal hut, glancing up as Chris came into land. Both his wheels were down, he noted wryly, watching as the Spitfire seemed to float down to settle on the ground. The Yank had had a rather dodgy run of bad luck a few months ago, leading to a particularly hairy landing without wheels. Ever since, they had all got into the unconscious habit of checking for the landing gear, especially when Chris came in to land.

"What is it, Ainsworth?" he called, raising his eyebrows as Rob waved his arms to get him to hurry.

"They've invaded Denmark and Norway!" Rob called back. "The Germans are finally on the move!"

The amusement disappeared and Miles stared at him, dumbfounded.

"What?"

"Denmark and Norway," Rob repeated as Miles drew closer. "Jerry invaded them this morning! It's all over the wireless."

Miles quickened his pace. "When?"

"At dawn." Rob turned and went towards the dispersal hut, increasing his pace to match Miles' long stride. "They hit both Denmark and Norway. Denmark surrendered immediately."

"And Norway?"

"The news is just coming on now. Come and hear for yourself."

Miles nodded and pulled off his flying gloves as he followed Rob into the hut. The rest of the squadron was there already, sprawled in the available chairs. Someone had brought in a wireless radio and hooked it up at the back, turning the volume up loud enough for them all to hear. Miles nodded in greeting to the dispersal sergeant and leaned against the wall just inside the door as the BBC news program began.

"This is a special broadcast of the BBC Home Service. German forces invaded Denmark and Norway early this morning, taking the

Night Falls on Norway

northern countries by surprise. At 5:20 this morning, German envoys in Oslo and Copenhagen presented the Norwegian and Danish governments with an ultimatum, demanding that they immediately accept the protection of the Reich or be prepared to go to war with Germany. The ultimatum was accompanied by an invasion force of German troops. Denmark agreed to surrender immediately, allowing German forces to proceed into the country unopposed. In Oslo, Norwegian Foreign Affairs Minister Halvdan Koht returned the following reply: "We will not submit voluntarily. The struggle is already underway." An hour before the ultimatum was handed to the Norwegian government, a German cruiser carrying invasion troops was hit and sunk in the Oslofjord by Norwegian defenses. German troops are landing in Norway, while the Luftwaffe is bombing strategic targets ahead of the advancing troops. The harbor towns of Stavanger, Bergen, Trondheim and Narvik are all involved in the fighting, in addition to Oslo. Norwegian King Haakon and his entire government has escaped Oslo while Norwegian forces try to repel the invading forces."

Miles glanced at Rob to find him staring at the floor while he listened, his lips pressed together.

"So that's that, then," said Slippy, one of the pilots closest to the wireless set, when the news had ended. "Hitler went after Norway. Here we all thought he was going to go into Belgium and Holland."

"Oh, he will, don't worry," Rob said, lifting his head. "This is just the beginning."

"What's Jerry want with Norway?" Hampton drawled from near the window. "Aside from snow, what have the Norwegians got?"

"A way to get iron," Miles said. "Jerry gets his iron from Sweden, and trains carry it through Norway when the ports in Sweden freeze over in the winter."

Slippy tilted his head and looked at Miles. "How do you know that?"

"I pay attention to world affairs."

"Rotten luck for the Norwegians," Slippy muttered. "All of that for some iron that's not even theirs?"

"Why is everyone crammed in here?" An American voice interrupted and Miles turned to watch Chris step into the hut. "What's going on?"

"Germany's gone and invaded Denmark and Norway," Miles told him, turning to leave the overcrowded hut. "The others will fill you in."

He stepped outside and looked up at the clear blue sky, exhaling.

"Strange to think that while it's such a peaceful, perfect day here, the Germans are overrunning Norway further north," Rob said, joining him outside. "It doesn't seem real, somehow."

"Just as it didn't seem real when they did it to Poland?"

"Exactly." Rob shrugged. "Even though that's what started all this off, Poland seemed very far away. So does Norway."

"I don't suppose it feels far away to them," Miles said, turning to start the long walk back to the main buildings of the airfield. Rob fell into step beside him and they trudged through the grass together, their hands in their pockets. "Just yesterday they were making a fuss over us dropping mines in their neutral waters. Perhaps if we'd done it sooner, they wouldn't be facing the Germans right now."

"Hitler really doesn't give a fig for international laws or neutrality, does he?" Rob said disgustedly after a moment. "Both Denmark and Norway had no intention of getting drawn into this war. Why not just let them be?"

Miles glanced at him. "Do you really think he ever had any intention of stopping with Poland?" he demanded. "Hitler has always wanted only one thing: to dominate Europe. Poland was only the beginning."

"I suppose so. I did rather hope that it would all fizzle out, to be honest. Of course, I knew it was unlikely, but there you are." Rob threw his head back and looked up at the sky. "At least now all this damn waiting will be over. I don't know which is worse, waiting for the storm to break or the storm itself."

"We won't have to wait long for the storm," Miles predicted. "Hitler will move towards Belgium and Holland. Norway does surprise me, but only because of the timing. I really expected him to attack the west first."

"Obviously so did the Norwegians. Do you think they can win?"

"I have no idea. I know if they don't, it will give Hitler a huge advantage in the Atlantic, as well as uninterrupted access to supplies and materials that Germany can't produce itself." He shook his head. "We'll have to send troops to help them. I just hope they're not too late."

"You think Chamberlain will commit to fighting in Norway?" Rob asked skeptically. "He didn't commit to helping Finland."

"Finland wasn't as strategically important. I don't doubt that Chamberlain would love to simply ignore Norway, but he won't be able to. There's too much at stake. He should have done more before now to help protect them, but he didn't, and so he will have to try to correct that error."

"Yes, and at what cost to us?"

"That's the thing, isn't it?" Miles scowled. "This probably could have been avoided if we'd acted sooner. I'll tell you this much, though. I feel very sorry for the poor sods stuck in Norway at the moment. Things are going to get a lot worse before they get better."

Chapter Twenty

Grindal, Norway

Evelyn got out of the car and walked around the front to stare at the smoke pouring out from under the hood. She had pulled to the side of the road as soon as it started, shutting off the engine, but white-gray vapor was still seeping from inside the engine compartment. Peder and Anna joined her, and they all stared at the smoke in dismay.

"I don't know much about automobiles, but that doesn't look good," Anna finally said.

"It's not," Peder replied with a sigh. "I just hope it's something I can fix."

He turned to go to the back of the car, opening the luggage compartment to pull out a toolbox.

"It might be something simple," Evelyn said, glancing at Anna. "If so, we'll be on our way in no time."

"And if it isn't?"

"Well, then, that's another issue."

Peder came back with the box and set it on the ground before walking to the side of the engine where the smoke was coming from. After gingerly touching the metal hood, he shrugged and looked at them.

"It's not burning hot, so at least we know it's not on fire," he said with a quick grin before lifting the side of the hood to reveal half of the engine. More vapor and smoke poured out as he opened it and he waved his hands in front of his face, trying to disperse it. The acrid smell of smoke didn't bode well for something that could be easily patched up on the side of the road.

Evelyn walked over to join him, looking into the engine compartment almost fearfully. She and Rob had spent many hours with their chauffeur, learning the ins and outs of the engine that powered their Lagonda. It was a necessary skill to learn if you intended to drive yourself around the country. If the car broke down, it was up to the driver to get it going again. While she knew the basics, she had only been forced to repair her engine once in the three years that she'd been driving. Wallace was very good at keeping all the Ainsworth automobiles in pristine working order. When the Lagonda had failed on her, it was a blown valve, she remembered. Wallace had promptly replaced all of them and neither she nor Robbie had had an issue since.

"That's not a valve," she murmured, peering into the engine. "I had one go on me once, and it was nothing like this."

Peder glanced at her in surprise. "Do you know engines?"

She nodded. "A little. My brother and I share a car. We learned very quickly that we had to know how to fix it."

Peder bent down and opened the tool box.

"Hopefully it's just a hose that's come loose," he said. "It happened once last summer and smoke poured out like this. I was able to reconnect it and then replace it later."

"Is there anything I can do to help?"

"Not yet." He straightened up with a tool in his hand and leaned over the fender into the engine. "I'll have to find the problem first, then we'll see what can be done."

Evelyn nodded and moved away to give him more room. She looked at Anna and saw the concern in her eyes. They were on a main road and they had no way of knowing if German troops were right behind them or coming from another direction. The road appeared to be going through a valley, with heavily wooded forests on either side ascending up into a steep incline. They were in the middle of a mountain pass, and were sitting ducks with nowhere to go if the Wehrmacht came rolling through.

"Where are we?" she asked.

"In Grindal," Anna replied. "We're a few hours south of Trondheim."

"Do you have a map?"

She nodded and went into the car, emerging a moment later with the road map she had been using to help navigate. She carried it over to the other side of the hood and spread it out, pointing to where they were located.

"This is where we are," she said, "and here is Trondheim."

Evelyn studied the map with a frown. They were closer to the coast than she had realized and her heart sank. If the Germans had succeeded in landing along the coast, they were in danger of being trapped between the troops coming in from the ocean and those coming up from the south.

"Where is Narvik?" she asked.

Anna pointed to a spot much farther north. "Here."

"And we know the Germans landed troops there. So we have to assume that they will come south from there, and in the meantime, we know they will come up from Oslo and Bergen." Evelyn shook her head. "We're right in the middle."

"They haven't made it here yet," Anna pointed out, "and they have to get past the army first. Let's not panic just yet."

"I'm not panicking. I'm stating facts. If we don't keep moving, we'll end up trapped." Evelyn straightened up and leaned against the car. "Peder, have you heard anything on the radio about the Swedish border?"

"Only that people are swarming towards it," he answered, his voice muffled from inside the engine. "No one has said whether or not they're letting people in."

"I wish we could get through to London," she said in frustration. "Perhaps I should risk it and head for Sweden."

Anna was silent for a long moment, then she sighed.

"If Peder still can't get through to London the next time he tries, then I'll take you to the border," she relented. "I don't think it's a wise choice, but I suppose we're running out of options now. We can continue and take refuge in the mountains, which would buy us some more time until you can reach London. If the Germans do make it past the army, it will take them weeks to secure the mountains, if at all."

"This is all assuming I can get this car going again," Peder muttered, straightening up. "I've found the problem. It's not a hose."

"What is it?"

"I think there's a crack in the head gasket."

Evelyn's heart sank even further. If that was the case, this car wasn't going anywhere soon. At least, not safely.

"Is that bad?" Anna asked, looking from Evelyn's grim face to Peder's. "What does that mean?"

"It means we're not going anywhere right now," he replied. "If I can figure out a way to…"

He broke off abruptly and stared at something behind them, his eyes widening and his face paling. Evelyn felt a shiver streak down her spine and she spun around quickly. Four men in uniform and carrying rifles had emerged from the trees a few yards away. Her heart thumped, then settled down as she noted that the military uniforms were not German, and no iron cross was in sight.

Anna let out a gasp beside her and began running towards the soldiers.

"Erik!" she cried, leaving the road and running through the brush and over frozen grass towards a tall man in the middle.

Night Falls on Norway

Evelyn looked at him curiously. Anna's brother looked nothing like her. Where her hair was dark, his was blond, and where she had a slender frame, he was solidly built with broad shoulders. He stood a few inches taller than the three soldiers with him, and Evelyn had the distinct impression that he was someone who would be ruthless in a physical altercation.

Now, however, a huge grin was spreading over his face, and he broke away from the others, moving forward quickly.

"Anna!" he exclaimed, holding out his arms. "Anna, thank God!"

He caught her up in a hug and half swung her around, laughing.

"I've been so worried!" he said, setting her down. "We heard they've taken Oslo. What are you doing here?" He looked over to Evelyn and Peder. "And who are they?"

Anna took his hand and pulled him towards the car. "Erik, this is my friend Marlene. She works at the embassy with me. And you remember Peder?"

Erik Salvesen stared at Peder, recognition dawning on his face. Another grin spread over his lips and he moved forward quickly, holding his hand out.

"Peder! I didn't recognize you at first! How are you?"

"As well as can be expected, I suppose," Peder replied with a smile and a shrug, shaking his hand firmly. "And you?"

"The same." Erik turned to nod in greeting at Evelyn, then looked at Anna. "But why are you here? Where are you going?"

"I don't really know," she confessed. "We fled Oslo before the Germans arrived. Peder found out about the invasion and came to tell me late last night. We collected Marlene and then we drove to a rise over the fjord. We saw the German warships waiting just outside Oslofjorden."

Erik stared at her, then glanced at Evelyn. "You saw them? You saw the ships?"

"Yes. They were just sitting out there, silently. I realized that they were waiting for dawn to attack, and so we left. Marlene is trying to get out of Norway and back to England. She wanted to try for the Swedish border, but I wasn't sure they would allow people through once they realized what was happening."

Erik made a disgusted sound in his throat.

"They're not," he said shortly. "They turned the King away, or so we heard."

Anna's mouth dropped open and they all stared at him, aghast.

"What? They refused refuge to King Haakon?!"

Erik nodded grimly and looked at the open side hood of the car. "Yes. The last we heard he was going north to the mountains. At least he and the ministers are safe, for now. What's wrong with the car?"

"I think it's got a cracked head gasket," Peder said. "I don't know if I can fix it."

Erik glanced back at his fellow soldiers, then looked at the three of them.

"This isn't the best place to be stranded," he said grimly. "The Germans landed at Trondheim. There was no real fight. We had no warning and were caught completely unprepared. They've taken the city and are moving into the surrounding areas. Soon these roads will be patrolled by Germans and it won't be safe."

"What about the army?" Anna asked. "What about your regiment?"

"We're scattered around. We retreated and my commanding officer was killed, along with several others. We're trying to team up with another unit in the north, but we've been busy avoiding capture."

"Are the Germans close, then?" Evelyn asked, breaking her silence.

He looked at her. "Close enough. They're coming up from Bergen, and in from the coast. We're in a safe pocket right now, but I don't know how long that will last. They're meeting almost no resistance to slow them down. If we can contact one of the other units with a radio, we might be able to coordinate something, but we've been separated from our signals team."

Peder looked up. "A radio? I have my radio with me."

Erik raised his eyebrows. "What? You brought it with you?"

"Yes. I've been trying to reach London for Marlene."

"And were you able to?"

"Not since we saw the ships in the fjord. I got through then, but haven't been able to since. If you give me the frequency, I can try to reach your unit."

"That's the best news I've heard all day," Erik said with a grin. He looked at the car again. "If this has a cracked head gasket, you'll never find somewhere for parts to fix it before this road is flooding with Nazis."

"But what else can we do?" Anna asked.

Erik was quiet for a moment, his brows drawn together in a frown. He glanced back at this companions.

Night Falls on Norway

"Wait here for a minute," he finally said, turning to go back to the other soldiers.

Evelyn watched as they talked together in low voices. Peder shuffled from one foot to the other, his hands in his pockets as he kept one eye on the small group of soldiers and another on the road.

"What do you think they're discussing?" she asked.

"Knowing Erik, probably what's the best way to help us," Anna replied. "He won't want to leave me, but unless there's someone with them who's a skilled motor mechanic, he knows we won't be able to continue."

"Even if we could continue, if the Nazis have taken Trondheim, where will we go?" Peder asked. "If the Swedish border agents wouldn't even allow the King through…"

He didn't finish, but he didn't have to. Evelyn was well aware that if a king wasn't allowed into Sweden, the odds of her getting through were not good. Not unless she snuck through between border checkpoints.

"You need to get through to London," Anna said after a moment in a low voice. "You and I will be all right in the end, but Marlene is an enemy. We have to get her out of Norway."

"All I can do is try, which is what I've been doing," he retorted.

"And I appreciate it," Evelyn said with a smile. "I know you're doing your best."

Erik turned and came back to the trio by the car.

"I've talked it over and they agree with me. You can't stay here, and there's no way to get your car running again safely," he told them. "If you come with us, you'll have a better chance at avoiding the Germans."

"Come with you where?" Anna asked, glancing over to the other soldiers.

"Into the mountains. There are five more of us. We came down to scout and see if the Germans were on the road yet. Leave your car and come with us. It will be safer than on your own."

Peder was already turning to close the hood of the Volvo. "I don't have anything but my radio," he said, "but the girls have bags."

"We can easily carry them," Anna said.

"Hurry and get them, and then let's get off the road and back into the trees," Erik said briskly. He glanced down at Anna and Evelyn's feet. "Do you have any better shoes? There's snow higher up and as we go north, it will get deeper."

"I have some boots," Anna said, turning to go towards the back of the car. "Marlene, do you have anything?"

"Not boots," Evelyn said, following her. "I have a pair of sturdy loafers, but I don't know how much use they'll be in the snow."

"They'll be better than what you're wearing," Anna said, glancing at the fashionable pumps on Evelyn's feet.

She nodded and pulled her suitcase out of the back of the car, setting it on the ground and crouching down to undo the straps. While Erik waited, she and Anna quickly changed their shoes as Peder stowed the toolbox in the back of the car. He pulled out the case with his radio, the basket of food Else had packed for them, and a small toiletries case.

"Is this yours, Marlene?" he asked, holding it up.

Evelyn glanced up from redoing the straps on her case and nodded. "Yes. Thank you."

"I'll carry it if you like," he offered. "My case is not heavy."

"I don't want to be a bother," she protested, standing. "I can manage."

"Let him take it," Erik advised behind her. "We have a steep climb ahead and it will be rough going already."

Evelyn looked at Peder and nodded reluctantly. "Thank you."

He smiled at her and turned to lock up the car. "You're welcome."

Once the car was securely locked, they turned to start towards the trees. As she stepped off the road, Evelyn had the strangest feeling of leaving safety behind. She pressed her lips together and glanced back at the black Volvo. They would be safer with a group of Norwegian soldiers than on their own on a main road with an advancing German army. So why did she suddenly feel as if she was walking into danger, rather than away from it?

Reaching the trees, she paused and turned to take one last look at the car, pulled to the side of the road.

"It looks so forlorn, doesn't it?" Anna asked beside her, following her gaze. "Almost as if we're abandoning it."

"Do you think I'll ever see it again?" Peder asked, pausing and looking back with them.

"Perhaps." Evelyn looked at him and her lips curved. "If anyone tries to take it, they'll quickly realize why it was left there."

"Perhaps it will still be there when you can return with a mechanic," Anna agreed.

He nodded and turned to follow the soldiers into the woods. "Perhaps."

Night Falls on Norway

Evelyn followed, stepping into the trees. As she went deeper into the forest, following the others, she couldn't help but wonder if she wasn't now putting nine more innocent people in danger simply by being here. Anna and Peder were the only ones who knew and understood the true danger if Evelyn were to be caught. The others had no idea that they were assisting a woman who was on the SD's radar. If they did, she doubted they would have been so quick to agree to help them. Erik, especially, would be horrified to think that he had aided a British spy who had put his sister's life in danger. Yet she had no other choice. She had to find a way out of Norway.

And she needed them to help her do it.

Knutshø

Eisenjager left the small shop behind the petrol pump and walked to his car parked near the edge of the road. The black Volvo had stopped to refuel a few hours before. After a nice chat with the woman behind the counter, he learned that two women and a young man were in the car. One of the women had gone into the shop to pay for the petrol while the other had got behind the wheel. The man, who had been driving when they arrived, stayed in the back seat. The woman seemed to be of the opinion that he was ill because he was hunched in the seat and remained that way even when the car pulled back onto the road.

Eisenjager didn't care if the man was ill. What he cared about was that the shop owner had described Jian perfectly. He was on the right road, and they were only a few hours ahead of him.

Sliding behind the wheel, he started the engine and pulled onto the road, accelerating. The woman had known about the invasion taking place. She had asked him if he had seen anything on the roads and whether or not she should close her shop. It never once occurred to her that he might be German himself. She had accepted his polite explanation that he was Danish, traveling through Norway and separated from his companions. His accent was nothing like a Danish accent, but she hadn't seemed to notice. Funny how people found it easier to accept a lie than to question a small thing like a strange accent.

He waited until he passed through the small town and was back in the countryside before pulling the car to the edge of the road and shutting off the engine. Getting out, he walked to the back and lifted the storage compartment, pulling out a deep, square case. He carried it around to the passenger side and got back in, holding the case on his lap. Lifting the lid to reveal a radio, he pulled out a wire with a special adapter on the end and leaned over to pull the cigarette lighter out of the dash. Inserting the adapter into the lighter opening, he turned the key to restart the engine. As the engine came to life, so did the radio in his lap.

Eisenjager straightened up and lifted out the paddle to begin transmitting a code to the SS unit that had already landed at Trondheim. According to the woman at the filling station, the black Volvo had been going north. The woman who paid for the petrol mentioned trying to reach Trondheim. She obviously had no idea that the Germans had taken it this morning, along with all the other main ports along the western seaboard of Norway. That was all to his own advantage. He had plenty of time to alert the Gestapo and the SD in Trondheim while he pursued them from the south. Once the SD were notified of a British agent trying to escape the invasion, they would work with the SS to ensure that the trio didn't make it past Trondheim.

And then he would capture the English spy known as Jian.

Chapter Twenty-One

London
5pm

The hard soles of Bill's shoes echoed along the corridor in a rapid tattoo as he hurried towards the radio room. Evelyn had finally managed to make contact. They had rung his office just moments before, as he was preparing to go out and grab a bite to eat. Thank God they caught him before he left. After waiting all day, he would have been very annoyed indeed if he had missed her.

"Where is it?" he asked, striding into the small radio room unceremoniously.

"Here, sir." A young man turned, removing his headset and holding out a piece of paper. "I just finished decoding it."

"Thank you."

He took the message and scanned it quickly.

AM IN THE MOUNTAINS SOUTH OF TRONDHEIM WITH ANNA AND NORWEGIAN SOLDIERS SEPARATED FROM THEIR UNITS. GERMANS HAVE TAKEN TRONDHEIM AND ARE ADVANCING THROUGHOUT NORWAY. WON'T MAKE SWEDISH BORDER. AWAITING INSTRUCTION - JIAN.

Relief flooded through him. She was still safe, at least for now. He pursed his lips thoughtfully, then looked at the young man who had handed him the message.

"Can I have some paper?" he asked. "I'll write out a return message."

He nodded and passed him a notepad and pencil. Bill took it and moved a few feet away to an empty station. Seating himself, he quickly composed a reply instructing her to stay where she was, glancing at his watch when he was almost finished. He added another line telling her to try to make contact again in two hours, then got up and took it over to the radio operator.

"Send that immediately, please. How long are you manning this station?"

"Until midnight, sir."

"Good. I'll be expecting another message in about two hours. As soon as it comes in, I'll have another message to send. Understood?"

"Yes, sir. Will you be in the building or shall I call you at home?"

"What? Oh no. I'll be in my office." He started to turn away, then changed his mind. "Actually, I'll wait to see if there's an immediate reply."

The young man nodded and put on his headset, turning to the radio before him. He set the message Bill had written out on a clipboard and proceeded to tap out the code.

Bill watched him, his lips pressed together. It was just plain bad luck that Evelyn was caught in Norway right now, but it did drive home to him the need to get her fully trained on sending radio transmissions back to London and, more importantly, using the code process that they had in place for agents overseas. The basic code she was using now was sufficient enough to get the job done, but it was far from secure. If the Germans knew what to look for, they would break it in no time.

He just had to hope and pray they weren't listening for outgoing transmissions yet.

"It's done, sir."

Bill nodded and waited. When ten minutes had passed with no reply, he laid a light hand on the man's shoulder.

"Thank you. Let me know as soon as the message comes in later."

He nodded and Bill turned to leave the small room. He started down the corridor, then slowed as he changed his mind. Turning, he went in the opposite direction until he reached the stairs. He ran up them lightly, pulling out his identification for the guard at the top.

"Evening, Mr. Buckley," the man said, glancing cursorily at the offered ID. "Are you getting ready to leave for the day, sir?"

"Hardly, though I am going to pop out for a bit of supper," Bill said, tucking away his identification. "Is Montclair still in his office?"

"Yes, sir." The man moved out of the way. "He's been there all afternoon."

Bill nodded and continued down the hallway until he reached the corner office at the end. He knocked once, then reached for the handle when he heard the command to enter.

Night Falls on Norway

"Hallo Bill," Jasper said, looking up from a sheaf of papers spread over his desk. "You're still here? I thought you would have gone for dinner by now."

"I'm just going now," Bill said, advancing across the office. "I just received word from Jian."

"Good! How is she?"

"Safe, for now. She's in the mountains near Trondheim. She said the Germans have taken the city and are advancing through the country."

"She's in the mountains, eh?" Jasper sat back. "Is she alone?"

"No. The translator is with her, and so are several Norwegian soldiers. They got separated from their regiments, more than likely."

Jasper frowned thoughtfully. "How did she manage to team up with soldiers? Not that it's not convenient, but it seems like awfully good luck."

"Not as lucky as it seems," Bill said wryly. "The translator's brother is in the army. I'd guess that she went looking for her brother."

The frown on Jasper's face cleared and he nodded. "Ah, that makes much more sense. Do we know anything about the brother? Can he be trusted?"

"That I don't know. Let's hope so."

"Yes. Well, at least she is safe for now." He stood up and went over to the wall where an over-sized map of Norway had been hung next to one of Denmark. "She's outside Trondheim, you say?"

"Yes, but if the Germans have secured the port and the city, there is no possibility of her getting through," Bill said, joining him in front of the map.

"No. No, you're quite right. It's out of the question." Jasper studied the map for a moment. "I've spoken to the Lord of the Admiralty. He's assured me that the Marines will arrive in Namsos by the 14th, and the captain of the cruiser taking them has agreed to take her aboard. She's quite a distance from Namsos, though. Do you think she can make it?"

"I know she'll do her best, but whether or not she can make it depends entirely on the Germans."

"Quite so. Norway is mountainous, and that can work in her favor, especially if she's with soldiers well acquainted with the terrain. The Germans will be slowed down by the unfamiliar mountain ranges. If they're careful, she just might make it. Once she's in Namsos, the captain guarantees her safety, as long as our ships get there and take the port before the krauts. When she arrives, have her contact Lieutenant

Commander Wheeler. He's the captain's right-hand man. He's been briefed and will get her onboard. They'll take her to Scapa Flow."

"Very well. Is there anything specific I should tell her?"

Jasper glanced at him. "Yes. Tell her to stay alive and make that ship on the 14th. If she doesn't, I can't guarantee that there will be another opportunity. This is our only real shot to get her out."

Bill nodded, staring at the map grimly.

"Understood."

Mountains north of Grindal, Norway
7pm

Evelyn grimaced when an icy wind smacked her in the face as she moved out of the trees into an overgrown area that used to be a yard surrounding a crumbling, stone building. They had come across the structure an hour before and, after Erik and the others had scouted the entire area, determined that it was the abandoned remains of what most likely used to be a barn. Foundations of what appeared to be a house weren't far from the area, through the trees. What had happened to the small farm in the mountains was a mystery, but they were grateful for the meager shelter with the temperature rapidly descending.

Evelyn carried the armful of wood that she had collected to the opening of the barn and went inside, exhaling in relief as she stepped out of the biting wind. Most of the roof to the structure was gone, but the outer walls and back corner still had enough of it left to provide shelter from the worst of the elements. Any hay or straw was long gone, but one of the soldiers had managed to forage enough underbrush to provide something of a cushion for the two women. Anna was in the process of stacking it in the back corner of the structure.

"There's more, but this was all I could carry," Evelyn told Erik, dropping her armful of wood onto the ground beside the fire pit he and the others had dug in the center of the barn. "I'll go back out."

"That's fine," he told her. "There are others out gathering it as well. Rest for a moment."

"I can't rest while everyone else is working," she protested.

"Everything is under control," he said with a shrug. "I'll have a fire going soon and Rolf is out hunting for something to cook. There is nothing more that can be done."

Night Falls on Norway

"We have a basket of food that the landlady of the boarding house where I stayed packed for us," she offered. "It's not much, some bread and cheese and smoked fish, but it's something."

Erik looked at her, surprised. "Your landlady packed you a basket?"

She nodded. "Anna woke her up when she came to warn me and she realized what was happening. She's very kind. I hope they are all right."

Evelyn turned away to move to the back of the barn where Anna was trying to make the area where they would sleep as comfortable as possible. She looked up as Evelyn approached.

"It's not much, but at least we won't be directly on the cold ground," she said with a shrug, motioning to the piles of soft spruce branches she had arranged. "If we spread some clothes over them and use our coats for blankets, we should be all right."

Evelyn nodded, eyeing the area with a feeling of dismay. The temperature had dropped significantly and while the stone walls protected them from the worst of the wind, it still howled and whistled through the gaping holes where the roof used to be. Anna saw her face and smiled faintly.

"Don't worry. The fire will help a lot, and we can start a smaller one over here as well. You won't freeze."

Evelyn was betrayed into a short laugh. "Are you trying to convince me or yourself?"

"Both." She straightened up and looked around the back of the structure. "Why don't we gather some of these old rocks and stones and put them in a circle? We can set a fire inside them and not risk it spreading."

Evelyn nodded and turned to begin gathering the largest rocks she could find. Her feet were throbbing and she didn't think she would ever get warm again, but moving helped keep her mind off both the cold and her predicament.

"Marlene, I'm actually getting quite a good signal over here," Peder called from the other side of the barn where he had settled down with his radio. "I should be able to get through to London again. I'm going to try, anyway."

"Thank you!" She glanced at her watch, squinting in the darkness. "It's been two hours, hasn't it?"

"Yes."

Erik looked over from where he was arranging the wood in the makeshift fire pit.

"What have you learned about the German troops?" he asked. "Anything?"

Peder shook his head. "Only that Oslo is occupied and they are moving north and west."

Erik nodded and was silent, going back to the fire. Evelyn carried two very large rocks over to set them down near their corner.

"Once you get instructions from London, we'll be able to make a plan," Anna said, dropping a few more rocks onto the growing pile. "Don't worry. We will get you out of Norway."

Evelyn looked at her in surprise. "What makes you think I'm worried?"

"You look as if you're heading for the gallows," she replied with a laugh. "It's not that bad yet. If we stay in the mountains, we'll be fine. The Germans won't come into them until they've secured all the low-lands."

"Perhaps not, but we have to be on our guard," Erik said, overhearing. "We're going to keep guard in shifts through the night. Three of us will patrol the area while the rest sleep. We've already discussed it. You will be safe enough tonight."

"I appreciate everything you're doing for us," Evelyn said earnestly. "Thank you."

"It would be done, regardless of whether you were here or not," he said dismissively. "There is no need to thank us."

She swallowed and went back to looking for appropriate stones. Anna's brother wasn't very friendly, but she supposed she wouldn't be either if she'd been separated from her unit in the midst of a German invasion.

"Don't mind Erik," Anna said in a low voice. "He isn't very happy with the English these days, and I'm afraid he's not being very friendly towards you. Please don't take it personally."

"I'll try not to." Evelyn hesitated, then glanced at her. "Is it because we dropped mines in the waters?"

"Among other things. He seems to think that the invasion is England and France's fault, and perhaps it is. But there is no point in blaming anyone now. I told him as much earlier, but he is stubborn." Anna shrugged. "He will warm up once he gets to know you."

Evelyn was silent. She wasn't particularly bothered by Erik's coolness towards her, but it was obviously weighing on Anna's mind. He hadn't been impolite or rude, he just wasn't overly friendly, and that was fine. She wasn't there to make friends. She was there to get out of Norway as quickly as possible, and with the least amount of exposure. If he could help her do that then that was all that really mattered.

Night Falls on Norway

"Marlene!" Peder called to her a few minutes later and waved her over. "I've got through."

Evelyn went over to him quickly, Anna close behind. Out of the corner of her eye, she saw Erik look over sharply, but he made no move to join the small group on the other side of the barn. Peder was listening intently to his headset, one hand pressing it against his ear while the other reached for his pencil and paper. Anna switched on a flashlight and held it over his shoulder to give him light while he was writing, and Evelyn watched as he scrawled an illegible short hand over the page. It looked like a mix of Morse code and his own peculiar brand of coding. Whatever it was, she was very relieved to see it. At least now she would have a course of action to follow that didn't consist of simply running without a destination in mind.

"I hope he can decipher that," Anna whispered, "because it looks like Greek to me."

Evelyn grinned. "It's coming through in Morse code, but he's obviously got his own shorthand that he uses as well," she said.

"So then, if the Germans intercept the message, they can read it?"

"Hopefully not. It's encoded, but I'm afraid it's a very basic code. Let's hope the Germans have other things on their mind at the moment and aren't monitoring wireless messages."

Anna looked at her in disbelief. "That's it? We're just going to hope they're not listening?"

Evelyn nodded grimly. "I don't have the code that...others use in these situations," she said in a very low voice. "I was never supposed to be in this position yet, you see. I'm sure that will be corrected when I get back."

"That doesn't help us now," Anna muttered.

"That's all of it," Peder said, removing his headset and bending over the paper. He went through the message and translated it into the basic code that Evelyn would be able to transcribe. After a few minutes, he turned around and handed the paper to her. "I'll send your reply. They're standing by."

She nodded and took the paper. Anna held the light over it and she scanned it quickly.

PROCEED TO NAMSOS IMMEDIATELY. CRUISER WILL ARRIVE ON 14TH. ASK FOR LT. CMDR WHEELER ON ARRIVAL. THIS IS YOUR ONLY CHANCE TO EVACUATE. GOOD LUCK AND GOD SPEED. ACKNOWLEDGE RECEIPT.

Evelyn looked at Anna. "I have to go to Namsos," she said. "How far is that from here?"

Anna frowned. "Quite a way," she said, turning to go back to the corner where their bags were stacked. "I'll get the map."

Evelyn turned back to Peder.

"Can I have the paper and pencil?" she asked. "I'll write out the reply."

He nodded and handed her the pad. She took it and crouched down to write a message and encode it.

INSTRUCTIONS ACKNOWLEDGED. PROCEEDING TO DESTINATION - JIAN.

She was just finishing encoding the short message when Anna returned with the road map from the car. Evelyn handed Peder the pad and turned to watch as Anna spread the map out on the ground.

"We're here," she said, pointing. "Namsos is…here. It's north of Trondheim. If we were driving, it wouldn't be far. Perhaps four hours."

"But we're not driving," Evelyn said with a frown. "How long will it take to walk there?"

A shadow fell over the map and they looked up to find Erik standing behind them.

"Namsos?" he asked. "That's where you're trying to go?"

Evelyn nodded. "Yes."

Erik crouched down beside them. "The most direct route is here, through Trondheim and then follow the fjord up to Framverran, crossing over the water here. But if the Germans still have Trondheim, that route may be blocked. And there is also the question of getting across the water, both at Trondheim and Framverran. The Nazis will have ships in the fjord."

"What do you suggest, then?" Anna asked, looking at him. "We have to get her to Namsos by Sunday."

He looked at them for a moment, his face unreadable, then turned his gaze back to the map, studying it for a long moment in silence.

"If you stay in the mountains, you can make it to just outside Trondheim without going down into the valley," he said finally. "By the time you reach Melhus, you will know if that route is accessible or not. If it isn't, you will have to go around to the east and follow the fjord up on this side. It will add much more time to the journey."

"Why do you say if?" Evelyn asked. "Do you think the Germans will leave Trondheim?"

"Not without being forced out," he replied bluntly. "But if the British…"

Night Falls on Norway

His voice trailed off and she suddenly understood. If the Royal Navy attacked Trondheim from the water, the Norwegian troops could mount an attack from the land. If that happened, Trondheim might be open to them.

"If we have to go around, how much longer will that add?" Anna asked, looking at the map.

"Perhaps another day," Erik said, shaking his head. "It's hard to tell. It depends on how quickly you can cover the ground, and whether or not the Germans have it blocked along the way."

"Do you think we can make it there by Sunday?" Evelyn asked after a moment.

Erik looked at her. "Yes, but you will have to cover much ground during the day. It will not be easy, and the further north you go, the more snow you will have to go through. That will slow you down."

She nodded, trying to ignore the anxiety threatening to overwhelm her. They would make it. They had to. This was her only chance to make it out of Norway.

"We will make it," Anna said, glancing at her. "Don't worry. We will find a way."

Erik looked from one to the other.

"What's in Namsos?"

"There will be a ship that can take me back to England," Evelyn said reluctantly.

"And it will be there on Sunday?"

She nodded. He pressed his lips together and his dark eyes probed hers, his face once more unreadable. Evelyn held his gaze, resisting the urge to look away. He knew, she thought suddenly. He knew she wasn't simply an embassy clerk panicking and trying to leave Norway in the midst of the invasion. She could see it in his eyes. Yet he made no comment, and instead, looked back at Anna.

"I will take you as far Trondheim," he decided. "Once there, you will have to continue alone. I have to try to rejoin whatever is left of the army. But we can at least get you that far."

"Thank you."

He nodded and stood up.

"Come and eat something, and then I suggest you all get some rest. We leave at first light."

Chapter Twenty-Two

Evelyn shifted and tried to get comfortable on what she was convinced was the most *un*comfortable bed she'd ever laid on. She had spread a few woolen skirts over the soft spruce branches and folded her raincoat into a pillow, but no matter how she laid, the needles managed to poke into her at some point on her person.

With a sigh, she looked at the small fire burning in the rock enclosure she and Anna had constructed. The flames were low but threw out enough heat to warm her. At least she wasn't freezing.

"This is not even a little comfortable," Anna muttered. "I'm being stabbed by something, but I can't seem to arrange myself around it."

Evelyn choked back a laugh and lifted her head to look at her friend. They were laying at opposite angles, their heads only a few inches from each other, affording them both maximum exposure to the fire. Anna caught her look and grimaced comically.

"I suppose it's better than the floor, but I'll admit that I'm jealous of Erik's kit."

Evelyn nodded. The Norwegians had kit bags that contained a rolled-up flat mattress that they could sleep on, and a warm woolen blanket.

"I'll second that."

Anna shifted again on her bed. "Are you warm enough?"

"Yes. The fire is throwing out a lovely amount of heat." Evelyn returned her gaze to the flames. "Once we get comfortable, we'll be able to sleep."

"We have a long road ahead of us," Anna said after a long minute. "Are you scared?"

"Of the Germans?"

"Of not making it to Namsos in time."

Evelyn thought for a moment, then sighed.

"If I allow myself to consider it, then I am," she said. "I'm trying to focus on what I can control, and right now that is simply to cover as much ground each day as humanly possible. If I don't make it, there will be time enough to be afraid then."

"Peder told me while we were eating that he is worried. He's afraid that you will be stranded here. He thinks we should have tried for the border after all."

"There's no use thinking about that now. We're here and I have a way out being arranged for me. This is at least guaranteed, if I can get there in time. Sweden was never guaranteed."

"True." Anna fell silent for a few minutes, then she shifted again. "I keep thinking that perhaps it's my fault that we're in this position."

Evelyn lifted her head to peer at her in the firelight.

"How can it be your fault?" she demanded. "Did you tell Hitler to invade? Don't be ridiculous. None of this is your fault."

"If I hadn't talked you out of the border, you could be in Sweden now."

"Or I could have been turned away and we would be trapped between the border and Oslo. That would be much more dodgy than this. At least here we have Erik, who is willing to take us as far as Trondheim. This is the best place we could be, all things considered."

"I suppose you're right." Anna didn't sound convinced. "At least you're getting to see some of Norway," she said after a moment with a short laugh.

Evelyn grinned. "Yes, I am."

They fell silent again and then Evelyn propped herself up on her arm.

"Anna?"

"Yes?"

"Why don't you come with me?"

Anna looked at her, surprised. "Go with you? You mean to England?"

"Yes."

"But...I can't! The ship is for you, not me."

"They won't turn you away, not if I tell them you're a valuable asset," Evelyn said in a low voice. "Think about it for a moment. You'll be safe in England. You've done so much for me that the least we can do is offer you refuge."

"Marlene, I can't leave Norway," she said after a moment, shaking her head. "If we can't repel the Nazis, we will need people willing to resist them. I can be of use here, in my own country."

"But if they succeed and occupy Norway, you will be trapped here," Evelyn pointed out. "You'll be forced to live under Nazi rule, and the Gestapo will take over your police. They'll remember you from last fall. You will have nowhere to hide."

"I doubt the same men will come here, but that's a chance I'll have to take. There will be people willing to fight and resist, but they will need guidance and leaders. You've already begun a network. I can finish it, and ensure that we can get valuable information out to your agency."

Evelyn considered her thoughtfully. She was right, she admitted to herself. Anna was in a perfect position to continue what she had started over the past few days. If the Germans weren't forced back and out of Norway, they would need people on the ground who could pass intelligence out. They would also need people who would continue the fight from within. Anna was both. She had already proven that she was willing to work with the English in the war effort, and her help would continue to be invaluable if Norway was lost to them. She was someone they could trust, and who would do what needed to be done.

"Are you sure?" she asked softly. "It won't be easy, and you will be shot if you're caught."

Anna met her gaze and nodded. "I'm sure," she replied just as softly. "This is where I belong."

Evelyn nodded slowly and laid back down. She had offered, and Anna had refused. There was nothing more to be said. And the other woman was right about one thing: Norway would need people willing to resist the Nazis, and Anna was certainly one of them. She had proven her willingness to do whatever was necessary to oppose the Germans last fall, and again over the past few days. Evelyn knew that they would be very lucky to have her on their side.

She just hoped and prayed that Anna would be able to evade capture. If the Gestapo got hold of Anna Salvesen, not only would the fledgling network be doomed, but Evelyn's identity would be at risk once again. Anna may not know her real name, but she had learned a lot over the past few months that the Germans would be thrilled to pry out of her.

And then no one would be safe.

April 10

Evelyn stepped outside and looked around. Dawn had broken, casting the clearing into deep shadow, and bringing with it a cool, crisp breeze. Anna and Peder were still sleeping inside, but Evelyn couldn't stay on the uncomfortable bed one moment longer. When she got up, Erik and the rest of the soldiers had already rolled up their beds and left the barn. Now, stepping outside, she saw that Erik and two others were talking several yards away, near the trees. When she walked outside, they turned to look at her and Erik lifted a hand in greeting. She waved back and started across the clearing towards them.

"Good morning," she called. "Where is everyone?"

"They've gone to patrol ahead to make sure the path is clear," Erik replied. "Once they confirm that no Germans are advancing into the mountains, we can be on our way."

"And if they are?"

"Then we find a different way."

Erik turned his head to say something in a low voice to the other two. They nodded and turned to head into the trees.

"Where are they going?" she asked, watching them leave.

"To check behind us," he said shortly, turning to walk back towards the barn with her. "Are the others awake yet?"

"Not yet." Evelyn glanced at him. "I can go wake them, if you like."

Erik shook his head. "Let them sleep a little longer. We can't leave until the others get back, and we have a long day ahead of us. There is no reason to wake them yet."

Erik was silent for a long moment, and then he stopped and turned to look at her.

"Why are you here?" he asked.

She raised her eyebrow. "What do you mean?"

"Why are you in Norway? I know Anna said that you work at the embassy, but why didn't you stay in Oslo? The embassy staff are protected under international law. You could have remained in the embassy and the Germans would have guaranteed your safety until your government made arrangements for an evacuation. Instead you fled the city with Anna and Peder. Why?"

"It seemed like the best thing to do at the time," Evelyn said with a shrug. "If I had stayed in Oslo, it may have been months before

I could leave. My work at the embassy was temporary, and I need to be back in London as soon as possible. I don't have months to wait."

"Temporary? How temporary?"

"I was due to leave by the end of the week," she said smoothly.

Erik was silent for a moment, then he shook his head. "Bad luck. If they had held off another week you wouldn't be in the middle of this."

Evelyn was silent and he looked at her.

"You're involved with the war effort?"

"Yes."

"What made you get involved in this war?" he asked, glancing at her.

"What made any of us get involved in this war?" Evelyn countered. "Why did you?"

He smiled dryly. "I wasn't involved in it until Hitler picked this fight," he pointed out.

She made a face. "Good point," she said sheepishly. "Well, I couldn't just sit by and do nothing while others went off to fight. And so I decided to do something instead."

"And you ended up in the middle of a German invasion," he said. "Not exactly what you were expecting when you arrived in Oslo, was it?"

"Not exactly, no."

"And how do you feel about being in the war now?"

"When I first began, I wanted to do something for my country. I wanted to do something that would matter," she said slowly. "Everyone I knew was joining the RAF or the Navy. I wanted to contribute as well."

"And now?" Erik prompted when she paused.

"Now I've seen what the Germans are willing to do, and how far Hitler will go to expand his territory. I want to do what I can to stop them. Your country should not be going through this, just as Poland shouldn't have gone through this. This is no longer about making a contribution for my country, it's about fighting to protect all of Europe."

"Protect all of Europe? You mean as your country protected Finland?" Erik shook his head. "There is no protection from the Nazis. They're running rampant all over Eastern Europe and Scandinavia and no one has lifted a finger to stop them, most especially your government. You have very ideological views, and they are to be commended, but they won't get you very far in this war. You cannot protect Europe, just as you cannot protect Norway. If you and others like you continue to think that you can, this war will end very quickly with France and England's defeat. You are on the defensive, and that is how you must think. You must be prepared to fight, not to protect, but to survive."

He walked over to the door of the barn and reached inside, grabbing something. He turned to walk back to her, a rifle in his hand.

"Do you know how to use this?" he asked, handing her the gun.

Evelyn took the rifle. "Yes."

He raised his eyebrows skeptically. "Show me."

She looked at him for a moment, then turned her attention to the rifle in her hands. It was a standard carbine and, although it was one she had never handled before, Evelyn was well acquainted with bolt-action rifles. The magazine was different from the top-loading setup that she was used to, and it took her a moment to figure out that the cartridges were loaded from the side directly into the receiver. She opened the hinged compartment and saw that it was fully loaded. Closing it again, she lifted the rifle to her shoulder and peered down the sight.

"What kind of rifle is this?" she asked. "It's different from anything I've used."

"It's a Krag–Jørgensen M1912/18. Norwegian-made."

She lowered the rifle and walked a few feet into the clearing, looking around. Spotting the edge of an ancient and rotting fence in the distance through the trees, she pointed to it.

"Do you see that fence?"

"Yes."

"The second-to-last post, the one that is lower than the others," she told him, raising the rifle and settling it against her shoulder.

Erik crossed his arms over his chest and nodded. "All right."

Evelyn braced her legs and peered down the sight again, aiming at the post. After a moment, she exhaled and squeezed the trigger. The shot cracked out and she lifted her head with a frown. The bullet had gone wide. She immediately lowered her head again, adjusted her aim, and fired again. This time, her shot hit the second-to-last fence post.

Lowering the rifle, she turned to hand it back to Erik. He unfolded his arms and shook his head, his face softening just slightly.

"Keep it. You're a better shot than the soldier who was assigned that gun," he told her. "It will be better served with you."

Evelyn frowned. "Then what will he use?"

"He was killed yesterday by a German sniper. He has no need of it anymore."

She swallowed. "I'm sorry."

"Don't be. We're at war now. This is how war goes." His dark eyes met hers. "I wish you, Anna, and Peder didn't have to be caught in the middle of it, but you are. There is no helping that. You take the gun and keep it by your side. It is not for protection, but for survival. If you see a threat, use it."

"I will. You don't need to worry about me."

Something resembling a smile twisted his lips, softening his harsh countenance once again.

"I'm not worried about you. Not now. Just be sure to shoot straight the first time."

She made a face. "It was my first time firing this model of rifle!" she protested.

"How's your shoulder?"

"It hurts like the devil."

That surprised a bark of laughter out of him.

"Yes. The Krag has a nasty kick until you get used to it. Next time, it won't hurt as much. You will be prepared for it." He looked towards the trees as four soldiers burst through, panting. "It's all right!" he called. "Just some target practice!"

"My God, Salvesen, you could have warned us!" One of them exclaimed. "We thought…"

"It's my fault," Evelyn called. "I wanted to try out the rifle and Lt. Salvesen was kind enough to agree. I'm so sorry!"

She gave them her best smile and they all stared at her, then rushed to assure her that it was quite all right and there was nothing to worry about. Erik watched as his men came forward as one, hastening to make themselves agreeable to the blonde woman in their company. He shook his head partly in amusement and partly in disgust before turning away to go to the barn.

"I'll wake the others. It's time to get moving," he said over his shoulder. "Philip and Sal, go and find the others. They were doubling back to make sure we don't have any Germans following us. We leave as soon you return."

Night Falls on Norway

London, England

The man exited the building and walked down the steps to the sidewalk. He went to the curb and lifted his black umbrella, flagging down a taxi. One slowed and pulled to the curb, stopping before him.

"Whitehall," he said, getting into the back.

"Aye," the driver nodded, easing back into traffic.

The man turned his attention out the window, watching as men and women hurried along the pavement. It was early and they were likely hurrying to begin their day, but his day had begun four hours before when he was called into the shabby building on Broadway Street.

He pressed his lips together grimly. The Germans had invaded both Norway and Denmark the day before, demanding that both countries accept the protection of the Reich. Denmark had agreed, but Norway had not. Fools. German troops were rolling over the limited and weak opposition, taking the country anyway. Norway would fall quickly, with a loss of lives that was unnecessary. King Haakon should have surrendered when he was given the chance. Instead, he chose to resist. Hadn't any of them learned yet that resistance was futile against the might of the Third Reich?

But it wasn't the invasion that had him frowning thoughtfully. It was the mad scramble that had begun late yesterday afternoon and was still ongoing. MI6 was in a controlled frenzy, undertaking what could only be an extraction from the west coast of Norway. An order had gone out to one of the cruisers accompanying the British troops on their way to assist the Norwegians in repelling the invasion. The cruiser was to evacuate a civilian from Namsos and transport them back to England. Now why would that be considered a priority in the middle of an invasion?

As far as he knew, MI6 had no existing agents in Norway, nor in Denmark. In fact, most of their operatives had been exposed after the Venlo Incident, which was a downright embarrassment. They were still struggling to rebuild the European networks, and he hadn't heard of any moves to go into Scandinavia. So who were they so interested in getting out of Norway?

The taxi turned a corner and Westminster Abbey loomed on his right. His eyes narrowed as he stared at the landmark without seeing it. There was only one agent that he knew of that had been sent to Oslo: Jian. She would have been trapped when Germany launched their invasion. Oslo fell within six hours, as did all the main port cities. Sweden had closed their borders almost immediately. MI6 had to be trying to get her out.

The man clenched his hand around the handle of his umbrella, his knuckles turning white. He hadn't been able to find out any information on her since they locked everything down in November. The SD agent, Herr Sturmbannführer Renner, had bungled the whole operation so badly that there was no doubt that the leading powers in Broadway Street were now suspicious of a spy in their midst. Almost immediately, the entire section Jian worked in was classified and closed off from everyone except a very select few. From that day forward, he had had absolutely no idea where she was located. As far he knew, she had simply disappeared.

His grip on the umbrella relaxed slightly. This could be the chance they needed to finally capture the elusive British spy. He could hand the Gestapo their prize virtually gift-wrapped. All they had to do was stop her from making it to Namsos.

He would contact Berlin and alert them to the fact that an evacuation was being planned for Namsos on the 14th. He would offer the possibility of it being Jian, but make it clear that it was by no means certain. If, by some strange chance, it wasn't her, he didn't want to endanger his newfound status in Berlin by giving them false information. He had only just managed to get back into their good graces by passing on her codename. He had no intention of falling out of them again.

Chapter Twenty-Three

Mountains north of Grindal, Norway

Before Erik could reach the door to the barn, Peder loomed into the opening, his hair standing up on top of his head and his shirt half tucked into his trousers. His eyes were wide with excitement and he skidded to a stop when he saw Erik only a few feet away.

"The British have come!" he cried, a grin spreading over his face. "They're here!"

Philip and Sal stopped and turned to look while Erik stared at him in astonishment.

"What?"

"Five British destroyers sailed into Narvik, trapping the German ships. They sank two of the German destroyers!"

"At Narvik?" The soldiers came forward quickly. "Are you sure?"

"Yes. It sounds like the British suffered losses as well, but two of the Germans ships have sunk."

"What about the others?" Erik asked quickly.

"No word yet, but it's a beginning."

"Yes, it is," Anna said, coming out behind him. "That's fantastic news."

"How did you come by it?" Erik demanded. "How did you hear this?"

"I've been listening to the Norwegian army frequency since last night," Peder told him.

"You've been what?!"

Peder flushed and ran a hand over his hair, smoothing it down self-consciously.

"I didn't want to tell you because I knew you'd look at me like that," he said. "You never did like it when Kristian and I listened in on things you thought were none of our business."

"That's because it always landed you both in trouble and I had to get you out of it," Erik retorted. "How did you get onto their frequency?"

Peder shrugged and turned away. "I'm not telling you," he said over his shoulder. "Anyway, even if I did, you wouldn't understand a word of it."

Evelyn bit back a grin, eyeing Anna's brother out of the corner of her eye. He looked somewhat dumbfounded.

"What else have you heard?" Philip asked. "Have you heard anything about Trondheim?"

"The Germans still have it, but there are pockets of fighting around it." Peder paused in the door of the barn. "Most of your troops are making their way north."

"Peder?" Erik stopped him when he would have continued into the barn. "Did you hear anything about the German positions?"

"I know they're holding Trondheim and moving west and north along the fjord."

"And south? Are they moving south as well?"

"Not that anyone's said. There's a formation moving up from Bergen, but they haven't crossed Sognefjorden yet."

Erik nodded slowly. "Good. That's good." He turned to look at Philip and Sal. "Go find the others. I want to get going."

They nodded and turned once more to leave. He turned back to Peder.

"Keep listening, Peder. If we can find out where the Germans are, we can avoid them."

Peder grinned. "That sounds good to me."

He ducked into the barn and Evelyn glanced at Erik.

"Do you think we can avoid them and get through Trondheim?" she asked.

"Doubtful, but we may be able to navigate through their lines and go around."

"If the British have ships in Narvik, they may also have ships going to Trondheim," Anna said. "Maybe the Germans will be forced out."

"If they are, they will be forced right into our path," he replied grimly. "I don't think we want that."

"No, but this is still good news," Evelyn said slowly. "Ships are already arriving with troops and supplies. You're not alone anymore."

He gave her an unreadable look. "Perhaps."

"Oh Erik, stop being so dramatic," Anna exclaimed. "You're always looking at the bad side of things. Two German destroyers were sunk! This is a reason to celebrate, not look like we're about to be shot."

"I'll celebrate when we kick the Nazis back to Germany."

"That's a fair statement," Evelyn said. "Two sunk destroyers are good, but more would be better."

"Oh don't you start as well!" Anna threw up her hands. "Am I the only one who thinks this is fantastic news?"

"No. I think it's wonderful news, but I can see your brother's point," Evelyn said with a shrug. "If all the German ships were sunk in Narvik, then we'd be going in the right direction."

"This is a start!"

"Yes, it is." She turned to go into the barn. "I'll get my things together. Do you have everything ready to go?"

"Yes. I just have to grab my bag."

"Hurry and get ready to leave," Erik said. "The others will be back any minute. If you're going to make Namsos by Sunday, we have a lot of ground to cover."

London, England

Bill looked up when his office door opened and raised his eyebrows in surprise when Montclair walked in.

"Jasper!" he exclaimed, setting down the communication in his hand and standing up. "I thought you'd gone up to Whitehall for a meeting."

"I did," Jasper replied, walking over to one of the chairs before the desk. "I've just come back."

He sat down and looked at Bill, his eyes sharp and keen. "How are you, Bill? Have you had lunch?"

Bill retook his seat and looked at him quizzically.

"It's a bit late for lunch now," he replied. "I'll wait for dinner. I'm dining with Marguerite at Claridge's."

"I've heard from Wesley and a few of the others that you're putting in long hours every day."

"So are you. We all are. There's a war on."

"And it won't be ending any time soon, not if Adolph Hitler has anything to say about it," Jasper said, crossing his legs. "We're in for the long haul, and exhausting ourselves this early in the game won't do our people any favors. How many agents do you have abroad now? Ten?"

He nodded.

"I wonder if it won't be best to move a few of them over to another handler. I don't want you becoming overwhelmed and burned out, nor do I want Marguerite to begin to hate me. And she will, you know. The less she sees of you, the more she'll resent me."

"It's only been a few days, Jasper. This is hardly business as usual. The Jerries caught us all off-guard with Norway, and I've got two agents still in Copenhagen. Marguerite understands that my work will keep me away at times. This is one of those times."

Jasper studied him for a long moment. "This will become business as usual if we allow it to," he finally said. "How many agents do you have in France?"

"Five, if you're not counting people like Josephine Rousseau, who work for the Deuxième Bureau."

"And Jian will make six?"

"Yes."

"Where are the others?"

"Two in Copenhagen, one in Switzerland and one in Belgium."

"I'll move them to another handler and leave you the ones in France," Jasper decided. "Get me their details and I'll decide who will be best to oversee them."

"I don't know if they will work for someone else," Bill protested, sitting back in his chair.

"They won't have a choice. Bill, my mind is made up. After the meeting I've just had, I'll need you to be solid and at the top of your game for the entirety of this war. I won't have that if you continue at this pace. And before you start to point fingers as I can see you're about to, I'm also making some changes to my own schedule."

Bill stared across the desk at him, then sighed.

"All right. I'll have Wesley gather the details together for you."

"I appreciate it. We'll make the transition as smooth as possible for the agents. Don't worry." He made no move to get up. "Have you had any further communication from Jian?"

"Not since last night. She acknowledged the instructions to make her way to Namsos."

"Do you have a schedule for her to check in?"

"No. I think it's rather dependent on whether or not they can get a signal out. I don't know what they're using for a radio, but it's not one of ours."

Jasper was quiet for a long moment, then he raised his eyes to Bill's.

Night Falls on Norway

"If she's captured by the Germans, the Gestapo will turn her over to the SD, along with everyone she's with. We'll lose our only eyes and ears in Norway."

"I'm aware of the stakes, Jasper, and so is she."

"GC&CS has been intercepting more and more coded messages from the Germans coming into England." Jasper shifted in his seat and recrossed his legs. "They've been passing them on to MI5."

Bill frowned. "That sounds ominous. That sounds as though they still have agents in England; agents that we haven't located yet."

"It does, doesn't it? That's what MI5 thinks as well. We all thought that we'd turned all the ones the Jerries sent over, but now they've got us wondering. MI5 has been busy setting up more security nets to try to catch any that might come in." Jasper hesitated, then sighed. "It's inevitable that Hitler will send over more spies. I was surprised at the amount of traffic GC&CS has been intercepting, though."

"This was the first you've heard of it?"

"Yes. You know Vernon doesn't like to share his information with us. That isolationist view is also embraced by all of his officers."

"What happened to change that?"

Jasper smiled wryly. "They came across something that pertains rather significantly to us."

"Oh? What's that?"

"They believe they've discovered the codename for our mole here in London."

Bill stared at him and Jasper's smile grew at the look of astonishment on his face.

"I thought that would get your attention," he said.

"I should think so! Who is the bastard?"

"We don't know yet, but this moves us further ahead than we've been. GC&CS have been decoding messages coming through on a regular basis to a man called Henry. MI5 are convinced that Henry is right here in London. There have been one or two incidents where something was mentioned in the message that was quite obviously referring to landmarks here in the city. But the references were such that it was more likely directed to a resident, rather than someone who comes in to visit from the country."

"And you think it's our spy?"

"I do. After being informed of the existence of the messages, I demanded to see all of them. One of the earlier ones makes reference to information passed on to Oslo."

"That could be anything."

"The message was intercepted on November 5th, the day after Jian arrived in Oslo. In that message, they referred to something, or someone, called Rätsel. In February, there was another mention of the name."

Bill frowned thoughtfully. "Rätsel? That's German for mystery, isn't it?"

"Or enigma, but yes. MI5 thinks it's a reference to a person rather than to their coding system, and that's why they finally passed the information on to us. After going through the messages, I believe it's what the Germans are calling Jian."

"If it is, then Henry is the one who alerted them to her presence in Oslo in November."

"Yes."

"Are there any clues to his position in London?"

"None. MI5 can't discern anything about the man other than the fact that he resides in London."

Bill was silent for a moment, then he pushed back his chair and got up restlessly.

"And we know that he holds a position of some note within the government," he said slowly. "It's not much, but it's something. As you say, we're further along than we were."

"When Jian gets back, make sure that she's aware of the development as well as the name." Jasper stood up. "The more people we have looking for Henry, the better."

"And MI5?"

"They've passed the whole thing over to us. GC&CS will forward all future messages to me." He turned towards the door. "In the meantime, continue to keep all Jian's operations as close as possible. Once we're sure he's as much in the dark as everyone else, we can begin releasing false information and see where it leads us. But let's make sure we've plugged all the holes before we start flooding the boat."

Bill nodded. "I will."

"Now, for God's sake, get out of here and go to dinner with your wife. There's nothing more that can be done for any of them today." Jasper paused at the door and looked over at him. "If anything comes in from Norway, you'll be notified immediately?"

"Yes."

"Good." He opened the door. "The rest is in the hands of Providence, then."

Chapter Twenty-Four

Somewhere near Leinstrand, Norway
April 11

Evelyn grimaced as she thrust her hands into the freezing water of a small stream that ran across the corner of the clearing. She cupped up water and splashed it on her face, shivering violently as the icy water hit her skin.

"At least it is clean water," Anna said beside her.

They were kneeling next to the stream as the gray light of dawn streaked the sky above. The night before, exhausted and near to falling over, the group had come across a small farm in the lower hills. After scouting the area for any signs of enemy forces, Erik had approached the house and knocked on the door. After a short discussion, he returned to tell them that the farm was owned by an older couple who had agreed to allow them to take refuge in their shed overnight. The party had been overjoyed to find an ancient, wood-burning stove inside that still worked. The man had brought out firewood for them and a pile of blankets. When he saw Anna and Evelyn, he seemed startled until Erik explained it was his sister. Upon hearing that, the man had visibly relaxed and gone away again, wishing them all a good rest.

Evelyn had never been so grateful for rough woolen blankets and a wood stove in all her life. Erik had kept up a grueling pace, stopping only when absolutely necessary. By the time they came upon this farm, she was convinced that she couldn't go another step. She had been completely exhausted, and so cold that her limbs had ceased to have any feeling in them. Once she and Anna were huddled together beneath the blankets near the stove, the feeling had slowly returned to her legs and feet. And so had excruciating pain. Her feet, raw from hiking in loafers not meant for rough terrain, had swelled as soon as she removed the shoes. This morning she had fished in her suitcase for thicker socks and resolutely put the loafers back on, ignoring the pain. There was nothing else she could do.

"Grrrrgh, that's cold!" Anna gasped, splashing water on her face.

"Anna!" Erik called from behind them.

They turned to find him standing near the shed with a plump, older woman dressed in a long skirt with an apron tied around her. He motioned for them to come and Anna looked at Evelyn.

"That must be the farmer's wife," she said, standing. She picked up her suitcase beside her. "Come on. Let's go see what's going on."

Evelyn stood up, grimacing again as she picked up her bag and began walking back towards Erik and the older woman.

"Are you all right?" Anna asked, catching the expression.

"I'm fine."

Anna looked skeptical but remained silent.

"Anna, this is Mrs. Hansen," Erik said as they approached. "Mrs. Hansen, this is my sister, Anna, and her friend, Marlene."

"Good morning," the woman said with a smile and a nod. "My husband just told me you were part of the group that took shelter in our shed."

"Thank you for allowing us to camp in there," Anna said with a smile. "The stove and blankets were very much appreciated."

"Yes, it was very kind," Evelyn agreed. "Thank you."

"You're welcome. I came out to ask if you would like to wash up in the house? That stream is freezing and you'll catch cold. Come. We have hot water and a tub where you can wash properly."

Anna looked at Erik and he nodded.

"Go. We will wait. Just don't take too long."

"Oh, that would be lovely!" Evelyn exclaimed. "Are you sure you don't mind?" she asked the woman.

"Yes, yes, come!" She turned to lead the way to the farmhouse some distance away. "It is no trouble."

"Thank you again," Anna said.

"Please. These are frightening days. If we don't help each other, then we're no better than the Germans," Mrs. Hansen said. "How do you come to be with your brother's unit?"

"I'm from Oslo and we fled when the German ships were coming into the fjord. We worked at an embassy there. We didn't really know where to go, so we just went north. When our car broke down near Grindal, Erik found us."

"Oslo!" She looked surprised. "You don't sound like you're from the city." She looked at Evelyn. "You do," she added with a nod, "but you don't."

"I grew up near Trollheiman," Anna said.

"Ah! That explains it." Mrs. Hansen beamed. "Are your parents still there?"

"Yes."

They came to the back of the house and Mrs. Hansen led them inside. They stepped into a narrow corridor that led into a large and sunny kitchen. The smell of coffee filled the air, and Evelyn's stomach rumbled in response.

"Please. Sit down," Mrs. Hansen said, motioning to a round wooden table. "The tub is in the back room, through there. Mr. Hansen is filling it with hot water now. It's not much, but it is better than an icy stream, no?"

"Heaps better!" Anna agreed, sinking into a chair at the table.

"You can take turns once he's finished." Mrs. Hansen turned to the counter. "And while you're waiting, you will have some breakfast."

"Oh no!" Evelyn protested despite the growling in her stomach. "We couldn't impose on you any further."

The woman waved her protest away and turned to set two steaming cups of coffee before them.

"Don't be silly," she said briskly. "You will eat something before you start off again."

"The water's ready." Mr. Hansen emerged from the door at the back of the kitchen, nodding to the women at the table. "Good morning. I hope you slept all right out there."

"We did. Thank you for allowing us to use the shed."

"Now, there is a stack of clean towels next to the tub," Mrs. Hansen said, "and soap is on the shelf."

Anna looked at Evelyn.

"Would you like to go, or shall I?"

"You go first," Evelyn said, picking up her coffee. "I'll enjoy my coffee."

Anna grinned and got up, picking up her case and turning towards the door. "I'll be quick," she promised over her shoulder.

She disappeared into the room and closed the door, leaving Evelyn alone with Mr. and Mrs. Hansen.

"I'll take coffee to the men outside," Mr. Hansen said.

"I've put it all on that tray there," Mrs. Hansen said, motioning to a square, handled tray. "Be careful."

He nodded and picked up the tray, turning to go out of the kitchen. Mrs. Hansen watched him go, then carried a thick brown loaf of bread over to the table.

Evelyn sipped her coffee, looking around the comfortable kitchen.

"This is a lovely kitchen," she said. "How long have you lived here?"

"Oh, over forty years now," Mrs. Hansen replied with a smile. "We came here just after we married."

"Do you have children?"

"Three daughters and a son. They are all grown now and married." She went back to the long counter along the wall and picked up a plate with yellow cheese. "None of them live far."

"You're very kind to be so generous to us."

Mrs. Hansen smiled and shook her head.

"I would not be able to sleep knowing that I had a chance to help someone and chose not to," she said. "The coming days will be hard enough. My husband said you're trying to reach the Norwegian army?"

"Erik is, yes. He's trying to rejoin his unit. When the invasion began, they were scattered."

"And you?"

Evelyn shrugged. "I am trying to reach the Swedish border," she lied.

The older woman looked at her for a moment, then pushed the bread and cheese closer to her.

"Eat something," she urged, sitting across from her. "You won't get very far if you don't eat." She watched as Evelyn smiled and reached for the brown bread. "Are you on foot the whole way?"

"Yes."

She shook her head and frowned. "You are not dressed for that. There is more snow coming. You will freeze in those clothes. Don't you have anything warmer with you?"

Evelyn swallowed and shook her head. "No. I'm afraid when we left Oslo, we weren't expecting to be going by foot. We were in a car, but it broke down."

Mrs. Hansen was silent for a long moment, then she reached out and patted Evelyn's hand.

"I'll be right back. You eat, and drink your coffee," she said, pushing herself up out of the chair and turning to leave the kitchen. "There is more cheese at the side there if you finish that."

Evelyn watched her go and reached for another slice of bread. Her stomach was still rumbling, but the bread was thick and hearty, and the cheese rich and smooth. She bit into another piece, grateful for the coffee and the food. The basket of food that Else had packed for them had been finished last evening, leaving them at the mercy of whatever they could find in the mountains as they went. She thought suddenly of home and of the large breakfasts served in her parents dining room. Eggs, thick rashers of bacon and ham accompanied by toast smothered with rich, creamy butter were standard fare on most mornings, and Evelyn suddenly felt very far from home. Would she ever get back?

A wave of desperate melancholy rolled over her, robbing her of breath, and she set down her half-eaten bread and cheese. Raising trembling hands, she covered her face and took a deep, ragged breath. What if she didn't make it to Namsos in time? What if she was stranded in Norway? She would be forced to remain with Anna, putting her in danger, until she could find a way across the Swedish border. Every hour that she spent with Anna was another hour that could lead the Gestapo to them both. If the Germans suspected Anna of helping a British agent, there would be nowhere she could hide that would be safe.

Evelyn dropped her hands, staring across the kitchen blindly. She couldn't do that to Anna. Not after everything the woman had already done to help her. If she didn't make it to Namsos in time, she would part company with Anna and find her own way. The prospect was a terrifying one, but she saw no other alternative. She would have to make her way to the border and try to find a way across it. She could change her appearance, and her Norwegian was apparently strong enough not to raise any questions in the local populace if Mr. and Mrs. Hansen were anything to go by. She could find a way. She would have to.

Reaching for her coffee, Evelyn took a long, steadying breath. Everything would be all right. She would figure it out.

She was just finishing her third piece of bread and cheese when Anna opened the door and came back into the kitchen dressed in clean clothes and looking refreshed.

"That was heavenly," she announced, dropping into her seat and reaching for her coffee. "The water's still hot, but you'd better hurry."

Evelyn nodded and pushed her chair back to stand. She was just heading for the back room when Mrs. Hansen returned with a stack of clothing in one arm and a pair of sturdy brown boots hanging from her hand.

"One of my daughters is about your size," she said, nodding to Evelyn. "Or at least, she used to be. These are some of her old clothes. There's a pair of warm pants and a sweater, and a few shirts. Try them on. If they fit, take them. They will keep you warmer than that skirt will. I also found these boots. If they fit, please take them as well."

She handed Evelyn the boots and a stack of clothing, keeping a few of the sweaters. Those she handed to Anna. "I thought these might fit you," she said. "You're more of a size with my oldest. This is all that is left here of hers."

"Oh, we couldn't!" Anna exclaimed. "Really, this isn't necessary!"

"Please take them! If they fit, make use of them. They will do you more good now than they will sitting in a trunk upstairs indefinitely."

Evelyn stared down at the pants and boots. "This is very kind of you," she said. "You must let me give you something in return."

Mrs. Hansen shooed her towards the back room.

"Don't be silly. Go and try them on. I hope the boots fit you. Those shoes you're wearing will do you no good on foot through the mountains. Go now!"

Evelyn looked up when a knock fell on the door fifteen minutes later.

"Marlene? Can I come in?" Anna called.

"Yes."

The door opened and Anna poked her head around it cautiously, then smiled and came in when she found Evelyn fully dressed in the pants and one of the sweaters.

"Oh they fit!" she exclaimed. "Good!"

"Yes. The pants are a little large, but nothing a belt didn't fix," Evelyn said, looking down at the heavy work pants and warm sweater. "I feel like a bit of a fool, but this is much more appropriate to hiking through trees and underbrush."

"Yes, it is." She tilted her head. "And you don't look like a fool. You look like a woman who works on a farm. There's nothing wrong with that. In fact, it is perfect if we do end up running into German soldiers. They won't have any clue that you're not a Norwegian."

"Let's just hope it doesn't come to that," Evelyn said, sitting on a stool and reaching for the clean pair of socks she had pulled out of her suitcase. She looked up sharply when Anna let out a loud gasp. "What?"

"Your…your feet!" Anna stammered, staring at her feet in horror.

Night Falls on Norway

Evelyn followed her gaze and grimaced. Her feet did look terrible. They were red and bleeding where several blisters had formed, burst, and then been rubbed raw by the walking yesterday.

"Yes. I sincerely hope the boots fit." She pulled on her socks, covering the sight and reached for the boots. "If they don't, I dread to think what my feet will look like by tonight."

"You can't walk like that!" Anna exclaimed. "Why didn't you say something?"

"What good will it do?" she demanded, looking up. "I have to get to Namsos, and this is the only way."

"But…you won't be able to walk at all if you continue!"

"I don't have a choice, Anna. I must. They feel much better since I washed them in warm water."

"Wait." Anna turned towards the door. "I'll see if Mrs. Hansen has any kind of bandages. We can at least wrap them to protect the worst parts."

"It's fine!" Evelyn protested. "Don't bother her! She's already done too much!"

But Anna was already gone and she knew it was useless to argue. Once the kind woman with the big heart heard she was injured, there would be no stopping her. She let out a loud sigh and slid her right foot into one of the boots to see if it fit. She let out another sigh, this time one of relief, when her foot nestled comfortably in the old work boot. It fit. Thank God!

She slid the left one on and stood up gingerly, surprised when a dull throbbing was the only protest her poor feet made. She would try to pay the Hansen's for the boots. It was worth any price not to have to put those loafers on again!

"She had some linen and some salve." Anna was back, followed closely by Mrs. Hansen. "What are you doing? Do the boots fit?"

"Yes, they do." Evelyn looked at Mrs. Hansen. "They're perfect. You must let me pay you for them."

"I wouldn't dream of it," she said, shaking her head. "They were sitting in a trunk, doing nothing. You have need of them. Now, take them off again and let's take care of your feet. Anna says you have blisters all over them."

"It's quite all right," Evelyn said, dropping back onto the stool.

"It's not quite all right," Anna said briskly. "Use the salve and wrap them up. Trust me. I grew up with this stuff. It works miracles."

"It does," Mrs. Hansen agreed, unscrewing the lid to a short, fat tub. "Though it smells terrible."

Evelyn took off the boots and her socks and reached for the tub of salve. She knew when she was outnumbered. It was useless to protest. The quicker she did as they asked, the quicker they could be on their way.

"Oh goodness!" Mrs. Hansen gasped when she saw the raw and bleeding skin. "How were you walking around?"

"I'm stubborn," Evelyn replied, wrinkling her nose as she scooped out the foul-smelling salve. "Ugh!"

"Yes, it smells very bad, but it will heal those up. Put it on nice and thick." Mrs. Hansen turned towards the door. "That won't be enough linen strips. I'll get some more."

She left and Anna handed Evelyn the stack of linen strips when she finished with one of her feet.

"I would wrap multiple layers," she said, grimacing as Evelyn gingerly began wrapping her foot. "The more padding you have around it, the better. Will the boot still fit once it's all wrapped?"

"I think so. There was some room in them."

Evelyn grit her teeth and worked quickly, wrapping the linen strips around her foot and around her ankle. She was just finishing when Mrs. Hansen returned with another stack of bandages. She passed them to Anna and nodded in satisfaction when she saw that Evelyn had one foot finished already.

"Very good," she said approvingly. "I'll leave you to do that and I will go finish in the kitchen. I think your brother is getting impatient," she told Anna as she turned away. "You'd best hurry."

Anna nodded and watched as Evelyn applied the salve to the other foot.

"Don't worry about Erik," she said once Mrs. Hansen had gone. "I'll explain that we were bandaging your feet. He won't be angry once he knows what's taking so long."

"I want to get moving quickly as well. I understand his concern. We're trying to stay ahead of one wave of troops and avoid another. We need to be on our way."

Anna was silent for a moment.

"I will get you to Namsos in time," she finally said quietly. "I promise. If I have to steal a car, I'll get you there. As much as I would love for you to stay, I know how dangerous it is for you."

Evelyn looked up and held out her hand for the other stack of bandages.

"Hopefully, that won't be necessary," she said with a wry smile. "I will make it to Namsos, but it's not your responsibility to ensure that

I do. If it becomes too dangerous, I will leave you and Peder, and go alone."

"What? No you won't. That was never the plan!"

"Anna, we never had a plan," she pointed out, beginning to wrap her other foot. "If there is any risk of the Germans finding out who I am, or that you are with me, I will leave. It's far too dangerous for all of you. You know what's at stake. I won't risk you any more than I have to."

"Don't be ridiculous," Anna muttered crossly. "I'm not going to let you make your way through German lines to Namsos all alone. We will do it together, and we won't be caught. That is all."

Evelyn looked up to argue, but changed her mind. Anna already looked anxious and worried enough. There was no point in making it worse by arguing with her over this. Time would tell whether or not she would have to leave her friends and continue alone.

And if that time came, she would do it and not look back.

Chapter Twenty-Five

11th April, 1940

Dear Evelyn,

Well, Herr Hitler finally moved, but not in the direction anyone was expecting. Did you see that invasion coming? I suppose it makes sense strategically, but I still thought he would attack the low lands and France first. So much for Norwegian neutrality. And so much for my luck in the pool. It got up to over two hundred pounds in the end.

Denmark gave up without a fight, but I don't really blame them. They had no hope of putting up any kind of resistance against the Germans. I'm surprised Norway is fighting, to be honest. I don't know much about their army, but I was rather under the impression that they were no match for the Wehrmacht either. I sincerely hope I'm wrong. If Norway is lost, Hitler's U-boats will have free rein in the Atlantic. They're already causing quite enough damage as it is.

Belgian forces have been put on alert all along the border. It won't be long now before Hitler moves west. He'll try to take France before setting his sights on us. Now that he's finally moving, I think it will happen quickly. At least the waiting is finally over and now we can get down to the business of fighting this war.

Our patrols have increased since all this began. I'm flying every day now, sometimes three patrols in a day. Tomorrow, though, we're getting a bit of a change of pace. Our squadron is scheduled to do a reconnaissance flight over Hun territory. I'm not worried about telling you because by the time this letter gets to you, it will be done and over with. Anyway, I'm trusting that you won't tell Jerry we're coming to take pictures of his backyard. Rob's rather chuffed about it. He's itching to get a shot at them, but I don't think we'll get the chance. Our orders are to fly over, take the photos and get out as fast as possible. That's why they've fitted out Spits with the cameras. They're taking advantage of our speed and maneuverability. Well, at least it will make a change from what we've been doing.

I hope you're doing well. When do you finish your training stint? It should be soon, I think. Perhaps when you get back to your station, we can meet at a pub somewhere.

I'd better put the light out. Long day ahead tomorrow. Take care of yourself.

Yours,
FO Miles Lacey

Steinan, Norway

Evelyn looked up and stopped abruptly, grabbing Anna's arm to prevent her from continuing through the trees. Erik was ahead of them, holding up his hand in a signal to stop moving. She frowned and glanced behind her at Peder. He had come to a halt a few feet behind them and he nodded to her, indicating that he had seen the signal to stop. Bringing up the rear of the group were two of Erik's men, their rifles in their hands and their faces grim. As everyone stopped, they shifted their grips on their rifles and took a protective stance at the back.

Erik motioned with his other hand and the two soldiers directly behind him moved forward slowly, flanking him briefly before disappearing into the trees ahead. As soon as they had gone ahead, Erik turned and motioned for Anna, Evelyn and Peder to move off the trail and into the trees.

Evelyn swallowed and she and Anna moved to their right, stepping between the trunks of the towering pine trees. Peder followed, moving behind a particularly old and wide trunk. He set down his case and looked at them questioningly. Evelyn shrugged in response and peered around the tree closest to her, watching as Erik moved into the trees to the left of the trail. They had been following a lower ridge for about two hours now, but Evelyn hadn't seen or heard anything to cause alarm. The mountains were quiet and peaceful, giving the impression of walking through a protective canopy. Yet something had obviously disturbed that peace and quiet.

223

"This can't be good," Anna whispered after a few moments. "They're still not back."

"No, but I haven't heard any sounds of struggle or alarm," Evelyn whispered back.

Anna nodded in agreement and leaned up against her tree.

"How are you doing?" she asked. "How are your feet?"

Evelyn shrugged. "I'm fine. The break we had for lunch helped. It was so kind of Mrs. Hansen to pack that food for us."

"Perfectly timed as well," Peder said with a grin, keeping his voice low. "We'd finished the bread and cheese your landlady sent with you."

"Erik tried to pay them as well," Anna said. "They wouldn't take it from him either, so don't feel bad about her refusing your money."

"I hope and pray they aren't hurt by the Germans," Evelyn said. "I wish there was something I could do for them."

"They will face the Nazis as we all will, and they will be all right. You must stop worrying about us. You are the only one you should be concerned about," Anna advised in a low voice.

"You sound like your brother," Evelyn muttered. "If I stop caring for others, then there is no point at all to what I do."

"I'm not saying to stop caring. I'm cautioning you against making decisions based on emotion rather than reason." Anna shrugged. "In the end, we all have to take care of ourselves. If we have help along the way, that is a wonderful thing, but none of us can count on it."

"She's right," Peder said unexpectedly. "We all must learn to think differently now. We must fight, of course, and do what we can to help to each other, but we can't get so caught up in the plight of others that we neglect our own interests. There will be pain and sorrow. We cannot stop that. Many people have already died, and many more will follow. As heartless as it sounds, we must learn to become immune to it if we are to survive."

Evelyn looked from to the other. "When did the two of you become so wise?"

"When I saw the ships in Oslofjorden," he muttered. "Part of me didn't want to believe that it would come to this, but the other part of me knew that it would happen eventually. That's why I told you I would join your network if the Germans came. Now they are here and we all must do what we will do. I have chosen to resist. There will be many who will not, but I can't let that affect my choices. Just as you can't let your compassion affect yours."

Evelyn's lips twisted. "Point noted."

"Here's Erik," Anna said a few minutes later, peering through the trees.

Evelyn straightened up and turned to look. Erik and Philip moved across the trail towards them. There was no sign of the others and, as they drew closer, Erik motioned for them to follow him.

"What's happening?" Anna asked as they joined him on the trail once again.

"We're near Steinan, southeast of Trondheim. I've sent the others on a sweep to make sure we're not walking into any surprises. I think we're all right for now, but below...it's not good. Come. See for yourselves."

He turned and led them off the trail in the opposite direction. They moved slowly, pausing frequently, until at last they reached a ridge. He motioned for them to get down and, once they had all crouched low, he moved them forward until the forest floor angled sharply into a steep descent into a ravine. There he stopped and handed Anna a pair of binoculars.

She took them and looked out over the expanse of land below. Her lips tightened and, after a long moment, she silently handed the binoculars to Evelyn.

Evelyn caught her breath as she stared out over the valley. Their position on the mountain afforded them an outstanding view of the immediate valley and the miles beyond, stretching to the water in the far distance. Trondheim was marked by the remnants of a thick, black cloud of smoke hanging overhead, the result of a Luftwaffe bombardment that had accompanied the invasion two days before. While that sight was chilling enough, it wasn't what drew her attention and made her blood run cold. It was the sight of columns of German troops, tanks and trucks forming a mechanical river out of the port city and into the surrounding areas. The Nazis were moving, and they were moving quickly.

"Panzers!" she breathed. "Already?"

"Yes." Erik sounded grim. "This is the first wave of reinforcements. They're moving east. They're probably going to meet up with the divisions coming up from the south. Or they're heading north. Either way, it's clear Trondheim is well and truly lost. We can't retake it now, and there's no way you can go through it or cross the fjord."

Evelyn stared at the ominous sea of gray uniforms and Stahlhelms, the distinctive rounded steel helmets worn by the German military. She tamped down an almost overwhelming surge of terror and swallowed, forcing herself to breathe deeply. There were so many of them! It was like a never-ending swarm pouring into the countryside.

"Marlene!"

She started and tore her gaze away from the sight to find Anna and Erik both staring at her. She had no idea how long she'd been staring at the spectacle, but she'd obviously missed something that was said.

"What?"

"Are you all right?" Anna asked. "You're very pale."

"I…I'm fine."

"Erik was saying that we'll have to go around to the west and follow the fjord up to Steinkjer. We'll be able to cross there."

"The mountains are deeper as you go north, and they will provide very good protection," Erik said.

Evelyn swallowed, stole one last look at the advancing troops, and then handed the binoculars back to Erik, turning resolutely away from the ridge. She followed the others back to the trail and looked at Peder.

"Did you see?" she asked.

He nodded. "I saw enough."

"I wish I had been wrong five days ago," she said in a low voice. "I wish none of you had to go through this, but I'm glad you and your radio are with us and not still in Oslo."

Peder smiled and reached out to squeeze her shoulder gently. "So am I."

Evelyn returned his smile and turned to Erik. "Thank you for bringing us this far. I appreciate it more than you can know."

He nodded brusquely.

"You're welcome, but I'm continuing on with you," he said. "After seeing what will be right behind you, I can't leave you three alone. It is too dangerous, and none of you are as familiar with the mountains as I am."

"But…what about your men?" Anna asked. "What will they do?"

"They will continue to move north and join up with what's left of our battalion. I'll join them after we've seen Marlene safely to Namsos."

"What about Anna and Peder?" Evelyn asked. "What will they do when we reach Namsos?"

"I have an uncle not far from there," Peder said suddenly. "He is in Gartland. We can go there until we decide what's best to do."

Erik looked at him for a moment, then nodded. "Yes. That is a good plan. It will give you time to see where it will be safe to travel."

Philip emerged from the trees ahead and whistled. Erik turned to look, then motioned for them to move back into the trees.

"I'll be right back," he said, turning towards Philip, "and then we'll get moving again."

Evelyn moved off the trail with the other two and watched as Erik stood talking to Philip. While they talked, the other soldiers joined them.

"Do you think the way ahead is blocked?" Peder asked in a low voice. "If it is, we will have to go east, further into the mountains. That will take more time."

"I hope not," Anna said, glancing at Evelyn. "I don't think your feet will allow us to go too far off course."

"They're fine," Evelyn assured her. "That salve is wonderful. I'll leave the bandages on, and it will be all right."

Anna looked skeptical but was silent.

"What's wrong with your feet?" Peder asked.

"The shoes I wore weren't made for hiking in mountains," Evelyn said dryly. "My feet are covered in blisters. But the woman at the farm this morning was kind enough to give me these boots and some salve and bandages. I'll be fine."

Peder grimaced. "I'm sorry. I had no idea. And you've been carrying that heavy suitcase too. Here. Give it to me and I'll give you the small case back. It is lighter and smaller."

"No. You have your radio." She smiled at him. "Thank you, but really, I can manage."

"I think they're finished," Anna interrupted them. "The others are leaving."

Evelyn turned to look, watching as Erik shook hands with the other soldiers. Then they all nodded and waved to them before turning to fade into the trees, all except one. Philip turned and began walking back with Erik.

"Is he staying too?" Peder asked.

"I don't know," Anna said, moving out from behind her tree and back onto the trail.

"Philip has agreed to continue on as well," Erik told them. "It will be better with two of us. He is willing to put off joining the others until we get you safely to Namsos."

Evelyn looked at the young soldier and smiled. "Thank you."

He nodded. "You're welcome. It will be safer with two of us." He looked at the rifle draped across Evelyn's torso and smiled faintly.

"And, of course, three guns are better than two. Lieutenant Salvesen says you're quite a shot."

"She is. But come. We must move. Let's get ahead of those Germans now while we're in a position to do so. If we move quickly, we can cover another forty kilometers and reach Skatval." Erik glanced at Evelyn. "Anna told me about your feet. It's about an eight-hour trek. Will you be able to do it?"

She met his gaze steadily.

"What's the result if I can't?" she asked.

"You won't make Namsos by Sunday."

"Then I don't have a choice, do I?" She smiled wryly. "Let's get started."

Bialystok, Poland

Vladimir folded his paper neatly and reached for his coffee. He swallowed the last gulp, then got up from the table. The small restaurant was nearly empty, the only other occupant being an old man who looked as though he had spent his entire life in the fields. He sat hunched over his plate, his eyes down, and paid no attention to the people around him. Not that there were many this early in the day.

Tucking the paper under his arm, Vladimir turned towards the door and left the small café. It was looking bleak indeed for the Norwegians. The German troops had taken control of all the airfields in Norway on the first day of their offensive, allowing the Luftwaffe unlimited reign over the skies. They used the advantage in true Blitzkrieg fashion, attacking the people of Norway with abandon as they paved the way for their troops. There were reports of villages burning as the German forces swept, virtually unchecked, north. The King, Crown Prince, and all their ministers were in retreat, having escaped Oslo before the Germans landed, and were being ruthlessly pursued by the highly trained German paratroopers. What was left of the Norwegian army was in disarray, scattered and ill-equipped to face the elite forces of Hitler's Wehrmacht. They wouldn't be able to hold out very long, and if the King and the other royals were captured, there would be an end to Norway.

Vladimir turned to stride up the street. After Grigori had alerted him to Evelyn's presence in Oslo, he had made some very discreet inquiries of his own. The NKVD had two men in Oslo who kept them well informed, and one of them had confirmed the arrival of the British agent at the airport outside of Oslo on the second of April. Had she still been in the city when the Germans landed in the early hours Tuesday? More importantly, had she been able to get out of Norway before the bulk of the German troops arrived? Or before Eisenjager found her?

He hadn't forgotten about the German agent who, by all reports, had been set on her trail. If, by some chance, she was still in Norway, she would have to avoid, not only the advancing soldiers and the accompanying SS detachments, but also one of the deadliest men in Hitler's Third Reich. While he had absolutely no doubt that she *could* find a way to survive, what concerned Vladimir was that she would get the opportunity to do so. If Eisenjager knew she was in Norway, then so did the SD, and therein lay the problem. They had standing orders regarding the British agent, as Vladimir well knew. He had been informed of the orders by his own protégé firmly entrenched in Berlin. The young agent was up against formidable odds, made more so by the indubitable fact that she had no idea of the threat.

Striding up the street as the gray light of dawn gave way to early morning sun, Vladimir knew that he had a decision to make. He could continue as he had been, watching from afar and allowing MI6 to blunder their way through this war with embarrassing ineptitude, or he could step in and take Evelyn in hand himself. He had almost decided to do just that the day he left Moscow. The news in the paper today decided the issue for him; Norway wouldn't last much longer. If Evelyn was still in the country, something had to be done now, while there was still a chance to get her out.

He would contact his man in Oslo and put him on her trail. Without realizing it, Grigori had given him the perfect excuse for a revived interest in the British agent. Grigori pushing for the NKVD to get hold of her gave Vladimir a valid reason for keeping track of her himself. Not that he would need one. He had so many operations in play that his own superiors had long ago tired of keeping track of them all. If he thought something could be useful to them in the future, he laid the groundwork for it. The British agent would be considered just another of those contingency plans.

Glancing at his watch, he turned the corner and headed back to his hotel. He would contact Mikhail now and by nightfall, the Soviet agent would either tell him the British agent had made it out of Norway, or he would say he was on her trail. Either way, Vladimir would then have some idea of how to proceed.

Under no circumstance could she be allowed to fall into Eisenjager's hands.

Chapter Twenty-Six

Near Skatval, Norway

Evelyn nodded to Philip and ducked into the abandoned barn where they had taken shelter for the night. Erik and Philip had kept up a grueling pace throughout the afternoon and evening, stopping only once for half an hour to eat some of the food that Mrs. Hansen had sent with them. It wasn't until after ten o'clock that they had come across this farm. It was in good repair, but had obviously been abandoned for quite some time. After checking the old house and the smaller out-buildings, Erik had decided that they would take refuge in the barn. He built a fire to chase away the frigid temperatures and, after eating again, the others had fallen into an exhausted slumber.

When Evelyn had gone out a few moments earlier to answer to nature, Philip was posted outside for the first watch. He had nodded to her and warned her not to go far. It was a cold night and there were wolves in the area. She had done as he suggested, starting at every slight noise until she had hurried back to the barn. Wolves. Fantastic. Just one more thing to worry about.

Coming out of the harsh wind, she went to the fire, holding out her hands to the welcome warmth. If she wasn't such a stubborn woman, she reflected, she would be close to giving up. The road seemed to be getting longer and more difficult with each passing hour. Yet what other choice did she have? What other choice did they all have?

"It will snow before morning," Erik said in a low voice behind her.

She turned in surprise to watch him come out of the shadows near the door and move towards her.

"I thought you were asleep," she said.

"I should be, and so should you." He sat down near the fire and pulled out a cigarette case. "We still have a long way to go."

Evelyn sat next to him and accepted the offered cigarette.

"Will we make it by Sunday?" she asked.

231

"It's possible. If it weren't, I wouldn't be pushing us so hard." He lit her cigarette, then his own. "The snow will slow us down."

"I looked at the map with Anna earlier. It looks as if we're not even halfway there."

Erik glanced at her, his lips curving faintly. "We still have two days. Don't panic yet."

Evelyn was silent for a long moment, smoking her cigarette and staring into the flames.

"Who are you?" he asked after a long silence.

Evelyn looked at him to find dark eyes studying her in the firelight.

"What do you mean?"

"The Royal navy wouldn't arrange to evacuate a simple embassy clerk from a port miles away from Oslo," he said calmly. "They would wait until the entire embassy could be evacuated. Yet here we are, hiking across Norway to get you to a rendezvous with a British ship. Anna is determined that you not come within earshot of the Nazis, and Peder is risking much to contact London for you on a regular basis. So, I ask again. Who are you? Really?"

Evelyn swallowed. She supposed it had been inevitable that Erik would realize that she wasn't exactly who he had been led to believe. He was right. The embassy employees would be interned in the embassy until such a time as England could send transportation to evacuate them. The fact that she was risking a cross-country trek to meet a ship willing to take her now was telling.

"Does it matter who I am?" she asked, glancing at him. "Would knowing make any difference?"

He looked at her for a long moment.

"I suppose not, but it would appease my curiosity," he said. "You speak Norwegian very well, but I think you are English. I suppose you could be French, but I would be surprised if that were so."

"Why is that?"

"In general, I don't find that the French display the amount of courage that you've shown in the past two days."

Evelyn was torn between a feeling of insult on behalf of her French relations and amusement. She couldn't stop the wry smile that curved her lips.

"I've shown no more courage than everyone else," she replied. "We are all doing what we have to do right now, as best as we can manage."

Erik turned his gaze into the fire and they were quiet for a few moments.

232

Night Falls on Norway

"It hasn't escaped my attention that you've made a very close ally of Peder and his radio," he finally said in a low voice, "or that Kristian also appears to be firmly on your side. Anna said the two of you went down to visit him in Drammen. There's only one reason that I can think of that someone from the British embassy would want to make friends with wireless radio enthusiasts."

Evelyn was silent. It was obvious that Erik had worked out her real purpose for being in Norway, but she wasn't about to confirm or deny it.

"Anna has changed over the past months, and she's obviously become very fond of you," he continued. "I'll admit that when she told me she was going to work for the embassy, I tried to talk her out of it. I didn't understand her reasons for working for another government. Now I'm beginning to see why she chose to."

"I believe she was offered a very good salary," Evelyn murmured, drawing an amused look from him.

"No doubt, but Anna has never been interested in money," he said. "Tell me something. How did you convince her that the Germans were a very real threat? Because that is the only thing that would have driven my sister to work so closely with the British."

Evelyn glanced at him and sighed.

"I didn't," she told him. "She saw it for herself."

Erik nodded slowly and turned his gaze back to the fire.

"Then she's more perceptive than I," he murmured. "I didn't become convinced until they sailed into Trondheim."

Evelyn hesitated, then tossed her cigarette butt into the fire.

"There's no shame in that," she said. "Many men far higher up than you failed to see this invasion coming, regardless of the signs. Everyone hoped Hitler would stop with Poland. There is nothing wrong with hoping for peace."

"There is when it causes you to be blind to what is happening around you." Erik finished his cigarette and tossed it into the fire. "But now that we've learned that lesson painfully, it won't happen again. If we fail to win this battle, the Germans will have to contend with a very different type of Norwegian than they're expecting."

Evelyn looked at him sharply. "You're speaking of resistance?"

"If it becomes necessary." Erik looked grim. "I will do whatever I must to get my country back. So will many others. So will Anna, which is why I want you to convince her to go with you on Sunday."

"What?"

Erik looked at her, his face unreadable. "If Anna stays here, she will start down a road that she cannot possibly reach the end of. I'm afraid that she will begin something that will get her killed. If she goes with you, she can be spared all of this."

"She wants to fight."

"She can do that from the safety of another shore. There are ways for her to help us without being here."

Evelyn nodded slowly, acknowledging the truth of his words.

"That is true, but I don't think she thinks of it quite in the same way," she said slowly. "I've already asked her to come with me. Her answer was quite firmly no. She wants to stay and do what she can here."

"That is her immaturity talking," he said disgustedly. "She was always reckless, and this is just another example of it. She needs to leave and be safe, not throw herself into the front lines."

"You're not leaving," she pointed out. "What makes Anna different?"

"Anna is not trained for this."

"Then train her." Erik looked at her, surprised, and she shrugged. "If that's your only argument, it is easily remedied. Anna can be trained, just as I…"

Evelyn broke off suddenly, biting her lip.

"Just as you've been trained?" he asked softly. "I'm not surprised. You handled that rifle too well, despite the fact that you'd never seen a Krag–Jørgensen."

She was silent for a moment, then looked at him. "I'm more than willing to bring Anna with me, but I've already spoken to her once, and she declined. If you can convince her otherwise, I'll do what I can. But I think you must be prepared for the fact that she doesn't want to leave Norway."

"Then she will die."

"I wouldn't be too quick to predict that," Evelyn said after a moment. "She is surprisingly resourceful, and she knows the risks. She won't make foolish mistakes. I think you might be surprised."

"If I can convince her, you will take her with you?"

"Yes."

He nodded. "Then I will convince her."

Evelyn glanced at him. "Good luck with that."

They were quiet again for a long moment, then she turned her head to study his profile.

"Are you serious about forming some kind of organized resistance if Norway is lost to Hitler?" she asked quietly.

Night Falls on Norway

"The King has made it clear that we are to fight," he said. "I will do so until my last breath."

"If you do, you won't be alone," she said slowly. "I'm confident that we can offer aid and supplies to help."

Erik looked at her. "And how would you know that?"

She smiled slowly. "You'd be amazed what a lowly embassy worker can know."

He was surprised into a short laugh.

"If it comes to it, that would be welcome, and necessary," he said after a moment of thought. "All of our weapons and equipment have been seized by the Germans. All we have left is what we carried with us. Do you think you can get weapons to us?"

"It's possible."

"If that is so, then I will make sure that any and all information about the German troops and plans that we come across is forwarded on to your government."

"That's a fair enough trade," she said. "I would ask that, if Anna stays, you allow her to continue with what she's already begun."

Erik looked at her sharply. "What do you mean?"

"It's the only way I can guarantee the supplies you'll need," she said calmly.

He scowled. "I knew she was up to something," he muttered. "I should have realized that she'd already begun."

He was silent for a very long time, staring into the fire, and Evelyn waited. If he agreed, she knew Bill would get the supplies they would need. Whatever resistance Erik organized would be considered part of the network she had built, and therefore was guaranteed MI6 support. But he had to agree to allow Anna to continue what they started in Drammen, otherwise there was no point to any of it. Resistance was key, but so was the intelligence that they would be able to gather.

And Anna was the only one she trusted to do that.

"Very well," he finally said. "If she insists on remaining here, I'll ensure that she is properly trained and that she can continue what she's already started. But if she agrees to go with you, I will take her place here. Agreed?"

"Agreed."

London, England
April 12

Bill looked up when a short knock fell on his door, and it opened almost immediately. Wesley entered, carrying a stack of papers in his hand.

"Good morning, sir," he said cheerfully. "I have the morning's transmissions here, and Roger stopped me in the corridor. He was bringing a message from the radio room, so I told him I'd bring it to you. I know you've been waiting to hear from Jian."

Bill nodded, holding out his hand for the sheaf of papers. "Yes, I have. Thank you."

He dropped the rest of the papers and tore open the message from the radio room.

WE'RE MAKING GOOD TIME AND HAVE BEEN ABLE TO STAY AHEAD OF THE INVASION FORCES. SHOULD REACH STEINKJER BY NIGHTFALL. ON TARGET TO REACH DESTINATION ON TIME. WILL TRY TO MAKE CONTACT AT 10PM IN CASE OF FURTHER INSTRUCTIONS. - JIAN

"Good news, sir?"

"Well, it's not bad news," Bill replied, setting down the paper and rising from his chair. "Is the map of Norway still up there?"

"Yes." Wesley turned to the map taking up part of one wall of the office. "What are you looking for?"

"Somewhere called Steinkjer," Bill said, joining him. "It will be between Trondheim and Namsos."

Wesley nodded and studied the map for a moment. "Here it is, sir," he said finally, pointing to a spot on the map. "Looks like it's the only place to cross the water."

Bill stared at the map with a frown. "Yes."

"Is something the matter, sir?"

"What strikes you about that point on the map, Wesley?"

Wesley looked at the map for a moment. "Just that it's the only land-crossing for miles."

"Exactly." Bill turned away from the map. "And if the Germans have an ounce of sense, they'll make a beeline for it and secure it."

Wesley turned and watched as Bill went back to his desk.

"That's where Jian is going, isn't it?" he asked.

"Yes. She says they've been able to stay ahead of the Germans, but if the Huns manage to get to Steinkjer first, she'll be walking right into them." Bill dropped into his chair. "Get Bigsby on the line, will you? See what he can tell us about enemy movement, specifically in the region around Steinkjer."

"Yes, sir." Wesley turned towards the door. "I'll go try him now."

Bill watched him leave, then reached for the stack of morning transmissions on his desk. There was nothing he could do to help Evelyn physically in her flight across Norway, but he could warn her of any additional unforeseen complications. If the Germans were moving in that area, old Bigsby would know of it. His lips curved despite himself. Thank the good Lord that the old battle-axe had come over to work with them at the start of the war. He and Bill had known each other since before Bill had married Marguerite. If there was any possibility of Evelyn running head first into the Huns, Bigsby would tell him.

As he turned his attention to other matters, he was conscious of a feeling of relief. At least she was still able to get word out and, at least as of now, she was avoiding the advancing troops. For a novice agent who had found herself suddenly in enemy territory, Evelyn was doing exceptionally well.

Jian was going to make a damn good spy. They just had to get her out of Norway.

Trondheim, Norway

Eisenjager watched as another column of trucks carrying troops rumbled by. He had entered the city easily enough after showing his credentials at one of the many checkpoints set up around the perimeter. After filling the tank of his car, he had gone into a café filled with fellow Germans. He had ordered a coffee and open sandwich from a stone-faced man behind the counter, taking it with him back to his car. He would eat and then continue on his way.

There was no possibility that Jian had come through Trondheim. She would have seen that it was secured and impassable. She would have been forced to go around it. The question was whether or not she was still heading north, and how. He had seen the Volvo at the side of the road near Grindal. Either they had obtained another vehicle, or they were proceeding on foot. He sincerely hoped it was the former. A car he could track. If they were moving on foot, there was no way he would find them.

He finished his sandwich, still watching the rows of troops moving from the harbors out of the city. After a moment, he turned and reached for the case on the floor of the passenger's seat. He would contact Berlin and see if they had any information for him, then he would continue on his way. If the Englishwoman was in a car, they would have stopped for petrol somewhere around Trondheim. Perhaps he would get lucky.

He set up the radio and sent a signal, prepared to wait for an answer. When it came almost immediately, his eyebrows shot into his forehead and he reached for his codebook. They had been waiting for him. That meant they had news, and urgent news at that. He decoded the incoming message quickly, his brows drawn together in concentration, the trucks bearing troops out of the city forgotten for the moment.

INFORMATION RECEIVED AN EVACUATION WILL BE ATTEMPTED AT NAMSOS ON 14TH. LIKELY TARGET JIAN. USE ALL AVAILABLE MEANS TO PREVENT EVACUATION.

His lips tightened thoughtfully as he stared at the decoded message. She was still heading north, then. Reaching into the backseat, he grabbed the folded road map he'd been using and opened it up, spreading it out over the steering wheel.

After studying it for a moment, he located Namsos, a town on the coast of what looked like an inlet from the ocean. Eisenjager pursed his lips thoughtfully. It was quite some distance north, but well within range for her to reach by Sunday. But how? What route would she take?

He studied the map for a long time before he finally came to the conclusion that there was only one spot that she would be likely to pass, no matter which way she went. Waterways separated the land between the coast and this side of Norway all the way up. With the German navy controlling the Trondheim fjord, the next possible crossing was a town called Steinkjer. There was another possibility further north, near Snasa, but that would take much longer. If Jian had to be in Namsos on Sunday, Steinkjer was the most likely crossing point.

A cold smile crossed his lips. There were battalions of SS troops moving north on the other side of the Trondheim fjord. He would contact them. They were in a position to reach Steinkjer quickly and could set up a net. Once that happened, they were all but assured to catch Jian and her two companions. They just had to get there before she did.

Eisenjager reached for the radio again. He would tell Berlin he was closing in, and then he would contact the commander of the SS troops. With any luck, he would have Jian by nightfall.

Chapter Twenty-Seven

Evelyn crept forward with Anna when Erik waved for them to move through the trees and join him and Peder. They were crouched on the edge of a ridge, and Philip had gone ahead after seeing whatever was below, silently disappearing into the trees. Whatever they were staring at couldn't be good.

As Erik had predicted, snow had fallen through the night and morning, covering the mountains with a soft, cold blanket on top of the already existing hardened snow. Winter was still alive and well in the mountains, and while it was cold and made progress slower, it also deadened the sound of their movement, allowing them to pass through the forests almost silently. Philip had taken the rear, erasing signs of their progress with a long fir branch as they went, ensuring that no tracks could be traced to them. At least, not by an ordinary observer.

Evelyn and Anna crept forward noiselessly and joined Erik and Peder by the tree line at the edge of the mountain ridge. Far below them, a road wound its way through the mountain pass. The fresh snowfall hadn't made the road impassable, indicating that it had been cleared recently, but the massive tree laying across it would prevent any vehicles from proceeding.

"What is it?" she whispered to Erik.

"Someone has blocked the road," he told her in a low voice. "Philip has gone down the mountain to see if he can find out what's going on."

"Why do you think someone did that?" Anna asked after a moment. "Couldn't the tree have simply fallen across the road?"

Erik pointed to the base of the trunk and passed her his binoculars. "Take a look."

Anna took them, looking down at the fallen tree. After a moment, she sucked in her breath and wordlessly passed the binoculars to Evelyn. Evelyn gazed through them at the tree and her lips tightened. The trunk had been cut cleanly.

"Who would do that?" she asked, passing the binoculars back.

Night Falls on Norway

"It could be the Germans wanting to prevent anyone from getting in or out," Erik said with a shrug. "Or it could be my countrymen trying to keep the Germans from passing. Either way, it tells me that someone expects troops to come through here."

Evelyn looked back at the road far below them. There was ample space between them and the blocked pavement, but even so, she felt a shiver go down her spine. She frowned at the feeling, knowing that it didn't bode well. That particular feeling never did.

"Will Philip be all right on his own?" Peder asked after a long, silent moment. "Shouldn't he have stayed with us? If it was the Germans who put the tree there then it's dangerous for him to be down there."

"No more dangerous than it is for us up here," Erik told him with a faint smile. "Philip knows how to be silent and invisible. He's one of the best at it."

"Perhaps we should keep moving," Anna said after a moment. "If it is the Germans, the longer we stay in one spot, the more chance we have of them realizing we're here."

"As soon as Philip returns, we'll continue. We can't move without knowing who blocked the road. If it was the Germans, we will have to alter our route." Erik glanced at Evelyn. "And if we have to do that, it will put us behind even more."

She nodded to acknowledge the warning. If they were put very much further behind, she wouldn't make Namsos in time. And at that point, she would have no choice but to try for the Swedish border.

Before Anna could reply, something caught Evelyn's attention and she turned her head sharply, staring down at the road below. Erik reached out and quickly took the binoculars from her, raising them to his eyes as shadows emerged from the distance. Vehicles were approaching the road block.

"Buses. It looks like German troops," he said after a moment, lowering the binoculars and glancing up at the overcast sky. "There's no sun, so they won't see any reflections from anyone in the trees."

"At least we know who blocked the road," Peder said. "The Germans wouldn't block it if they had troops coming through. It must have been our people."

"Let's hope so." Erik pulled back away from the edge of the ridge and motioned for them to do the same. "Pull back into the trees. I'm sure we're too high up to be seen, but it's best to be safe."

Evelyn slipped behind a tree and watched as the black shadows moved along the road towards the fallen tree. As they progressed, she was slowly able to make out the long, narrow outline of three buses.

241

There were no other vehicles with them, no tanks or motorcycles. Just the buses. She began to frown, then that same chill went down her spine and she stiffened.

"Where does that road lead?" she asked suddenly, looking over at Erik. "Where are they going?"

He met her gaze and a light of appreciation leapt into his eyes.

"You are much quicker than I expected," he murmured. "That pass leads eventually to Steinkjer. It is the only road along this mountain ridge that goes there."

Evelyn turned her eyes back to the buses far below them. It was as she thought, then. The Germans were catching up, and would soon be ahead of them. Their journey had just become even more dangerous. If those buses were heading for Steinkjer, then others were as well. There was no way they would reach the town before the Germans.

"If they take over Steinkjer, they will control the route to the coast," Anna breathed. "We'll never make it to Namsos."

Erik glanced at her. "Never say never. There's always a way. And we don't know that they've taken it yet."

"Look!" Peder interrupted, nodding to the road below. "They're stopping."

Erik raised the binoculars, training them on the vehicles slowing to a stop in the distance. Despite the distance, Evelyn could see enough to know when the buses had come to a complete stop.

"They're getting out," Erik said a moment later. "Two officers just got out of the lead bus, and another one is coming out of the second. They'll go to examine the blockage and see what they need to do to remove it."

"Can they do that, do you think?" Anna asked.

"It depends on what they have on the buses with them," he said, lowering the binoculars. "If they have some axes, possibly. It will take hours, though. More than likely, they'll call for a tank if there is one close enough. Otherwise, they will look for another route."

More dark specks emerged from the buses and moved towards the tree laying across the road. Even though they were far below them, Evelyn felt a strange kind of terror at the sight of the enemy soldiers. They would find a way past the obstacle, and then they would continue to Steinkjer and beyond. There would be no stopping them.

Just as the thought entered her mind, the hushed silence of the mountains was suddenly shattered by a staccato of cracks, almost like...

"Gunfire!" Anna cried, staring down the mountainside.

Erik had the binoculars up to his eyes again, but Evelyn didn't need them to see the chaos unfolding below. Tracers of bullets were arcing out of the trees, onto the road and the hapless buses. The sound of machine gun and rifle fire, delayed by distance, seemed disjointed and almost theatrical as it echoed up the cliffs to reach them, at odds with the scene below them.

More troops were pouring out of the buses now, firing back into the trees as a virtual hail of bullets rained down upon them from the surrounding hills. As the sounds of the battle reached the party high up on the ridge, they saw the dark shadows around the buses begin falling to the ground.

Evelyn watched in shock as the lead bus suddenly went up in flames a few seconds before the sound of the explosion reached them. The front of the bus lifted up into the air briefly before the whole vehicle rolled over, engulfed in flames. And still the gunfire continued from the mountains as the German soldiers tried to take shelter behind the other two buses.

"Oh my God," Anna breathed beside her, her eyes wide in a pale face and her voice sounding almost strangled.

Evelyn watched, her throat closing in horror, as more and more shadows became motionless against the white snow. She struggled to breathe while still unable to tear her eyes away from the grisly sight. Just as she was sure there would be no end, she saw something flutter above the second bus. Someone had raised a white flag, signaling defeat. Another one appeared near the last bus and she began to breathe a sigh of relief. It was over.

Except it wasn't over. She and Anna stared, horrified, as the gunfire continued from the trees.

Evelyn felt the blood drain out of her face and her heart pounded against her chest as she tried to understand what she was witnessing. The soldiers trapped between the buses were surrendering! Why didn't the shooters stop firing? They were supposed to cease fire at the sight of the international symbol for surrender.

But the gunfire continued and, one by one, more and more shadows became motionless in the road until, eventually, there was no more return fire. The white flags had disappeared into the snow, released as the ones waving them fell to join their comrades.

The unholy silence that descended upon the mountains once again was deafening as the last rifle fell silent from the trees. Staring down into the mountain pass, Evelyn felt a surge of nausea roll through her. There was no movement around the buses now, and the flames of the burning shell in the front were licking towards the tree blocking the road. Seeing the motionless bodies lying in the snow, and listening to the awful silence, she took a deep, ragged breath.

"I…don't understand," Anna whispered brokenly. "There was a flag. They were surrendering. Why didn't they stop?"

Evelyn had no answer, turning to look at Erik. His face was pale and his lips were pinched together grimly, but he offered no words of explanation. He looked at them and opened his mouth to say something, but then closed it again without saying a word.

"Lieutenant Salvesen!" Philip emerged from the trees breathlessly. "It's our own troops!"

Erik turned to him quickly. "What?!"

He nodded, trying to catch his breath. "Yes. I saw several I recognized, but they've been joined by many I don't know. They aren't wearing uniforms."

Erik scowled. "New recruits?"

"More than likely."

"How many?"

"There had to be at least fifty on this side alone."

"Did they see you?"

Philip shook his head. "No."

"Good. We can't take the time to explain what we're doing." Erik turned to look at the others. "We need to keep moving. We must try to make it to Steinkjer before the Germans take it. After this, they will come looking for a fight."

Anna made a choking sound and his face softened slightly. He reached out and put his hands on her shoulders.

"Look at me," he commanded. When she lifted her face to his, he brushed tears off her cheeks. "You should never have seen that. I'm sorry that you did."

"Why did they keep shooting?" she demanded. "They massacred those men."

He nodded slowly. "Yes."

"But why?"

"Because if they hadn't, those same men would have massacred us," he said softly. "Perhaps not today, or tomorrow, but eventually. I don't say that I agree with the order to continue firing, or that it's an order I would have made, but I understand it."

Evelyn swallowed her nausea and turned to make her way back to the path, forcing herself to focus on moving instead of the horror she had just witnessed.

"I will never understand it," Anna said, shaking her head and pulling away from him. She turned to follow Evelyn back to the trail. "If a man surrenders, you take him prisoner. You don't kill him. They're no better than the Germans!"

Night Falls on Norway

Erik made no reply but turned to follow the others back to the trail. He looked at Peder.

"Are you all right?" he asked.

Peder nodded grimly. "Let's just get moving," he said shortly.

Erik nodded and turned to lead the way, his eyes meeting Evelyn's briefly. In that brief second, she saw her own horror reflected in his dark eyes. He may understand the reasoning behind what had just occurred, but he was just as disturbed by it as they were.

Somehow that eased her own shock and grief and she turned silently to follow him. This war was just that: a war. And she had just witnessed the senseless slaughter that accompanied war. It was the first time she had ever seen someone die, let alone a large group of someones. They were brothers, fathers, sons and husbands. It didn't seem to matter that they were the enemy. It was just horrible.

As she trudged through the snow next to a silent and visibly upset Anna, Evelyn knew that she would never forget what she'd just seen. She also knew that it was just the beginning and she would undoubtedly see more men, and women, killed before this war came to an end.

She just hoped and prayed she had the strength to make it through it all.

London, England

Bill looked up when a shadow fell over the table. He was sitting towards the back of the Savoy Grill, enjoying a solitary lunch. The only person who knew where he'd gone was Wesley, but it wasn't Wesley standing next to his table.

"Jasper!" he exclaimed, setting down his knife and fork. "What are you doing here?"

"I hope you don't mind but Wesley told me where to find you," he said. "May I join you?"

"Of course."

Bill watched as he pulled out the chair across from him and sat down. Jasper's bushy eyebrows were drawn together in such a way that he instinctively knew that this unexpected lunch date was not a purely social one. Suppressing a sigh, he sat back and considered his boss, resigned.

"What's happened now?" he asked.

A wry smile passed over Jasper's face. "Is it that obvious?"

"You prefer to eat alone as much as I. If you've searched me out, there must be a reason, and given the current climate, I can't imagine that it's a very good one."

"Quite right." Jasper looked up as a waiter approached and glanced at Bill's lunch of poached fish. "How is the fish today?"

"Very good."

"I'll have the same," he told the waiter, "and a whiskey and soda."

The waiter nodded, moving away, and he turned his attention to Bill.

"I'm glad to see you out of the office for lunch," he said. "I know I'm not one to cast stones in this regard, but it really is necessary to get out of that building once in a while."

"Good for the soul?" Bill asked, his lips twisting as he reached for his knife and fork again.

"Something like that, yes."

"I suppose it does me good to clear my head a bit," he admitted, cutting into his fish. "Of course, now you're here to clutter it up again, I'm sure. Do you plan on telling me what brought you, or shall I guess?"

"GC&CS decoded another message," Jasper told him.

Bill looked up sharply. "Henry?"

Jasper nodded but remained silent as the waiter approached the table again, bearing his whiskey and soda. Bill watched as the man set the drink down in front of Jasper before turning to leave again.

"They know about Namsos," he said, once the waiter was out of earshot. "At least, they know there will be an evacuation attempt, and they believe Jian is the intended target."

Bill stared at him, his lunch forgotten.

"How the bloody hell did they find out?" he demanded in a low, fierce voice, his brows snapping together. "You said the entire operation was classified!"

"It is." Jasper reached for his drink, his face grim. "Not only was it imperative that no one know about the extraction of your agent, but no one is supposed to know about the landing that will take place at the same time. If the Germans realize that troops will be landing, it will be like shooting rats in a barrel for the Luftwaffe."

Bill set down his utensils again and reached for his own drink. "Do you think that's a possibility?"

"I just don't know. It sounds as if they don't know how the extraction will take place. If that's the case, then they still have no idea that ships are coming into the harbor."

"What did the message say? Exactly?"

"That the information received was being acted upon. They have someone pursuing Jian and arrangements have been made to stop her before she reaches Namsos for the evacuation."

Bill was silent for a long moment, his lip pressed together in a thin, unpleasant line.

"What makes you think they don't know how the extraction will take place?"

"Because they're trying to stop her before she reaches Namsos. If they knew ships were coming in, they would be planning an all-out attack, and they wouldn't be worried about stopping her before she got there. They know the Luftwaffe can decimate the entire town, and they would also get her in the process."

"I still don't follow how that indicates they're unsure of the method of extraction."

"They know their Luftwaffe controls the airspace, so sending an airplane to fetch her is out. They know that. That only leaves something like a fishing boat to carry her out to a waiting ship, or a ship itself. But if the Germans thought for one second that ships were going to sail into Namsos, they would be planning an aerial bombardment. The message makes no mention of that."

Bill thought for a moment, then shook his head.

"Would it, though?" he asked. "I agree that if they suspected what was really planned, they would be making defensive plans, but would they tell Henry? There's no reason for him to know. As far as he's concerned, the only thing that is relative is Jian."

"Well, that's why I'm concerned," Jasper admitted. "It's too late to call the operation off. Even if I thought the cabinet would listen to me, there isn't enough evidence to warrant pulling the troops back or moving them to a different landing point. If they are planning to attack, there's nothing we can do to protect the ships, the troops or your agent."

Bill exhaled and pinched the bridge of his nose.

"They know we've been mining the waters," he said after a long moment. "What would be the most logical way to get an agent out of Norway at the moment?"

Jasper raised an eyebrow. "What are you thinking?"

"I'm thinking what I would be thinking if I were in their position. They know we had mining ships off the coast as recently as three days ago. They know we have destroyers in the area because we sunk three of their ships in the port at Narvik."

"Yes. So?"

"So I would assume that a fishing boat or trawler was going to carry the agent out to a ship waiting offshore," Bill said with a shrug. "It's virtually impossible to locate a fishing boat in the dark without knowing where or when to look."

"And if that's what they believe the likely scenario will be, then they would try to prevent her from reaching Namsos and risk losing her before they can apprehend her," Jasper said slowly, nodding. "So you agree with me, that they're unaware of what's coming."

"I think so," Bill said after a moment. "There's no reason for them to believe we're sending ships into Namsos. If anything, they will be looking for us to try to land at Trondheim. That's the larger target."

Jasper grunted. "Which is precisely why we're landing at Namsos. The plan is to take Namsos, then move south and take Trondheim back."

They fell silent as the waiter returned with Jasper's lunch. As soon as he had withdrawn again, Jasper picked up his knife and fork, preparing to cut into his fish.

"Have you heard from Jian?"

"This morning." Bill pushed his plate away, his appetite gone, and reached for his drink. "She expects to make Steinkjer by nightfall. But knowing that the Germans are aware of her presence, as well as where she is going, makes me very uneasy."

Jasper glanced up. "Why is that? I mean, aside from the obvious?"

Bill sipped his drink and leaned forward.

"Steinkjer is the only real point to cross the water and move towards Namsos for miles. Every crossing before it is controlled by the Germans in Trondheim fjord," he said in a low voice. "If they know she's heading for Namsos, they know she'll have to go through Steinkjer."

"And they'll be waiting."

"Yes."

"Can you warn her?"

"She will try to make contact tonight, but it may be too late."

Jasper looked at him for a moment, then lowered his gaze back to this lunch.

"You said she's with a Norwegian soldier, correct?" he asked.

"Yes."

"Then you must trust that he will be able to move them through the lines without detection. Regardless of what happens, there is nothing more that can be done. Warn her when she makes contact, but whatever happens after that is out of your hands."

"It doesn't make it any easier."

Jasper smiled faintly. "I know. It would be better if she wasn't Ainsworth's girl, wouldn't it? We all feel some kind of responsibility towards her. It's complete rubbish, you know. She knew the risks when she agreed to come onboard."

"As you say, though, she's Robert's daughter."

Jasper nodded. "Yes."

They were silent for a long time as Jasper ate his lunch and Bill nursed his drink. Finally, Jasper raised his head from his food.

"The pressing question, of course, is who is Henry?" he said. "And how the hell did he find out about Namsos?"

Chapter Twenty-Eight

Toulouse, France

Miles climbed out of the cockpit and jumped down off the wing. He looked over to where Rob was shutting down his engine, then raised a hand to shield his eyes from the sun as he watched Mother and Slippy come in to land.

"Morning, sir," a young sergeant saluted as he came over ahead of the refueling tank. "Good flight over?"

"Yes, thanks." Miles nodded and turned to watch the refueling tank pull up to his Spitfire. "Glorious weather today."

"Yes sir."

He turned and began walking towards Rob's Spit as the other two came in to land behind them.

"Ashmore is heading over to talk to the Intel Officer," he called as Rob climbed out of the cockpit. "Not much to do until they've refueled us and we get the all clear."

"It's France!" Rob retorted, jumping down. "There's always something to do."

He looked over and watched as Mother and Slippy coasted down the landing strip, staggered from each other.

"That's the last of us," he said. "Where are the others?"

"Already went into the officer's mess, more than likely," Miles turned to walk with Rob towards the buildings not far in the distance. "They were all headed that way when I came in to land."

Rob pulled his cigarette case out of his breast pocket.

"I hope they get us refueled and on our way quickly. I want to get over there and get back. I don't trust the Jerries as far as I can throw them."

"We'll be all right. It won't take them long to get us going again. We'll just have time for a quick cup of tea, I expect."

"Lacey! Ainsworth!" Chris called from the doorway of the building ahead. "Get a move on!"

Night Falls on Norway

"What's got the Yank so riled?" Rob wondered. "They really are excitable, aren't they?"

"Who? The Americans?"

"Yes. Chris is always on about something."

"I expect it's got something to do with their breeding. A lot of Italians over there."

"Can you guys walk any slower?" Chris demanded in exasperation as they drew closer.

"Where's the fire, old boy?" Miles drawled, raising his eyebrows.

"No fire, and no reconnaissance flight, either," Chris replied, turning to go back into the building. "Come and find out for yourself. We've been grounded."

"Grounded?!" Rob exclaimed, tossing his half-smoked cigarette away and following Chris into the large, square building. "We've only just arrived!"

"Tell me about it!"

Miles frowned and followed them across a short hallway and through another door that led into the officer's mess where the rest of the squadron was gathered. They looked up when Miles and Rob entered, and Ashmore, their CO, set down his cup of tea and moved towards them.

"Has Chris told you the news?" he asked.

"That we're grounded?" Miles asked. "Yes. Why? What's happened?"

"There's cloud cover over the targets in Germany. We've been told to wait it out for a couple of hours to see if it clears."

"A couple of hours!" Rob scowled. "What are we supposed to do for a couple of hours?"

"Precisely." Ashmore shrugged. "Nothing we can do about it, though. Jenkins, the CO here, says there's a rather good watering hole down the road that serves a tolerable lunch. Or we can stay here, of course. If anyone decides to try the local attraction, he's offered one of the cars for transportation."

Ashmore wandered away on that statement and Rob looked at Miles.

"Well how do you like that?" he demanded. "Bloody RAF can't even get its weather reports straight. Before we left, they said clear skies over the target!"

"I don't suppose they can control the weather," Miles murmured, turning towards the table at the back where huge steel canteens filled with hot tea were set up. "As Ashmore said, there's nothing we can do about it. No point in getting all upset."

"You're not even a little bit annoyed?" Rob asked. "To have come this far and not be able to continue?"

"No one said we wouldn't continue, only that we had to wait a few hours," he pointed out, reaching for a cup and saucer.

"If we have to postpone it, we'll be right back here again tomorrow," Rob muttered, picking up a cup for himself. "What a nuisance. I would rather be flying endless patrols."

"Really?" Miles glanced at him. "I'm getting rather tired of staring at the North Sea. At least we got a change of pace today."

"We did, and now we're back to sitting around with nothing to do. I thought all the waiting was over."

"Not to beat a dead horse, but there's no way to control the weather, old boy."

Miles poured tea into his cup and sipped it. A grimace crossed his face and he looked down into the cup before setting it down. Rob raised an eyebrow.

"That bad?" he asked, laughing at the answering look Miles gave him. He put his empty cup back. "I'll pass, then."

"Wise choice." Miles turned away and sighed, looking around the room. Most of the seats were taken and Ashmore was deep in conversation with a tall man whom Miles assumed was Jenkins. "What in blazes are we going to do for a couple hours here?"

"Maybe some of the others will want to go to that café Ashmore told us about," Rob suggested after a moment. "At least we'll get a decent cup of coffee there."

"Do you think so?"

Rob grinned. "I'm half French, remember? If there's one thing the French do well, it's coffee."

"That sounds like a plan, then," Miles decided. "I'll go round up the Yank and some of the others. You go find Mother and Slippy. Between us, we really should be able to find some way to make this layover bearable."

"God I hope so. Maybe there'll be some lovely little local ladies hanging around, looking for some laughs. Otherwise we'll all die of boredom."

"If there are, you can all have at it."

Rob made a face. "Good Lord, you're becoming a real old stick in the mud, you know that?" he demanded, poking him in the chest for emphasis. "If I'd thought for one second that this is what would happen to you, I would never have introduced you to m' sister."

"You didn't. She introduced herself," he retorted with a grin.

"It'd serve you right if she was in Northolt hob-nobbing with that pilot fellow you went to school with. What's his name? Dutton?"

"Durton. And I very much doubt that she is. She's on a training course."

"Which means she's just as bored as we are!" Rob turned to go towards the door in search of Mother and Slippy. "Lord help us all if this war doesn't get going soon!"

Outside Steinkjer, Norway

Evelyn shivered and tried in vain to burrow deeper into her coat. The combination of snow and frigid wind was taking its toll on her and her fingers were numb inside her fur-lined gloves. Darkness had fallen hours ago and Erik had finally agreed to stop long enough to allow Peder to try to get through to London.

"Anything?" she asked, looking over Peder's shoulder. He had cleared off a hollowed out tree trunk and was sitting astride it with his radio case open in front of him.

"No."

Evelyn bit her lip and tried to see her watch in the moonlight. She could barely make out the little illuminated hands, but she thought it was just after eleven.

"Could it be because we're late?" Peder asked, looking over his shoulder. "We told them ten."

"Keep trying," she told him.

He nodded and turned his attention back to the radio. After watching for a second, she went over to where Anna was sitting on her suitcase and using a tree as a back rest.

"Anything yet?" Anna asked as she joined her.

She shook her head and dropped down onto her own suitcase. "Not yet." She looked around. "Where's Erik?"

"He went to scout around ahead." Anna leaned her head back against the tree trunk. "He doesn't trust Steinkjer to be clear of German troops. He and Philip are both trying to determine the best route to take to minimize the risk of running into them."

"I'm so sorry you're in the middle of this," Evelyn said in a low voice after a minute. "I've said it before, but it bears repeating. If you want to part company, I completely understand and will go the rest of the way alone."

"Don't be ridiculous," Anna said crossly. "We're not leaving you."

"It's getting too dangerous."

"Which is exactly why we won't leave you. Now stop suggesting it. You're stuck with us." Anna threw her a tired smile. "Besides, where would I go? We're going to Peder's uncle after Namsos, so we have to keep moving in this direction anyway."

Evelyn nodded and tried to adjust the woolen scarf more securely around her neck to block out the cold wind.

"I don't think I'll ever get warm," she said after a long moment. "And it doesn't seem like we'll be able to find anywhere to take shelter."

"Erik thinks that we'll find somewhere outside Steinkjer. He just wants to get past it first." Anna stifled a yawn. "I'll tell you this, though, I'm more worried about finding somewhere to get food. We've only got a few pieces of bread left and no cheese."

Before Evelyn could respond, Philip emerged from the trees nearby and glanced at them. He looked around, then came over to them.

"Your brother's not back yet?"

"Not yet. Why? Did you see something?"

He shook his head, a frown on his face. "No. Everything seemed clear, but I feel like something is wrong."

Evelyn looked up sharply. "Wrong how?"

"I don't know. I can't explain it." He looked at the rifle hanging across her body, nodding to it. "Get that loaded and ready. It's better to be prepared."

"It already is," she assured him. "If needed, I'm ready."

He nodded and seemed a little comforted by that. Brushing snow off a log nearby, he dropped down onto it and looked towards Peder a few feet away.

"Is he still trying to get through to London?" he asked.

Evelyn nodded. There had been no way to prevent Philip from finding out who Peder was trying to contact, not once he and Erik were the only two left. Erik had assured her of the other man's discretion, and she had no other choice but to trust him, but she still wasn't happy about it.

"How long has he been trying?"

"About twenty minutes."

Philip frowned. "I hope the Germans aren't nearby. If they are, and they realize a wireless signal is going out close by…"

Anna frowned and looked over to Peder. "Is that possible?"

Night Falls on Norway

"It is if they know to look for one," he said without lifting his head from the radio. "Otherwise, they need special equipment to scan for it, and then they have to be within a certain range. I wouldn't worry too much."

"I hope you're right," Philip said.

"If we can't get through soon, we'll stop," Evelyn said after a moment. "If it wasn't important, I wouldn't continue to try."

"I know." Philip sighed and rubbed his face, then pushed himself to his feet. "I'll go see what's keeping Erik."

He was just turning away when Erik came through the trees on the other side of Peder.

"I'm here," he said. "How are things behind us?"

"They're fine, but I don't have a good feeling," Philip replied. "What about ahead?"

Erik looked grim. "It's the same."

Anna looked from one to the other.

"What does that mean?" she asked when neither of them seemed inclined to elaborate. "Either you saw evidence of German troops in the area or you didn't."

"I didn't, but something isn't right," Erik said, stepping over the hollowed out tree trunk where Peder was seated. "I can't explain it. We need to be on our guard and as quiet as possible."

"Do we continue on this course?" Philip asked.

He nodded.

"Yes. I don't know that changing course now would do anything other than slow us down. And time isn't on our side." He looked at Peder. "How long have you been trying to get through now?"

"Almost half an hour."

Erik's frown grew and he went over to stand next to Evelyn.

"That's too long. If there are enemy troops in the area, they could intercept the signal and realize we're here," he said, looking down at her.

"Peder doesn't think that's likely," Anna told him. "He said that they would have to know to look for the signal."

Erik never took his eyes off Evelyn's face, staring at her steadily.

"Is there any possibility that they could know to listen for a wireless signal?" he asked, his eyes boring into hers.

Evelyn swallowed. Of course there was a possibility. She knew it and Anna knew it. But was it likely? She was about to open her mouth to say no when she suddenly remembered Oslo last November.

255

It wasn't likely then for anyone to know of her whereabouts, yet both the SD and the NKVD had.

"Perhaps," she said reluctantly.

He nodded, seeming to be satisfied that she had admitted to it.

"Peder, shut it down," he said, turning away. "You can try again later when we're past Steinkjer."

"Just another minute," he protested. "Just give me another minute."

"Every minute you're on that thing is another minute that the Germans can intercept it! Do you *want* to be a guest of the Huns?"

"No, but—" Peder stopped abruptly, grabbing his headset and pressing it against his ears. "I've got something!"

Erik turned impatiently, his lips pressed together tightly. He watched as Peder grabbed a pad and pencil and began writing furiously while he listened. Turning his head, he looked at Philip and made a movement with his hand, motioning for him to fall back and prepare to move. Philip nodded and tightened his hands on his rifle, turning to move back into the trees behind them.

Evelyn stood up and picked up her case. Some of Erik's uneasiness was transferring itself to her and she moved forward to stand next to Peder, looking over his shoulder and willing him to go faster. Her heart began to beat a little faster as his pencil moved over the paper steadily. Once he had the message, he could shut the radio down and they would move. It would be all right. It had been so far.

She felt Anna come up behind her, and Erik moved to stand in front of Peder, his attention directed to the trees in front of them. As soon as Peder was finished, he was ready to move. And, suddenly, Evelyn was just as anxious to get moving.

"Here!" Peder tore off the paper and passed it to her. "It's done."

He quickly unplugged the radio from the strange, oblong box that he used as a power source, and began putting everything back into the case. While he was closing it up, Anna shone her torch onto the paper, allowing Evelyn to read the message quickly. Her blood ran cold when she decoded the words.

ENEMY MAY KNOW OF YOUR PRESENCE AND DESTINATION. PROCEED WITH EXTREME CAUTION. MAKE CONTACT IN 10 HOURS.

"What is it?" Anna asked, seeing the look on her face.

"We have to move," Evelyn said urgently. "Do you have your lighter handy?"

Night Falls on Norway

"Yes. It's right here." Anna switched off the torch and pulled a lighter out of her coat pocket.

Evelyn took it and flipped it open. It took a few tries with her numb fingers before she managed to get it lit, but then she held the flame to the paper in her hand, burning the message as she had all the others.

"What do you mean we have to move?" Erik demanded, coming back to them.

"Just that. We need to move. Quickly."

Erik stared hard at her then nodded once, turning towards the trees. He had only taken two steps when he froze and held up his hand, motioning for silence. Evelyn felt a streak of awareness shoot down her spine and she caught her breath.

The wind whistled through the trees, carrying the faint sound of voices. Her heart pounding, she froze and listened, her lips parting on a silent gasp. Erik turned his head sharply and his dark eyes met hers as she suddenly made out the words on the wind.

"Schnell! Das signal kam aus dieser richtung!"

Chapter Twenty-Nine

"That was German!" Anna hissed as Erik inserted his fingers in his mouth and let out a low, owl-like whistle. Evelyn nodded and grabbed her rifle, pulling the strap over her head and hooking it over her shoulder with one smooth motion. Anna wordlessly grabbed Evelyn's suitcase, freeing both hands for the rifle. Evelyn nodded her thanks and turned as Philip silently emerged from the trees in response to Erik's whistle.

Erik motioned with his hands and then pointed up, indicating that they would have to ascend higher to avoid the enemy. Philip nodded and turned to cover their rear flank as Erik led the small group through the trees and up the incline. Anna went up in front of Evelyn while Peder remained behind her, ready to brace her if she slipped going up the snow-covered hill.

Evelyn's breath came fast and shallow as she gripped the rifle tightly, listening for the sound of pursuit. There was none. They hadn't been heard or detected yet. But the voices were still floating on the wind and she found it strangely calming to focus on the German. They were arguing, she realized after a moment. While one was reiterating that the radio signal had come from this direction, the others were complaining that all that was out here was snow. Listening to them bicker, a strange sort of calm descended over her and Evelyn realized that the trembling in her limbs had stopped. It was almost as if she was moving and living in another person's body, observing from the outside as the group moved rapidly into the hills above.

They reached the next ridge and she realized that the voices had faded into the distance. Scrambling over a fallen tree, she landed on a flat path and looked behind her. Peder was just going over the tree with Philip behind him, sweeping away their tracks from the snow, when she heard it: the sound of multiple boots crunching through snow. Turning her head swiftly, through the trees she saw blinking flashlights in the darkness. They had escaped one threat only to run in front of another!

Night Falls on Norway

Her heart surged into her throat as she listened to the marching footsteps coming from the right. Erik grabbed Anna's hand and shoved her into the trees on the other side of the trail, motioning for Evelyn to follow. Then he turned and waved Philip and Peder back. Philip nodded and grabbed Peder's arm, pulling him down and out of sight behind the fallen tree. As soon as he was hidden, Philip hurriedly swept away the tracks in the snow by the trail before diving down next to him, disappearing from view.

Evelyn's heart pounded painfully against her chest as she crouched behind a mound of underbrush, watching as Erik cleared their tracks as best as he could while the sound of the marching enemy drew closer. They could hear them clearly now, the sound of their voices carrying down the trail. She couldn't see Anna, who had taken cover behind a spruce tree that looked as if it had been struck by lightning at some point. While the bottom trunk was still thriving, the top had split and fallen sideways, there to remain until time and nature reclaimed it. At the present, though, it offered the perfect protection for Anna.

Erik finished on the trail and silently moved past Evelyn, disappearing into the trees behind her. A moment later, she couldn't see him either.

No sooner had he melded into the darkness than the German voices became louder and a short burst of laughter rang out on the trail. A group of four soldiers dressed in gray Wehrmacht uniforms came into sight, walking in pairs, and Evelyn shrank down even lower behind the brush. Her throat constricted, and she held her breath, listening as they tramped towards them.

They had stopped talking for the moment. Instead, she heard the sound of their heavy breathing as they moved quickly along the ridge, their steps in time with each other. One of them coughed suddenly and she started, biting her bottom lip to keep from gasping. They were very close to her now, passing just on the other side of the copse she huddled behind. Her blood pounded in her ears, and all she could hear was the sound of her heart thumping until she was afraid they would also hear it.

"This is a waste of time," a voice said directly next to her. "We haven't seen anything in these mountains."

"Hauptsturmführer Beck wants to be sure," another replied. "He's been informed that a high value target will be moving through Steinkjer tonight or tomorrow."

At the mention of the superior's rank, icy fear, sharp and swift, sliced through Evelyn and her throat constricted. Holding her breath and knowing that she should remain perfectly still, she nonetheless turned her head to try to peer through the underbrush at the trail that passed a few feet from her hiding place. The four soldiers were just passing the brush, and she could smell the leather of their boots and stale cigarette smoke on their long coats.

At the sight of the dark gray coats, she raised her eyes, searching for the lapel insignia. She already knew what she would find, but she had to be sure. Even prepared for it, the sight of the sinister silver SS sent another shaft of terror through her, and Evelyn lowered her eyes quickly.

"A high value target?" The first soldier scoffed. "Unless it's the Norwegian king, no target is worth this cold."

"Shall I tell Hauptsturmführer Beck your thoughts? I'm sure he will be interested to hear what you have to say."

That appeared to silence the disgruntled soldier, and the group fell silent again, continuing along the trail. Evelyn's chest burned as she tried not to breathe, terrified that she would end up sneezing or making some noise to give away their position. Her hands tightened on her rifle and she clung to the comfort of the cold steel. At least she wasn't completely helpless if they *were* discovered.

"If anyone is out here, they will be holed up somewhere to wait for morning," one of the other soldiers said. "Only a fool would still be moving with more snow coming."

"Perhaps."

They were moving away now, putting distance between themselves and the concealed group in the trees. Evelyn watched them go, afraid to tear her eyes away in case that was the second that one of them saw something. Her mind was spinning, trying to grasp that her worst fear had come true. The SS had learned of her presence here. How was immaterial for the moment. What mattered was that now Anna and the others were in even more danger than before. The regular German army was bad enough, but Hitler's SS troops were another matter altogether. They were his death squads, and the SD was their intelligence branch. Not only did they know she was trapped in Norway, but they had learned that she would have to pass through Steinkjer. Which could only mean that they also knew where she was going. Her lips tightened and a slow anger began to chase the paralyzing fear away. There was only one way they could have learned she was heading for Namsos; they had to have heard it from London.

"Do you think it's true that it was Eisenjager who contacted Beck?"

Night Falls on Norway

The question floated back to her and Evelyn frowned. She knew that name, but she didn't remember how.

"Eisenjager? That's a myth. He doesn't exist."

The voices were fading now and Evelyn strained to hear the response.

"...say he...most dangerous...Himmler..."

It was no use. They were too far away now and the wind was carrying their voices in the opposite direction. Evelyn scowled, trying to remember where she had heard or seen that name before. Iron hunter. That was what it meant. But how did she know it?

The men passed from view along the trail, but still no one moved. Evelyn remained where she was, waiting for Erik to give some kind of signal. She listened to the new silence that fell over the mountainside, shivering in the cold. She could hear nothing now aside from the howl of the wind and the occasional howl of a distant wolf. Her heart stopped thumping against her chest, and she took a deep, ragged breath, sucking air into her starved lungs.

After what seemed like an eternity but was in fact only a few minutes, Erik moved out from the trees and motioned for them to join him. Evelyn tried to stand and found that her legs had cramped from cold and fear. Pain shot down them from her hips and she grit her teeth, using the rifle butt to help push her to her feet. Once she gained her balance, she moved towards Erik, biting her lip as her feet screamed in protest. Out of the corner of her eye, she saw Philip and Peder move up the rise on the other side of the trail, and she exhaled. It was a miracle that none of them had been seen.

Anna joined Erik and looked at Evelyn, her face pale.

"You were right next to them!" she hissed. "I thought for sure you would be discovered!"

"I don't know how I wasn't," she confessed in a whisper.

"You're a high value target?" Erik asked softly, his dark eyes boring into hers. "Did you know this?"

Evelyn swallowed painfully. "You understood them?"

"I speak German as well as my sister. Did you know?"

"No."

Anna cast Evelyn a sharp, warning glance before turning to face her brother.

"We don't even know it's her they're looking for," she argued. "It could be anyone and we just happen to be here as well."

"That would be a very big coincidence."

"They do happen. If Marlene knew she was a target, she would never have allowed me to come with her."

Erik looked at her in silence for a moment, then the grim set of his mouth relaxed a bit and he glanced at Evelyn.

"Those were SS troops," he said in a low voice. "They are specialized and highly trained, more so than the regular soldiers. We must be very careful."

"There are more above us," Philip whispered as he and Peder joined them. "I saw the lights when were behind the log. We can't go up any further. We'll run into more."

"They're spread out through the hills," Erik said. "They've cast a net around Steinkjer."

"They how do we proceed?" Peder asked, looking from one to another. "Should we find somewhere to shelter and wait for morning?"

"No. By morning there will be three times as many of them. We must go through them."

"How?" Anna demanded.

"We have to get into the valley," Erik decided after a long moment of thought. "There are houses and villages there where we can conceal ourselves."

"We will lose the protection of the hills," Philip pointed out.

"We have already lost it. The valley is the only way through now."

Philip frowned. "That means going along the ravine," he said slowly. "We'll be putting ourselves in a kill box."

"Do you see another way?" Erik asked. "If you do, please offer it. I don't want to go down there any more than you do, but I can't think of another way."

Philip was quiet, thinking, then he finally shook his head. "No. Even if we stay in the hills, we will have to descend to pass through Steinkjer, and that's what they'll be expecting. That's why they've cast such a wide net, to force us where they want us to go."

Erik nodded. "Then let's get moving. We'll move quickly and without light. Stay close together. Philip, you take the back and Marlene, you stay in the middle. We'll keep the fire power even between us."

Evelyn nodded and took a deep breath as the small group moved out of the trees and onto the trail. Erik led them to the opposite side and they began a silent descent, moving to the left of the area where they had first heard the German soldiers approaching. She listened to the silence around them, straining for sounds of voices in the darkness. While she didn't much like the thought of descending into something referred to as a kill box, she realized that they had very limited options. She had to trust Erik.

Night Falls on Norway

They moved as quickly and quietly as possibly, stopping frequently while Erik or Philip checked for the SS patrols. Each time they stopped, Evelyn gripped her rifle a little tighter, knowing that both the Norwegian soldiers were counting on her ability to fire if needed. Anna was still carrying her suitcase for her, allowing her to have both hands to handle the gun. While she felt guilty for her carrying two heavy suitcases down a mountain covered in snow, Evelyn was glad to have both hands on the rifle. She wasn't entirely confident in her ability to hit any target with her frozen fingers, but if it came down to it, she had no choice. At least she knew she was a good shot. Hopefully that would hold true despite the frigid temperature.

Erik held up his hand, halting the group, and Evelyn stood still, listening. She couldn't hear anything in the darkness, but something had made him stop abruptly. Twisting her head, she strained to see any tell-tale specks of light. They had seen several on their descent, some quite close to them, but now all she saw was darkness. Clouds had covered the moon, robbing them of what little pale light it had afforded. Her eyes, accustomed to the darkness, made out the tall shapes of trees around them, but nothing else.

She reached forward to touch Anna's arm questioningly, but before she could touch her, she heard what it was that had made Erik stop so suddenly: voices.

Evelyn frowned in confusion. They seemed to be coming from above them, but then the wind shifted and she could swear they were coming from behind them. They were too far away to make out the words, and she turned to peer behind them, trying to make sense out of the muffled sounds.

Peder was right behind her and when she turned to look, his eyes were wide in a pale face. She gave him a reassuring smile and reached out to squeeze his arm, offering what strength she could. He smiled faintly as they stood perfectly still in the deep shadows, listening. And waiting.

Evelyn was never to be quite sure what happened next, or what caused the chaos that erupted around them. All she was sure of was that the silent darkness was suddenly shattered by the crack of a pistol somewhere in the hills above them. Whether they had been sighted or if the shooter had seen something else was something they would never know. As soon as the shot rang out, Evelyn's heart surged into her throat and Anna visibly jumped in front of her. As she did, her foot slipped on the snowy incline and she began to lose her balance. Erik turned swiftly to grab her, latching onto her arm and steadying her. She regained her balance, but one of the suitcases slipped from her grip. They all watched helplessly as it launched down the incline, crashing through the undergrowth before slamming into a tree. The sound echoed around them, almost deafening in the darkness, and then silence fell again. Evelyn sucked in her breath silently. The voices in the distance had stopped and, for a split second, there wasn't a sound in the night.

Bright light suddenly pierced through the blackness, arching down from above and sweeping back and forth a few feet in front of them. Looking up, she saw several tall figures illuminated on a ridge far above them. Her heart surged into her throat and she watched as several more bright lights joined the first, searching for the source of the unnatural noise in the night.

Peder's hand closed around hers and squeezed warningly and Evelyn turned to see more lights coming from the trees behind them. These were on the same level as them, and they were closing quickly. She looked at Erik just as one of the lights above illuminated the suitcase laying on its side at the base of a tree.

The lights from the German soldiers showed the ravine only a few yards below them. In the spring, it would be flooded with water from the melting snows above, but now it was dry, covered with only a dusting of snow. The trees on the banks above it offered some protection from the hills above, and Erik motioned towards it as a shout echoed from above. The Germans had seen the suitcase.

"Run for the ravine!" Erik gasped, shouldering his rifle and turning to take aim at the ridge above them. "Marlene, go! Protect them in the ravine!"

As soon as Anna, Evelyn and Peder began half-sliding and half-running down the mountain towards the gorge, Erik and Philip began firing. Within seconds, gunfire lit up the mountainside, deafening as it echoed around them. Evelyn didn't remember running for her life, she only remembered the terrifying feeling that the next shot she heard would be the last. Gripping her rifle, she dodged between trees and around underbrush, gasping for air as she ran for all she was worth. Anna was a few feet to her right, ducking behind trees as they heard the ping and thud of bullets spraying around them.

Diving behind a thick tree, Evelyn stopped to peer around it, looking back as she tried to catch her breath. Erik and Philip were behind them, returning fire from behind the cover of trees as enemy soldiers were sliding down the mountainside after them. The Germans were far enough away that Evelyn had no doubt that they would make it to the ravine before them, but she also knew they weren't the only SS soldiers. There had been at least one group on the same ridge as they were when all hell broke loose, and those were the ones that she knew could stop them.

Almost as if fate had heard her, a burst of rifle fire erupted from her right and she saw several shadows moving a few yards away in the trees. Looking over her shoulder, Evelyn saw that Anna and Peder had reached the bank of the ravine. She jerked her head in the direction of the ravine, shouldering her rifle.

"Go!"

Anna looked at her and nodded, her eyes wide with terror. She turned and leapt off the bank with Peder close behind.

Erik and Philip were pinned down a few feet behind her by gunfire coming from the soldiers to the right. Unable to leave their cover, Evelyn knew they wouldn't last long. She turned and aimed at the closest enemy shadow to Philip and braced herself, firing. The shadow ducked back behind a tree and she fired again at another shadow close to him. A cry of pain echoed through the trees and she knew that her bullet had found its mark.

It's just an animal, they're just animals, she told herself as she aimed again. *They're not people. They're not men. You're just out hunting, and Dad always said you could hit anything. Just take the shots. Don't think about the people. Just take the shots. If you don't, Erik and Philip will die.*

Evelyn repeated the words to herself over and over again as Erik and Philip made a break for the trees where Anna and Peder had been moments before. As they ran, Evelyn fired again as a tall SS soldier emerged from behind a tree with a machine gun. The lights from the soldiers rapidly descending from above flooded over him and Evelyn watched as her shot went into his chest. She caught her breath as he was thrown backwards, a crimson stain spreading across his uniform under his open coat. She stared, paralyzed, as he fell back to hit a tree before sliding into the snow, the machine gun falling out of his hand. Something akin to shock rolled through her, crushing her chest and blurring her vision, and she felt rooted to the spot, unable to move.

Oh my God. I just did that. I just killed a man!

The thought broke through the haze in her mind and her empty stomach rolled over as a wave of nausea gripped her. She was frozen, still staring, when a strong hand grabbed hers. She stumbled as Erik yanked her towards the ravine.

"Move!" he commanded harshly. "Let's go!"

With that, he gave her a shove over the side and Evelyn felt herself flying down into the gorge, her feet barely touching the sides of the bank. As soon as she landed at the bottom, she sucked in some air and Erik and Philip joined her. There were a few blessed seconds without gunfire as they sprinted along the ravine bed. Anna and Peder were ahead, and Evelyn breathed a sigh of relief when she saw them safe.

"Behind you Philip!" Peder yelled as they approached.

Philip spun around and fired just as a tall shadow on the top of the bank let loose a stream of bullets. Evelyn reached Anna and turned as a German soldier tumbled into the ravine, blood pouring from a wound in his stomach. She forced down a strangled cry and heaved the rifle up to her shoulder as a row of enemy soldiers appeared on the bank, their rifles aimed at them.

"Run!" she cried over her shoulder as she, Erik, and Philip began firing.

Bullets rained down into the ravine and she stopped breathing as she fired repeatedly at the shadows above. She hit two of them before Erik got her moving again. She had been in one spot for too long and a bullet whizzed by her head, narrowly missing her and hitting the opposite bank instead. She gasped and turned to stumble along the gorge before resolutely turning to take aim again.

Before she could get her shot off, there was a cry behind her and Evelyn turned to watch in horror as Peder stumbled and fell.

"Peder!" she cried, running towards him.

He had dropped his radio case and was clutching his thigh, writhing in agony.

"It's my leg," he gasped as she dropped down beside him.

Evelyn pulled his hands away and stared at the blood pouring through his pants. A gaping hole in the fabric left no doubt as to the extent of the injury and she shook her head, her eyes filling with tears.

"No, no, no!" She shook her head and began to pull the scarf from around her neck. "We'll tie it up. Philip or Erik will help you."

Peder took one look at her face and shook his head, reaching out to still her hands.

"No. I can't walk, and you can't stay," he said, his voice surprisingly firm. "I did what I could. Now it's up to others. My time is done."

He reached for his radio and shoved it into her hands.

"Take it. Leave me. Don't let them get that," he said urgently. "Use it and get home!"

Erik dropped down on his other side. He took one glance at the leg and looked at Evelyn.

"He's right. He can't continue," he said. "We've stopped them for now, but the rest are coming. We have to move."

Night Falls on Norway

"We can't just leave him here!" Evelyn protested.

"You must!" Peder looked at her and smiled tremulously. "It's been a pleasure, Marlene. I would have loved to continue working with you, but it's not to be. It will be up to Kristian now."

Erik reached into his coat pocket and pulled out a pistol, pressing it into Peder's hand.

"Here. It's loaded and primed. For God's sake, don't shoot yourself."

Peder let out a strangled laugh and waved them away.

"Will you get out of here?" he demanded. "Get Anna and get away while you still can. I'll do what I can to slow them down."

Erik pulled Evelyn to her feet.

"Come. We must leave him," he said urgently. "We haven't much time."

She nodded and stared down at Peder, tears rolling down her cheeks.

"I'm so sorry, Peder," she whispered. "I'm so sorry I got you into this."

"I got myself into this," he retorted. "You have nothing to be sorry for. Now go!"

Erik grabbed her hand and pulled her away, turning to run along the ravine bed. Philip had gone ahead and caught up with Anna and, as they ran towards them, she turned and saw Peder still on the ground behind them. She let out a cry and tried to run back but Philip grabbed her arms, stopping her.

"No, we must leave him!"

"We can't leave him!" she cried frantically. "Oh my God, Peder!"

"He can't walk, Anna," Erik said, not ungently, as they joined them. "It was his choice. He wants us to go on."

Anna looked at Evelyn and saw the tears pouring down her face. She gasped and looked back at Peder, her own eyes filling with tears. As if sensing the struggle he couldn't hear, Peder raised his hand in a wave, then made a motion for them to go.

"We have to get out of this ravine," Philip said urgently. "They'll be sending troops ahead as well as coming after us. I told you this was a kill box. If we stay here, we die."

Erik nodded in agreement and motioned to a bend ahead. "There."

They sprinted to the bend and rounded the corner, out of sight from their pursuers. Erik led them for a few yards, scanning the steep bank, then motioned for them to climb out. He stood guard until they had all reached the top, then scrambled up after them.

They stood in dark and silent trees for a moment, and then he began moving again. Evelyn followed numbly, her rifle hooked over her shoulder and Peder's radio clutched against her chest. Suddenly, through the silence, they heard two pistol shots, one after the other. Evelyn gasped and stopped, listening. After a second of silence, the unmistakable sound of machine gun fire responded.

It lasted only a few seconds, then silence fell again. Erik and Evelyn looked at each other and he reached out and took her hand, squeezing it tightly.

"If I know Peder, he just took at least two of them with him," he said in a low voice.

Evelyn's throat squeezed shut and she nodded mutely, clinging to his hand, shaking. Anna wrapped an arm around her shoulders, tears again flowing down her face.

"God took him quickly," she whispered brokenly.

Erik allowed the two women a moment to grieve, but then he gently turned them towards the trees.

"Come. We must move before they pick up our trail. Peder did as he promised he would and bought us some time. Let's not waste it."

Chapter Thirty

Asp, Norway

Evelyn collapsed in the corner of the old, crumbling stone structure. At one point in time, it had been a home, but now it was empty and falling apart. Anna had told her that there were many of these types of buildings in the mountains. Most were still owned by the original families, but had been either long forgotten or minimally maintained over the years. This one fell into the latter category as there were still doors on the structure and the fireplace in the center of the far wall was intact. The windows were gone, but the wind had died down now, and there wasn't much of a breeze coming through the two empty openings. Even if there had been, she reflected, she was too tired to care.

After checking the chimney and finding it miraculously clear of debris, Erik was preparing to set a small fire in the heart with the wood Philip had carried in from the trees. She watched him numbly for a moment, wondering how he could be so calm and still continue to move when the rest of them were half-dead on their feet. At least, she and Anna were.

She looked over to where Anna had dropped onto the hard stone floor near to the fireplace. Her face was streaked with dirt and her hair had come out of its braid and was hanging in tangles around her face. She seemed completely unaware of any of it as she watched her brother work to get a fire going. Anna looked the way she felt: utterly defeated.

The door to the cabin squeaked on rusty hinges as it swung open and Philip came through with another armful of tree branches.

"We should be safe here for a few hours," he said, dropping the wood beside the hearth. "There's no sound for miles, and we're deep enough into the hills that they won't see the smoke."

"Even if they do, they will assume it's a local," Erik said, sorting through the fresh wood, looking for pieces that weren't damp. "They'll expect us to go towards the town, not into the wild again. You get some rest. I'll take the first watch this time."

Philip nodded. "You won't get any argument from me," he said tiredly, turning to look around the small space. Seeing Evelyn in the corner, he went to the opposite corner near the door. "I'll just clean and reload first." He glanced at Evelyn. "You'll want to do the same," he told her.

"I already gave her the kit," Erik said over his shoulder. "She knows."

Evelyn nodded mutely and reached for the box Erik had handed her when they first arrived. Inside were rags and a long brush to clean the barrel of the rifle. Another box of ammunition cartridges was beside it.

"Can't she rest first?" Anna demanded, looking at Erik. "She's exhausted."

"We all are," was his only reply.

Anna exhaled loudly and dragged herself to her feet tiredly to go over to Evelyn. She dropped beside her and leaned back against the wall, turning her head so she could watch her.

"Are you all right?" she asked. "Can I help you?"

Evelyn smiled faintly and shook her head, beginning to dismantle the rifle. "No. It won't take long."

"I don't see why you can't sleep first," she muttered. "If we're so safe here, it shouldn't make a difference."

"They're right. It's best to do it now. Just in case."

"You mean just in case we're not as safe as they think?"

"Yes."

Anna was silent for a moment, then she rubbed her face.

"Do you think he died quickly?"

Evelyn swallowed. "Yes. There was more than one machine gun firing. I'm sure he went quickly."

She looked at the radio beside her and her hands trembled momentarily as a wave of sorrow washed over her. That radio, Peder's pride and joy, was all that was left of him now. And it was the very thing that had led to his death.

"Part of me still can't believe he's gone," Anna whispered. "We just left him there, and then…how could we just leave him?"

"We had no choice," Philip said from his corner, glancing up from his own rifle. "He couldn't have made it out of the ravine."

"He knew and understood," Erik added, turning to look at them from where he had finally managed to get a fire started. "He told us to leave him. It was a very brave thing that he did. He died with honor."

Anna stared at him for a minute, then nodded tiredly. "I suppose he did," she agreed.

"We're not going to make it, are we?" Evelyn asked suddenly, looking up. "How can we? We're all exhausted. We have no food left. We've lost Peder. I have his radio, but no idea if I'll be able to get it to work. The German SS are looking for us, and are probably all over the mountains by now. We'll never make it to Namsos."

"That's the exhaustion talking," Anna said. "You'll feel better after some sleep."

"I don't think I will. I don't know if I have the strength to continue...or the will."

"Why? Because you saw what this war is really about?" Erik demanded. "This is what happens in war. People die. Men die. Boys die. Women and children die. It's never pretty and it always takes its toll. Peder died well. I wish that we all could go as quickly and with little fuss."

"It's not just Peder," Evelyn said, her voice shaking. "I shot and killed a man. I...I watched him die!"

"Yes, and you will watch many more men die," he retorted harshly. "Do you know why? Because you'll have to. You chose to be part of this war. You believed in something, and you chose to fight. Well, this is what that means. It means you will do things you find repulsive, and you will witness atrocities you never thought possible. You will be forced into situations that are unimaginable, but you will continue. You won't have a choice. You'll hate it, but you *will* continue to fight."

"Erik!" Anna protested weakly. "Can't you see she's upset?"

"Yes, of course I can," he muttered. "But you both need to understand that this isn't a game. We're in it until the end now, whether or not we like it, whether or not we want to be, and whether or not we think we can do it. The sooner she realizes that, the sooner you realize that, the better off you'll both be."

Evelyn took a deep, ragged breath and felt her hands steady as she stared across the small space at Erik. Everything he said, while cold and harsh, was also true. She had offered to serve her country, and to fight. She had been trained to fire guns with the intent to kill. Sifu had trained her to use her body as a weapon and her hands for the same intent: to kill. MI6 had trained her to detect and silence enemy sentries. All of it, everything she had learned and been trained for, had led her here. This was the path she had chosen that long ago day in a chateau outside of Paris.

271

"You're right," she said after a long moment, her voice cracking. She cleared her throat. "I'm sorry."

"Never apologize," he said gruffly after a long moment of staring back at her, "not for being human. Finish reloading that gun and get some sleep. It's after one in the morning. We continue at eight."

Steinkjer, Norway
April 13

Eisenjager slowed and pulled to the side of the road, shutting off the engine. Dawn was streaking the sky with gray and purple, casting shadows across the make-shift barrier blocking the road. A soldier in a long coat walked towards his car, a machine gun hanging over his shoulder, while two others watched from a few feet away. They had their hands on their rifles, ready to fire if needed.

"Herr Manfrit Gruber?" he asked, bending slightly to peer into the window.

"Yes."

Eisenjager pulled out his papers and passed them to the SS soldier. He watched as the young man examined them carefully before passing them back. He clicked his heels together respectfully as he straightened up.

"Hauptsturmführer Beck is waiting for you, Herr Gruber," he said politely, opening the car door for him. "If you would come with me?"

Eisenjager climbed out from behind the wheel, tucking his papers back into his inside coat pocket. He turned to follow the soldier across the road and into the trees a few yards away.

"The others will watch your car," the young man said over his shoulder. "This is one of the main roads into Steinkjer, and no one is allowed in or out. It will be quite safe there."

"I'm really not worried about it," Eisenjager replied. "Have you secured the town?"

"Yes, but we haven't gone any further. We're waiting for additional support."

Eisenjager raised an eyebrow but said nothing more as he was led through the trees. They walked for some minutes before they came to the edge of what looked like a dried out river bed. Below them in the ravine were several bodies covered with gray blankets, laid out in a row. Black boots covered the uniform trousers to just below the knee.

"Those are our dead," a deep voice said from the left.

Eisenjager turned to face the tall man walking out of the trees towards them. He had dark hair and pale skin, but his eyes were sharp and keen. They swept over Eisenjager quickly as he approached.

"They killed seven of my men in total," he continued. "Five here and two back there in the trees." He jerked his head in the direction he had come from. "And we only got one of them. I am Herr Hauptsturmführer Wilhelm Beck," he added, holding out a gloved hand. "You must be Herr Gruber."

"Yes." Eisenjager gripped his hand.

Beck nodded and looked at the soldier who had escorted him. "You may return to your post."

The soldier clicked his heels and saluted, then nodded to Eisenjager and turned to make his way back through the trees. Once he was out of earshot, Beck turned back to look at him assessingly.

"Or should I call you Eisenjager?" he asked softly.

"I prefer Herr Gruber at the moment."

Beck smiled faintly. "Yes, of course. It's an honor to meet you. I was beginning to believe the rumors were true, and that you were only a myth. It's reassuring to know that they're wrong."

"Why is that?"

"Because we need men like you," he answered candidly, turning to walk over to the edge of the ravine. He began to make his way down the steep incline into the river bed. "Especially after what happened last night."

"What did happen last night?" Eisenjager asked, following him.

Beck glanced behind him. "I'm still trying to work that out," he muttered. He reached the bed and turned to watch as Eisenjager slid the rest of the way down the incline. "As far as I can tell, your British agent was right where you said she'd be."

Eisenjager stopped at the bottom of the incline, a surge of satisfaction rolling through him.

"She was here?"

"I think so, yes." Beck turned and led him past the covered bodies and along the ravine. "There were four men and one woman. At least, that is what I'm told. Three of the men had rifles. They're responsible for that." He waved his hand to encompass the bodies behind them. "They were outnumbered, out-positioned and out-gunned, yet they still managed to kill seven of my soldiers. We believe they are Norwegian military."

"And the fourth man?"

Beck motioned ahead. Eisenjager turned to look and saw another body lying alone further down the ravine.

"He shot and killed one more of my men, and severely wounded another in his stomach. I don't expect the one with the stomach wound to last the day. That will bring the number of dead to nine."

Eisenjager's lips tightened and he strode forward, covering the distance to the body quickly with his long legs. They had covered it with a blanket like the others, but he could see that the black trousers and shoes were civilian.

"This one is not army?" he asked, stopping beside the body.

"No. He was Norwegian, but a civilian. Peder Strand, according to his identification. He lived in Oslo." Beck bent down to reach for the edge of the blanket. "It's not pretty," he warned before pulling it back.

Eisenjager stared down at the lifeless face, taking in the multiple bullet wounds over his torso and head. The man was riddled with machine gun fire, the price he paid for shooting two SS troopers.

"Why did he stay behind?" he asked after a moment.

"He was shot in his leg and couldn't continue. When he was approached, he opened fire with this." Beck pulled out a pistol and handed it to Eisenjager. "It's a Norwegian standard-issue sidearm."

"One of the others gave it to him," Eisenjager said, examining it. "Probably for defense." He looked up. "What happened to the others?"

"They escaped that way," Beck pointed down the ravine. "They went around the curve. By the time our soldiers got there, they were gone."

Fury streaked through Eisenjager, white and hot, and his fingers clenched around the pistol in his hand.

"I thought I made it clear that the woman had to be stopped and detained?" he said, his calm and quiet tone belying the angry glint in his cold eyes.

"You did not make it clear that she was accompanied by three trained soldiers," Beck retorted. "My men were not prepared for them."

"Are you making excuses for the failure of your men?"

"No. I'm stating facts. They were not adequately briefed on the nature of the mission. They were told to look for two women and a man, all civilians. What they found were three soldiers and a man

274

familiar enough with pistols to kill one of my men and fatally wound another."

Eisenjager stared at him in cold silence for a long moment, then he handed the pistol back to him and turned his attention to the body at their feet.

"Was there anything else on him?" he asked. "A notebook? Anything?"

"No. Just his wallet and identification."

"Scheisse!" Eisenjager turned away from the body. "That's of no use to me then!"

He started to stride towards the curve in the ravine in the distance, then turned and went back to Beck instead.

"What's in that direction?" he asked, pointing.

"Steinkjer. The ravine runs along the edge of the town."

"And you've sent men in pursuit of them?"

Beck frowned. "No. I don't have the men to send." He turned and motioned to the bodies behind them. "They killed half of the men I sent to look for them. My orders are to wait for reinforcements."

"When will they arrive?"

"Tomorrow."

Eisenjager let out a frustrated exclamation. "Tomorrow is too late!" he spat. "That is why I told you to stop them here."

"I cannot send my platoon on a hunt through enemy territory," Beck told him stiffly. "We haven't secured the area, only the town. We know there are enemy forces in the area. My orders are to wait."

Eisenjager stared at him for a moment, then exhaled.

"And you must follow your orders," he said grudgingly. "I understand."

Beck inclined his head and they turned to walk back to where they had come down into the ravine.

"You aren't the only one interested in this agent," Beck said, breaking the silence after a few minutes.

Eisenjager looked at him sharply. "Oh?"

"I received a message this morning from Obersturmbannführer Hans Voss, in Berlin. He also stressed the importance of apprehending her. Are you aware of the SD's interest?"

"I am. They do not concern me."

Beck grunted and smiled faintly. "Perhaps they should. They are obviously still keeping an eye out for her, and they have resources everywhere the SS go. If they find her first, you will lose for the first time in your career."

The hint of smug arrogance in his voice indicated that the possibility was satisfying to the Hauptsturmführer. Eisenjager noted it, and the smile he gave him was chilling.

"Unlike the SS, I do not lose my prey. I can assure you, they will not find her first."

London, England

Bill hung up the telephone and stared at it with a frown. He raised his eyes to the clock on the wall of his study, and the frown deepened. It was two hours past the time when Evelyn was supposed to have made contact, but still nothing. He had rung the radio room to make sure, and they confirmed that no new messages had been received yet. She still hadn't checked in.

He picked up his glasses and put them on, turning his attention to the reports on the desk in front of him. Even though it was Saturday, he still had work to do. Marguerite had gone to a luncheon with the Women's Institute, leaving him to get done what he had to do before they went to the theater this evening. If he didn't finish, he would have a very annoyed wife on his hands. His lips curved despite himself. She had been looking forward to this evening all week and he wouldn't disappoint her.

Nevertheless, a few minutes later his mind wandered again, and a heavy sense of foreboding fell over him. The navy had sent a group of destroyers to Narvik along with air support in the form of an aircraft carrier with the aim of defeating the enemy there and gaining a foothold in northern Norway. They were expected to arrive today and engage the Germans. Tomorrow, more ships were arriving in Namsos, carrying the Royal marines. By Monday, if everything went to plan, the Germans would be engaging Allied troops up and down the coast. Evelyn had to be out of there before that happened. Once the battles began, she would be in more danger than ever.

Where was she?

Bill exhaled and dropped the report in his hand, flipping the folder closed over it. He got up impatiently and turned to go over to the wall of bookshelves alongside his desk. Pulling down a large world atlas, he carried it over to a reading table and set it down, opening it and turning to the pages for Norway. In her last transmission, Jian had said that she was outside Steinkjer. He had warned her that the Huns knew she was in Norway, but he hadn't received a reply. Hardly surprising, and he hadn't been concerned last night. They had received confirmation that the message was received, and that was all that he was concerned with at the time. He had no way of knowing how reliable the radio was that she was using, or even if it would continue to be able to transmit. Therefore, when no reply came, he assumed that they had simply lost their signal again. After all, he had told her contact again in ten hours. He hadn't told her to acknowledge the message. He had wanted to keep the messages as short as possible. The shorter the message, the less time it took to decode, and the less time the Germans had to intercept a location on the radio.

But now the ten hours had been and gone, and there was still no word from her.

After some searching, he found Steinkjer on the map and studied the area with a frown. The town was located in the middle of a bottleneck where Norway narrowed, bridging the north and the southern portions of the country. It was about two-thirds of the way between Trondheim and Namsos. He shook his head. Without knowing how she was traveling, he had no way of beginning to estimate when she would reach Namsos. In fact, without knowing where she was now, he couldn't be sure that she *would* reach Namsos in time. The cruiser would be in the harbor tomorrow, and the captain was under orders to unload his cargo and then return to England. If Evelyn wasn't there by the time he finished unloading the troops, he would leave, and she would be trapped in the middle of a battle for Norway.

A battle that was never supposed to have occurred in the first place.

He let out a frustrated grunt and followed a line from Steinkjer to Namsos with his forefinger. If the party had made it through Steinkjer last night, it would have been after midnight or even after one or two in the morning. They would have stopped for what was left of the night. Asp looked like a possibility. It was the next sizable town after Steinkjer. They would probably have been able to find somewhere to stop there. If that was the case, they would be far enough away from the water that the likelihood of running into enemy troops would be lessening. They would be able to move more freely as they got away from the bottleneck, and drew closer to Namsos. All the current surveillance photos showed the German troops concentrated around Trondheim and moving north along the fjord to join up with the forces coming south from Narvik. They were staying in the middle for now. They would worry about the smaller coastal ports once they joined up with the other divisions.

And that might just be the thing to save Jian. If she'd made it through Steinkjer, she had the whole western swath to Namsos to navigate without much risk of interference from enemy forces.

If she'd made it through Steinkjer, he reminded himself, straightening up and removing his glasses to rub his eyes. And he wouldn't know that until he heard from her again.

He turned to go back to his desk, a frown settled on his face again. So far, she had been extremely punctual in contacting when she said she would, but of course, he had no way of knowing what kinds of delays she was running into. All he could do was wait.

And pray.

Chapter Thirty-One

Spillum, Norway

Evelyn leaned against the post of a wooden fence and felt her eyes trying to close. She forced them open again and looked at Anna, sitting on a tree stump a foot away. She looked as half-dead as Evelyn felt. They had been hiking through the mountains since eight this morning, moving through progressively deeper and deeper snow until she was convinced her legs couldn't take one more step. She had lost all feeling in her feet and ankles hours before, and her calves and thighs were screaming from the effort of slogging through at least two and a half feet of snow. Her rifle was back to being slung across her body and she carried Peder's radio and her toiletries case, switching hands when she lost feeling in the one carrying the heavy radio. Anna still carried her suitcase, her own left behind on the incline outside Steinkjer. She had her feet propped up on it while she sat on the tree stump, waiting for Erik and Philip to finish checking the immediate area.

They had come upon the outskirts of Spillum, a town just south of Namsos, and Erik was checking to make sure it was clear and safe for them to pass through. So far they hadn't run across any indication that the German forces had made their way west, but they all knew that could change in an instant. If the town was clear, they would look for somewhere to take shelter in the hills. If not, they would have to go around. Evelyn grimaced at the thought and fought back a wave of helpless tears. She honestly didn't think she could go much further, perhaps no further at all. She was falling asleep on her feet, and so was Anna. They had to stop soon.

"It looks quiet," Erik announced, coming out of the trees with Philip beside him. "I don't think they've come this way yet. We should be safe to look to for shelter for the night."

"Oh, thank God," Anna said. "I don't know how much further I can go."

Erik nodded. "I know. Come on. Philip thinks there might be some old farms up that way."

Anna nodded and struggled to her feet, picking up the suitcase. Evelyn bent to pick up her cases again and, as she did so, a shiver of warning went down her spine. Through her exhaustion, instincts she didn't even know she had took over and, instead of picking up the cases, she straightened up with her rifle in her hands. Seeing her swing the gun into her grip, Erik and Philip both did the same, spinning around to look for the threat.

"What is it?" Anna asked in alarm, looking around.

Before Evelyn could answer, a man stepped out of the shadows near the end of the fence. He carried a shotgun, but at the sight of three rifles pointed towards him, he raised his arms in a placating motion.

"Whoa, easy there!" he said, keeping his grip on his shotgun, but stopping well away from them. "Who might you be?"

"Who might you be?" Erik countered.

The man looked at him for a long moment, then lowered his arms and his shotgun.

"That's my property behind you," he said, nodding at the expanse of land behind the fence Evelyn had been leaning against. "I was out checking on the goats when I saw you."

Erik lowered his rifle, Philip and Evelyn following suit.

"My apologies," Erik said. "We ran into some German troops yesterday and it's left us nervous."

"Germans? Where?"

"Near Steinkjer."

"Ah. We'd heard they were moving north from Trondheim." The man nodded and moved forward, holding out his hand. "My name is Jørgen."

"I am Premierløitnant Erik Salvesen, and this is Sekondløitnant Philip Andersen," Erik said, shaking his hand. "This is my sister Anna, and her friend Marlene."

Jørgen nodded to them. "It's a very cold night to be out, and more snow is on the way. Where are you headed?"

"Namsos, but we won't make it tonight. We were going to look for somewhere to take shelter in the hills."

Jørgen scratched his neck under his chin, looking at them thoughtfully.

"Not likely to find much up there," he finally said. "Most of the old homesteads up there were torn down years ago to make way for the logging. How long have you been on the road?"

"Since early this morning."

He shook his head. "You must be near to frozen. I've got some room. Not much, mind you, but enough. If you don't mind the floor, you'd be quite welcome."

Erik glanced at Anna and Evelyn, then looked back at Jørgen. "I thank you. We'll be on our way at first light."

The man waved his hand dismissively. "My son is away and won't be back until Monday. It is only me in the house, so the company will be welcome. Come."

He turned and motioned for them to follow him and Evelyn looked at Anna, relief flooding through her at the prospect of imminent warmth. Anna smiled and hooked her arm through hers as they followed the men.

"Perhaps this is a sign that things are looking up," she said, leaning against her tiredly. "We just might make it after all."

Evelyn looked up as Erik sat beside her at the wooden table. She had Peder's radio open in front of her and had been tinkering with it for the past fifteen minutes trying to make it work, all to no avail.

"No luck?" he asked.

She shook her head. "I think it must have been damaged, perhaps when he was shot and it fell. It powers on, but the switch isn't working. I can't search for a frequency."

"So you have no way of contacting London," he said in a low voice.

"No."

Erik stared at the radio pensively for a moment. "Kristian would be able to fix it," he said. "His is just like this. They built them together, you know, while we were in school. Over the years, they added and changed things, made what they called upgrades, but they're still essentially the same machines."

"But Kristian is in Drammen," she said, "so that is of no help to me now."

Erik glanced at her. "What do you want to do? Do we continue to Namsos?"

"Yes. I have to assume everything is still the same. If I get there and find otherwise, then that's another problem I'll face then."

"Peder gave you the radio. Will you take it with you?"

Evelyn looked at him thoughtfully for a moment. "I hadn't thought that far ahead, to be honest," she admitted. "I don't think I really thought we'd make it this far. Jørgen says that Namsos is only about an hour walk from here."

"Yes, provided the Germans haven't destroyed the bridge. If they had, though, Jørgen would have told us." Erik looked at the radio thoughtfully. "If you leave it with me, I could get this to Kristian and he will get it working again. Then I will have a way to get information out and back to England."

Evelyn glanced behind them. They were quite alone. Anna was washing up in the back room and Philip was helping Jørgen in the large kitchen on the other side of the small house. She returned her gaze to his face.

"Erik, you realize how dangerous that will be?" she asked in a low voice. "I know what you're determined to do if the Germans succeed in occupying Norway, but please consider carefully. Peder is dead now because of this radio."

"And many Norwegians are dead now because of the Germans," he replied evenly. "I know the risks. I knew them the other night when we discussed this, as did you."

Evelyn's lips twisted as she thought of how naive she had been even two nights ago, thinking only of how useful it would be to have Erik and Anna here on the ground in Norway. Now she understood just what would happen to them if they were caught by the Germans.

"Watching Peder…" Her voice cracked and she cleared her throat.

"Made it all real," he finished for her. "I understand. Yet this is our world now. This is what we have to survive in. This radio will help us do that to some extent."

"Were you able to convince Anna to come with me?" she asked suddenly.

He shook his head. "No. You were right. She is determined to stay here and fight, with us."

Evelyn sighed and rubbed her eyes. "I didn't think you'd be able to talk her into it, but I admit that I hoped you could."

"Hoped he could what?" Anna asked, walking into the living room.

Her face was scrubbed clean and her hair was brushed out and re-braided. She no longer looked like a homeless vagabond, and Evelyn smiled, turning in her chair.

"Nothing," she said. "It's not important."

"Did you get it working?" Anna asked, walking over to stand by the table and looking down at the radio.

"No."

"What now, then? How will you know if the plan is still the same?"

"I won't, not until I get there tomorrow."

Anna looked at her for a moment, then shook her head and reached out to lay a hand on her shoulder.

"If something goes wrong, you'll stay with us," she said. "No arguments. We'll find a way to get you to the Swedish border."

Evelyn swallowed. She had no intention of staying and keeping them in such danger, but she knew it was no use to say as much to Anna.

"Let's hope it doesn't come to that," she said instead, forcing a smile.

"Come into the kitchen and eat," Jørgen said from the door, drawing their attention. "It's not much, just hot soup and toasted bread, but it will fill you. You all look half-starved."

Evelyn and Erik stood up and she closed the radio case, locking it securely.

"Hot soup sounds like heaven," she murmured, turning away from the table. "Are you an angel in disguise, Jørgen?" she asked.

The man grunted. "I'm no angel, Miss, but I will help where I can," he said brusquely. "While you eat, I will build up the fire in here and get some blankets. It won't be fancy, but you all should be comfortable enough."

"Perhaps you're not an angel," Anna said with a smile, "but as far as I'm concerned, you're a hero. Thank you for all of this."

He flushed and waved them towards the kitchen.

"No need to thank me. Go and eat before Philip eats it all. He had almost finished a bowl already before I came in here."

Evelyn followed the others towards the kitchen, pausing to watch as Jørgen went over to the large fireplace in the center of the wall and began to pile more logs onto the low flame. Suddenly and irrationally, she knew that Norway would be all right. Whether or not the Germans succeeded in occupying the small country, the people would survive. People like Jørgen, the Hansen's, and the Kolstad's in Oslo would keep helping where they could, spreading hope when there would seem to be none. People like Anna, Peder, Kristian, Olav, and now Erik would fight, and die, to make sure that the country survived. No matter how dark the days got, there would always be hope.

As Evelyn turned away to go into the kitchen, she grasped that hope and held on to it. She had to believe it or she would never be able to get on a ship tomorrow and leave Anna and Erik to their fate.

London, England
April 14

Bill looked up as Wesley entered his office, a newspaper in one hand and a stack of folders in the other.

"Good morning, sir," he said, closing the door behind him and crossing to the desk. "Have you been here long?"

"No. I've just arrived," Bill said, reaching for the folders. "Sorry to have you come in on a Sunday. It will only be for a few hours."

"It's all right, sir. I understand." Wesley cleared his throat. "Have you seen the papers?"

Bill glanced up from the folder he was flipping through and raised his eyebrows.

"Not yet, no."

Wesley handed him the newspaper. "I think it might cheer you up. I know it did me."

Bill took the paper and opened it to read the headline.

GERMAN DESTROYERS AND U-BOAT DESTROYED AT NARVIK.

"Oh, that *is* good news!" he exclaimed, scanning the article. "Eight destroyers sunk and one U-boat."

"If it's accurate, that's a big chunk of the Kriegsmarine destroyer strength," Wesley said.

"I'd say it's half, if the numbers we have on their naval strength are accurate. That's jolly good news!"

"I thought you'd enjoy it, sir." Wesley smiled. "We were due for some good news."

"Yes, we were." Bill finished reading the article and set the paper down. "Still nothing from the radio room?"

"No, sir."

He frowned and took off his glasses, rubbing his eyes.

"Where the hell is she?" he muttered, not expecting an answer. He got up and walked over to the map of Norway on the wall. "Lieutenant Commander Wheeler is in Namsos now. He has orders to leave as soon as the marines are safely ashore."

"How many ships are with him?" Wesley asked, joining him at the map.

Night Falls on Norway

"Two more cruisers and ten destroyers." Bill scratched his head as he gazed at the map. "They're remaining in Norway, and Wheeler is leaving to rendezvous with another cruiser and three destroyers heading back to Scapa Flow. He can't remain any longer than absolutely necessary. It's too dangerous for a cruiser to be sailing alone with the U-boat threat."

Before Wesley could offer a comment, a knock fell on the door and he turned to open it, admitting a young man in uniform.

"Good morning, sir," he said respectfully. "This just came through for you. It's from the *HMS Cardiff*."

Bill held out his hand, taking the folded message from the young man. "Thank you."

He nodded and turned to leave as Bill went back towards his desk, his head bent over the paper as he scanned the message quickly. Wesley closed the door behind him and turned to look at Bill.

"What does it say? Do they have her?" he asked.

"No." Bill dropped into his seat again and laid the message on the desk. "They're docked and unloading. Wheeler wants to know if his passenger is coming. I have absolutely no idea what to tell him."

He lapsed into silence and Wesley was quiet, waiting. After a few moments, Bill sighed heavily and sat forward, reaching for a pad and pencil.

"There's not much I can do at this point but try to buy her some extra time and pray that she presents herself," he muttered, scrawling a reply on the pad. "Have this reply sent back. If he hasn't had any contact by mid-afternoon, he's to depart as planned."

"And Jian?"

Bill tore off the paper, folded it and handed it to Wesley, his lips pressed together in a grim line.

"Will have to find another way home."

Chapter Thirty-Two

Spillum, Norway

Evelyn bent over the table and studied the map spread out before her. Erik stood next to her, his brows pulled together thoughtfully as he, also, studied the map. It was late in the morning and they hadn't left at first light, as had been their intention. When Jørgen went out to tend the animals, he had discovered that the fresh snow had caused a large section of fir tree to fall, blocking the entrance to the barn. Because he had been kind enough to give them shelter and food, Erik and Philip had spent part of the morning helping him cut and move the obstruction. By the time they had finished, Jørgen insisted on giving them breakfast as well.

"I think this will be the best route here," Erik finally said, pointing. "From what Jørgen said, the roads will be clear, but there's no reason to risk it. We can cross the mountain here and avoid the road altogether until here, where we will have to take it. This will take us to the bridge. Once we cross the bridge, there are a few different roads to take, and we can easily avoid the main one."

"I don't even know where I'm going," Evelyn muttered, staring at the map helplessly. "With no way of reaching my contact, I don't know which harbor to go to. From what I can see, there are three."

Erik glanced at her. "Yes. There are more, but these three would be the only ones capable of docking a large ship. What kind of ship are we talking about?"

"A cruiser," she said after a moments hesitation.

"Definitely one of those three, then," he said thoughtfully. "You will be able to see them well enough when you get there." He looked at her and gave her a small smile. "You will find them. Don't worry. Namsos is not like London, or even Oslo."

Evelyn nodded, taking strength from that small smile. She had learned over the past few days that Erik gave them rarely. He was trying to encourage her and give her hope. They were so close. *She* was so close. And yet so much could still go wrong.

"Well? What have you two decided?" Anna asked, coming into the room with Philip close behind.

"We'll stay off the main road and stick to the mountains until we have to cross the bridge," Erik said. "Once we get to the bridge, we have no choice but to be in the open."

"There are no German troops in the area yet," Philip said. "If we take the main road, it will be faster and easier."

"There are no troops that we know of," Erik replied. "It's not worth the risk if we're wrong."

"That's true," Anna agreed, glancing down at the map. "How much longer will it take to go through the hills, though?"

"With the added snow? Perhaps an extra hour."

Anna looked at Evelyn sharply. "It's almost ten now. That will put you in Namsos after one."

Evelyn nodded. "I know."

She had no way of knowing when Lt. Commander Wheeler would leave, but Erik was right. It wasn't worth taking the risk to go along the main road. If the SS troops had followed them, they could very well be watching the roads into Namsos, waiting for them. And they would be looking for two men and two women traveling together.

Philip pulled out a chair and sat down, leaning his elbow on the table while he studied the map.

"If we go that way, we'll reach the bridge at mid-day," he said slowly. "The sun will be at its highest and any reconnaissance flights will have a very clear view." Then, as if echoing Evelyn's own thoughts, he continued, "The SS will be looking for two couples. If they see us on the bridge, there will be no mistaking us."

"That's why they won't see us on the bridge," Evelyn said, her voice even.

"What? How is that?" Anna demanded. "Do you have a plan to become invisible?"

"Not invisible, no," she said with a laugh. "But not what they're looking for. You see, we won't be crossing the bridge together."

Anna and Philip stated at her blankly, but Erik grasped what she meant immediately. He frowned, his dark eyes probing hers.

"That wasn't the plan," he said. "I told you I would see you into Namsos. I told you I would get you there safely."

"And you have," she told him with a smile. "I would never have got this far without your help and guidance. For that, I owe you a great debt. If ever I have the opportunity to repay it, know that I will do everything in my power to do so."

"Do you mean you're leaving?" Anna suddenly gasped, her eyes flaring wide. "Is that what you mean? You're going on alone?"

"Yes."

"No!" Anna glared at her, her face flushing. "We've come this far together. We will go the rest of the way as well. There is no reason for us to give up now."

"I'm not giving up. I'm being practical. Anna, there is nowhere between here," Evelyn pointed on the map, "and here where we can take cover from aerial reconnaissance. We will be completely exposed, and if the Germans are out there, the only defense we have left is to separate."

"She's right," Philip admitted reluctantly after a moment of silence. "Dressed as she is, she can be mistaken for a farmer's wife going into town. If they're watching, they won't see anything they haven't already seen several times already."

"*If* they're watching. Jørgen said they haven't come this far yet. He hasn't heard of any in the village, or even passing on the road."

"That doesn't mean they haven't," Evelyn said. "Anna, be sensible. We've come this far, and I have put you at more risk than you had any reason to be. I won't do it any longer. I'll go the rest of the way alone, and you will be far safer without me. You all will. You know that."

Anna shook her head. "I don't care about that," she argued. "I promised to get you out of Norway. I can't just leave you to fend for yourself now."

"You're not," Evelyn said with a quick grin. "I am. I'm the one making the decision, not you."

"If you continue alone, and Philip goes on his own, then we will all cross the bridge at different times and enter Namsos with very little risk, even if they have someone watching the bridge and the city," Erik said, nodding. "Philip can meet up with us once we're in Namsos. It is good. That is the best approach, I think."

"I am out-voted, then?" Anna looked from one to the other, ending with Evelyn. "I'll do what everyone else thinks is best, but I am not happy with this decision at all."

Evelyn nodded, smiling sadly. "I know."

"When we reach Namsos, we can get a message to our battalion and find out where and how to rejoin them," Philip told Erik.

"Yes. Anna, I'll make arrangements for you to get back to Rindal and our parents," Erik said with a nod.

"You don't have to make arrangements for me," Anna retorted, tossing her head. "I can make my own way."

Night Falls on Norway

"How? You don't drive and the trains are too dangerous. The Germans are bombing the tracks and the stations."

"I'll find a way."

"You're being stubborn."

"I think I'm entitled to be stubborn after everything we've been through," Anna shot back.

Evelyn watched the two siblings arguing and felt an acute stab of homesickness. They reminded her forcibly of herself and Robbie, and suddenly all she wanted was to get home and see his freckled, laughing face.

Philip made a face and got up from his seat, turning away from the table.

"While you two have your argument, I will tell Jørgen that we'll be leaving shortly," he said over his shoulder. "If we're going to make it there today, we need to get started."

"He's right," Erik said, rolling up the map. "Now that we have a plan, it's time to leave. Marlene, you will stay with us through the mountains. Once we reach the road, I'll give you this map and we will separate."

She nodded, avoiding looking at Anna.

"Let's get moving."

14th April, 1940

My dear Evelyn,

How are you? I think of you often. Now that this war seems to be moving in the direction we both knew it would, I wonder if you're as anxious for it to get going as I am. I feel as if we've been waiting indefinitely, and now we're still waiting. I suppose this is the normal progression of things, but I really must admit I wish I could just jump into the fight. I'm sure you feel the same way, stuck traveling to other stations in the middle of nowhere. You're probably bored silly. Don't worry, though. You'll be back at your home station any day now and I'm sure Durton will bring some kind of excitement to your daily grind. But not too much, I hope!

I survived my first recon flight. We took off at four-thirty in the morning and landed to refuel just in time for breakfast. We were supposed to continue immediately, but lo and behold, there was heavy cloud cover over our target. So

CW Browning

instead we were told to stand down for a few hours to see if it cleared. Eventually it did, and we got underway again. It was an extremely nerve-wracking flight, I don't mind saying. We flew over three different points, taking photographs from a special camera fitted onto the belly of our Spits. We really did expect to run into some enemy fire, but we didn't see even one wingtip to shoot at. I honestly don't think the Jerries even knew we were there! We did our sweep and flew back to base without any trouble whatsoever. In the end, it was all rather dull.

Rob was thoroughly disgusted with the whole thing, and so was the Yank. As much as I want the war to get underway at last, and for all this waiting to end, I was rather glad that we all got back without any incidents. Does that make me a coward? On the one hand, I'm more than ready to get to work and meet the enemy head-on, but on the other, I'm rather glad it didn't happen the other day. I don't know what that means, really. Everyone else was very upset not to have had a great scrap.

Did you see the news out of Norway? We sunk eight of Jerry's destroyers and one of her U-boats at Narvik yesterday! It's absolutely fantastic! The U-boat was actually bombed by a catapult plane off a battleship. The CO thinks it might be the first time that's ever happened. We did have an aircraft carrier there, as well. All said, it was a much-needed victory, and one that will hopefully show Hitler that we mean business. I just hope it's not too little, too late. The Germans have control of all the airfields in Norway, and their paratroopers are the best in the world. I want to believe that we can take Norway back, but I know that it will be a very hard fight to do so. If we'd gone earlier…but I suppose there's no point in looking back. At least Chamberlain is finally showing some teeth. Not many, mind, but some.

I do feel sorry for the Norwegians. I saw some photos in the newspaper of the bombings the Luftwaffe have been hitting them with. It must be like living in a nightmare to have enemy troops pouring into your towns and not being able to do anything about it. I can't even begin to imagine how they're coping with it all.

Oh! I almost forgot. While we were whiling away the time waiting for our reconnaissance flight to get underway, Rob and I and some of the others went round to their local café for some coffee. I can't tell you where we were, but I will say that we

290

were eating madeleines. While we were there, Rob fell to talking with one of the locals. They didn't seem to very concerned at all about the possibility of an invasion. It seems that most of them think that the Maginot will protect them. I was rather surprised that no one over there seems very worried. It made me think of the fun side of your family, in Paris. Are they of the same mind? Or will they leave France? Rob seems to think they'll stay, even though your mother would be thrilled to have them come here. Do you think they will? I'd love to meet them.

I hope you return soon. I miss you. I'll drive down to see you. Just let me know when.

Always yours,
FO Miles Lacey

Outside Namsos

Evelyn looked through the binoculars at the wide river below separating her from the port town of Namsos. The bridge spanning it looked clear, and there was no sign of a German truck or soldier in sight. She breathed a silent sigh of relief. Turning her head slightly, she looked to the left where she could just make out large shapes in the distant harbors.

"They're there," she said, lowering the binoculars and passing them back to Erik. "I can just make them out in the harbor."

"Yes." He took them and passed her a folded road map. "Here. Take this in case you need it. This was from Peder's car. It's not as good as the one we've been using, but it will help you in a pinch."

"I hardly think I'll need it," she said with a smile, taking it nonetheless. "It's a straight shot across the bridge and through the town to the docks. I'll be fine, but thank you."

She began to remove the rifle slung across her body, but he laid a hand on her arm to stop her, shaking his head.

"No. You keep it. You may have need of it yet."

"It does look odd, though," Anna said with a grin. "A woman walking through town dressed in farming clothes, carrying a suitcase, and wearing a gun. I would look twice."

Evelyn looked down at herself and, for first time since this five-day ordeal had begun, seemed to realize just how ridiculous she looked. She grimaced comically, wondering what on earth her London crowd would say if they saw her now. The grimace turned into a faint look of horror and she was suddenly very grateful that she was hundreds of miles away.

"I look a sight," she agreed, shaking her head. "You don't think I'll be stopped, do you?"

"Not likely," he assured her with a smile. "There are too many people fleeing the Germans with nothing but what was on their backs. You may look odd, but so do many others."

Anna grinned. "We're a long way from the Hotel Bistro, ja?"

Evelyn met her eyes and couldn't stop the laugh that sprang to her lips. "A very long way," she agreed. "Oh God, it's probably filled with Germans troops now. What a ghastly thought!"

She handed Anna Peder's radio, taking her suitcase in return. Smiling sadly, she glanced down at the radio case.

"Promise me you'll get that to Kristian and get it fixed and working again," she said. "It seems like the least we can do for him."

Erik smiled faintly. "We will. It will honor his memory when we continue to use it," he promised. "Don't worry."

"How will I contact you once it's working again?" Anna asked.

Evelyn swallowed the sudden lump that came to her throat. This was it. She was really saying goodbye to the companions that had been through so much with her in such a short amount of time. It was like saying goodbye to family, only worse because she knew she would never see them again.

"I could give you the frequency, but I have a feeling that will change when I get back," she said. "But our people in London will know the call sign of this radio. We'll reach out to you."

Anna nodded then smiled, her eyes meeting hers. "Be sure that you do," she said. "I fully intend on continuing what we started together."

Evelyn nodded. "I know you will. Thank you." She hesitated for a moment, then, "And thank you for everything you've done since I arrived. I'm so sorry it all turned out this way, and I'm so very sorry about Peder. I never meant for…"

Anna shushed her, shaking her head and putting a hand on her shoulder.

"None of us did. This was never supposed to happen. But it did, and we must all do the best we can with what time we have now. Peder made his choice when he came to tell me about the ships outside Oslofjorden. He was not your responsibility. You must stop feeling that he was. The Germans would have come, whether you were here or not. I'm just happy I was in a position to be able to get you this far."

She gave her a fierce hug then pulled away.

"You take care of yourself, Marlene, and I'll see you the next time you come to visit."

Evelyn nodded and smiled, not trusting herself to speak. Instead, she turned to Erik.

"I think I owe the most to you," she said, holding out her hand. "Thank you."

He gripped her hand and nodded brusquely.

"You're welcome." His fingers tightened on hers suddenly when she would have pulled her hand away. "It was an honor. You're a very brave woman, and much stronger than some of the men I've known. Hold on to that strength. It will get you through this war. And you *will* get through it, of that I have no doubt. There are very few who can see what you've seen, and keep going. Never doubt yourself again."

Evelyn swallowed again, pushing down the feeling of sorrow that threatened her composure and made her throat tight.

"Thank you. I won't." She smiled tremulously. "At least, not as badly as I did the other night."

He nodded again and released her hand, one of his rare smiles crossing his lips as he did so.

She turned and held her hand out to Philip. "Take care of yourself, Philip."

"And you as well," he said with a smile. "It was a pleasure to fight by your side. You're a remarkable woman. God speed you on your way."

She nodded and released his hand, turning away to look back over the river below them.

"We'll rest and give you a head start," Erik said, turning to look out over the water with her. "Remember, if you see any Germans, don't panic. They'll think you are a Norwegian. Just continue as normal and don't draw any attention to yourself."

Evelyn took a deep breath and nodded. Then she glanced behind her, gave Anna one last smile, and started down the snowy hillside towards the road below. She reached the bottom a few minutes later and turned to look up. All three of her companions were still standing in the trees at the top, watching her. A stab of sorrow went through her and she wondered if they would survive the coming weeks. She knew now how quickly it could all end in a storm of bullets. And if the Germans ever discovered they had been the ones to help her...

She turned away resolutely, tucking her last sight of Anna and her brother away in her mind. There was no way she could ever repay Anna for everything she had done for her, and now she was just as much indebted to her extraordinary brother and his friend, both of whom who had risked the wrath of their battalion to help get her to Namsos safely. They had all risked so much when they didn't have to. It seemed terrible and heartless to be leaving them to an uncertain future as she went towards safety and freedom. Yet she had no other choice, and she knew both Anna and Erik understood. It was why they had risked so much to get her this far.

Evelyn glanced back over her shoulder a few moments later to find the ridge empty, and a strange feeling of loneliness rolled over her. She was alone.

She shifted the rifle to hang at her side and tightened her grip on her suitcase and toiletries case. The bridge to Namsos was about a quarter mile up the road. She just had to get across and then she could make her way through the town to the docks. The bridge was the only place she would be exposed. There would be nowhere to hide if a truck of SS soldiers came rumbling towards her.

She took a deep breath, forcing herself to calm down. Erik was right. Even if she did come across German soldiers, there was absolutely no reason for them to suspect who she was. She was dressed as a Norwegian, she spoke as a Norwegian, and she had Norwegian papers with a false name, courtesy of Olav Larsen, thank God. She would be fine.

She just had to make it across the bridge.

Chapter Thirty-Three

Bialystok, Poland

Vladimir crossed the lobby of his hotel and nodded to the man behind the desk.

"Are there any messages for me?"

The man nodded and turned to pull a sealed telegram out of a cubby hole behind the desk.

"This telegram arrived for you this morning, shortly after you left, Comrade Lyakhov," he said, handing it to him.

Vladimir nodded and turned to stride towards the stairs. The lift was broken and had been since he arrived, but he didn't mind taking the stairs to his room on the fourth floor. He had always much preferred the stairs. He felt as if he was trapped in a box when he took the lift.

He went up the steps quickly, one gloved hand on the railing, the clip of his boots echoing off the aging tiled walls. At one time, the hotel had been a respectably furnished, up and coming establishment that catered to those who could afford a little more than the ordinary lodgings. But time, and the coming of another war, had dampened any such aspirations. In another year, the tiled walls would begin to show the wear of neglect, necessitated by the stringent economic policies of the Soviet Union. It was inevitable, and was already beginning if the broken lift was any indication.

Vladimir reached the fourth floor and turned to stride down the long corridor to the last door on the left. A moment later, he was closing the door and tossing his hat onto a chair. He unwound the scarf from his neck and began to pull off his leather gloves.

He'd spent a long morning combing one of the southern neighborhoods of the city, looking for the sailor who had been working with the German SD. Once he found him, he could interrogate him, eliminate him, and then get back to Moscow. And that would be another case closed.

Throwing his gloves onto the chair with his hat, he unbuttoned his coat and shrugged out of it before carrying the telegram over to the small desk in the corner. He sat down and tore it open, scanning it quickly.

AGENT STILL IN COUNTRY. SS CORNERED HER IN STEINKJER BUT FAILED TO DETAIN. WHEREABOUTS UNKNOWN. SHE MAY BE HEADING TO NAMSOS. WILL CONTINUE TO PURSUE LEADS. CONTACT AGAIN SHORTLY.

Vladimir set the telegram down on the desk and tapped it thoughtfully, his lips pressed together in a frown. Mikhail had been looking for Evelyn for two and a half days now. The man was one of the NKVD's best agents, and he had no doubt at all that Mikhail was using Eisenjager himself to track down the British agent. The very fact that he still had no idea of her location was both a blessing and a curse. If Eisenjager didn't know where she was then she was relatively safe for now. However, if Mikhail didn't find her soon, her luck wouldn't continue to hold out.

He got up and went over to the bed, reaching down to pull out a square case from underneath. He had been hoping to hear that she was safely away from Norway, but that didn't appear to be so. Vladimir unsnapped the case and flipped it open, removing the folded shirts and setting them on the bed. He lifted out the false bottom to reveal a variety of papers and codebooks. After quickly sorting through them, he extracted a codebook and replaced the false bottom, closing the case.

If she was heading for Namsos, it could be that she was on her way to an extraction point. He sincerely hoped that was the case, but if it wasn't, all was not lost. Mikhail had his orders. If he found her before Eisenjager, he would get her across the border into Sweden, where Vladimir would meet them himself. It wasn't ideal by any means, but it was far better than the alternative if Evelyn was trapped in Norway with Eisenjager.

Crossing back to the small desk, Vladimir set down the codebook and opened the drawer to pull out a telegram pad. It was time to send a message to the imbeciles in London. They were very close to losing an extremely promising young agent through their utterly careless stupidity. They had been given numerous warnings that Hitler was about to invade Norway, and yet they had disregarded all of them. Worse, they had sent a green agent, with no field experience in enemy territory, into Oslo. Vladimir was well aware of the so-called training MI6 provided its agents. It was deplorable, not to mention dangerous. She would have absolutely no idea how to navigate through German occupied territory and not be seen. It would be a complete waste. If Evelyn could only be properly trained, then she would be a force to be reckoned with, and one that would be unstoppable.

But first, she had to get out of Norway, and out of Eisenjager's path.

Namsos, Norway

The man known as Mikhail leaned against a lamp post and bit into a sandwich, seemingly taking a break. His eyes, however, darted from one street corner to the other, memorizing every face that moved along the main street just blocks from the water. British troops had been marching through the small town for the past few hours, unloading from the cruisers and destroyers that had sailed into the fjord. The town was bustling, and an unsuppressed excitement buzzed through the streets. The British had come to help fend off the Nazis.

Yet he wasn't interested in the streams of Royal marines pouring in from the quaysides. Instead, he was searching for a face that he had glimpsed all-too-briefly just outside of Steinkjer the day before. A face that no one could describe because, to his knowledge, no one had ever knowingly seen it before.

When Comrade Lyakhov contacted him and told him to find a British agent whom he believed was being hunted by the notorious Eisenjager, he had been skeptical. They all knew about Eisenjager; the man was a legend. But Mikhail had always been of the opinion that that was all he was: a myth. Yesterday all of that had changed.

His hunt for the woman had seemed doomed to lead him across Norway with only one dubious lead and nothing else. Mikhail was a stubborn man, though, and when Comrade Lyakhov told you to do something, you did it. Unless, of course, you preferred to spend your last days rotting in the Gulag. And so he had persisted, turning his attention instead to looking for a man who might also be pursuing the British agent. And yesterday that persistence had paid off.

Mikhail shook his head as he chewed. Following breadcrumbs left from Oslo to Trondheim and beyond, he had come to the roadblock on the way into Steinkjer yesterday. Recognizing the car stopped at the side of the road from a description given by a couple in a petrol station in Knutshøe, he had pulled his motorcycle into the woods and had gone the rest of the way on foot. Concealed in the trees, he had listened to the three SS soldiers talking at the barrier.

That was when he'd realized the man in the car was, indeed, Eisenjager, and he was most definitely on the trail of a woman. Less than twenty minutes later, Mikhail knew exactly what had happened in the ravine the night before, and he watched as Eisenjager returned to his car and was allowed through the checkpoint to continue on to the town.

Mikhail finished his sandwich and crumpled the paper, tossing it into a wastebasket nearby. He knew Eisenjager was here, looking for the woman. He had followed him here, losing him only after crossing the bridge into Namsos. And as soon as Mikhail had seen the ships in the harbor, he realized that the British agent would be trying to board one to leave Norway. If she wasn't here already, she soon would be. Or, at the very least, Eisenjager thought she would be.

Brushing a few breadcrumbs off his coat, Mikhail began moving along the sidewalk. His orders were very clear: prevent Eisenjager from gaining control of the British agent, and ensure that she departed Norway safely. Failing that, he was to take control of her himself and get her to Sweden. He tucked his hands into his coat pockets and hunched his shoulders against the wind coming off the water. Before he could do that, he had to find her. And Eisenjager was his only hope to do that. The description Lyakhov had given was useless. It described half the women in Norway. No. Eisenjager was his only hope now.

His eyes narrowed sharply when a tall man in an unremarkable brown coat turned the corner, walking towards him. Mikhail waited until he had passed before stopping to look in the window of a shop on the corner. It was him. Eisenjager.

Mikhail shot a look sideways and watched as he stopped near the end of a building, looking across the street before turning the corner. As soon as he disappeared from sight, Mikhail moved quickly, retracing his steps until he reached the corner. Instead of going around it, he leaned against the building and pulled out a pack of cigarettes and a lighter with a mirror finish. Bending his head to light a cigarette, he angled the lighter slightly to give him a small view around the corner. Not seeing the tall man reflected, he turned the corner, pausing to slip the lighter back into his pockets. His eyes swept the narrow street quickly just in time to see Eisenjager disappear into an alley halfway towards the waterfront.

Casting another glance over the street, he crossed it quickly and moved down the road until he was opposite the alley. As he passed it, he glanced across the street and into the narrow space between the buildings. Eisenjager was leaning against one of the buildings, looking at the end of the street where a bevy of activity surrounded the entrance to one of the wharves. British soldiers swarmed around a makeshift checkpoint that had already been established to prevent unauthorized people like himself from getting anywhere near the cruiser docked there.

A small smile curved Mikhail's lips as he continued down the street towards the wharf entrance. Eisenjager had obviously determined that if the British agent was going to try to leave Norway, she would do so from that wharf. How he had figured it out was immaterial. If Eisenjager was watching the only approach to the wharf, he clearly expected his prey to come by.

Reaching the end of the street, Mikhail turned left to double back to a narrow lane he hoped would lead to the other end of that alley. He would have to be quick. If the German agent was in position, he didn't have much time.

Evelyn thanked the newspaper vendor and turned away, relief rolling through her. According to the wizened old man, the British had been unloading troops and supplies for the past three hours down at the docks. Not only had she made it into Namsos, but it seemed as if everything was still on schedule. She just might make it out yet.

Tucking the newspaper she'd purchased from him in thanks for the help under her arm, she ran across the street and started up the sidewalk. He'd told her to turn left at the corner and then follow the road straight to the wharves. The smell of saltwater filled her nostrils and she breathed deeply in the tangy scent of ocean…and freedom. She was almost there.

Turning the corner, Evelyn found herself standing at the top of a long, narrow street that ran at an angle down to the water. The sight of the familiar brown and green uniforms that greeted her caused another wave of emotion to wash over her, and she felt her throat tighten in response.

Switching her suitcase to her other hand, Evelyn self-consciously tucked the rife to her side as she began to make her way down the street. She had no idea what ship Lt. Commander Wheeler was on, nor how to find him, but that didn't seem to matter right now. She had made it this far, through the mountains and the snow, through the SS unit that had cost Peder his life, to end up here, just yards away from freedom. She hadn't thought she would make it, and if not for

Erik and his tough truths, Evelyn suspected she would have given up the night Peder died. Yet here she was, garnering a mix of shocked and curious looks from men and women alike as she made her way through the waterfront town toting a rifle over her shoulder and a battered suitcase and toiletries case that looked as if they had been through the wars.

Her lips twisted suddenly as she caught sight of her reflection in a window and a shot of amusement went through her. What would Miles say if he could see her right now? Good heavens, she would be mortified if anyone she knew saw her like this, but especially Miles! Not that he would even recognize her. No trace of the genteel aristocrat was visible. She looked more like a homeless vagabond than the wealthy socialite that she was. She shook her head and tightened her grasp on the toiletries case. It would be interesting trying to get someone to take her seriously once she reached the dock. It would be a miracle if she could get anyone to listen to her, and who would blame them?

A large group of marines were marching towards her, and Evelyn looked around. There was nowhere to move out of their way, so instead she ducked into the street, crossing to the opposite pavement. Once she reached it, she paused and turned to watch them march on, a strange feeling of pride going through her. Sending up a quick prayer for their safety, she turned to continue on her way, her eyes on the entrance to the wharf ahead of her.

British soldiers and officers were moving in and out of the quay in organized chaos while two Royal marine guards stood watching everyone who approached the entrance. The checkpoint was reinforced by two automatic rifles mounted on walls of packed sandbags, one on each side of the entrance. She could just see the helmets of the men manning them over the tops of the barriers. As she approached the end of the road, army trucks rolled up from the quayside and stopped at the entrance before pulling out to turn and head into the town. The British were already well on their way to establishing themselves.

Evelyn swallowed and looked across the street, then took a deep breath and crossed to the checkpoint. As she approached, silence fell among the soldiers and she felt dozens of eyes staring at her in astonishment. Ignoring the almost overwhelming feeling of embarrassed discomfort, she kept her eyes on the guard closest to her. As she drew closer, he caught sight of the rifle at her side and shifted his own gun into his hands, frowning and stepping forward warningly.

"The wharf is off limits, miss," he said in English, glancing behind him. Another soldier moved forward to join him, repeating the same thing in Norwegian.

Night Falls on Norway

Evelyn smiled and came to a stop in front of them, setting her cases down in the snow.

"I'm a British subject," she said, speaking English for the first time in over two weeks. It seemed strange to hear her crisp, upper-crust accent after so long.

The two men facing her looked startled, and the one who had spoken first slowly released his rifle, his brows furrowing.

"I'll need to see your papers," he said. "Do you have them?"

"Yes. They're in my small case. Just a moment."

Evelyn bent to open her toiletries case. She lifted out the top tray that held her hairbrush, hair pins and other personal items to pull out her English passport. Looking up, she passed it to him with one hand as she replaced the tray and closed the case with the other.

Both men peered down at her passport, studying it before looking back at her in astonishment.

"Thank you, Miss," the one said, handing it back to her. "What are you doing here?"

"I'm looking for Lieutenant Commander Wheeler, actually," she said with a smile. "I do hope I haven't missed him. The infuriating thing is that I have absolutely no idea which ship he's on!"

Both men stared at her, clearly unsure how to react to the obviously aristocratic tone and inflections that were coming from a woman dressed in the clothes of a farmer and carrying a rifle. Just when she was sure that she would have to try someone else, a tall officer approached from behind them.

"How do you know Lieutenant Commander Wheeler?" he asked, his blue eyes sweeping over her. "What is your business with him?"

"I don't know him. I was told to ask for him, and my business is my own," she said, returning his gaze evenly.

"And who told you to ask for him?"

"Sir William Buckley, in London."

The officer didn't show any reaction to the name but he reached out his hand for her passport. She handed it over, watching as he examined it.

"Why do you carry a Norwegian Defense Force rifle?" he asked, not lifting his eyes from her identification.

"I don't know if you're aware, but there appear to be an awful lot of Germans with guns running about," Evelyn said dryly.

Her response got his attention and he raised his eyes to hers swiftly, a laugh lurking in their depths.

"I was fortunate enough to have a Norwegian Lieutenant escort me here from Trondheim. He gave me the rifle for protection after seeing that I could handle it."

"You can fire that rifle?"

"Yes, of course I can. I've been hunting since I could walk," she said briskly.

A faint smile crossed his stern face and he closed her passport, handing it back to her.

"You will have to unload it and surrender it to the corporal here before you can come through," he told her. "It will be returned when you leave. I'm sure you understand."

Evelyn nodded and lifted the strap over her head, opening the side chamber and extracting the rounds that had fed in from the cartridge. Once the rifle was empty, she held it out to the corporal.

"Please do be careful with it," she said. "I've grown rather attached to it."

The corporal couldn't stop the grin that crossed his face as he took the gun.

"Yes, miss."

"If you would come with me?" the officer offered, holding out his hand politely to motion her forward. "I'm Lieutenant Barker. I'll be happy to assist you in locating the Lt. Commander."

Evelyn picked up her cases and joined him beyond the barrier, walking with him towards a small hut near the quayside.

"Thank you. I'm afraid I have no idea which ship he's on, or even if he's arrived yet," she confessed.

Lt. Barker glanced at her. "No? How is that?"

"I'm afraid I was caught in Oslo when this all began and in the ensuing chaos, I lost communication with Sir Buckley before he could give me all the information. The only thing I was told was to present myself here today and ask for the Lt. Commander."

"You've come all the way from Oslo?" he demanded, shocked. "How on earth did you make it?"

"Not without challenge," she replied tiredly. "Thankfully, I was ahead of the advancing troops for most of the journey."

"Good Lord, how extraordinary," he murmured, opening the door to the hut and holding it for her. "Now the rifle is making much more sense."

Evelyn stepped into the small hut to find a desk on one side and two folding chairs on the other. He motioned her into one of the chairs, leaning against the desk once she was seated.

"When did you leave Oslo?"

Night Falls on Norway

"In the early hours Tuesday morning, before the Germans launched their attack."

"You've been traveling since Tuesday?"

"Fleeing would be a more appropriate term," she said dryly. "I didn't think I would make it, but here I am."

He shook his head, clearly amazed and stood up.

"If you wouldn't mind waiting here, I'll go and try to hunt down the Lt. Commander. He's on the *HMS Cardiff,* and she's still in the harbor." He turned to the door. "I'll be as quick as I can. I know they were planning on weighing anchor soon."

"Thank you."

Evelyn watched him disappear through the door, closing it behind him. A small, wood-burning stove sat in the corner and she got up to go over to it, shivering. Reaching her hands towards the warmth, she exhaled and tried to make her shoulders relax. The ship was still here. She hadn't missed it.

No matter how many times she repeated it to herself, her body refused to relax. Letting out a deep sigh, she turned to pull the chair over to the stove and sat down again tiredly.

She would relax once she reached London.

Chapter Thirty-Four

Mikhail moved silently through the back entrance to the narrow alleyway. The buildings on either side blocked the noise from the street, giving an eerie feeling of being isolated from the rest of the town. That suited him perfectly, and he felt right at home in the shadows as he paused behind a wooden staircase rising to an upper level entrance. At the other end, Eisenjager still leaned against the wall, his back to Mikhail. There were no other obstructions between him and his target after the staircase, but the alley narrowed significantly about halfway down. He would have to be silent and move quickly once he passed the stairs. While he had no doubt that his training was as good as the German's, he had no desire to draw attention to the alley with the noise of a struggle.

After watching the man at the end of the alley for a long moment, Mikhail moved out from behind the stairs. Something had drawn Eisenjager's attention in the street, and he had shifted so that his back was to the rest of the alley. As Mikhail moved forward, Eisenjager pulled something out of his coat pocket, bending his head to check it briefly before turning his attention back to the street.

Mikhail eyed the pistol in Eisenjager's hand as he crept forward, staying in the shadows of the building to his left. It was a Browning HP-35, a high powered pistol that, in the hands of an experienced shooter, was capable of picking off a target up to fifty meters away. There could be no doubt as to Eisenjager's objective. He had absolutely no intention of detaining the British spy.

So much for Lyakhov's belief that the Germans wanted the woman for themselves.

His shoulders stiffened when Mikhail was less than three feet away, and Mikhail braced himself for the possibility that he would turn and see him, but the German agent was too focused on his prey. He raised his firing arm, steadying his wrist with his other hand, his eyes locked on his target in the street. Following his gaze, Mikhail watched as a blonde woman dressed in heavy pants, boots, and a long winter coat at odds with the rest of her attire stopped on the pavement, turning to watch a group of British soldiers march up the street. She had a rifle slung over her shoulder and carried a suitcase and smaller, square case. In that split second, he knew Eisenjager would never get a more perfect shot.

Mikhail closed the gap between them swiftly, slicing his left hand in a downward arc to slam into the bundle of nerves below his ear. As his left hand made contact, his right wrist hit the arm holding the pistol, forcing it down before the German could take advantage of the perfect, stationary target. Eisenjager let out a gasp before his eyes closed and he fell sideways into Mikhail's waiting arms.

Easing the tall, unconscious man to the ground, Mikhail slid the pistol from his fingers and tucked it into his own pocket. Straightening up, he looked out of the alley. The woman had turned to continue down the street, her eyes fixed on the flurry of activity by the entrance to the quayside. Moving out of the shadows and to the corner of the alley, he watched her go, pressing his lips together thoughtfully.

It had to be her. The description, while it matched half of the women in Norway, was exact. Coupled with Eisenjager's obvious attempt to assassinate her, it had to be the British agent, but she was nothing like what he would have expected of one of Lyakhov's targets. She was young, very young, and despite the strange, mismatched clothing, she was very beautiful. Who was she? And why was Comrade Lyakhov so determined that she get out of Norway and away from the SS with all speed?

He shifted his gaze to the entrance of the wharf and the makeshift checkpoint. She was headed straight for it. Was she going to try to get out of Norway by getting on a ship? Or did she already have an extraction set up?

Leaning against the corner of the alley, Mikhail partially hid the inanimate form on the ground behind him from view, and reached into his coat to pull out his cigarettes. There would be nothing unusual in the sight of a working man taking a break to smoke in the mouth of an alley. He lit a cigarette, never taking his eyes from the woman reaching the end of the street and crossing to the checkpoint. He would wait to see what happened. If she remained in Namsos, he would do as Lyakhov had ordered. How he would convince her that he could get her safely to Sweden was another matter entirely, but he would find a way. He always did.

When she was led past the barriers a few minutes later and shown into a small hut on the quayside, Mikhail dropped his cigarette butt and put it out with his boot. Turning his head, he looked down at

Eisenjager dispassionately. The man was still out cold, but he would come around shortly. When he did, he would find his target out of reach and no sign of his assailant.

Bending down, Mikhail picked up the extinguished cigarette butt and palmed it before moving out of the alley and turning to walk up the street. It was time to contact Comrade Lyakhov and return to Oslo. The British agent was safe in the hands of her own people.

His work here was finished.

Evelyn looked up, startled, when the door to the small hut opened without warning. She had been sitting near the wood stove for over an hour now, alternating between dozing and fretting over whether or not the Lt. Commander had already weighed anchor and was gone. The thought of going back out there and trying to find another way home filled her with hopeless despair, and so she continued to sit in the little hut, hoping that *HMS Cardiff* was still there.

Now, as she stared up at an officer of medium height with black hair graying at the temples, she knew her wait was over. He looked at her briefly, then closed the door to the hut before crossing over to stand in front of the desk.

"Miss Masters?" he asked. "Miss Jenny Masters?"

Evelyn nodded, relief rolling through her. The name on the passport she had handed the guard was Laura Masters. Jenny was never mentioned on the papers, but was the codename that went with the identification. The only way this man could possibly know that name was if MI6 had told him.

"Yes."

His face relaxed into a smile. "I'm very pleased to meet you. I'm Lieutenant Commander Wheeler. You've had us on pins and needles all morning, wondering if you were going to make it in time."

"I'm terribly sorry about that," she said with a small smile. "I lost my radio operator, you see. I had no way of contacting London."

A shadow crossed his face and his eyes met hers, surprisingly kindly for a complete stranger.

"I'm sorry to hear that. Well, at least you're here now. You've come just in the nick of time, as well. The captain's ready to give the order to weigh anchor. I'm to get you aboard without delay. He's anxious to be underway, as I'm sure you are as well."

She nodded tiredly. "Yes, indeed, thank you. There is just one thing, a small matter of my rifle. I believe it's being held at the gate."

Wheeler was betrayed into a grin.

"Ah yes, the infamous rifle. I'm told you walked up with it slung over your shoulder. Gave the boys at the entrance quite a turn."

"I'm afraid I look a fright," Evelyn admitted with a laugh. "I don't blame them for being leery of me. I've been walking through the mountains for four and a half days. Fashion took second place to practicality, you see."

The Lt. Commander stared at her. "Four and a half days?" he repeated, stunned. "There's four feet of snow out there!"

She nodded. "Yes. I'm well aware."

"Where did you come from?"

"Oslo."

"Oslo! But they took Oslo on Tuesday!"

"Yes. I left a few hours before they arrived in the city. I've been moving ever since."

"How on earth did you do it? The Nazis are advancing everywhere and have taken control of all the airfields. How did you avoid them?"

"I had a very good guide who knows the terrain well, and I had a companion who knew the importance of getting me here in time to catch your ship."

Wheeler shook his head and straightened up, bending to pick up her suitcase.

"My dear girl, you may have your rifle back with my compliments. I'll have Lieutenant Barker ensure it is delivered to the ship immediately. You've earned the right to carry whatever weapon you desire as far as I'm concerned."

He smiled down at her and, despite herself, Evelyn felt her eyes fill with tears at his kind tone that reminded her so forcibly of Bill and her father.

"Come. Let's get you aboard ship and settled," he said gently, seeing the tears shimmering in her eyes. "It's time to go home."

Bialystok, Poland

Vladimir looked up when a knock fell on his door and a sealed telegram slid under the gap along the floor. Raising his eyebrow, he crossed the room to pick it up. There was no noise in the corridor, but he opened the door and looked out anyway. He was just in time to see a hotel uniform disappear around the corner at the end of the hall.

Closing the door, he locked it again and turned to carry the telegram over to the desk. He had been pouring over maps of the city, looking for a particular street that had been mentioned during his manhunt. Pushing the maps aside, he tore open the telegram, reading it quickly.

MISSION COMPLETED. SHORES ARE CLEAR. DEPARTING NAMSOS FOR OSLO.

A slow smile curved his lips and he tossed the telegram onto the desk. Evelyn was on her way home. She had made it.

He got up and went to the window, pulling the curtain back and looking out over the dark city below. He'd known Mikhail would find her. Even in the midst of an invasion, the man could find anything, or anyone. Even so, Vladimir was conscious of a feeling of relief. Eisenjager had complicated things, causing some worry, but now it was over, and Robert Ainsworth's daughter was on her way home.

Now that she was safely away from the Nazi invasion in Norway, his own plans could proceed. He stared out the window, his lips pressed together thoughtfully. The message he'd sent for MI6 to intercept earlier would get the ball rolling. He had no doubt of that. They wouldn't have a choice, not if they wanted to continue to receive the information he was passing on to them. And, given their present situation with a mole in their midst, they wouldn't have much basis to argue.

Yes. Things were progressing nicely in that quarter, now that the little hiccup with Evelyn had been resolved.

Vladimir dropped the curtain and turned to return to the desk. It was time to get back to work. The sooner he tracked down his target, the sooner he could leave Poland and focus on the British agent.

The coming months were going to be vital, and he had every intention of using them to his advantage. While this incident in Norway had been unforeseen, it was just possible that it would end up being a key to what was to come.

And a large part of unlocking the enigma that was Evelyn Ainsworth.

Chapter Thirty-Five

London, England
April 20

Bill got out of the back of the sedan and went up the shallow steps to the glossy black door of the stately home on Brook Street. He carried a bag filled with groceries from the market in one hand and his umbrella in the other. The sky had been overcast all morning, threatening rain that had yet to appear. As he pressed the bell with the handle of his umbrella, he cast a glance to the heavy clouds overhead. It was coming. There was no doubt about it. London was in for deluge.

Wesley had called him at home a few hours ago to tell him that the train bearing Evelyn from Scotland had arrived at Waterloo station. The fact that his assistant had volunteered to spend his Saturday morning at the train station waiting to ensure that Jian arrived back in London safely was telling. He had been just as concerned as Bill was himself when they hadn't heard anything from her leading up to her evacuation. It had been with great relief that they received the message from *HMS Cardiff* that the package was onboard. A rough crossing in the North Sea, complicated by a close shave with a German U-boat, had delayed her arrival in Scapa Flow. Then a violent storm had once again delayed her moving onto the Scottish mainland and beginning the final leg of her journey back to England.

But now she was home, and Bill had stopped to get her a few provisions on his way over, knowing that the Ainsworth residence in London had been standing empty. This at least would save her having to go out for dinner on her first night back after what must have been, in the end, a harrowing experience.

When the door opened, his ready smile froze on his face and his eyes widened in shock. Evelyn was dressed in wide-legged black trousers and a white blouse with flowing sleeves, but the clothes did nothing to conceal the fact that she had dropped a significant amount of weight in the three weeks that she had been gone. Her hair was pulled back into a chignon at the back of her head, giving him an unimpeded view of an extremely pale face and very deep, dark hollows under her eyes.

"Bill!" she exclaimed, her eyes lighting up and a smile spreading across her face. "How lovely! Come in!"

She stepped back so that he could enter the house, closing the door behind him.

"Welcome back, Evie, my dear," he said with a smile, recovering his composure quickly. "I've brought you a few things to help tide you over until you can get to the shops."

"Thank you! All I've got in the larder is tea." She moved to take the bag from him but he shook his head and pulled it away.

"I'll carry it in for you," he told her. "You must be exhausted."

"Not so exhausted I can't carry a few groceries," she replied with a laugh. "Very well. Let me take your hat and coat, at least."

Bill handed her his umbrella and hat and shrugged out of his top coat.

"How was the train down?"

"It was very uneventful, which I appreciated very much," she said, turning to hang his coat in a closet inside the door. "I came on the Flying Scotsman, which was a first for me."

She closed the closet door and turned to lead the way down the hall to the kitchen in the back of the house.

"Well, you've had enough starts and stops over the past few days, haven't you?" he asked, following her into the large kitchen. "You deserved a non-stop trip. How long did it take?"

"A little over seven hours." She turned to take the bag of groceries from him and motioned him into a seat at the table. "I slept some of the way. There's something about trains that always makes me sleepy."

Bill sat down and crossed his legs, watching as she unpacked the bag on the counter a few feet away. Her movements were much slower than normal and he hadn't missed the strange gait as she preceded him down the hallway, as if she was nursing a bad foot. She hadn't limped, precisely, but she definitely wasn't moving with her usual confident energy.

"It's the rocking, I expect," he said. "What time did you get in?"

"Just over an hour ago. I'd just finished unpacking when you came." Evelyn turned with a packet of sausages in her hand. "This is wonderful! Thank you! And you even bought eggs!"

Night Falls on Norway

"I seem to remember that the Norwegians are like the French in that they don't eat a good breakfast," he said with a faint smile. "It looks like I made the right choice. You look half starved, my dear."

She grimaced and turned to put the sausages on the counter while she reached into the bag to pull out the rest of the groceries.

"That's due more to my flight across Norway than the bread and cheese breakfasts," she said over her shoulder. "Believe me, when I could get it, that bread and cheese was wonderful!"

"When you could get it?"

"Food was...scarce," she said, emptying the bag. She turned to reach for the kettle on the stove. "We had to go on foot through the mountains, avoiding the villages and towns where we could have bought food. We weren't sure where the Germans were, you see. It was safer to avoid them and not risk being caught between the advancing troops. Else, the landlady at the boarding house in Oslo, packed us a basket with bread and cheese when we left in the middle of the night, which was very kind and generous of her. But once we met Erik and the others, it didn't go very far."

Bill watched her fill the kettle with water, his eyes narrowing when she swayed slightly and had to grab hold of the edge of the counter to steady herself. He waited until she had finished filling it, then he stood up and took it from her hand.

"I'll do this," he said, gently guiding her into a seat at the table. "Sit down. You look as if you're about to fall over."

"I just got a little light-headed," she protested. "It's nothing."

"I'm very glad to hear it, but I'd feel better if you sat. I'm quite capable of making a cup of tea, I assure you." He lit one of the gas burners and set the kettle over the flame, turning to look at her. "When was the last time you ate?"

"I had a few biscuits on the train."

"I mean a real meal. When was the last time you had something substantial?"

Evelyn thought for a moment. It was a brief moment, but it was too long for him. The fact that she had to think about it brought a frown to his face and he studied her silently for a long moment.

"I had dinner when I arrived in Scapa, but I'm afraid my stomach was upset after the crossing," she finally said. "Given the horrid weather, I didn't want to eat before getting on the boat to go across to the mainland. When I reached John o' Groats, it was mid-morning and I just had time for a scone and some tea before my train left for Inverness."

"So you're saying you haven't had a decent meal since you left Scapa?"

She shrugged and rubbed her temples. "I suppose not. To be honest, I hadn't given it much thought. I've felt so…well, it really doesn't matter, does it? I'm here now, and you've brought plenty of food to make a lovely dinner of eggs, sausage and beans. I'll make up for it."

"You said you went by foot?" Bill asked. "You mean to tell me you *walked* all the way from Oslo to Namsos?"

"Not quite all the way. We had a car part of the way until it broke down south of Trondheim. While Peder, that's the man whose car it was, tried to figure out what was wrong, Anna's brother Erik came out of the hills. He's in the Norwegian army, and he had a few of his men with him. They were separated from their battalion when Trondheim fell. He advised leaving the car. By then, Peder had decided it was most likely a crack in the head gasket, so the car was dead anyway. That's when we started hiking."

"Who is this Peder?" Bill asked after a moment.

"He was a friend of Anna's. He went to school with Erik. He was a radio enthusiast, and I'd met him a few days before. He'd agreed to join the network to get information to us, but only if the Germans really did try to invade Norway. When he learned there were ships in the fjord outside Oslo, he went to warn Anna. They came to get me."

"And it was his radio you were using to contact us?"

"Yes."

"What happened?" he asked after a moment.

Evelyn was quiet for a moment and he thought she wasn't going to answer, but then she spoke, her voice flat and emotionless.

"He was killed outside Steinkjer."

The kettle began to whistle and Bill turned to look for cups. Finding them behind the second cabinet door he opened, he pulled out two.

"The tea is in that one over there," Evelyn said, pointing.

He opened the indicated door and pulled out the tea. "And the radio?"

"He gave it to me when…well, when it was clear he couldn't continue. But I think it must have been damaged when he fell because I couldn't get it to work." She watched as he fixed the tea, a silence falling over them. After a moment, she continued. "I kept trying, but it was no use. In the end, Erik took it and said he would contact another friend of his who would be able to get it working. He promised to use it to contact us with information on German activity if the Nazis do end up occupying Norway."

"And Anna?"

"She will continue building the network we started."

Bill handed her a steaming cup of tea, frowning when her hands shook as she took it from him.

"How was Peder killed?" he asked gently, taking his seat with the other cup of tea.

"The SS were waiting for us outside Steinkjer." She sipped her tea, then lifted her eyes to his. "They knew I was there. They knew where I was going."

He sighed, his face grave.

"Yes, I know. MI5 has been intercepting messages between the spy in London and Berlin. We were only made aware if it after you were already on your way, and by then it was too late to warn you. I notified you as soon as I could."

"Your message came as we ran into an SS patrol," she said after a moment. "In a way, it may have saved us. We were already moving when we realized they were there. If we hadn't received that message when we did, it could have been worse."

Bill looked at the shadows in her eyes and the hollows in her face and wondered how much worse it could possibly have been. The woman sitting across from him was a stranger, a completely different person from the one he'd sent on her way three weeks before.

"There is one thing," she said suddenly, her forehead creasing thoughtfully. "We heard some of the soldiers talking and they mentioned a name I've heard before, but I can't remember where or how."

He raised his eyebrow. "Oh?"

"Yes. Eisenjager." She looked across the table at him. "It means—"

"Iron Hunter," he said, a chill going through him despite the hot liquid in his cup. "Are you certain?"

"Yes." She stared at him for a minute. "You know it as well. Who is it?"

"What did you overhear?" he asked, avoiding the question for the moment.

"Only that they thought it was Eisenjager who informed their superior that I would be passing that way. They were moving away from us at that point, and I couldn't catch much else. Something about Himmler, and a bit about Eisenjager being a myth, but it didn't make much sense."

"And you've heard the name before?"

"Yes, but I don't know where or how." Evelyn rubbed her forehead tiredly. "I just know that it isn't the first time I've come across it."

Bill drank his tea, his mind spinning. If Eisenjager was involved, many more things were beginning to make sense. It explained why the Nazis had sent an SS unit so quickly to Steinkjer and how they knew she was coming. His lips tightened suddenly. If the notorious German assassin-turned-spy was involved, it was a bloody miracle Evelyn was sitting across from him now.

"What do you know of him?" Evelyn asked, her eyes on his. "Who is he?"

"He's a German agent," he said reluctantly, setting down his cup. "As far as we know, he began in the SS, trained before the war and hand-selected by Himmler himself. We think he was an assassin, a member of one of the death squads. However, recent information indicates that he has moved over to the Abwehr, Hitler's intelligence division."

"So now he's a spy?"

"We believe so, yes, and a very dangerous one." Bill shook his head. "If he was the one who informed the SS that you were in Norway, he must have been there as well."

"And this is all because of a spy right here in London," she muttered, pushing her empty cup away. "How did they know I was there? I thought you and Jasper had ensured that no one knew of my movements."

"We're working on it. To be honest, I don't see how he could have known for sure. I'm of the opinion that he guessed."

"Guessed? Well his guess was not only correct, but it cost the life of an innocent civilian who was doing everything he could to help me," Evelyn said, her voice shaking with anger.

Bill nodded. She was right, and there was absolutely nothing he could say to defend it. Whoever this Henry was, he had caused an inordinate amount of damage already. It was only luck and fate that had brought Evelyn home, especially if Eisenjager had been put on her trail.

"We will find him."

She sighed impatiently and stood up. "But in the meantime, I'm—"

She cut off abruptly as her face drained of color and she swayed on her feet. Bill jumped up, catching her just as she pitched sideways towards the counter. Her eyes had closed, her body a dead weight in his arms.

Night Falls on Norway

"Evie!" he exclaimed, patting her face. "Good God, Evie!"

She didn't respond and he scooped her up into his arms, striding for the door. He carried her down the hallway to the front parlor where he knew from many previous visits that there was a long couch. A moment later, he laid her gently on the sheet-covered cushions. As he straightened up, she made a noise in her throat and came awake with a start.

"Oh!" she gasped, her eyes flaring wide.

Bill laid a firm hand on her shoulder when she would have tried to sit up.

"Oh no you don't," he said, shaking his head. "You stay right where you are."

"What happened?"

"You fainted," he told her bluntly. "You're ill. I knew as soon as you opened the door."

"Fainted?" she stared up at him, aghast. "Impossible! I've never fainted before in my life!"

"Well, you have now. Not surprising, really, after what you've been through." He turned towards the door. "Is the telephone working?"

"Yes. Yes, I think so," she said, frowning. "It was the last time I stayed here."

"I'm calling for a doctor, and then I'm going to have one of the nurses from the agency come round. She can help you upstairs and into bed."

"Oh for heaven's sake!" Evelyn protested. "That's hardly necessary! I probably just need some rest, that's all."

He paused at the door and looked back at her.

"You may be right, but right now you're having a doctor look at you to make sure. You can debrief once you're well again. You're absolutely no good to me dead, you know."

She pulled a face but made no attempt to get up again.

"Bill!" she called as he was halfway out the door. "Why me?"

He frowned and turned back, looking at her questioningly. "Pardon?"

She was looking at him soberly from the couch, her eyes troubled.

"Why did you choose me last year? What made you think I would be good at this?"

Bill exhaled and met her gaze steadily.

"There are a number of reasons," he said slowly, "but the one that matters right now is that you were made for this."

She stared at him. "What?"

He smiled faintly. "You may not feel like it now, but you are one of the few who can handle this life. I saw it in your face when we had lunch and you spoke of Hitler and how important it was that he be stopped. It takes a certain kind of person to weather the kind of storm we're going into, and you're that person."

"I don't feel like I'm strong enough to weather anything," she whispered. "I don't know how I made it to Namsos. I really don't."

"And that, my dear, is precisely why you *are* strong enough. Strength isn't something you're aware of. It's something that shows itself when there is no other choice." He looked at her for a moment, then walked over to stand beside the couch. "You've changed drastically in the past three weeks. I can see that. Yet here you are. That is what I saw in Paris last year."

"I killed a man, Bill," she blurted out, her eyes dark and haunted. "I shot him and watched him die. Then I shot…oh, I don't know how many more! Peder died because he was shot in his leg and couldn't continue. We just left him there! And then, when we were away, we heard the Nazis open fire on him. They used machine guns, Bill, on a wounded man."

He swallowed, his chest tightening at the pain in her eyes and the grief in her voice. The sheltered, young socialite had become a soldier somewhere in the mountains of Norway, and there was nothing he could do to ease her growing pains. That was something she would have to deal with herself. But she didn't have to do it alone. Crouching down next to the couch, he took one of her hands in his.

"You've seen the ugly side of war, I'm afraid, and there is no unseeing that," he said gently. "You should never have been in Oslo when the Nazis invaded, but this would have happened eventually if the war continues for any length of time. This is what it means to be at war. You did what you had to do, what everyone who is called to fight must do, and because you did, Peder is the only one who lost his life. Make no mistake, Evie. They would have killed all of them to get to you, and that will never change. You will always be the target, and you will always have to protect those who are working alongside you. But don't let it define who you are. Accept what happened in Norway, grieve for it, but leave it on that mountainside outside Steinkjer. It's over, and it cannot be undone. You will continue, and you will be even stronger for it. I promise."

Evelyn clung tightly to his hand for a long moment, tears shimmering in her eyes, then she slowly exhaled and nodded, releasing his hand.

Night Falls on Norway

"Erik said much the same thing when I left them. This is what I get for wanting to fight like a man, I suppose," she said after a moment, a hint of dryness in her tone. "I was never cut out to knit jumpers and make jam for the soldiers, but this seems to be quite the other end of the scale."

Bill smiled faintly and stood up. "You'll find your spot in the middle, Evie," he said, looking down at her. "It's a long road we have before us, but it won't all be like Norway. Now, I'm going to ring the doctor and get a nurse over here."

He turned to leave the room again, pressing lips together as soon as his back was to her. It was a long road ahead indeed, and Hitler was just getting started. But as Bill left the parlor and went towards the telephone on the small table in the hallway, he felt oddly optimistic. Herr Hitler might be just getting started, but so were they.

And Jian was about to become the thorn in Hitler's side.

Epilogue

22nd April, 1940
Dearest Miles,

How are you? I returned from training, but was sent immediately to London for a few days on an advanced course. It's a pity we can't have dinner together while I'm here, but I shan't have the time. I'm due back on the 25th. I do wish I could see you, though. I feel as if it's been simply ages.

Thank you for all the letters that I had waiting for me. You can have no notion how much they cheered my spirits. The training trip was very challenging and, in the end, took a lot more out of me than I expected. The hour I spent reading through your letters made me feel almost like myself again.

I was very glad to hear that you made it over enemy territory and back without incident. I know you're all itching to shoot down some Jerries, but it will come soon enough. For now, I am just thankful that you and Robbie are safe.

It doesn't look as if things are going very well in Norway. I read today that our forces are in danger of being surrounded by German troops. The Luftwaffe is bombing relentlessly, destroying our supplies and communications. I don't see how we can last much longer. We may have won at Narvik, but the Nazis have the entire southern portion of the country overrun. I think it's only a matter of time before we must retreat. Then what will happen to the Norwegian people?

I'm beginning to see everything that I was afraid would happen if Hitler was allowed to continue. We allowed him to become powerful, and now he can't be stopped. His Blitzkrieg is the stuff of nightmares, rolling over everything in its path. He'll turn his attention to France soon, and the Maginot line will not stop him. I've also heard people in Paris say that the Maginot will protect them. That seems to be a common theme among the French, and it's rather infuriating, to be honest. They refuse to acknowledge that the Maginot was never finished! France didn't want to violate Belgian borders, so it never went to the sea as had been intended. That leaves the entire border of Belgium open to attack, and Hitler is a fool if he doesn't take advantage of it.

My family at least sees the danger. They will leave Paris at the first sign of any German offensive. My aunt and uncle will most likely come to stay with my mother, so you may get the chance to meet them. My cousins, however, are reluctant to leave France. I suppose I can't blame them. I'd want to stay and help England if she were invaded. Tell Robbie that Nicolas and Gisele are at least considering coming to England with their parents, but I don't hold out much hope. He wants to stay, and Zell will never leave him. I hope it doesn't come to them having to make that choice, but I'm very afraid that it will.

Will I see you when I get back to my station at last? I do hope we can work something out. I miss you dreadfully, you know.

Sincerely yours,
Evelyn

Author's Notes

1. **Replica Enigma Machine**. In 1939, six days before Germany invaded Poland, a British Military mission (MM-4) arrived in Poland posing as civilians. Their aim was to get a team of Polish code-breakers out of the country, along with their replica Engima machine. The team made contact with Gwido Langer, Marian Rejewski, Jerzy Różycki and Henryk Zygalski and escaped with them when Poland was invaded. They went across the border into Romania, and from there onward to Western Europe, where they passed their decryption techniques on to the French and British. It was only because of the advanced work performed by these men, and the successful extraction by the British team, that Alan Turing was able to complete his extraordinary work and ultimately crack the Enigma code. One of the members of the British team was a woman named Vera Atkins. She went on to become the assistant to section head Col Maurice Buckmaster of the SOE (Special Operations Executive), and was responsible for the recruitment and deployment of female British agents into occupied France. (Wikipedia: https://en.wikipedia.org/wiki/Vera_Atkins)

2. **Government Code and Cypher School (GC&CS)**. This was the organization responsible for intercepting, decoding, and distributing foreign cyphers and intelligence. During WW2, they were located at Bletchley Park, a country mansion north of London. Bletchley was purchased by Hugh Sinclair in 1938 to be used as the wartime base for SIS and GC&CS. However, SIS, now renamed MI6, ultimately moved back to London before the outbreak of war, leaving Bletchley to the codebreakers. The GC&CS was renamed to GCHQ after the war in 1946. They are, of course, most well-known for the work of Alan Turing and others in breaking both the German Engima and Lorenz codes, which some argue shortened the war by several years. There were several sections of the GC&CS during the war, including the Air Section, Naval Section and Army Section. For the purposes of this series, when referring the GC&CS, it is in relation to the codebreaking activities that occurred at Bletchley Park.

3. **Mechelen Incident (aka Mechelen Affair)**. January 10th, 1940. A German aircraft with two officers on board crashed in Belgium, near the town of Mechelen-sur-Meuse. One of the officers, Major Helmut Reinberger, had the operational plans for the airborne attack on Belgium in his briefcase. When they realized they were in Belgium and not Germany, Major Reinberger revealed to his pilot that he had secret documents that must be destroyed. He went behind a thicket to burn the documents, but two Belgian border guards had arrived on bicycles and saw the smoke coming from the bushes. One of them rushed over to save the documents from being destroyed. The Germans were then taken to the border guardhouse, where they were interrogated. During the interrogation, Reinberger once again attempted to burn the documents by stuffing them into a burning stove. He yelled with pain while doing so, however, and the documents were once again saved from the fire. Much of the content was illegible after two attempts to burn the plans, but that which remained was enough to give the British a clear snapshot of what Hitler had planned for the low countries in the coming weeks. (The Second World War, Martin Gilbert, p 38) (HistoryNet: https://www.historynet.com/the-mechelen-affair.htm) (Wikipedia: https://en.wikipedia.org/wiki/Mechelen_incident)
    -When Hitler was told of the crash, he said, "It is things like this that can lose us the war!" Yet, he still intended to proceed with the invasion as planned on January 17th. Due to weather, the invasion was postponed for three days to Jan. 20th. By that time, it had become clear that the Belgian and Dutch forces had begun to mobilize, most likely because of the leak of information from the crash. Despite this, it appears that it was only the bad weather that finally caused Hitler to postpone the invasion of France until the spring. (The Second World War, Martin Gilbert, p 38)

4. **Altmark Incident**. On February 16th, 1940, sailors from the British destroyer *Cossack* boarded the German supply ship *Altmark* in Norwegian waters, rescuing 299 British soldiers and merchant seamen who had been taken prisoner by the Germans in the South Atlantic. Prior to engaging the *Altmark*, the British, believing the prisoners-of-war to be onboard, demanded that the vessel be searched by the Norwegians. Afraid to risk their neutral status with England and France, they reluctantly agreed. However, the prisoners were concealed below the hatches and they were missed in three separate searches. Not finding any prisoners-of-war, the *Almark* was released. However, British aircraft located the *Altmark* on February 15th and the *Cossack*

was sent in pursuit. They found the German ship being escorted by Norwegian ships, who warned that they would open fire if the *Cossack* made any attempt to board the *Altmark*. Upon seeking instruction from the admiralty, First Lord of the Admiralty, Winston Churchill, instructed them to board the ship if the Norwegians refused to escort it to Bergen in cooperation with the Royal Navy, where they could then inspect the ship themselves. It was at this point that the *Altmark* ended up being most helpful to the British. They tried to ram the *Cossack*, but only succeeded in running aground, whereupon the British promptly boarded her. In doing so, they violated Norwegian neutrality. After a short fight that left four German sailors dead, the British prisoners-of-war were located and released, and the *Cossack* made a dash to the Baltic sea before any retaliation could be made by either the Norwegians or the Germans.

-The entire affair was a much-needed moral victory for the British, but it ended up having very severe repercussions for Norway. Because of the incident, Hitler became convinced that Norway was not neutral and that the British would take over bases in Norway in an effort to prevent him from accessing the Atlantic and the much needed iron ore from Sweden. While the planning for the invasion of Norway, codenamed Operation Weserübung, was already underway in Berlin, the *Altmark* Incident convinced Hitler to make the invasion a priority.

-The Norwegians made a formal protest, stating that their neutrality had been violated against international law. The British Government responded by saying that Norway itself had violated international law by allowing the Germans to transport British prisoners-of-war through its waters and back to Germany. Germany, not to be ignored, demanded reparations from Norway as well, claiming that they had sided with the British and allowed the *Altmark* to be boarded, leading to the deaths of German sailors. (The Second World War, Martin Gilbert, p 42-43) (British Intelligence in the Second World War: Its influence on Strategy and Operations Vol 1, F.H. Hinsley, p 105-106) HistoryHit (https://www.historyhit.com/1940-altmark-incident/)

5. On March 15th, 1940, two British bombers flew across the North Sea, Denmark and the Baltic to reach Warsaw. Their mission was to drop somewhere between six and seven million propaganda leaflets on the former capital of Poland. After making their "bombing" run, both planes were low on fuel, which necessitated returning across Germany to land at airbases in France. One of the planes landed by accident in Germany when the pilot thought he had crossed over into France. In

front of astonished peasants, he managed to take off again and land safely in France the following morning. On that same day, March 16th, the Germans aggressively attacked the British fleet at anchor in Scapa Flow. Fifteen German bombers dropped bombs on the port, killing three officers on the heavy cruiser *Norfolk*, and also killing a civilian who was standing at the door of his cottage, watching the raid. Two days later, Winston Churchill told the War Cabinet that, "There was considerable feeling in the country that while the Germans used bombs, we only dropped leaflets." (The Second World War, Martin Gilbert, p 49)

6. **The Spitfire's Wooden Propellers**. The early Mk I Spitfires were powered by a 1,030 hp Merlin Mk II engine. These engines had a ten-foot diameter two-blade wooden fixed propeller which weighed 83 lbs. But the two-blade propellers severely limited take-off distance and climb rate. And, as you can imagine, there are several reports of other issues with the wooden propellers. They were susceptible to dry rot, and on more than one occasion a propeller would snap during routine flight. In this book, one of the pilots experienced just that. However, from the 78th production airframe, the wooden propellers were replaced with three-bladed, two-position metal propellers, which improved take-off performance, maximum speed and service ceiling on the Spitfire, making it the only fighter capable of successfully competing with the German BF 109 at higher altitudes. To incorporate the new propeller on already existing MK I Spitfires, a kit was developed and teams went to the air bases to replace the propellers. By August 16th, 1940, every Spitfire had been modified with the new metal propellers.

-Interestingly, wooden propellers were to return by 1941, as the war caused a shortage of the duralumin metal used to produce the propellers. This led to the application of the Schwarz process, where "special machinery pressed a hard metal mesh coating and cellulose sheet" over propellers made from soft wood. This ended up producing very hard, composite wood blades which were used until the end of the war. These were the Rotol Propellers, which were contant-speed wood and metal blades. (Smithsonian National Air and Space Museum (https://airandspace.si.edu/collection-objects/rotol-spitfire-propeller-blade-constant-speed-wood-and-metal/nasm_A19601413000) (Wikipedia https://en.wikipedia.org/wiki/Supermarine_Spitfire_(early_Merlin-powered_variants)#cite_ref-32)(Key.Aero – Spitfire MK I, II and IIA's

Prop Fittings https://www.key.aero/forum/historic-aviation/89374-
spitfire-mk-i-ii-and-iia-s-prop-fittings)

7. **Vidkun Quisling**. A Norwegian military officer and politician. In
1933, Quisling left the Farmers Party and founded the National Union,
a fascist party. His party did achieve some popularity, but failed to win
any seats in government and was still only active on the fringes in 1940.
In 1934, he met Nazi ideologist and theorist Alfred Rosenberg. By
1936, Quisling had hardened his anti-Semitic stance. By 1939, he was
delivering lectures entitled "The Jewish problem in Norway" and he
openly supported Adolf Hitler in the growing European conflict. He
sent Hitler a 50th birthday greeting thanking him for "saving Europe
from Bolshevism and Jewish domination." In the summer of 1939, he
was invited to tour Germany and was well-received, with Germany
promising funds to boost his party in Norway and help spread pro-
Nazi sentiment. In December, he met Hitler, gaining a promise from
the Fuhrer to respond to any British invasion of Norway pre-emptively
with a German counter-invasion. On March 31st, he was summoned to
Copenhagen to meet with Nazi intelligence officers, who asked for
information on Norwegian defenses and defense protocols. He
returned to Norway on April 6th, and Germany invaded on the 9th.
That afternoon, Quisling was told by the German liaison that if he set
up a new government in Norway, it would have Hitler's personal
approval. Quisling created a list of ministers and then accused the
legitimate government of having fled. By 5:30pm, Oslo was occupied
by the Germans, and Norwegian radio ceased broadcasting at the
command of the Germans. With their support, Quisling entered the
NRK studios in Oslo and broadcast a message. He announced the
formation of a new government with himself as Prime Minister, and
revoked the earlier order made by the King to the Norwegian army and
civilians to fight the German invasion. Within 24 hours, Hitler officially
recognized the new government under Quisling.

 -Quisling's success, however, was short-lived. On April 10th,
Germany's ambassador traveled to Elverum where the legitimate
Norwegian government sat and demanded that King Haakon appoint
Quisling head of a new government. In that way, they could secure a
peaceful transition of power. King Haakon refused, saying that he
would rather abdicate than appoint any government headed by
Quisling. Upon hearing him take a stance, the Norwegian government
unanimously voted to support the king, and urged the Norwegian
people to continue their resistance. Germany retracted its support of
Quisling's government when it became clear that he did not have the

backing of the country, choosing instead to build its own independent governing commission. By April 15th, a new German governing body was instituted by Hitler. Today, the word Quisling is a term used in Scandinavian languages and in English for a person who collaborates with the enemy – a traitor. (Wikipedia: https://en.wikipedia.org/wiki/Vidkun_Quisling)

8 **Norwegian ambush**. After the surprise invasion of the German forces on April 9th, the Norwegian forces were temporarily scattered as they were overrun by the superior Wehrmacht. They were loyal to the King, however, and refused to accept the Quisling government's submission to German rule. They regrouped and prepared to fight, accepting thousands of young Norwegian recruits who joined the units taking up positions along the narrow mountain roads. One of these young Norwegians was a recruit by the name of Eiliv Hauge, a clerk by trade. On April 11th, he saw action for the first time when a column of German buses filled with troops wound its way inland towards his unit's position. The Norwegians had blocked the road with tree trunks and, as the Germans began to leave the buses, the Norwegians opened fire. "Within minutes, Hauge later recalled, the buses were ablaze. Dead and wounded Germans lay in the road. White flags of truce were waved – in vain." The historian of this episode wrote, "Coming shamefully of age, Hauge and his comrades fired on these too, until two hundred Germans lay silent in the snow." (The Second World War, Martin Gilbert, p 49)

-This is an actual event that took place on April 11th in the mountains of Norway. I maintained the event and the details in their entirety, neither to glorify the act nor defend it, but only to illustrate the desperation and horror that the men and women in Norway faced in those dark days as German forces overran their country.

9. **Landing at Namsos.** On April 14th, two cruisers and ten destroyers sailed into Namsos, landing Royal Marines in Norway. However, everything else surrounding the town and events in the book is fictional. To my knowledge, no civilians were taken off shore, and none of the ships left immediately. They remained and, on the 15th, were under heavy fire from the German Luftwaffe. Namsos itself was bombed relentlessly in the following days.

10. **King Haakon.** When the Oscarsborg Fortress at Drøbak fired on the leading German ship, *Blücher*, the resulting battle and retreat of the remaining ships enabled King Haakon to escape Oslo with the Royal

family and his entire government. They fled to Hamar, but the rapid advance of the German troops forced them to move to Elverum. They met with the German ambassador in Nybergsund on the 10th, a small town outside Elverum where the government was staying. When the King famously refused to appoint a government with Quisling as head, the Luftwaffe attacked the town the following day, destroying the village, but failing to kill any member of the government or royal family. Neutral Sweden was only 16 miles away, but the Swedish government had decided that it would "detain and incarcerate King Haakon if he crossed their border" (something King Haakon never forgave). With Sweden closed to him, the King and his son, the Crown Prince, fled north with their ministers. What followed was two months of harrowing travel around Norway as they tried to stay ahead of the Germans, and their bombers. Under fire and almost caught several times, they continually moved to avoid being captured or killed. One hundred highly trained German paratroopers were ordered to pursue the royals, capture the government, and kill the King. Hitler knew that without their King, the Norwegians would end resistance. King Haakon's desperate flight finally ended when the King and his party were taken onboard the British cruiser *HMS Glasgow* at Molde and transported 620 miles north to Tromsø, where a provisional capital was established on May 1st. The Royal Family and Norwegian Government were evacuated from Tromsø on June 7th aboard *HMS Devonshire* with a total of 461 passengers.

     -This evacuation became extremely costly for the Royal Navy when German warships *Scharnhorst* and *Gneisenau* attacked and sank the nearby aircraft carrier *HMS Glorious* with its escorting destroyers *HMS Acasta* and *HMS Ardent*. *Devonshire* did not rebroadcast the enemy sighting report made by *Glorious* as it could not disclose its position by breaking radio silence. No other British ship received the sighting report, and 1,519 British officers and men and three warships were lost. *Devonshire* arrived safely in London, and King Haakon and his Cabinet set up a Norwegian government in exile in London.

     -Unlike in the book, the Swedish did not refuse to allow the King to cross the border. However, they advised him that both he and his son would be detained and interned. Wishing to continue his rule and to lead his country, the King chose to remain in Norway with the Crown Prince. Interestingly, Crown Prince Olav's wife, Crown Princess Martha and the three royal children (including today's King Harald) were driven over the border to her homeland of Sweden, where they were allowed refuge. (Wikipedia: https://en.wikipedia.org/wiki/Haakon_VII_of_Norway)

Night Falls on Norway

(News in English.no: https://www.newsinenglish.no/2015/04/08/the-kings-defiance-and-chaotic-escape/)

Other Titles in the Shadows of War Series by CW Browning:

The Courier

The Oslo Affair

The Iron Storm

Into the Iron Shadows

Other Titles by CW Browning:

Next Exit, Three Miles (Exit Series #1)

Next Exit, Pay Toll (Exit Series #2)

Next Exit, Dead Ahead (Exit Series #3)

Next Exit, Quarter Mile (Exit Series #4)

Next Exit, Use Caution (Exit Series #5)

Next Exit, One Way (Exit Series #6)

Next Exit, No Outlet (Exit Series #7)

Games of Deceit (Kai Corbyn Series #1)

About the Author

CW Browning was writing before she could spell. Making up stories with her childhood best friend in the backyard in Olathe, Kansas, imagination ran wild from the very beginning. At the age of eight, she printed out her first full-length novel on a dot-matrix printer. All eighteen chapters of it. Through the years, the writing took a backseat to the mechanics of life as she pursued other avenues of interest. Those mechanics, however, have a great way of underlining what truly lifts a spirt and makes the soul sing. After attending Rutgers University and studying History, her love for writing was rekindled. It became apparent where her heart lay. Picking up an old manuscript, she dusted it off and went back to what made her whole. CW still makes up stories in her backyard, but now she crafts them for her readers to enjoy. She makes her home in Southern New Jersey, where she loves to grill steak and sip red wine on the patio.

Visit her at www.cwbrowning.com
Also find her on Facebook, Instagram and Twitter!

Printed in Great Britain
by Amazon

65673006R00196